"Are you going to tell me who or what the hell you are?"

Ana snarled and shook her head, waiting for the perfect moment, and then she sprang forward, her arms wrapping around his shoulders as she took him down, hard.

They rolled together, his body pinned tight to hers, and she grunted loudly as her head connected with the iron fence that bordered her home. She felt his hand against her stomach while the other went for her throat.

Declan's fingers burned hot—the energy licked her skin and the pain that radiated out from them was substantial. That—the pain—she could handle, but having him so close, feeling his flesh against hers brought up all sorts of stuff she didn't have time to deal with.

The smell of his blood drove her insane. It had been one of the reasons she'd always kept her distance from Declan.

In her three hundred years no one—human, vampire, or otherworld—had awoken such longing, such need.

By Juliana Stone

WICKED ROAD TO HELL
HIS DARKEST SALVATION
HIS DARKEST EMBRACE
HIS DARKEST HUNGER

Forthcoming

KING OF THE DAMNED

Novellas

WRONG SIDE OF HELL

JULIANA
STONE

WICKED ROAD TO HELL

A LEAGUE OF GUARDIANS NOVEL

AVON

An Imprint of HarperCollinsPublishers

This is a work of fiction. Names, characters, places, and incidents are products of the author's imagination or are used fictitiously and are not to be construed as real. Any resemblance to actual events, locales, organizations, or persons, living or dead, is entirely coincidental.

AVON BOOKS
An Imprint of HarperCollins*Publishers*
10 East 53rd Street
New York, New York 10022-5299

Copyright © 2012 by Juliana Stone
Excerpt from *King of the Damned* copyright © 2012 by Juliana Stone
Excerpt from *Wrong Side of Hell* copyright © 2012 by Juliana Stone
ISBN 978-0-06-202264-6
www.avonromance.com

First Avon Books mass market printing: May 2012

Avon Trademark Reg. U.S. Pat. Off. and in Other Countries, Marca Registrada, Hecho en U.S.A.
HarperCollins® is a registered trademark of HarperCollins Publishers.

Printed in the U.S.A.

10 9 8 7 6 5 4 3 2 1

This book is dedicated to Tracy and Shelli,
my Sunday/Thursday night TV buddies.
Good times, my friends . . . may they never end.

ACKNOWLEDGMENTS

Once more I'm so very humbled by all the talented people who work behind the scenes to get my books out there. Esi Sogah, my lovely editor, Pam Jaffee and Jessie Edwards, the publicity ladies. Tom, who outdid himself with this cover. Hell never looked so good, eh? Adrienne Di Pietro, I just adore you. The girls at HarperCollins Canada, it was so lovely to meet!

I also need to give a shout-out to my readers for *Wicked:* Tracy Stefurak—thanks for all your input and enthusiasm. Amanda Vyne—again, best roomie ever, and your sharp eye is much appreciated.

Again, I'm so thrilled to have met such an amazing group of paranormal authors at HarperCollins. The Supernatural Underground ladies rock and everyone should check out the blog!

Lastly, a huge THANK YOU to the readers who've embraced my jaguars. Thank you so much for your e-mails, they mean a lot!

WICKED ROAD TO HELL

CHAPTER 1

Declan O'Hara stepped into the middle of the crossroads, a lonely stretch of pavement on the outskirts of town. The moon was barely visible, yet a thin ribbon of light bled through, basking the low-lying fog in an eerie glow.

He glanced to his right as a series of subtle vibrations shot up his legs.

Company was coming.

His hands were loose at his sides and he cracked his neck in an effort to relieve some tension.

Declan smiled in anticipation. *It was about time.*

His eyes pierced the gloom. An image wavered and solidified not more than three feet from him and the smile vanished, leaving his expression blank. He studied the newcomer for a few moments, relishing the fear he sensed.

"You're late." Declan's voice was low, the tone conversational, yet the hard glint in his eyes told a different story.

His visitor, a slight imp of a man, took a step backward and shook his head. "I got away as soon as I could." His voice was thin and there was a nervous edge to it.

Declan paused, welcoming the whisper of magick that rippled over his skin. "Where is he?"

The newcomer swallowed thickly, his Adam's apple protruding in a rapid jerk. "He's no longer in Los Angeles."

At Declan's frown the man continued. "He now has a protector . . . a vampire."

"A protector?" *Interesting.* "That's all you got?"

The slight man nodded slowly.

Unbelievable. Declan swore under his breath and turned away. What a complete waste of time. For fuck sakes, he'd given up a bottle of merlot and a hot blonde for this? His irritation was surpassed only by his desire to get back to the lady and salvage at least part of his evening. He stepped away.

"What about payment?"

Declan paused, letting the energy inside him gather until his fingertips hummed with the heat of his power. He glanced back, eyebrows raised. "Payment? You didn't give me anything I don't already know. I wanted the location."

"But I warned you of the protector—"

He laughed, though he wasn't amused. "You think I need to be warned?" The ground beneath them trembled and danger swept in on the breeze. Declan was pissed. He had no time for this shit.

"There's talk . . ." The man licked his lips nervously. "There's talk that he's been taken to New Orleans."

"Fact or fiction?" Declan was fast losing patience. It didn't take much to trigger his dark side these days.

"I can't be certain."

Declan turned once more to face him, his face hard, his eyes cold.

"I risked a lot to come here, to meet with you. If they find out . . ." The small man's eyes glowed, a tinge of red burning through the gloom as he snarled in anger. "Samael will kill me."

Declan's surprise at the informer's words was kept hidden. Samael? If the demon lord was involved, the game had just changed big-time. Declan's fingers twitched, his nostrils flared as the energy in his hands sparked.

"What does Samael want with him?"

"I will give you no more." The informer widened his stance and hissed. "I want payment."

There it was . . . the trigger.

Declan cocked his head to the side and gave his power free rein. Mist swirled ever faster, hiding the darkness he unleashed. Wind whipped along the surface of the road, moaning as it enveloped the informant in a blanket of death. Seconds later Declan stepped over the still form that lay at his feet.

"Consider that payment rendered." He grabbed his cell phone and hit redial.

"You get the intel?" Nico's rough voice filled his ear. The shifter was a jaguar warrior and Declan's partner.

"I'm headed to Louisiana. I'll let you know what I find when I get there. We don't have much time. Samael's involved now."

"Samael?" Nico sounded surprised. "That can't be good. Who the hell *is* this guy we're tracking? Do we have a name yet?"

Declan's eyes narrowed. "No name." He paused as an owl hooted in the distance. "Check out Los Angeles, see if you can pick up his trail or find a bread crumb that's bigger than a nibble."

The line went dead.

Guess he was heading to the Big Easy.

Declan arrived in New Orleans well past midnight the following evening. The moon was in hiding, the air was cool, and the energy in the city was powerful. Ancient magick lived here, fed not only by the great Mississippi River that slid by in silence, but by the souls of the dead who refused to leave.

It had been ages since he'd last been here. Another lifetime. He shook the melancholy that threatened and sought out the French Quarter. The Voodoo Lounge was located amongst a host of venues on Decatur Street.

Declan headed that way, his tall form sliding amongst the tourists with ease, his dark good looks drawing many a female eye. He ignored them all—even the busty brunette with the large doe eyes and plump, candy red lips.

There wasn't time for such frivolities when the world was going to shit.

Decatur was party central in the Big Easy, and the heat from the bodies in the streets and sidewalks created a blanket of mist that hovered inches above the crowd, as it mixed with the cooler air.

It was an eerie glow that somehow fit the chaotic undercurrent in the air. It was the chaotic undertone he was worried about. Something was off here in the land of crawdaddies and mint julep. He continued along Decatur until he spied the sign he'd been looking for.

It wasn't hard to miss, being a shade past puke green with a splash of orange and yellow. THE VOODOO LOUNGE. He smiled as he neared the club. He didn't remember it being so . . . gaudy.

There was a crowd gathered along the sidewalk, and by the looks of it, no one was getting inside. Typical night in the Quarter.

A mountain of flesh guarded the entrance; his bald head and heavy features were intimidating—as were the mess of tattoos that adorned his flesh. His shoulders were as wide as the door, the muscles bulging from beneath a tight T-shirt, and his legs were leather encased, his feet booted.

The dude was otherworld. It was in the energy that slithered along the man's frame, invisible to the human eye, yet vibrant to someone like the sorcerer.

The bouncer was a shifter, one of Ransome's clan, no doubt.

Declan nodded. "Nice evening."

The incredible hulk cocked his head to the side but remained silent.

"Ransome in tonight?"

"Depends"—the bouncer spit to the side—"on who's asking."

"An old friend." Declan flashed a smile that never reached his eyes. "Tell him O'Hara's in town."

The bouncer's eyes narrowed. He turned his head slightly, murmuring as he did so, obviously talking into a com device. Seconds later he stepped aside and Declan was allowed entrance.

The Voodoo Lounge had been in existence for as long as Ransome LaPierre's family had been in New Orleans, and that had been several generations. It was an eclectic bar filled with all sorts of otherworld and a mixture of human as well. They came together in a melting pot of bodies, music, and sex.

It was the kind of place that easily bred darkness. As Declan eyed the revelers he felt the potency of the energy surround him, and along with it, the familiar tug of want.

The dark side was a seductive bitch. He'd tasted her secrets. And though he was bound to the light, sometimes the lines blurred.

His gaze wandered the room as he slid through the crowd. It was hot, frenetic. He spied Ransome LaPierre immediately. It was hard not to. The alpha of the LaPierre pack was a handsome son of a bitch with a mess of hair the color of dark tobacco. The wolf was holding court in the far corner, surrounded by cheesy velvet sofas, jugs of beer, and—Declan grinned—lots of women.

The werewolf arched a brow and moved two women off his lap, a slow smile spreading across his features as Declan approached.

"You want one?" the wolf asked as Declan approached. He grinned and shoved a tipsy blonde Declan's way. "Or two?" He nodded toward the brunette and laughed, his N'awlins accent rolling off his tongue with devilish glee. "Bookends, no?"

Declan shook his head, though his eyes lingered on the generous rack that was nearly falling from the lady's too-small tank top. *Lady* being an extremely loose term.

"We need to talk." His tone was clipped.

Ransome's smile faded, and he stood in one fluid motion. The man was tall and had an inch or two on Declan, putting him near six-foot-six.

The blonde stepped in front of Declan, her hand falling to his chest. "What's the rush, sugar? Don't you wanna play?" She laughed softly. Her eyes were dilated, filled with the synthetic happiness of whatever kind of drug she'd ingested.

"Not interested." He removed her hand and followed Ransome, ignoring the expletives she shouted after him. The dense crowd parted like the Red Sea, allowing them easy access to Ransome's office located on the upper level of the bar.

The door closed behind them, muffling the heavy beat of the band. Declan exhaled slowly and watched as Ransome poured a generous tumbler of bourbon, but declined when the wolf offered him a glass as well.

Ransome smiled lazily, his slow Louisiana drawl falling from his lips like a melody. "So, what brings you back to these parts, my friend?"

"I'm looking for someone."

Ransome snorted. "Aren't we all?"

"This one's special."

Again the wolf laughed. "Aren't they all?"

Declan shook his head. "Not like this one."

The smile that graced the wolf's face fled immediately and his eyes narrowed. Declan nodded. Now he had his full attention.

Ransome took a long swig of bourbon, hissing as it went down, though his eyes never left Declan's.

"Where you been for the last two years?"

The wolf's question took him by surprise, and Declan was silent for several seconds. *To Hell and back.*

"Around," he answered softly as he eyed the shifter closely.

Ransome smiled though his eyes remained aloof. "It's a dangerous world, my friend, and we don't always know who the enemy is. A little elaboration would be welcome."

Declan didn't like where the conversation was headed. He had no time for posturing.

"It's common knowledge you broke ties with the Castille brothers, but the rumors of your whereabouts have been murky at best. You working alone?"

Declan wasn't surprised at Ransome's words. The werewolf had always kept a paw on the pulse of the otherworld. "No," he replied dryly. "I've got a new boss."

An image of Bill flashed in front of his eyes and he clenched his teeth together tightly. The little bastard was one of the Seraphim, angelic creatures who had absolute dominion over the upper realm. They also dipped into the affairs of humanity or wherever else they saw fit.

Two years ago Bill had pulled Declan from the bowels of Hell. Unfortunately his one-way ride out of darkness had come with a price. The Seraphim currently owned Declan's ass for several lifetimes to come. He was now part of a group of soldiers known as the Seraph. They did the bidding of the Seraphim, no questions asked.

"A name would be good."

"I don't have time to play twenty questions, LaPierre."

The werewolf studied him in silence and a slow burn of frustration hit Declan's skin.

"What does your boss want with this *person* who's *different*?"

Declan's anger spiked and rode the edge of pissed-off. "My new deal doesn't come with a lot of answers. I do as I'm told and move on."

LaPierre poured himself another drink, this time not offering the same to Declan.

"Nothing is ever as it seems, O'Hara."

"No shit," he answered, his voice tight. "Bill might be an arrogant little prick but he's Seraphim."

Ransome's eyes narrowed at that. "And how's that going?"

Declan grabbed a decanter of whiskey off the wolf's shelf and poured himself a double. "Don't ask." He downed the contents in one gulp, welcoming the fire as the liquid burned its way down to his gut. "You hear any chatter on the street? Otherworlders new to the area that don't belong? Or has my trip here been wasted?"

"A trip to Decatur Street is never wasted, O'Hara."

"Normally I'd agree, but I've no time to play and even less time to find this bastard."

"I might know something." A lazy grin spread across Ransome's face, and yet his eyes were dead serious as he focused on Declan.

"Might?" Declan asked.

"I've got a couple of conditions."

Declan eyed his old friend closely. "And they'd be . . ."

"I don't want a holy war running amok in my backyard. Keep your boss out of my city."

No worries there. Bill was with Azaiel. He was one of the original Seraphim but had fallen from grace centuries ago, lured from the upper realm by a beautiful eagle shifter. *Dumb fuck*.

He'd created a portal that had almost ripped a hole the size of Hell into the human realm. A lot of people had suffered, given their lives in order for the portal to remain hidden. Declan's own father, Cormac, had tried to get his slimy hands on the damn thing.

Azaiel had languished in the Hell realm for eons, but two years ago he'd been retrieved and now was on trial for his sins.

As far as Declan was concerned, the fallen was going to get what he deserved. Bill would be busy for days.

Declan nodded. "Done, and the second?"

Ransome grabbed a coat from the chair behind his desk. "I'm coming along."

"Not possible." Declan shook his head. "I'm working this one alone."

Ransome ignored him and slipped supple leather over his powerful shoulders. "You forget, sorcerer, that this is my town, and nothing of significance happens without my knowledge or involvement."

Declan's lips thinned but he remained silent. He could use dark magick to stop him, Ransome had no idea the kind of power that lived beneath his skin, but he couldn't deny the wolf was one hell of a tracker.

He nodded and stepped aside, following Ransome out the back door. He'd humor the wolf for the moment.

Besides, Bill would fucking hate the idea.

CHAPTER 2

The city of the dead—or Lafayette Cemetery No. 1—was quiet as Declan and Ransome walked by. It was nearing 3 A.M. and the souls of those still wandering between the concrete mausoleums were eerily silent.

Declan paused as his gaze passed over the rows of above-ground tombs, a macabre collection that stood in shadow. The dark gray, faded slabs looked forlorn and decrepit. He sensed the energy traces of those long gone from the earth, yet still bound to the physical world. Some stayed by choice and others because of unfinished business.

Either way it sucked to be in limbo. He should know.

"Where we headed?" he asked Ransome. They'd left the craziness of Decatur and Bourbon Streets, and were near the Garden District.

"A place on Prytania. It's been empty for years but was recently settled again."

Declan frowned. "By otherworld?"

"Yeah, a vampire." Ransome arched a brow. "And don't start with the Lestat jokes, they've been old since before '94."

Declan had no clue who the hell Lestat was but his interest was piqued. He'd not shared with Ransome the fact that this so-called protector was a vampire. Adrenaline flooded his cells. The hunt was on.

They passed several large mansions, all of them well-kept, reeking of old money and an era long dead. Shadows clung to the buildings, filled with whispers of energy that seemed out of sync.

The air was rank with pain, loss, and anger. Declan inhaled the ancient magick that lived and breathed in this part of New Orleans and smiled as it hit the cells inside his body. He could get drunk on the power, feed from it like candy.

He'd forgotten what the rush felt like.

Ransome stopped a few feet ahead of him, his large frame suddenly still. The wolf pointed toward a house in darkness. "The DeLacrux mansion."

The house was set back a ways, the entire property bordered by an intricate iron fence. The large trees in the front yard as well as the gardens and shrubs all looked overgrown, gnarled, and badly neglected. A run-down gallery ran the length of the home, with an upper level that mimicked the bottom.

Declan took a few steps closer and felt the unmistakable trace of a protection ward. "DeLacrux?" he asked, frowning as he continued to gaze upon the darkened home. The name was familiar somehow, but at the moment the reason for it escaped him.

He made a note to call Nico and have him check it out.

"The family has lived here for over two hundred years. They are the original owners and built this house, though for the last fifty or so it's been vacant." Ransome glanced toward Declan. "Until a few weeks ago."

"Any idea how many vampires inside?"

Ransome scented the air and nodded. "Just one." A smile lifted the corners of his mouth. "A woman."

Declan was surprised. "You've seen her?"

Ransome shook his head. "I can smell her."

Nice.

"You smell anyone else inside?" he asked sarcastically.

Ransome frowned. "There is someone, but I can't get a read on him." He looked at Declan. "I'm guessing this would be your person of interest."

Declan remained silent. He'd like nothing more than to put this baby to rest, grab the target, and take him back to holding until Bill could deal with him.

"The vampire? She around?"

Ransome shrugged. "Her scent is faint. She's probably hunting."

Declan took a few more steps until he was close enough to touch the iron fence. His hand lingered in midair and he closed his eyes as he visualized the wards that were in place.

They were intricate, filled with a power that surprised him considering the signature felt raw and untamed. He clenched his jaw together tightly. Something was way off. Things weren't right.

"Looks like we have company."

Ransome's voice was low, gruff, and Declan immediately fell back, though he was confident their presence was undetected. Shadows that he commanded slid across them as they melted into the darkness.

Several hundred yards down the road two forms emerged from the mist that hovered above the ground. They walked with purpose and lingered in the middle of the road, showing no fear, their long jackets unfurling in the wind.

One was demon; the stench was unmistakable. The other was vampire.

Declan loosened his hands and cracked his neck. It couldn't be coincidence they were here in New Orleans, on *this* street in front of *this* house. He smiled wickedly as his power unfurled. The sensation was like an intense jolt of energy.

It was *almost* better than sex.

"Guess you're not the only one looking for this prize."

Declan shook his head. "I guess not."

"I suppose it would be a shame to let them get close to him."

Declan grinned. "A total fucking shame."

"We should probably kick their asses then, no?"

Declan's hands burned hot, filled with power. "Copy that."

He took a step forward and halted just as quick. Shadows that clung to a large oak tree farther down the street began to swirl, wisps of energy that spun ever faster, and seconds later a small form appeared from the darkness.

A woman dropped to the ground and squared her shoulders as she looked toward the two men.

And there was no doubt that she was female; the round curve of her ass couldn't be mistaken for anything but. She was unaware of their presence, her focus on the two strangers. She shook out long hair that hung nearly to her waist and slowly walked toward the newcomers.

Something about the grace of her limbs as she glided over the road hit a nerve and Declan clenched his teeth. She moved like a dancer, effortless and sensual.

A twinge of unease sat low in his gut as he stared at the woman. There was something about her . . .

"That would be our vampire," Ransome murmured. "Sexy little thing."

The woman stopped a few feet from the two men in the street. She was too far away for Declan to hear her words, but her aggressive stance and clenched fists told him she was pissed.

He watched the three of them and then glanced at the house. The vampire was busy. Now would be a good time to slip inside and assess the situation. Was his target here?

"Go," Ransome whispered, a devilish grin in place. "I'll keep her busy if our visitors aren't up to the task." He laughed softly. "I wouldn't mind getting closer to that delicious piece of ass."

For whatever reason, the wolf's words irritated Declan, but he ignored them and began to draw charms in the air, his fingers flying with ease as the magick inside him flowed.

Though the ward was strong it was no match for him, and less than thirty seconds later he felt the gentle tug and pull as the protection charms evaporated. He should have been through them at once and yet he hesitated.

Declan glanced back once more. The female vampire was extremely animated in the way she talked, her hands moving constantly.

Goddamn but she was like Ana.

A flash of pain sliced through him and he hissed. Where the hell had that thought come from?

"What are you waiting for?" Ransome's slow drawl cut through his thoughts and Declan gave himself a mental shake. Revisiting the past and the memory of a woman two years dead was never a good thing.

He hopped the fence with ease, his long stride carrying him toward the gallery. Dark shadows lined the roof as he moved closer to the front door.

Declan eyed them carefully, his hands at the ready as the familiar burn of energy lit his fingers. Suddenly the dark erupted into hundreds of sharp teeth and flapping wings.

He raised his hands and reveled in the energy that flew from his fingers. It burned white-hot and the swarm of teeth and wings circled overhead, their cries of rage hitting a pitch that made his ears ring.

The little bastards couldn't reach him, and their confusion and anger were palpable. He eyed them closely as they continued to swoop about in a frenetic dance. They looked like rabid bats from Hell.

An enraged scream cut through the night and drew his attention. He whirled around and saw Ransome on the move.

One of the men, the vampire, had his hands on the female and they struggled. She deftly broke his hold and kneed him between the legs. His cry of pain echoed in the damp evening air, followed by a growl of fury.

The demon made an odd series of clacking noises, its body already morphing into its true form. It looked like the little vampire was going to have her hands full.

Yet it was the sight beyond that gave him pause. Several forms emerged from the fog and were moving toward them quickly, their bodies jerking in random motions, heads rocking to the side, arms flailing wide. It was unnatural.

They were unnatural. From the smell that drifted on the breeze he was guessing ghouls—the dead arisen.

Normally ghouls were slow and uncoordinated. But these ones were juiced up on some seriously dark shit. They were fast and he had no doubt they'd be dangerous. A powerful necromancer was in the area and it seemed he had business on Prytania Street.

Declan's night had just ramped from interesting to game on.

The legion of bats overhead flew toward the ghouls in silence, a deadly arc of fury. A few of them circled above Declan. With a flick of his wrist he knocked them hard and sent them flying.

There were no more barriers in place—nothing between him and the door. All he had to do was let himself in.

And still he paused.

The demon was now nearly ten feet in height, its human facade gone and replaced by its true form, which was scaly, slimy, and menacing. It hissed and breathed fire down at the small vampire, yet she stared up at it and yelled, "I'm going to bitch slap that ugly ass of yours all the way back to Hell."

This time he had no problem hearing her words.

"And then I'm gonna rip your face off, asshole."

Declan's blood ran cold. It wasn't so much the words themselves, but the tone and the defiance that bled through. She was so like Ana, it was eerie.

The rush of emotion that accompanied the thought pissed him off. He had no time to go down that path.

Ransome had shifted, and Declan saw the huge werewolf jump toward the demon. If the small vampire was surprised, there was no time to process, as the large group of ghouls was nearly upon them.

Declan had his chance and turned back to the door. His hand gripped the handle tightly and he pushed it open.

Inside it was dark—pitch black—as if a blanket of midnight had been thrown over everything. He quickly called forth an illumination charm and held his hand aloft, a soft glow falling from the tips of his fingers. He arced his hand slowly, watching the shadows recede and leaving bare to his eyes the old, tired wallpaper that adorned the walls. It was yellowed, a rose pattern, and brought to mind an era long gone.

A grand staircase dominated the foyer. The stairs looked worn, well used, and several of the spindles in the railing were missing.

He ran forward taking them two at a time and paused at the top to turn in a full circle. All the doors were open except the two at the front.

Good. That made things simple.

A god-awful screech ricocheted in the air outside, sliding in through the cracks of the windows, kick-starting his heart something fierce.

He moved with the stealth of a predator and opened the door on his right first. Empty.

He closed the door carefully and crossed over to the remaining room but before he could touch the handle, it was wrenched open.

"What the—"

Surprise furled his eyebrows and he felt a deflation of sorts as he realized almost immediately that this was not his target. It couldn't be. The person in front of him was not a man at all but a teenager.

"Who the hell are you?" The kid's tone was belligerent.

Declan sighed. A smart-ass, no less.

The boy's dark eyes narrowed. "How did you get in?" The teenager tried to see around him. "You shouldn't have been able to get in." The boy took a step forward and met his gaze boldly. "If you hurt her I'll kill you."

The air around the teenager shimmered and Declan took a step backward, not out of fear, but surprise. He frowned.

The young man was full of magick, deep, powerful magick that was on the cusp of maturing. And yet there was something else entirely different about him. Something he couldn't quite put his finger on.

"What are you?" His thoughts were whispered. It had been so long since he'd been truly puzzled.

The young boy smiled, tilted his head to the right. "I'm the dude who's going to kick your ass all over the place."

The kid's brash arrogance and cocky attitude totally needed adjusting.

Declan squared his shoulders. As much as he'd like to solve the mystery, he just didn't have the time.

He opened his mouth, a sarcastic retort on his tongue when the large stained-glass window behind him exploded, showering them both with shards of glass.

Declan's first instinct was to protect and he reached for the teenager, but the young man slid past him, his movements fast and graceful.

A ghoul had managed to climb to the upper level and though it was missing an arm, its eyes burned a fierce red. It slid forward. Behind it was another. The second monster lunged forward immediately, its dark, toothless grin dripping black gunk onto the faded wood floor.

"I don't think so, asshole!" the boy shouted, not fearing

at all for his safety. He pushed forward, his intent clear, and Declan swore as he followed suit. He pulled up the power that lay in his gut, relishing the sharpness of it as he did so.

The boy leapt over the stairs like an acrobat, landing on the other side in a quick move, and Declan knew in that instant that the teenager could hold his own. His slight frame hummed with energy.

The armless ghoul rushed Declan, black crap spewing out of its stump, and he barely had a chance to move away from the acrid spray. He turned quickly and sent a blast of energy into its chest, again jumping out of the way as it imploded, spilling the stench of death into the air.

The screech that fell from its mouth faded almost immediately as it disintegrated into nothing but a mess of liquid at his feet. Shouts, snarls, and mayhem crept up from below, echoing on the breeze that now flew in through the broken window.

"Ana!" the boy shouted, and hopped the railing before Declan could react.

A chill ran along Declan's skull and down his back. He faltered. *Ana?*

"What the—?" he growled. He turned and followed the boy's lead, flying down the stairs and running hard to catch up. The little bastard had skills, he'd give him that.

Declan burst out into the cool night air, and the sight that greeted him was unreal at best—a macabre banquet of black goop and body parts strung into the trees, the shrubs, and all over the road.

He swerved to avoid the crazed bats that swooped overhead, their protection absolute and ferocious, swearing once more as he narrowly missed stepping into a pile of the slippery shit. He spied Ransome several feet away. The wolf had shifted back into human form and was slowly gaining his legs with the help of the female vampire.

The teenager rushed to her and she embraced the young

man fully, her head turned slightly as she held him close. The boy meant something to her. His eyes narrowed and Declan's chest constricted painfully as he watched.

The curve of her cheek, the small tilt to her nose, and the subtle scent that wafted into the air—all of it sent his radar crashing into overdrive.

Ana.

She tensed as if she'd heard the painful whisper in his mind. He felt the vibrations in the air hang low, tight to the ground, as all sound faded into nothing. His chest was tight. His mouth dry.

Slowly she turned.

Declan's eyes widened in disbelief as his gaze ran over the delicate features, the generous lips, and the smattering of freckles that touched the bridge of her nose.

He felt like he'd been hit in the gut with a sledgehammer. The air was sucked from his lungs and he shook his head, not believing what he was seeing. *It couldn't be.*

"Declan." His name fell from her lips, two syllables that crushed him hard and twisted his insides painfully.

What the hell kind of shit was this? The image in front of him was not possible.

His anger unfurled—power rushed through him—and the ground around him started to tremble as huge cracks split the asphalt into gaping wounds.

She smiled, though her eyes glittered strangely, their blue depths like fragile sapphires. "Self-control was never one of your strong suits."

"Who are you?" he rasped, his mind wild and unsettled.

Ana was long dead, so how was that possible? He couldn't finish his thoughts. They were freaking crazy. Cormac had run a stake directly through her heart. *Two years ago.*

"She's dead," he muttered as he stared her down.

Laughter greeted his words, but the emptiness that rang with them couldn't be hidden. "You're right of course,

O'Hara. Technically I was born dead. Cradle to the grave on the same day."

Declan swore and took a step toward her. What the hell was going on? He didn't for one second believe that the vampire in front of him was Ana. *His Ana.* This was a sick joke, nothing more.

"Who are you?" He snarled again.

"Go back to the house, Kaden."

"I'm not leaving you with him."

"I'm not asking." The teenager protested once more but she silenced him with one look.

The boy glared at Declan, tucked his hands into the front of his jeans, and slowly walked toward the house, casting dark looks over his shoulder as he did so.

Ransome followed, an irritating smile hanging on his face as he passed by and scooped up his clothes. "See you back at the lounge"—he winked—"if you make it out alive."

Declan watch the wolf leave.

"You shouldn't have come here," the woman spit out, her eyes fully black.

"I'm not leaving until I get some answers," Declan answered fiercely.

"Well then." The vampire's fangs slid out as she hissed at him. "I have a problem with that."

And before he had time to react, she attacked.

CHAPTER 3

Ana DeLacrux was a pro at masking her true emotions. In the three hundred years she'd been alive, or rather, undead, she'd picked up a thing or two. Amongst them, never show surprise or emotion.

Sometimes it was the only thing that kept you alive.

Sometimes it was the only thing that kept you *sane*.

Declan O'Hara was a problem she'd not seen coming, and though her facade was one of cool indifference, anger even, inside she was a mess.

She felt her barriers sliding away, and the fear that accompanied such a loss of control was nearly paralyzing.

She couldn't go there. Not again. Feelings were something she'd never been good at navigating, especially when it came to the Irishman.

"Who are you?"

He was pissed and yet his voice was still the same, a bit of rasp, a touch of lilt, and a timbre that tore at her heartstrings.

In the space of a few seconds her mind whirled in what felt like a thousand different directions.

The fact that Declan O'Hara was here in New Orleans, with his ass parked in front of her home, was not good. It meant that he'd been sent by the Seraphim. She stared at Declan, her face stone cold.

They were actively hunting Kaden.

Why the hell hadn't she been warned? *Jesus fuck.* She gritted her teeth as she stared at the tall Irishman. She was so gonna kick Bill's ass the next time she saw him. Roly-Poly wasn't going to know what the hell hit him. He should have told her O'Hara was after the boy.

He should have told her the chance of a face-to-face was pretty damn imminent.

She'd warned Bill after that last time. Seeing Declan the year before, in the arms of some strumpet, and not being able to reveal herself to him had nearly killed her. *Again.*

Ana hissed and closed her mind to anything other than her job—protecting Kaden. If it meant hurting the man in front of her, so be it. It's not like she had much choice. No one could be trusted, and with the stakes this high . . .

At his refusal to leave her fangs slid out and she rushed forward, her body moving at a preternatural speed that most wouldn't be able to evade.

Except Declan O'Hara wasn't like most others. He was fast and she felt the heat of his power slide by, barely missing her left shoulder.

"Motherfu—" she yelped as another energy blast flew past, this time searing her flesh.

A grimace slid over her face. Things were going to get ugly.

She flipped in the air and landed just behind him, whirling around, and her hand jerked out as she shot a quick jab at his lower back. When in doubt, aim for a kidney.

Declan swore as she made contact and stumbled forward, but then recovered and kicked out to the side, his booted foot colliding with her midsection and sending her flying backward.

She heard him curse a string of foulness and rolled to the side as she went down, barely avoiding another energy blast.

She was up in an instant and stared at Declan, chest heaving, feeling strangely exhilarated at this dance. Her tongue ran along the edges of her fangs and she arched a brow. "What happened to never hitting a lady?"

"I don't see a lady anywhere. Only a vampire ramped up on crazy." Declan's eyes narrowed into twin slits of darkness and she saw the way the air around him shimmered. He'd been different two years ago, when he'd come back from Hell. She knew then he'd fed from a dark power. One that had changed him.

It made his blood all the more intoxicating. He was otherworld—his blood was naturally infused with heavy magick—but coupled with the darkness from below, it must be potent. Her mouth watered at the thought.

He smiled at her though his eyes remained flat. He cocked his head to the side. "Are you going to tell me who or what the hell you are?"

Ana snarled and shook her head, waiting for the perfect moment, and then she sprang forward, her arms wrapping around his shoulders as she took him down, hard.

They rolled together, his body pinned tight to hers, and she grunted loudly as her head connected with the iron fence that bordered her home. She felt his hand against her stomach while the other went for her throat.

Declan's fingers burned hot—the energy licked her skin and the pain that radiated out from them was substantial. That—the pain—she could handle, but having him so close, feeling his flesh against hers, brought up all sorts of stuff she didn't have time to deal with.

The smell of his blood drove her insane. It had been one of the reasons she'd always kept her distance from Declan.

In her three hundred years no one—human, vampire, or otherworld—had awoken such longing, such need.

She'd known instinctively that he was the one man who could break her—the one she could love. But he wasn't vampire. It was forbidden.

"Who the hell are you?" he asked once more.

"Why are you here?" she countered. "Who sent you?" She needed to keep him off balance.

Declan was breathing hard and nudged his knee between her legs as he leaned toward her. Energy flowed from his fingers and rolled over her skin. She smelled the heavy magick that clung to him and heard the blood rushing through his veins.

God, it was sweet, tantalizing.

She squeezed her eyes shut, not wanting to see the steady pulse at the base of his neck. And yet she immediately envisioned her lips against him, her teeth breaking skin, and her tongue lapping at the sweet nectar below his flesh.

Declan called to her basest nature, and her fangs throbbed painfully. Her eyes flew open and her gaze traveled over his handsome face. The dark eyes, square jaw, and full lips hadn't changed at all.

She needed to be away from him. He was a distraction she couldn't afford.

His hand tightened around her throat, just enough to cause pain. "Why did the boy call you Ana? She's dead."

She glared up at him, opened her mouth, but couldn't answer until he relieved the pressure. Slowly her fangs receded and she hissed, "Are you that dense, Declan? Did Hell fry your brains? Bill not doling out enough vitamins or what?"

His grip loosened for just a second and she grabbed the opportunity. Ana head butted him, *hard*, and brought her knees up sharply, smiling as she connected solidly between his legs.

Declan cursed and she kicked out once more, rolling to the side, and was up on her feet facing him in less than a second.

He glared at her as she continued to smile. "It's not possible." He spat.

"Really?" Ana was annoyed. "After everything you've been through, you would question the fact that I'm not rotting beneath the ground?" *How could he not know she was the real deal?* "You spent six months in the Hell realm and came back. Why do you find it so hard to believe that I managed my own miracle?"

Long moments of silence passed between the two of them.

His eyes were like liquid licorice. She'd always loved that.

"How are you alive?" he asked. She could tell he was wavering, on the cusp of belief.

Ana clenched her hands as she wondered how much to share.

"Freaky mojo, I suppose." She stared up at her home and her lips thinned as she spied Kaden watching from the upper level. "We're all players in a game much bigger than either of us can imagine. I was presented with an offer, life and servitude to a new master, or eternal death."

Ana turned back to Declan. "I chose life." She shrugged. "Well, my version of it anyway."

Declan moved toward her until he stood so close his warm breath touched her face. He stared down at her, and when his hand rose in the air she tensed. Not because she was afraid he'd hurt her—that would be easy to deal with. Physical pain at its most basic level was one-dimensional.

It was the other, the emotional pain that was hard to live with. It fragmented and grew until it became a monster. Hell, she'd done her best to avoid it for decades.

And yet as she stared up at him, her gut clenched tightly, she wondered if it would be worth it. To have the one thing she'd desired for so long . . . if only for this one moment.

His hand hovered, a whisper away from her cheek, and Ana's breath caught in the back of her throat. Her mouth went dry as her gaze focused on his lips.

It had been so long since she'd been touched. Her last

lover, Diego, had died fifteen years earlier. There'd been no one since. What was the point?

If only his scent wasn't so enticing. So far she'd been playing nice. Declan had no clue of the strength that lay beneath her small frame.

Ana groaned softly. She could do it. Take a drink.

Would that be so bad?

His eyes dilated until they were huge, round balls of ebony. He bent lower, so low that she could have opened her mouth and touched him with her tongue.

She felt that moment come, and God help her, her mouth parted slightly as desire flooded her, hot and heavy. His hands slid around her neck once more and she didn't care. They dug into the thickness of her hair, anchoring her body so that she couldn't move.

And then the warmth of his breath was on her lips.

"How the hell do you know Bill?" Each word was pronounced slowly, carefully.

Her eyes flew open. Shit. She'd fucked up. All desire fled until she was empty once more, and she gazed upon eyes that looked down at her with distrust and contempt.

Her lips tightened. "I don't—"

"Bullshit," he interrupted. "You mentioned him earlier and I'm guessing your Bill stands about five feet fuck all, with a gut as round as a basketball and a shiny bald head to match." He pushed away from her, and the ground began to tremble. "Does the sun shine out of his ass if he turns the right way?"

Ana opened her mouth to retort, but the ridiculous image Declan had just painted was so bang-on, she fought a hysterical giggle instead.

"Never mind." Declan hopped over the fence before she could stop him. "I know someone who will answer my questions. If he refuses I have no problem making him."

Fear sliced through her and Ana sprang after him, her

body flying past his in a blur until she stood between Declan and the door.

Kaden was just a boy—no match for a sorcerer with Declan's power.

"You will not touch him." She could barely get the words out, so great were her fear and anger. There was no way she'd let the Seraphim get hold of Kaden. She'd given her word that she'd keep him safe. "Do you not know what he is?" she asked, exasperated.

"Should I?" he retorted angrily, his eyes wavering from hers to drift upward. "Seems to me I don't know shit." He glared at her. "I watched you die two years ago. In my mind I buried you."

She watched him closely. Saw the myriad of emotions that crossed his face. His beautiful dark eyes flattened as his anger increased.

"Looks like I got that all wrong." Declan sounded bitter, and she winced.

Ana had a hard decision to make. Bill had entrusted Kaden's safety to her. She'd been his dirty little secret for the last two years, running covert missions Bill wanted no one to know about.

He was one of the Seraphim and they were hard-core. They believed the end always justified the means. In the constant war between good and evil they were willing to spill the blood of innocents if they thought it would further their own agenda.

Bill saw things a little differently. He knew the end didn't always justify the means, and though he wasn't always honest with her—he doled out information on a need-to-know basis . . . *his* need to know—Ana knew his cause was noble and in this instance he had her abject allegiance.

Ana would die protecting Kaden. In the space of six months the boy had come to mean everything to her. He was so like O'Hara it was eerie, and she supposed on some level, the teenager represented all that she would never have. A child . . . a family.

She exhaled slowly and rubbed her temple. What to do? The arrival of the ghouls this night told her that she was on borrowed time. Samael wouldn't be far behind—the damn demon lord had been dogging her every move for weeks now—and with the Seraphim finally showing interest things were going to get ugly.

Both Heaven and Hell were gunning for Kaden.

Right now Declan O'Hara was her enemy. He'd been sent by the Seraphim to retrieve the boy. It was obvious he had no clue who the hell he was hunting. She supposed she could thank Bill for giving him such vague orders.

She gazed up at the sorcerer. Would he try to take Kaden if he knew the truth?

"Come." She opened the door and stepped aside, her gaze wandering the quiet streets. The bats that protected her boundaries had made quick work of any remnants left in the street. It was clean of debris.

The night was quiet, serene even, as if nothing out of the ordinary had transpired. She thought of the humans tucked away in their beds, blissfully unaware of the drama that was unfolding. The world that should stay hidden was suddenly spilling into the human realm once more. Sooner or later they'd find out that their nightmares were true.

That monsters such as herself really existed.

"We need to talk," she said quietly, and held her breath as Declan's eyes narrowed.

He hesitated, ran his hands through the thick waves that hung over his left eye, and then walked past her without a word.

He moved with a grace that was sinful, his tall frame shrinking her world as she closed the door behind him. Declan's fists were clenched at his side, humming with dark energy.

He didn't trust her, and she supposed there was no reason for him to.

A soft creak drew her eyes upward. Kaden stood at the top of the stairs, his hand on the railing, about to take another step.

"Give us a few minutes." She knew he was going to protest—saw him square his shoulders. She raised an eyebrow and it was enough. Kaden shot an aggressive look toward Declan and then disappeared.

"Follow me."

She slid past Declan and headed to the kitchen located at the back of the house. She was edgy, still unsure if she'd made a huge mistake; however, there was no turning back now.

She flipped on the light, though the rusting fixture that hung from the center of the ceiling didn't do much to illuminate the room. The kitchen was as dated and tired as the rest of the house, with frayed, yellowed wallpaper and cracked linoleum. She rested her hip against the aluminum-framed table. The last time she'd sat at the damn thing it had been 1956. Elvis had been king, her brother had been home, and she'd been happy.

As always, thoughts of Jean-Charles conjured up memories best left alone. It seemed a lifetime ago, and for someone who had lived for over three hundred years that was saying something. She pushed all thoughts of her brother aside. There was no room for bitterness and melancholy. Not tonight anyway.

Ana straightened the cherry red vinyl chair and eyed the ancient fridge. Christ, she needed a drink. Badly.

"I work for Bill." Her words came out in a rush. "It was he who brought me back from the darkness two years ago."

Declan's eyes widened for just a second. "After the fiasco in Vegas? You've been alive all this time?"

His words were controlled, his tone conversational, yet

his hands were clenched tightly. She nodded and waited as long moments of silence followed.

"It doesn't make sense. If he pulled a Lazarus with you, why aren't you working for the Seraphim like Nico and I? Why did no one tell me?" His face was unreadable.

"Bill doesn't trust them."

Declan's eyes narrowed and he took two steps until he was inches from her. Ana's gut clenched and she wished he'd move away. His scent was irresistible, his heartbeat mesmerizing.

"*I'm* in New Orleans because I've been ordered by that little fucker"—his words were matter-of-fact and he watched her closely—"to bring someone in for the Seraphim, of which Bill *is* one, last I heard."

"You would hand over a boy to them? Do you even know why they want him?"

She saw the confusion on his face.

"Boy?" He rubbed his jaw.

"They want Kaden." Her voice trembled slightly and she was pissed at the show of emotion. "I'll die before that happens."

"Well that's kinda hard, isn't it? Since technically you're already dead."

His smart-ass tongue was starting to get on her nerves.

At Ana's growl Declan raised an eyebrow. "So, let me get this straight. Bill has *me* on the trail of a kid that he has *you* protecting?"

"That's about right." Ana was just as confused. "I don't know why he didn't warn me. He usually does." She paced as she spoke. "He plays nice with the Seraphim even if he doesn't always believe in their methods. Of course he sent you after Kaden. He was ordered to." She stopped and felt a wave of dizziness wash over her. God, she needed blood. "It's just . . . he usually warns me when the game has changed. If

I'd known you were on the hunt I'd have taken Kaden deep underground."

"Bill's away. He's been called to council for Azaiel's trial."

Ana was quiet as she digested that information. It made sense. If Bill was in the upper realm with the fallen, he'd have no way of contacting her. She shivered, suddenly so weary and tired of it all.

For the first time in a long while she wasn't sure she could carry out her mandate. She didn't know if she could keep the boy safe from both the Seraphim and now Samael.

The demon lord was like a dog, nose to the ground and tracking hard. It's probably why the Seraphim had finally made a move. They didn't want the demon underworld to get their hands on Kaden. They'd rather destroy the boy than chance it.

"How long will he be away?" she asked.

Declan shrugged. "I have no clue, but the last time he rode the golden elevator upstairs he was gone for months."

"I won't let you take him," she reiterated.

Declan ignored her comment. "Who is he?"

Ana pursed her mouth, her mind a total mess. What had she done?

"His name is Kaden."

"Yeah, I got that already. The kid have a last name?"

Ana shook her head. "No, just Kaden."

"He's full of magick." Declan's eyes narrowed. At Ana's tight-lipped stare he swore under his breath. "Where did he come from?"

She watched changing emotions flicker across Declan's face, and swallowed thickly. "He was abandoned as a toddler. As far as I know his parents are either dead or long gone."

"Where did you find him?"

Her gaze fell to the ground. "An orphanage in Los Angeles." She grimaced. "A real shithole of a place. He'd been there since he was two."

Declan's dark eyes bored into her. She felt them, the intensity, the anger.

"What does the Seraphim want with him?"

The vampire shrugged her shoulders. "I have no idea."

Ana met his gaze full-on but knew he wasn't fooled.

Declan O'Hara's eyes narrowed. "You're lying," he whispered dangerously as he took a step toward her.

Ana stared at him in silence.

O'Hara was right.

She was *totally* full of shit.

CHAPTER 4

Declan turned from Ana, not trusting himself. He glanced around the sparse kitchen and tried to focus on something other than the vampire.

It was no use. What the hell was going on?

He crossed to the window and stared into the backyard and though he tried to appear calm it was fucking killing him. He wanted to grab hold of Ana and . . . do what? Shake her until her head snapped? Kill her? Screw her?

He was confused as all hell, pissed beyond belief, and—he clenched his fists tightly—full of anger.

He'd watched the woman he loved die at the hands of his father. Every night when he closed his eyes it was Ana's face he saw. Lifeless, pale . . . dead. That had been on him. It was his cross to bear and he'd held it willingly.

Declan's jaw ached from tension and he blew out a long breath in an effort to center himself.

To find out she'd been alive the entire time and it was Bill, the little fuck, who'd brought her back was like a kick to the gut. *Unbelievable.* For two years no one had said a word.

Rage flickered inside once more, like a silent whisper. His heart was pounding and powerful energy slid along his skin. The glass window seemed to bow and liquefy but he forced the darkness away and the panes held firm. He would not lose control in front of her.

He'd deal with his anger later. Right now he needed to figure out what the hell was going on.

He turned around and glared at Ana. "You expect me to believe that kid is who the Seraphim are after?"

"I have no reason to lie," she retorted, her tone sharp. "And it's not just the Seraphim, Samael has been dogging me for weeks."

Ana walked past him and yanked open the fridge door. She grabbed a clear bag of blood and threw it in a microwave before turning back to him. He watched her closely and saw how her hand trembled as she waited for her blood to warm. She was definitely jonesing for a fix. Her skin was pale, her blue eyes huge in her face. She looked ethereal, though her small, tight form was dressed in kick-ass denim and leather.

She retrieved a crystal glass and filled it, glancing toward him before she took a sip. "His energy is strong." She finished the glass quickly. "But he doesn't know how to control it yet. He's untrained."

Declan frowned. He was hearing her words and yet none of it made any sense. He began to pace.

"So let me get this straight. That kid—"

"He has a name, use it," Ana hissed.

Declan glared at her. "*Kaden* is what, sixteen?"

"He'll be seventeen in December."

"He's a sixteen-year-old sorcerer with no clue where the hell he came from?"

Ana nodded but remained silent.

Declan paused in front of the fridge and yanked the door open. He wasn't sure what he was looking for but it sure as hell wasn't the bags of blood that lay upon the shelves.

"Sorry, I didn't know you'd be visiting. I'd have stocked up on Guinness."

Declan ignored her sarcasm and slammed the door shut. "I'm more into wine these days, but thanks." His eyebrows furled. "There's something off about him. I can't put my finger on it, but he's definitely got otherworld blood in him and it ain't all magick." He paused. "You gonna spill what that is exactly?"

She licked her lips and averted her eyes.

He took a step forward, not even sure what he was going to do, but the energy in him needed to be released. It burned so bad he felt nauseous.

"Stay away from her." It was the boy.

Declan paused, his gaze not leaving Ana's. He saw the concern, the need to protect that flickered in her eyes. *Interesting.* When they'd worked together at PATU, a paranormal antiterrorist unit, she'd been cold and aloof. It had driven him crazy. He used to fantasize about ways to break the glass that covered her skin.

Who knew a hormonal teenager would do the trick. He turned and faced him.

Kaden glared at him with the cocky bravado he'd shown earlier. Declan held up his hands. "It's all right. Ana and I go way back, like before she died for the second time."

The teen's hands were open at his side and Declan could "see" energy drifting over his palms. He tried to hide his amusement.

The boy thought to challenge him?

"Who are you? Why are you here?" Kaden's voice was deep, mature for a boy his age. Declan took a second to study him closely in the light. He was tall with the assured grace of an athlete and looked older than his sixteen years. His dark, wavy hair was worn long, touching the collar of his T-shirt, his features were well-defined, square jaw, high cheekbones. He was a good-looking kid, a natural leader.

"My name's Declan."

Kaden glowered at him. "We don't need you."

Declan dismissed the boy and his attitude. He nodded to Ana. "I'll ask once more. Why did you grab him?"

She filled her goblet again and took a long drink before answering.

"I was ordered to. Bill wants him protected, and like the obedient little soldier I am, I do what I'm told." She looked at the teen, and something stirred inside him. There'd been a time when he'd wanted that . . . the need to have her regard him in the same way.

As if he mattered.

Feelings . . . emotions . . . were a fucking bitch to navigate.

Declan's cell went off at that moment and he automatically pulled it from his pocket. It was Nico, the other sorry-ass son of a bitch who'd ended up signing his balls over to the Seraphim. They were both part of a supernatural A-team run by Bill.

"Don't answer it," Ana said quickly.

Declan ignored her, watching the two of them carefully as he put the device on speaker mode and set it on the table.

"You there?" Nico's rasp sliced through loudly. Declan heard wailing guitars and heavy bass in the background. He shook his head. The jaguar had developed a fondness for the heavier side of rock.

"Yeah, what'd you find out?"

"I managed to snag myself a demon, one with a huge chip on his shoulder. It didn't take much to get him to talk."

Ana and Kaden moved closer.

"He give up the goods?"

"Not the end game if that's what you mean but he did have some interesting information." The loud music in the background suddenly disappeared as if Nico had enclosed himself in a small room.

"And that would be?" he prompted.

"He said everyone was after a scrawny kid and that he was one of a list of seven."

Declan glanced at Kaden as Nico's words sank in. He didn't like the look Ana and the boy exchanged.

"I didn't get any names, though I was able to confirm that the vampire has taken him to New Orleans." There was a slight pause and some noise. He thought he heard Nico curse. "He wouldn't tell me why they wanted him."

"I know why," Kaden said.

"Not now!" Ana hissed.

"Who the hell was that?" Nico asked.

Declan glanced at Kaden for several long moments before he answered. "How fast can you get to New Orleans?"

"I can be there tomorrow. What the hell have you done now?" Nico sounded exasperated.

"I'll explain when you get here."

"For Christ sakes, Declan, the last time you said that, Bill had our asses guarding purgatory for months. What part of *going fucking insane* do you not remember?"

Declan snorted. "And here I thought we bonded in purgatory. I'll see you tomorrow. Meet me at the Voodoo Lounge on Decatur." Declan snapped his device closed and grinned as Nico's foul rant was cut short. The jaguar was pissed but he'd get over it. *Eventually.*

"Care to explain?" His manner changed abruptly as he raised an eyebrow. Kaden stared back at him, his face set, and remained silent. Declan turned to Ana. "I thought you said you had no idea why they wanted him."

Ana hesitated, and the burn beneath his skin flashed hot. The air around him vibrated and the energy wasn't all sunshine and roses. He was done playing games.

"If you expect me to lay my ass on the line for *you*, you'd better tell me everything." He tossed a dark look Kaden's way. "Or I'm outta here and I'm taking magick boy with me."

She hissed at him, her fangs fully extended once more as she moved in front of the now-protesting teenager.

The sight of her at the ready, willing to fight for a child, did all sorts of screwed-up things to him. She'd never looked more fiercely passionate—more alive.

His insides lurched and his fingers itched as a bolt of power slid through him unexpectedly. He shook his head and knew he was fast losing control.

"Don't threaten me, Declan," she hissed, "because I sure as hell won't play *nice*."

He arched an eyebrow and moved closer. "Is that a promise?"

Her eyes were now fully black—the woman was about to lose it, big-time.

"I have the mark," Kaden blurted.

Silence followed his words. "The mark?" Kaden had Declan's full attention.

"Bill said it was the mark of seven and I'm the fifth."

Declan stared at the teen in surprise. Ana's mouth was pursed tightly, her pale face nearly ashen.

"Kaden, what the hell? We agreed to keep that information private." Ana began to pace. "Unbelievable," she muttered.

Declan had heard stories about the mark of seven. Most he'd assumed were whispers of fantasy. Ana's pissed-off face told another story.

The mark of seven was real.

This changed everything.

He took the final few steps toward Ana, who'd stopped in front of Kaden. "Move."

Ana opened her mouth to protest and he shut her down quick. "You can't begin to comprehend what this means." He glared at her. "I won't hurt him." He meant it.

She eyed him warily and then reluctantly moved aside. He found himself inches from a teenager who stared at him with eyes that flashed anger, confusion, and pain.

"Let me see it," he said firmly. "I need to make sure." His words were pointed and it was obvious he wouldn't take any shit from the boy. The teenager slowly lifted his T-shirt over his head and turned around.

Declan's eyes were riveted to the intricate mark on Kaden's left shoulder. It was strangely luminescent, with red and black dominating—a symbolic etching with an eye in the middle, surrounded by vines in the shape of wings and horns.

"That's fine, you can put your shirt back on." He waited in silence as Kaden did so. Questions were firing off in his brain at a rapid pace.

Declan eyed the teenager closely. "Who else knows about the mark?"

Kaden shrugged his shoulders and averted his eyes. "No one."

Liar.

Declan was fast losing patience. "Don't screw with me, understand? I find it hard to believe that you've reached the age of sixteen without anyone seeing it."

"It didn't . . . the mark didn't show up until about six months ago."

This surprised Declan.

"Kaden, has anyone else seen the mark?" Declan asked once more.

Kaden's face darkened and his lips thinned. "Why does that matter?"

"It matters because you've got a pack of demons after you who answer to Samael and he's someone you don't want to mess with. Not to mention the Seraphim are interested as well. Someone tipped off those bastards."

"I just want it gone." Kaden's chest was heaving as he fought for control.

Declan shook his head. "Sorry, kid, I don't think this is the kind of tattoo you can have removed. You're stuck with it." The boy's face whitened at his words but Declan pressed forward. "I need to know who else has seen this mark."

The teenager rolled his shoulders and Declan noticed a telltale blush creeping up his neck.

"Was it a girl?"

Kaden's eyes stared down at his shoes and he shoved his hands into his pockets. "Yeah," he muttered quietly.

"And her name would be?" Declan continued.

Ana was once more by Kaden's side and she gave him a quick reassuring squeeze. "This is important, Kaden. Who saw the mark on your shoulder?"

"Claire." He looked up at Declan, his eyes dark with pain, rage. "She wasn't just my girlfriend, you know? She was my best friend." Kaden scuffed the floor with his sneakers. "She was the one they . . ."

"That they what?" Declan glanced at Ana. The pain in her eyes made his gut clench.

"They killed her. In my room."

Silence followed his words. Declan was stunned and didn't know what to say.

"Who killed her?" he prompted, his voice much more subdued.

Kaden stared back at him, his face filled with anger, the quiet, dangerous kind. "Demons," he spat. "She was waiting for me in my room." Kaden's eyes dropped to the floor. "I found her, after they'd . . ." His voice drifted into nothing and silence filled the room.

"Shit," Declan whispered

"What does all of this mean?" Ana was exasperated and began to pace the length of the room. "So he has a mark? So what?" Her arms were moving all over the place; animated didn't come close to describing her. "I have fangs, you have—" She stopped as their eyes met.

"Abs to die for?"

Ana growled, "You always were so . . . so . . ."

"Charming?"

"I was going to say flippant. This isn't a joke, Declan.

Kaden's life is on the line, as are the lives of six other people."

"I'm well aware of that." His tone was biting. His cut-and-dried mission had just fragmented into one hell of a problem and he had no fucking clue what he was going to do.

"I need to know that you're on our side." Ana stood beside Kaden and glared at him. "I won't let you turn him over to the Seraphim. I don't believe they have his best interests in mind, and obviously neither does Bill." She cocked her head to the side. "You have two choices, so what's it going to be?"

The world narrowed then, like all the air had been sucked from the room, leaving only him and the vampire. "Okay," he whispered, "I'll play . . . what are my choices?"

"You help us find the others on the list and breathe not a word to anybody."

He was at her side in an instant, smiling wickedly as she jumped. Good. He wanted her off-kilter. "What's the second?" His voice was rough and he watched her mouth closely as she spoke.

"If you don't . . ." Her hand was around his neck before he could react.

"If I don't . . ." he whispered, his eyes still glued to her lips.

Her nails dug into his flesh but he felt no pain. Slowly his eyes rose until they locked onto hers. Something flickered within their depths, a raw need and hunger that she quickly cloaked.

"If you don't I will suck every single drop of blood from your body and leave you to rot at the bottom of the Mississippi."

Declan burned inside and leaned down until his lips were beneath the soft lobes of her ears. He felt her shiver as his breath swept across her flesh. That they had an audience was forgotten. At that moment there was only Ana. He grinned wickedly. Oh, the things he could do to her.

"Promise? 'Cause, babe, you lost me after the word *suck* and I don't give a shit where you leave me."

She pushed him away. "I'm being serious." She was pissed, her color high, and Declan wanted to run his fingers through the thick auburn waves that fell down to her ass.

His gaze moved to Kaden and then back to her. He was done playing games.

"I am, too." He moved toward her, taking the last few steps until he'd crowded her against the rickety table. His eyes were flat and for the first time in what seemed like forever, he was relaxed. He had a plan. Declan O'Hara was going to take what he wanted and damn the consequence.

"I'll help Kaden because it feels right. He's just a kid. As for the others on the list, I'm game for that, too, but . . ."

The energy in the room shifted as Ana arched an eyebrow. She kept her eyes trained on him and she nodded toward the door. "Kaden, give us a few minutes." Her tone brooked no argument, though the underlying compulsion helped and the teenager left.

"What exactly do you want, O'Hara?" Ana asked when they were alone. Her eyes were huge, hung like jewels in her pale face, and her hair caressed her body like a silken blanket.

She looked like an angel but he knew the truth. She was a heartless witch who'd been yanking his chain for years. He smiled wickedly. He would never have an opportunity like this again. Declan O'Hara was gonna have his cake and enjoy eating every last fucking crumb.

His hand slipped along her jaw as he bent toward her.

"What I've always wanted," he said simply. "You."

CHAPTER 5

Ana should have pushed him away. Hell, she could have crushed his larynx in less than a few seconds if she wanted to.

She should have done a lot of things other than what she did do, which was to stare into his dark eyes and do . . . nothing.

His hand along her jaw sent electrical pulses rippling across her flesh and she shivered as they spread along her body. Declan's lips were inches from hers with only her rapid breaths between them.

His scent was heady, intoxicating, like a blast of rock and roll entwined with a shot of tequila. He was hard-edged and boldly passionate, an apt description for the man who on a good day irritated the crap out of her and on a bad day left her weak with want.

"I won't . . . we can't," she sputtered, hating the way her tongue was all tangled up.

"Just one taste," he whispered as his eyes bored into hers, a ghost of a smile lifting the corners of his mouth. "If you can handle it." He was daring her to refuse.

She felt his other hand slide along the back of her waist until it rested upon the curve of her butt, his long fingers splayed across her flesh possessively. Declan was tall, over six feet by several inches, and her small frame fit perfectly against his. He pulled her in close and she felt the hardness of his body as if it had been imprinted upon her own flesh.

Her muscles tensed, but then she relaxed.

Two could play his game. She moved against him, her hip rubbing suggestively along his thigh, and returned his smile as his body stilled.

She should have pushed him away, but she didn't. In her mind's eye she watched the two of them from across the room. She saw his darkness against the pale of her skin, saw his hands upon her body, and felt his urgent need. It was matched equally by the hunger he'd awakened inside her.

It was incredibly erotic and she began to pulse fiercely, the small bud of desire between the folds of her sex engorged and painfully aroused. Things were moving way too fast. She needed a full stop.

And yet she did nothing.

Ana hissed softly and felt the edges of her control slipping as his large hand at her ass dug in and crushed her against him.

She was on the verge of orgasm and Declan had barely touched her. He was breathing hard, they were both fully clothed, and he'd not even kissed her yet.

"What are you waiting for?" she asked hoarsely.

His hand slid to the base of her skull as his other cupped her from behind. In one graceful movement he placed her upon the counter and slid between her legs. The bright lights overhead dimmed, and for the first time Ana noticed the glittery energy that lit his dark eyes.

He was silent as he looked down at her, and everything inside her melted. Her hands crept up hard abs until they rested upon his chest and she felt the heat of his skin through the thin T-shirt he wore. God, did he have to feel as good as he smelled? She licked her lips and her mouth went dry at the thought of tasting him.

He was nearly flush against her and Ana felt the aggressive nature that was her vampire erupt from within. She wrapped her legs around him and pulled herself up until her breasts were crushed against his chest.

"I'm waiting," he murmured against her flesh.

"For what?"

Crap, don't you go there . . . His lips skated across her neck and she hissed at the sensation left in his wake.

"For you to ask nicely," he replied.

Her fangs lengthened, but she pushed them back. The darkness that always lingered around the edges of her mind was calling like a seductive whisper.

She couldn't taste him because she was afraid she'd never be able to stop.

"I don't think this is a good idea." She closed her eyes and stifled a groan as he suckled the flesh between the crook of her neck and her collarbone.

"Really." His mouth was nearly to hers, her head held in place by a hand on each side of her jaw. "I think you're lying."

Jesus, but she felt like she was coming apart, and it took nearly everything inside her to remain calm, to keep the beast at rest and yet . . . it had been so long since she'd fed for pure pleasure.

She opened her mouth to protest but his lips were there, sliding across her own with an assured ease as his tongue darted inside. *So much for waiting for permission.*

Her fingers dug into him and she tried to push him away, but his arms tightened around hers. He forced her head back as he attacked her mouth with an aggressiveness that teased the beast inside.

She growled against his lips and then opened fully beneath him, not caring of the consequence, only knowing that the fire Declan had started was going to be a bitch to put out.

Her legs were entwined around his waist and she clung to him like a child as he continued to kiss her long and hard, each pass of his tongue pulling on a chord deep within her that was so painful it was exquisite.

Erotic images played in her mind, of naked limbs and dark eyes. That he could do this to her with just a kiss was insane, and as she continued to gyrate against him, she ignored the alarm bells ringing in her ears.

She'd never had such a kiss, and though she'd envisioned this in her mind countless times as they'd been bunkered down working missions the world over, the real deal was so much more intense than she'd ever dreamed.

She groaned into him and when her incisors broke skin and slid out, she paused. Slowly his tongue lapped at their length, but then he pulled away, taking his warmth with him.

Outside the last of the cicadas played their sad lament, their song riding the breeze until the echoes faded into nothing.

Declan's eyes were like mirrors of chocolate. They shimmered with a brilliance that was mesmerizing. Silence fell between the two of them and they stared at each other for several long moments. His face was unreadable, closed.

He set her back down upon the counter and Ana hated that she felt empty. Cheated. His blood still sang to her, teasing with the unknown. His pulse was steady and she licked her lips as she eyed his jugular.

"I'll stay and help the boy." Declan pulled away and the moment was over. He was all business now.

"That's it?" Her nipples ached and they strained against the black tank top she wore. She fought the urge to run her hands along the taut peaks.

He crooked his head to the side and her eyes rested upon the classic bone structure that he'd been gifted with. Declan O'Hara was every woman's fantasy, every dark, tortured inch of him.

She couldn't help herself, and her gaze slid down the length of his body.

"Did you want more?" His voice was like silk and she saw the smirk that hugged the corner of his mouth. What the hell was wrong with her?

"No!" she protested much too quickly, and as his smile deepened Ana fought the urge to slam her fist upside his head.

"The next time I put my mouth on your body I intend to take my time and indulge."

Ana jumped off the counter. "There won't be a next time. You're not my type, remember?" *Liar, everything about him is your type.*

Declan was nearly out the door. "Yeah, and your eyes are not tattooed to my ass right now."

She blushed, which was something she'd not done in decades.

"Where are you going?" She winced at the whine that accompanied her words. Did she have to sound so desperate?

"Wards must be put in place if you're to be protected. I'll be outside." The door slammed, and it echoed into the now-quiet room.

What the hell had just happened? Wearily she rubbed her eyes, and it was saying something that she was in fact tired.

What the hell had Bill been thinking?

"If something happens to Kaden I'll never forgive myself," she whispered. In the space of a few hours her life had changed course in a way she'd never thought possible, all of it defined by two words, *Declan O'Hara*. He was a complication she wasn't sure she was strong enough to deal with.

She turned off the light and stood in the dark for a few moments, her fingers against her lips as she gazed out the window into the dark. She thought of her brother Jean-Charles, and her gut tightened as bittersweet melancholy hit her hard.

If she wasn't careful she'd end up just like him. Lost forever.

The damp was biting and fog was rolling in as Declan worked feverishly to get some heavy-duty protection wards in place. Latent energy hung in the air—it stank of demon and otherworld. He couldn't deny the potency of it, nor the pull he felt as he inhaled its stench and let it settle in his chest.

The darkness was seductive, powerful, and for the moment he'd use it, manipulate it for his own purposes. What the hell. He'd always been an opportunist, and right now he could use a bit of extra mojo.

Declan slipped between the shadows that bordered the large home, every sense alert as he carefully made his way to the backyard. The gloom was pierced by a ray of light that shone from a window above and yet the lower level now appeared to be in darkness.

He drew charms into the air, exotic designs that glistened in the darkness. They hung in luminescent shadow, like the thinnest thread of a spider's weave, and then disappeared as the magick took hold.

Declan concentrated and infused his spells with many intricate layers of protection. He knew they were strong—probably the strongest he'd ever conjured—but with a demon lord like Samael after Ana and the boy, he wasn't taking any chances.

No fucking way. He'd had a major hard-on for the vampire for so long it was stupid. He'd coveted and dreamed about her for years. When he was in the bowels of Hell her memory, her scent, and the need to see her again were what got him through.

He'd made a vow that when he made it out he'd claim her, tell her exactly how he felt, and explain to her why she needed to let him in. *To be with him.*

It was his sorry-ass luck that a week after he escaped Hell with Julian Castille she was dead at his feet and his butt had been signed over to the Seraphim.

He clenched his teeth so tightly that his jaw ached as he continued to work. He still could not think clearly of that day and the events that had led to her death.

Fate had pretty much kicked him in the ass, and yet now, two years later, he was getting a second chance.

Declan felt his groin tighten at the thought of her lips against his, and of the way she felt against his body—so small, compact, and fierce. He'd waited years for that kiss and though he'd acted cool and in control, the simple truth was, in that moment she'd wrecked him.

He was not going to let this opportunity slide by. He'd protect the teenager, something he'd have done regardless. He'd also do what he could for the others on the list.

But his ultimate goal was the vampire. He would have her.

His eyes flew open as a bolt of energy slid through him. It was only a question of when.

CHAPTER 6

Decatur Street was crazy. It was a typical Friday night in the Big Easy, yet the dark undercurrent that slithered beneath the crowd had Declan on edge. Everything was too loud, too frenetic. He could literally taste the chaos that rode the wind.

Sad to say it was a taste he could learn to love.

He glanced at Ana. She was tense. She'd deny it of course, but he saw it clear as day. Her hands were tight at her sides and her jaw was clenched as she scanned the crowd.

"You feel it?" he asked.

Ana nodded but remained quiet. She'd been like that since the night before. It wasn't something he was used to, and in fact he much preferred her biting tongue and sarcastic comebacks.

"Something isn't right." He nodded to the crowd. "*They're* not right."

"It's Samael. He's close by." She glanced up at him. "Are you sure the house is protected? I should have stayed home with Kaden."

He didn't like anyone questioning his power but was willing to cut her some slack. It was obvious she was worried. "No one will get through my charms."

"Samael is strong."

"No shit," Declan murmured, "and the pack of wolves Ransome sent over will keep him more than busy if he shows."

He spied the Voodoo Lounge and guided Ana through the dense crowd. The incredible hulk was once more on door duty, but this time stepped away and directed them inside.

The club was filled near to bursting, hundreds of bodies gyrating to the heavy music that blasted from the stage. The room was hot, the atmosphere even hotter, and he inhaled a blast of sweat, booze, and sex. He'd be lying if he said it didn't affect him. The energy was potent, just the kind he liked.

A tall shifter approached them, a wolf, but his eyes were only for Ana.

"DeLacrux."

Declan's jaw clenched. Who the hell was this?

Ana nodded. "Asher."

The wolf bowed. He was old school and carried a certain charm that wasn't present in today's world. Shifters lived longer than humans but maxed out around two hundred years. This shifter was mature and deadly.

"I'm O'Hara," Declan proclaimed as he moved so that he now stood between the two of them.

The werewolf turned his attention to Declan. "I know exactly who you are."

"Where's Ransome?" Declan asked.

The wolf ignored his question and moved to the side. He smiled down at Ana. "It's been what, fifty years?"

"Closer to sixty," she answered stiffly.

"How's Jean-Charles?" The wolf's eyes glittered strangely and Declan felt an immediate shift in the air.

Who the hell was Jean-Charles?

"I have no clue." Ana stepped closer to Declan. "Let's go," she said tightly.

"Really?" the wolf murmured. "I'm sorry to hear of your

estrangement, but then again he was always the wild one, no?"

"You're so full of shit," Ana said tightly. "If Jean-Charles walked in here today you'd crap your pants."

"Where's Ransome?" Declan asked once more, and took a step toward the wolf as he did so.

Asher growled, a low warning shot from deep in his belly. "You will give me some space, sorcerer."

Declan's fingertips burned with energy and he flexed them in warning. "I won't ask you again."

"Back off, Asher," Ana hissed. She took a step forward until she was at Declan's side. "Or I *will* rip your throat out."

Asher's eyes narrowed as a wicked smile cut across his features. The air around him thickened and Declan knew he was close to the change. "I think I might enjoy that but there's no time tonight." The wolf nodded toward the mezzanine. "Ransome is expecting you."

Declan grabbed Ana's elbow and guided her through the crowd. The heavy beat was fueling the crowd something fierce. They walked through the sweaty, writhing bodies and he could taste the decadence.

Ana yanked her arm from his grip and proceeded up the stairs, leaving him to follow. The jeans she wore were faded, soft, and worn, and they gripped her curves like a second skin. He tore his eyes away and glanced down at the crowd. Asher licked his lips and smiled up at him, though his eyes were on Ana once more.

Declan ignored him even though he wanted to smash the wolf's aristocratic nose. There could be no distractions. Not tonight.

Ana made her way toward the office, and it occurred to him that she'd been there before—she knew exactly where she was going. She didn't knock and he followed her into Ransome's office.

The wolf sat behind his desk, feet up, cigar in hand, and

looking totally relaxed—a direct contrast to the borderline chaos that threatened his club. Declan nodded in greeting but it was the large man leaning against his desk who grabbed his attention.

Nico.

"Holy fuck," Declan murmured. The jaguar warrior was dressed head to toe in leather and denim, but it was the blue Mohawk he sported and accompanying nose ring that had Declan's attention.

Nico pushed away from the desk. "O'Hara."

"What the hell happened to you?"

The warrior shrugged his shoulders. "A dancer at Ringo's. I thought it was time for a change."

"I see that," Declan answered. "For most of us a change might mean more or less hair product, some facial hair. You look like you belong on the freakin' A-team." He glanced at Ransome and grinned. "Seriously, Mr. T's got nothing on you."

The jaguar ignored him and turned his attention to the vampire. If he was surprised to see her, he gave no indication. Ana stood a few feet away, legs wide and hands held loose at her sides, though the fists were still clenched.

Nico nodded to her. "You're looking better than the last time I saw you in Vegas."

"Considering I'd just been staked I sure as hell hope so."

"Miss DeLacrux." Ransome rose. "Welcome to the Voodoo Lounge."

Ana arched a brow. "I'm sure Asher has told you I've been here before."

"Yes, he did, though fortunately I missed your last visit and the ensuing chaos it produced."

Declan frowned. He didn't like being in the dark but wasn't about to ask the question. "Are the two of you done walking down memory lane? Because last I checked we have a situation brewing"—he glanced toward Nico—"and when we don't return with the boy you can bet your ass the Seraphim will come looking as well."

"Boy?" Nico sounded surprised.

Declan nodded. "Our target isn't a man but a teenager."

"So you've found him." The jaguar studied him closely, "and we're not bringing him in because?"

Ana stepped forward. The tips of her fangs peeked from between her lips. She stood as tall as her five-foot-two frame allowed and hissed as she faced the jaguar warrior.

"First off you'd have to go through me, jaguar, and secondly, Declan has agreed to protect him."

Nico glanced his way and Declan winced at the fury in his eyes. *Shit, here we go.* With his newly shorn Mohawk, the jaguar looked like a deranged serial killer. "One word," the warrior hissed. "Purgatory."

Declan clenched his hands into fists, at the ready, just in case. He was never going to live down the Church of the Holy Fiasco but for fuck sakes he was getting sick of hearing about it. "Look, the whole purgatory thing was a mistake, but can we please move on? How the hell was I supposed to know the ladies were pure? That they'd been chosen to serve?"

Nico snorted, disgusted. "They were living in a fucking convent. That might have been your first clue."

Declan narrowed his eyes and faced the jaguar. "I will not hand him over. You know how the Seraphim work. Their motives aren't always pristine. We can't guarantee Kaden's safety."

"Kaden? You have a name, too?" Nico paced the length of the room and the air around him blurred. He'd always been volatile, and living on the edge of humanity for the last several years hadn't done him any favors.

Declan pulled up the energy that thrummed inside his chest.

Ransome growled a warning but it was Ana who defused

the situation. She was at Nico's side before anyone could move and placed her hand upon his arm. Declan watched closely, his hands at the ready. He didn't give a flying fuck that Nico was his partner, one of the Seraph. If the jaguar laid one paw on Ana he'd tear him apart.

"Nico." Her voice was soft, entreating. "He's a boy. A sixteen-year-old boy."

"Why do they want him?"

Ana exhaled slowly. "He has this mark." She paused and looked back toward Declan. "I don't understand all of it but he's one of seven who have it."

Nico's lips were tight as he glanced toward Declan. "It would be great if you could explain a little better than that."

"He's the fifth of the mark of seven." There it was. There would be no sugarcoating.

Silence greeted his words, long moments that stretched taut until Declan felt it clawing at him.

"Holy fuck." Ransome looked stunned. "This changes everything."

"The mark of seven," Nico repeated. The jaguar began to pace once more. "Shit."

Declan watched the jaguar closely. The mark meant nothing until Kaden joined with the others. Only then would the true power that was the mark of seven be revealed. The question, of course, was would they gravitate toward the dark or the light? Or hang somewhere in the middle.

"You do understand why we can't hand the boy over?" Declan's question was aimed at Nico, but he glanced at Ransome as well. The wolf was out of his chair and downed the remainder of his bourbon before meeting Declan's gaze.

"Where are the others?" Ransome asked. His eyes were flat and he was dead serious. "Because if you've dragged them here to my city, I'm going to insist that you leave." He bared his teeth and nodded toward the door. "I warned you that I want no part of a holy war."

Declan eyed the wolf carefully. "In answer to your question, we have no idea who the remaining six are, but as to the other . . ." His voice trailed off and he glanced at Ana. Her face was white, her lips pale. She turned to him, her eyes huge, and the worry that hung there tore at him.

He knew her. Knew how strong she was. To see the vampire so upset set him on edge.

In that second he knew nothing had changed for him. Who the hell was he kidding? He thought he'd use this whole exercise as a means for seduction? Fuck that. He'd walk through fire for her.

Ransome stepped around his desk, his dark eyes centered on Declan. "As to the other?" he prompted.

Declan pushed thoughts of Ana away. *No distractions.* "It's too late. We've already got a demon lord on our ass, and though he's yet to show his face, he's close by."

"A demon . . . *lord*." Ransome's face darkened.

There was a loud rap on the door and it flew open before the werewolf had time to allow entrance. "LaPierre, what the hell is going on?" A tall woman strode into the room, a towel over her shoulder and a cigarette dangling from between her teeth. She was hard-looking, with tired pale features and lanky blond hair that hung from a loose ponytail. She wheezed and took a long drag before exhaling loudly. "I just had Benny kick out three more wolves, and it ain't even a full moon."

"Benny?" Nico asked.

She turned toward the jaguar. "Yeah, the big-ass bouncer." She swung back to Ransome and put her hand on her narrow hips. The jeans that hung there were held up by the slimmest of belts, and the tank top she wore was emblazoned with the word *MOFO*. "Something weird is going on." She nodded back toward the door. "Can't you feel it?"

Ransome tossed an angry look at Declan and grabbed up the phone. "Hold on," he growled into the device. "Sarah, go back to the bar. Tell Benny to close up as soon as he can empty the place without starting a riot. Get Asher to—"

"Asher's left for the night."

Declan watched the way Ana flinched at the mention of the wolf. The two of them shared a history, one that involved the mysterious Jean-Charles. He wouldn't be able to rest until he knew the details, but first things first.

Ransome let loose a string of profanity that didn't abate until he barked orders into the phone and slammed it back down.

He glared at them all, and Declan moved toward Ana as the energy in the room darkened. The werewolf had gone from pissed off to deadly anger in less than a minute.

"Fuck me, O'Hara. Who the hell have you dragged to my town?"

"It's not his fault." Ana swallowed and took a moment. "I led the dark lord here. That's on me but I didn't know where else to go."

"The dark lord," Ransome repeated. "What is this? Harry fucking Potter?" The wolf glanced around the room. "Anyone here, I dunno, willing to give up a name?"

"Samael," Ana answered quietly.

Ransome stopped, speechless. He ran his hand through the tawny length of hair that hung across his forehead. "The demon of chaos," he whispered softly. Another loud crash sounded outside his door. Ransome shook his head and growled. "No shit."

"So what's the plan?" Nico asked.

Declan glanced at Ransome and the two men stared at each other for several long moments. They'd been through a lot, back in the day, and he hoped it would count for something.

He turned to Nico. "You on board?" he asked the jaguar. "I won't turn an innocent boy over to the Seraphim."

"How do you know he's innocent? From what I understand not much is known about the mark of seven other than the fact that once the pieces are put in play, look the fuck out. It's anyone's guess which way they'll swing." Nico laughed harshly. "Do they kick-start an apocalypse? Do they end one? We don't know."

"He's just a kid and I'm not willing to hand him over until I know more." Declan's voice hardened.

"He's under Bill's protection," Ana interjected. "That should be good enough."

"Bill?" Nico snorted. "I'm not sure I trust him, either."

Ana was silent. She looked tired.

They needed to get back to the house. She had to feed.

"We will protect him and find the others before the Seraphim do. But first we need to deal with Samael." Declan nodded toward the werewolf. "Can we count on your help?"

Ransome ran his hand over the rough stubble that shadowed his jaw. He took his time, walked around his desk, and straightened a few papers that lay there. When the silence became unbearable he finally looked up at Declan.

"The necromancer that called forth the ghouls last night . . . I'm assuming whoever the hell he is will be tied to Samael."

Declan had him. He tried not to smile, and nodded. "That's what I was thinking. The ghouls were the bastard's first strike. Demons are notorious for getting others to do their dirty work."

"He was testing me," Ana murmured, "with the demon, vampire, and the ghouls."

"Yeah, and you passed." Ransome shook his head. "He'll be coming at you with big guns next time." The wolf glanced at Declan. "Or he'll come himself."

"The necromancer might know who else is on the list." Declan raised a good point and they all nodded in agreement.

Another crash split the night, and this time the walls

shook from the force of it. Ransome swore under his breath and rolled his shoulders before striding past them to the door. He opened it and ducked; a beer bottle barely missed his head as it flew past and smashed into the wall behind him.

"I'll do some digging," he continued. "See if I can come up with a name, but until then . . ." He grinned wickedly at the three of them and cracked his knuckles. "I could use a little help."

CHAPTER 7

A crow flew past Ana and landed on the large stone angel that stood a few feet away. It stared down at her in silence, head cocked to the side as if it were about to talk.

She slid past the black bird, her feet gliding over the damp earth as she darted between the rows of graves. It was late, well on the wrong side of 4 A.M. The Voodoo Lounge had been an experience, an out-of-control crowd fueled by booze, loud music, and sex.

And a little bit of chaos. The aftereffects tingled along her spine and were the main reason she was so on edge.

It had been a mild taste of what was to come if Samael wasn't stopped.

They'd returned to the DeLacrux mansion only a half hour before, with the jaguar warrior Nico along for the ride. Declan had been correct. The wards were strong, the wolves were patrolling, and Kaden was safe.

She'd grabbed a bag of O neg and disappeared into the attic, which, unconventional as it seemed, was where she'd always felt the most comfortable. She needed space, time to be alone.

Christ, who was she kidding? *She needed to feed.*

Blood from a bag went only a small way in satisfying her hunger. It kept her alive, but didn't feed her soul the way fresh blood, *warm blood*, from a living human did. The essence fed her spirit and tempered the darkness that was part of her nature.

Most of the time it was an easy balance to achieve—walking that line between light and dark—but she could tell the next few days would test her like none before.

Being around Declan did nothing but make her crazy. She'd grown weak over the last two years. There was a time when she'd been able to resist the scent of his blood and block it out. Yet for the past twenty-four hours it was all she had thought about.

Her fangs slid out at the thought of him and she paused near the far end of the cemetery.

The crow flew by once more and swooped toward the largest of the mausoleums. The damn thing seemed to be following her and she frowned as she watched it glide gracefully through the air.

It landed atop the stone structure, but this time it was no angel it rested upon. The crow shook out its dark wings and stared down at her from the peak of the DeLacrux tomb. Its small, beady eyes glistened in the moonlight and it cawed sharply.

Ana winced as the sound cut through the heavy silence. She glared up at the bird and hissed, her fangs fully exposed. It continued to stare down at her as if issuing a challenge. She hissed once more and was at the foot of the tomb in less than a second, her body a preternatural blur. The crow flapped its wings and then disappeared into the night sky, leaving her alone amongst the shadows.

She'd been in New Orleans for almost two weeks but had not paid a visit to this particular corner of the city, otherwise known as the city of the dead. If the humans knew how many *undead* still walked between the tombs they'd surely stay away.

She felt silent eyes watching her, the heavy stare of souls

that still wandered. Her gaze swept the immediate area but there was no one willing to show themselves tonight.

She bit her lip and swallowed a sigh. The melancholy, the abject sadness that hung in her gut was painful. Ana had never felt so alone. So bereft. Seeing Declan again had stirred the pot, but running into Asher tonight, standing in the Voodoo Lounge once more, had set the damn thing to boiling.

She ran up the steps, her feet silent on the stone, and stood in front of the double doors. Names were engraved along each side, etched deep into the walls, and she traced them slowly. Her finger stopped at the last one. Jean-Charles DeLacrux. Her twin.

The whisper of a memory slid through her mind and she smiled to herself. Jean-Charles, or Jack as she'd called him, darting through the cemetery as a child and Ana fast on his heels. She leaned her body against the cold stone and rested her cheek upon the hard surface, her finger still caressing his name.

The last time she'd seen her brother had been nearly sixty years ago. He'd been covered in blood, mad with grief . . . and it had been her fault. If she'd kept her mouth shut . . . If she'd not been so jealous of his happiness . . . If Asher hadn't been there . . . maybe his lover, Cerise, would have been spared.

"You are dead to me, sister." They'd been the last words he'd spoken to her, and even now, the echo of them in her mind was enough to break her heart in two. Again.

He'd fled New Orleans, and his name had been etched into the stone by the local ruling council. It was a sign to all vampires that Jean-Charles DeLacrux was no longer welcome in their world. He'd committed a crime against their code and would be destroyed if he ever returned.

Ana grimaced as her fingers touched the other names that were there. So many of them. The DeLacrux were bad seeds. It was only a matter of time before hers was added to the list.

Bill wouldn't be able to pull a miracle like that out of his ass. She'd long ago accepted the fact that she was indeed cursed.

Hunger stretched and ached inside of her, gnawing at the emptiness that was there. She blew out a ragged breath. It was time to hunt. She needed more than the bagged blood she kept at the house. With Kaden to look after, she'd been keeping close and not hunting like she should.

"Nice digs."

Declan's voice startled her and she pushed away from the tomb, pausing as her fangs slid back out of sight before she turned around. The moon cast an eerie shadow across the cemetery and it cloaked Declan in a mist of ethereal light. He looked like a god, and in that moment she hated him—hated everything that he represented because it was something that she could never have.

"Stalker much?" she said. "I don't like being followed."

He ignored her sarcastic comment and rested his booted foot on the bottom stair. His gaze slowly traveled the building and paused at the peak.

"DeLacrux," he murmured. "What is this? Some kind of clubhouse for the undead?"

O'Hara had always been a smart-ass and she gritted her teeth as a muscle flexed sharply across her jaw. She supposed he was right. There were no actual bodies inside. Her immediate family no longer lived in New Orleans. Armand and Jacqueline DeLacrux, her parents, had left well over a century ago. It was never smart to stay in one area for too long. People tended to wonder about the folks who never aged past their early twenties. Last she'd heard, and this was nearly two decades earlier, they'd been in the South of France.

Ana's lineage could be traced back to the ruling queen,

Isobel. She'd been born vampire, as were most of the vampires in existence. To turn a human was forbidden and seen as the ultimate betrayal to their kind. Aside from the fact humans would dilute their bloodlines, most of them didn't come through the transformation well. They went mad, fueled bloody rampages, and had to be hunted, destroyed.

Jack the Ripper? Classic case.

In her world the rules were archaic. Marriages were arranged, alliances forged.

Ana had a fiancé. Somewhere out there. A reclusive bastard who'd rejected her on sight nearly seventy-five years ago. He'd been a tall Viking—Aleksander, an ancient who'd scared the crap out of her. And though she was grateful for the reprieve, she knew he was still out there, and if the queen wished it, his rejection meant nothing.

She sighed. It was just another thread of her life that was frayed, unfinished.

"Are you all right?" Declan's voice was quiet and he seemed genuinely concerned. She didn't want him to be nice right now. She much preferred the friction.

"I'm fine but I'd be way better if I was alone."

Liar.

His scent drifted lazily on the breeze and her eyes homed in on the pulse that beat at the base of his neck. Did he have to smell so damn good? Ana's mouth watered as she envisioned her teeth breaking his skin, her tongue lapping at the richness that would spill.

"It's not safe." Declan took another step.

No shit. If you were smart you'd book it out of here like yesterday.

She shook her head. "You're joking, right? I don't need a babysitter, Declan, so get over it."

He took another step and then another until he stood just below her. He stared up at her in silence, his dark eyes hiding all sorts of things.

"How do you know Asher?" His question surprised her.

"He's from New Orleans and I'm from New Orleans. It's a small community, Declan. Those who are otherworld tend to run in the same circles whether we like each other or not." She was being vague but really didn't want to discuss her past with the sorcerer.

Declan took one more step until he was eye level with her.

"Who is Jean-Charles?" His voice was lower, his eyes narrowed.

Ana clenched her jaw as another wave of need rushed over her. He was too close. His scent was intoxicating, earthy, with a hint of pine, or was that sandalwood?

"An ex-lover?"

His lips were open slightly and she focused on them, not really hearing his words. They were beautiful . . . his lips. A mouth made for pleasure. Heat coiled deep in her stomach and a slow flush crept across her cheeks. It was rare for a vampire to get hot, but at the moment, she felt like she'd slipped into a bed of molten lava.

She wanted to cup his chin and taste him. She wanted to pull him close and inhale his sweet fragrance. She wanted his hard body pressed against hers.

Ana licked her lips and growled softly as her incisors broke skin inside her mouth. Who the hell was she kidding? She wanted to sink her fangs deep into his jugular and take from him. Drink his essence and be done with it. Maybe then this longing, this absolute craving she felt for Declan would go away.

"Do it," he whispered.

She blinked and shook the madness that threatened.

"No." She turned from him and exhaled roughly. "You need to go, Declan." Her skin was on fire and the beast that was below the surface threatened. She would never forgive herself if she hurt him.

"What are you afraid of, Ana?"

Dammit, he'd cleared the last step and the heat of his body was at her back. She squeezed her eyes shut and fought for control but it was no use. Her fangs were now fully extended.

"Don't touch me." She barely managed to get the words out.

"You want me to touch you."

His hands were on her, his touch burning. Ana's eyes flew open and she whirled around, knocking his hand from her body as she did so.

"No." Her chest was heaving, her hands clenched into fists. "I don't want your touch, Declan, let's be honest here. I want to *eat* you." Ana said every word carefully as she glared at him. "There's a huge difference between the two."

She needed him to understand. She was not all puppies and rainbows. She was hard-edged and bad, with insatiable appetites that came with a price.

"Why is it so hard for you to admit that there's something between us?" He took another step, but this time Ana refused to back away. "That there's always been something there?"

She inhaled deeply, which was the wrong thing to do. Declan O'Hara smelled like decadence, passion, and *life*. Would it be so bad to take just a nibble?

The crow cawed as it swept by once more, swooping low, inches from their heads. Its sharp cry cut through their "moment" with the effective strike of a blade and Ana hissed in anger.

"There's never been anything between us, Declan. I don't know what fantasy world you were living in. I don't do men like you."

"You did Diego." His voice was harsh. "Many times, in fact."

I knew he could never break me the way you can.

"Seriously, Declan, this is getting old. There's something pathetic about a man who begs for sex." She laughed harshly. "And let's be honest here. That is what we're talking about, isn't it? Sex?" She took a step back. "I can spread my legs and we can go at it. Get it over with once and for all."

His face hardened at her words, his dark eyes narrowed into twin slits of ebony.

She reached for the waistband of her jeans and started to undo the clasp. "Is that what you want? A quick fuck in the cemetery?"

Declan cursed and she felt a hot sting of energy surround her tightly. It tingled along her arms and spread over her abdomen. She glanced up at him in surprise. She couldn't move. Ana struggled but there was no budging. What the hell?

Declan's hand slid around her neck and he bent low, his breath sizzling along her neck to tickle her in places that were hidden.

"When I finally have you"—his warm mouth was just below her ear—"it will be no quick *fuck* in a cemetery." She shuddered at the sensations that slid across her skin. "It will be a slow and thorough loving and I will taste every inch of you." His tongue flicked across her flesh. "I'll make sure I'm hungry."

Invisible fingers swept across her chest and her nipples hardened instantly. What the hell was he doing?

His hand slid along her jaw until he cupped her chin and forced her to look up at him. The raw emotion that hung in the depths of his eyes stirred something deep within her.

The man was dead serious. If she let go, let her desires have free rein, he would die. She wouldn't be able to stop at a taste, she wasn't strong enough. There would blood and sex and she would claim him.

How could she not? It's what her heart wanted, which ironically was the one thing she couldn't have.

The elders on council would hunt Declan until he fell.

It didn't matter that he was now Seraph—that he served a higher order and was considered immortal.

She knew the truth. Immortality was a myth. Everyone had an Achilles' heel.

"Please, let me go." Ana closed her eyes. There was no more fight in her.

Their lips were separated by a whisper and the hunger she felt was painful.

She licked her lips. "Declan, I—"

She was suddenly released and nearly fell as Declan moved away from her. He nodded toward the mausoleum. "Living in the past is a mistake. The ghosts that linger there will not keep you sane or feed the hunger you feel. You taught me that." He paused. "I'll see you back at the house."

Declan turned and disappeared into the darkness.

Ana shuddered and blew out a long, hot breath. The DeLacrux mausoleum stood in shadow and she crossed once more to the entrance, her eyes falling to the names etched into the stone.

Slowly her finger traced her brother's name.

Jean-Charles had been weak. He'd surrendered to the needs of his heart and it had ended tragically. The council had hunted his newly turned lover and murdered her. He'd been banished and Ana hadn't seen him since.

She liked to think that Jean-Charles lived and had found some kind of contentment. She wanted to believe she would *know* if her twin was dead.

Ana laid her cheek against the cold stone. God, how she missed him . . . and for the first time in nearly sixty years, she felt the sting of searing hot tears.

CHAPTER 8

It was nearly five in the afternoon when Ana made her way down from the attic. She'd slept a few hours and had been awake for the last several. Unlike popular modern folklore, vampires didn't require much sleep or go to ground during the day. They didn't reside in a coffin—well, she didn't anyway; her four-poster bed did just fine.

She did, however, have to avoid direct sunlight.

Her hand caressed the scar over her heart. And she definitely steered clear of stakes . . . when she could.

Shadows were just beginning to creep along the walls and she paused at the bottom of the stairs. Her home smelled musty with the heavy perfume of damp age. She glanced into the parlor and took a few steps until she was inside.

The faded cream walls were dirty, much closer to gray, and the huge mantel above the fireplace was covered in cobwebs. Her eyes drifted over the furniture. It, too, was faded, moth-eaten, and threadbare, nibbled at by whatever rodents had dared venture inside.

How different things had been before she'd stopped caring.

She closed her eyes as her chest tightened, heavy with the weight of memories and the sadness of what would never be.

She'd been happy here, many years ago. It had been easy to make herself forget and yet so damn hard to remember. But tonight, memories of a time and place long forgotten flooded her mind. Images of parties and dances and hot summer nights in the Quarter. Of Jean-Charles, his wicked sense of humor and his passion for living.

They'd been inseparable—she and her twin—their lives lived to the fullest. Until Cerise. Until it had been destroyed.

Ana should have known it would never last.

A sharp rap at the front door echoed into the foyer. It was Ransome LaPierre. His otherworld scent was hard to miss.

She opened the door just as he was about to knock once more. The tall wolf smiled down at her. He was golden light mingled with caramel-edged darkness. Power clung to him; there was no doubt that he was the alpha of his pack.

"Come in." Ana moved aside and closed the door behind him.

"Nice digs," Ransome said as he looked around.

Ana grimaced. "You're being too polite. The place is falling apart. I just don't . . ." She shrugged. "What's the point?"

Ransome turned in a full circle. "The foundation is good. It's the cosmetic stuff that needs repairing. I could hook you up with a few local contractors."

"I don't think so," she murmured.

"It wouldn't take much."

"What is this? *Extreme Makeover*? We gonna move a bus or something?"

Declan stood near the foot of the stairs and Kaden was just behind him. She nodded to Ransome. "Follow me. I'm assuming you have intel on the necromancer?"

She smiled at Kaden but chose to ignore Declan as she led the way toward the kitchen.

It was empty. "Where's Nico?" She crossed to the fridge

and grabbed a bag of blood, tossed it into the microwave, and then glanced back at the others.

Kaden slid his long legs under the table and slouched back in a chair. He picked up a half-eaten beignet and thrust the remainder into his mouth.

Declan arched a brow and answered. "He went to see a couple contacts he has in the area. Some voodoo woman in the Quarter. He hasn't returned yet. No worries. He'll hook up with us later."

She nodded and looked at Ransome. "So what did you learn?"

The werewolf glanced at the teen.

"It's okay," Ana prodded, "we've no secrets from Kaden. This *is* his life we're talking about."

"All right." Ransome nodded. "I called in a few favors, did some checking on my own, and have two possibilities. One is a guy named Al Deboer. He lives in Jefferson parish and has definite ties to the underworld. The other is Francesca DuRoche. She's a two-bit fortune cookie who has a place near Jackson Square."

"You got a feeling one way or another on these two?" Declan asked as he grabbed a beer from the fridge and tossed one to the wolf.

"I checked out Al's place earlier today. From what I can tell the guy's not been home for at least two to three days. I fed the asshole's cat for him." Ransome looked disgusted. "Dumb fuck."

"How can you be sure?" Ana asked, curious.

Ransome smiled and tapped his nose. "It's all here, baby. His scent was old, stale." He shrugged his shoulders. "Plus"—he winked—"the newspaper on his table was dated three days ago. Lead story was about a horse race in Florida that took place yesterday. I'm thinking old Al is a betting man."

Ana poured herself a glass of blood and forced herself to sip slowly. It was hard. Her hunger was beyond a regular thirst and it was difficult to act normal. Jesus, but she needed Declan to move away from her.

"So we find the girl." Declan drained the last of his beer and tossed the bottle under the sink.

"The sooner the better," Ransome added.

"I agree," Ana interjected. "Samael knows by now the ghouls weren't able to do his dirty work. He'll be coming after Kaden. Hell, we can already feel his presence."

"All right." Ransome looked at Declan. "She has a shop near Jackson Square and lives above it."

"Well, let's go." Kaden's chair scraped along the worn linoleum as he pushed it back and stood.

"I don't think so." Declan took a step forward and crossed his arms over his chest. "You need to stay put."

"No way." Kaden shook his head. "I'm not staying in this dump while you go out and have all the fun."

Declan's features darkened. The energy in the room sifted and churned. It slid across Ana's skin and settled around them all. Declan wasn't fooling around.

"This isn't up for discussion. You'll stay." He glanced at Ransome. "Your boys still outside?"

The wolf nodded. "Yeah, I've got two patrols on duty."

"Double it."

Ransome pulled out his cell.

Declan moved away. "Read a book or something. I don't care what you do, but if I find you anywhere other than in this house, I will kick your ass. Got it?"

Kaden remained stone-faced but was quiet.

"It's for your own good." Though Ana didn't like the thought of being away from the teen, there was no way in hell he was going out in the field. The safest place was her mansion.

"All right then. Hate to break up the drama but it's nearly six and the sun is setting." Ransome looked at Ana. "We're good to go, right?"

Ana set her now-empty glass on the counter and nodded. "Let's do this." Kaden turned his back to her as she walked by, and she sighed softly. *Teenagers.*

She grabbed a form-fitting leather jacket from the coat-rack in the corner of the foyer. Not because she needed it but because it projected a certain image she liked. Kick-ass, determined, and dangerous.

She was well aware of Declan a few feet behind, though the space between them felt as large as the Rio Grande. They'd never had an easy time, she and the sorcerer. Friction had always been a part of the equation.

Ana yanked the door open and stepped out into the crisp air. It was cooler than normal and though barely 6 P.M., very dark. There were no stars to light up the sky, no moon to shed her beams.

Declan moved past her and she watched his tall form slide between the shadows that fell across the path. The flag-stones were grossly overgrown with weeds, and for the first time since she'd been home, she felt embarrassed. Her home was an utter wreck.

The sidewalks were empty and the wind whispered against her cheek, bringing with it the voices of the dead.

"You all right?" Ransome stopped beside her, his nostrils flaring as his gaze swept the area in front of them. He heard them, too.

"I'm fine," she whispered. The dead souls who roamed New Orleans were many, and she often heard their sad lament. Most times she ignored them, easily blocking them out. But tonight they called to the sadness she felt.

"Let's go." They both looked up as Declan's terse voice cut through the gloom.

"I get the feeling there's unfinished business between the two of you," Ransome murmured as they started after Declan. "You planning on working that shit out?"

Ana's gaze fell to the sorcerer and she shook her head. "You're wrong. We're fine."

Ransome smiled down at her, but his eyes remained hard. "If I think either one of you is gonna get my ass burned because you can't keep it together . . . I'm outta this one. Understood?"

"Don't worry about it, we're cool."

"Yeah, that's what Anne Boleyn thought, and then she lost her fucking head."

"Whatever," Ana muttered under her breath.

They made their way toward Jackson Square in silence. Three bodies sliding through darkened streets that were eerily silent. So not the norm for the Quarter; it was Saturday night, after all.

There was the odd group of tourists and, yes, the weather was ominous, but still, the streets were much emptier than they should be.

"We don't have a lot of time." Declan looked down at her, and Ana nodded. He was right. Samael was close.

"You're sure the wards are going to hold?" She knew the question was redundant but couldn't help herself.

"They'll hold," Declan said softly. "I juiced them up good and strong. The magick that lives here is darker than any I've come across, in this realm anyway." He nodded once more. "They'll hold. Besides, the wolves will not let anything through. The LaPierre shifters are tough sons of bitches."

"There's the shop." Ransome pointed several feet ahead of them. They'd bypassed the nearly empty Jackson Square and had headed down a side street off the main walkway. Several colorful signs hung overhead proclaiming their wares, whether it was souvenirs, food, clothing, or, as in this case, fortune telling. Balconies lined the upper shops, indicating apartments.

They stopped just in front of Madame TuLeenie's. The shop was in darkness though the sign on the door still said OPEN. Declan tried the handle but it was locked. Above them a slip of dim light shimmered on the balcony.

"She's home." Ransome's nose quivered as he inhaled a shot of air. "I can smell her."

Ana shot a look of disgust at the wolf. "That is just wrong."

"Not really." Ransome smiled. "She smells like all kinds of right . . . for a necromancer."

Declan glanced upward. "There must be a fire escape around back. From what I can see the only way up is through the shop."

Ana moved in front of the men. "You guys find the alternate entrance. I'll take the balcony." She didn't hesitate and ran toward the brick wall, her body a blur of grace and agility as she jumped.

Seconds later she clung to the side of the balcony and grinned down at the boys. "I'll see you inside." She then arced her body through the air and landed in a defensive position out of sight.

Ana let her senses adjust and felt the human presence on the other side of the glass. Heavy purple gauze covered most of the window but light escaped from the far side where there was a two-inch gap. She slid along the wall and peeked inside the room.

She could make out the edge of a bed and it was covered with a mess of clothes; tops, jean, undergarments. A pair of boots and a bag lay on the floor.

Francesca was on the move.

A shadow passed and Ana stilled as she saw a curtain of crimson hair and a slender form draped in black. The woman paused and turned to the side, affording Ana a clear view of pale skin and delicate features. She grabbed the boots, tugged them on, and then left once more.

Ana tried the window but it was locked. She glanced over the balcony once more. Declan was nowhere to be seen. Damn but she could use his magic touch right now.

She squared her shoulders and faced the windowpane. Normally she preferred to be all silent and stealthlike, but when in Rome . . .

She kicked out her leg and was about to aim it dead center toward the glass when she saw a something fly past the window. The wall shook from the force of the hit and a large shadow stopped inches from her, its breadth huge on the other side of the curtain.

Ana wasted no time. She busted through the glass and rolled into a defensive position as shards rained down upon her. A sharp crack of pain split her skull, most likely from the fist that was attached to the asshole who lifted her body several feet into the air. She was thrown up against the brick wall as if she were nothing more than a rag doll.

Son of a mother . . . the pain was immediate and severe.

Long fingers dug into her shoulder before she had a chance to react. Ana saw a mess of red hair and tumbled limbs on the floor. Damn, *but she better be alive.*

She tried to twist from the intruder's grip, but even with her enhanced strength she was no match. Once more she sailed through the air, over the bed, to land on the floor with such force that several pictures fell from the wall.

She jackknifed her body and leapt up as her fangs slid from her mouth. A tall demon faced her, his face set in a toothy grin. He was in human form, though how long that was going to last was anyone's guess.

"Are you a fucking moron?" she shouted, angry that she'd been tossed about by a douche bag whose intelligence level looked to be subpar. Her jaw was killing her almost as much as her shoulder, and blood dripped down her face from the corner of her temple.

The demon's smile widened and she snarled in answer, her gaze moving beyond him to the now-stirring form on the floor. The woman groaned softly, and the demon paused.

She couldn't reach the girl before the demon. Jesus fuck! Where the hell were Declan and Ransome?

Ana grabbed a lamp from the table beside the bed and whipped it at the demon's head. It ricocheted off his skull with such force that it embedded into the wall beside him.

The demon turned its yellowish eyes onto her. Its face was contorted—the change was starting—it growled loudly and rushed forward. Ana leapt over the bed and met the bastard halfway, her booted foot aimed for the soft spot between its legs.

She connected hard and jabbed her long fingernails deep into its jugular as it roared in pain. The demon's legs buckled slightly but it recovered and its arms slid around her shoulders like a noose, its poisonous talons digging into her flesh.

She screamed in agony and hissed as it began to shake her but she didn't give up. She tried to crush its larynx while digging into its skin, all the while avoiding the poisonous spittle that was now dripping from its rapidly changing mouth.

Where the hell were the boys?

The demon roared and yanked her by the hair as it peeled her away and threw her once more. Ana landed hard near the girl and blinked rapidly as she stared up into the palest blue eyes she'd ever seen. Blood ran in rivulets down the woman's forehead, teasing Ana with the sweet scent.

The woman was dazed and shook her head. Her eyes widened, focused behind Ana, and she tensed.

Shit. Ana grimaced as she was grabbed and yanked into

the air once more. The woman yelled and tossed a deadly blade at her.

Ana's fingers gripped it hard and she bucked her body with all her might, twisting in the air like a gymnast. The demon grunted as she soared overhead. She screamed and landed, arms outstretched, the blade cleanly slicing through the bastard's head.

A gurgling sound escaped its mouth and then the head toppled forward. Ana sidestepped the carcass and stumbled. Her eyes were unfocused and she felt dizzy.

The door to the bedroom crashed open and she swung around, pushing a mess of long auburn waves behind her shoulder.

Now they decide to show. She hissed at them, pissed off. "Your nose is defective, wolf. Do you want to explain to me how in the hell you didn't smell that?" She pointed to the demon corpse.

Declan was at her side in an instant, his hand reaching for her. She yanked away. "Don't touch me." The rage and anxiety she felt wasn't rational. This she knew, and at the moment she didn't trust herself.

Ransome arched a brow. "Sorry, the demon must have been charmed. I still can't smell him." The wolf glanced around. "So where is she?"

Ana turned abruptly.

The space where the girl had been was empty.

A strangled sound fell from Ana's lips and she cursed.

"No worries." Ransome was near the window. He turned back to the two of them. "*Her* scent I can follow easily. I'll meet you back at the Lounge." He stripped the clothes from his body, shifted into his animal form, and jumped through the window.

Ana's body trembled. "I'll see you there," she said hoarsely, wincing as another wave of hunger swept over her.

"Ana, you're hurt. Let me help you."

Her fangs broke skin once more. Declan's scent was much too enticing. She averted her face. "Back off, O'Hara." She needed to be away from him. Like yesterday.

Ana slid past the sorcerer before he could react and jumped through the window that Ransome had cleared only seconds before. She landed, *hard*, and yelped as the jarring motion sent pain ripping through her shoulder.

She glanced up and saw Declan's silhouette. The hunger inside was unbearable. Ana turned and disappeared into the darkness.

She needed to feed, and tonight bagged blood wasn't gonna cut it.

CHAPTER 9

It was late, *again*, and nearing four in the morning when he heard Ana's footfalls. Declan tempered his anger as he sat in the darkened kitchen of the DeLacrux mansion. He'd been on edge all evening, had patrolled the perimeter of the lot several times. He couldn't shake the feeling that something was out there. Watching. Waiting.

His long limbs were tense, which pissed him off. He wanted to appear relaxed, as if he didn't give a flying fuck that the vampire had blown them off and disappeared for hours. It was hard. His fists were clenched tight, his back ramrod-straight.

The night had been a total bust and it sure as hell hadn't gone as planned. The necromancer had been of no use. She'd been half dazed from her tussle with the demon and subsequent fall from the balcony. Ransome had agreed to keep her until they could better interrogate her but that probably wouldn't be until tomorrow.

Nico had finally shown up at the Voodoo Lounge and the news wasn't good. His priestess had agreed to tap into the darkness and see what she could find out. She'd gone into a trance and come up with only one word. Apocalypse. She'd then gone into convulsions and Nico had barely managed to get the woman to the hospital.

She'd died shortly thereafter.

The jaguar warrior had left but Declan waited for the vampire. *For hours.* Like a wet-behind-the-ears schoolboy. The bartender Sarah had started passing him free drinks just so he'd get drunk and leave. It hadn't worked, though eventually he'd given up.

He heard Ana pause just beyond the doorway and then she swept into the kitchen with the assured grace of some- one very much in control.

He eyed her in silence as she crossed to the sink and grabbed a sorry-looking excuse of a plant off the window- sill. Carefully she ran some water over it and then set it back in place. She turned around and met his gaze full-on.

Light shone in through the window, a soft glow from the security lamp in the backyard. It left half of her features in shadow but the fullness of her lips beckoned and his body re- acted instantly. He felt the familiar ache inside, the one filled with need and want, and wished like hell it would go away.

He bit back the shitload of anger that was buried inside him and instead leaned back in his chair, propping his arms behind his head.

She smelled of rain, and he noticed the damp glitters of drops that glistened amongst the tangled hair that fell over her shoulder. She'd always hated the rain.

"Where've you been?" the words fell rapidly off his tongue but he didn't care.

"I had to feed." Her answer was simple, honest.

An image of her mouth pressed against some random man's neck flashed across his mind, and his face tightened in anger. "For the last eight hours? That's one hell of an ap- petite. I thought you were into bagged blood these days."

She shrugged. "It's not always enough."

"No, I guess not." He glared at her.

"Why don't you spill what's really on your mind and get on with it."

"You blew off an important interrogation," he snapped. Declan's fuse was burning fast and he kicked the chair back as he rose to his feet. It skidded across the floor and banged into the pantry.

Ana snorted, not backing down as he took a step closer to her. "What? You and LaPierre couldn't handle that skinny piece of ass? Are you kidding me?"

"You said you would meet us back at the Lounge." His tone was harsh and he took the last step until he was inches from her. Declan stared down into eyes that shimmered like glass. He saw his reflection deep within their depths. He looked like a man on edge, about to lose it.

Ana hissed and thumped him in the chest. "Give me some space, O'Hara."

He didn't budge but continued to glare at her, hating the way she got under his skin. He fucking wished she didn't smell so damn good, either.

"What is it that you really want to say, Declan? Because I sure as hell don't think you give a shit one way or another whether I was there to *interrogate* some bony-ass redhead."

She didn't get it.

His fingers trembled at his side and vibrations ran along the floor as he tried to temper his anger.

"There is a fucking demon lord gunning for your ass in case you've forgotten." Her eyes widened slightly. "And don't think for one minute you have a chance in hell against someone like Samael. He's ruthless, cunning, and stronger than anything you've come up against." He lowered his voice and whispered, "He's nothing like that piece of crap you dealt with at the necromancer's."

Ana opened her mouth to speak but then closed her lips tight. He sensed her mind at work, saw the way her eyes fell as she averted her gaze.

Maybe she was finally getting it.

"I won't let you pull a dumb-ass move and get yourself hurt, or worse."

Ana moistened her lips and exhaled a ragged breath. "I've been taking care of myself for the last three hundred years, Declan." She shook her head. "I've never had to rely on anyone."

"Trust me," he retorted as he backed away, "you meet that son of a bitch face-to-face, you're gonna want all the help you can get." Declan grabbed the chair from beside the pantry and thrust it back under the table. "I should know. He's no different than Lilith, and I held up her whipping post for nearly six months."

Declan strode from the room and headed toward the parlor. He'd found a half-decent blanket the night before and he tossed his long frame onto the short, uncomfortable settee. It wasn't his first choice; however, it was all there was. The habitable rooms were taken and the others were rank with mildew and age.

He groaned as he shifted his body and tried to get comfortable. His thoughts turned to Kaden and he grimaced. The boy's future was not a sure thing. He'd done some research. The mark of seven was legendary. They were both coveted and feared. If fear won out, the Seraphim would have them destroyed. If the demon underworld managed to get their hands on all seven, then who the hell knew what kind of weapon they'd control.

Declan sighed, closed his eyes, and tried to find some sort of peace. He was nearly there, too, but something woke him; a noise, a hint of energy in the air. Instantly he was on alert.

Someone was in the foyer.

The squeak of the doorknob turning echoed into the silence. Did she actually think he'd let her leave again?

Declan was up in a flash, his anger carrying him forward as he stomped into the foyer like a deranged person. But it wasn't Ana who stood there, frozen with the door half open. It was Kaden.

"Where the hell do you think you're going?" he snapped.

The teenager jumped at his words and Declan felt another tingle of energy charge the air as the boy turned to face him. He was dressed for outside with jeans, long-sleeved sweater, and a warm vest.

"I need to get out. I'm going crazy in here."

Yeah, join the fucking club.

"You guys won't let me leave or go anywhere. I've been stuck in this dump for days." Kaden shoved his hands into the front pockets of his jeans and lifted his chin in a defiant manner. "All I do is sit on my ass and think. I don't wanna think about things anymore. I don't want to remember Claire or what my life was like. I'm done with that." He turned back toward the door. "I need to breathe before I freak out."

"You're not going out there. " Declan took a step forward as Kaden tensed. "Alone." Every inch of his body protested. It had been days since he'd had proper rest. He might be one of the Seraph now but he was by no means like the rest of them. Some were of angelic origins, some otherworld, and others like Cale were a complete mystery.

Declan, on the other hand, still needed shuteye occasionally.

"Whatever," Kaden muttered. He yanked on the door and left it wide open as he disappeared. Declan glanced back at the settee and sighed before following the teen into the early-morning gloom.

It was quiet, eerily so. Declan stopped beside the teenager, his gaze sweeping the entire perimeter. Endless fog slithered along the paved road in front of the house, twisting like ribbons of smoke against the protection ward that lined the entire property.

The damp was biting and his breath hung in the air for

a few seconds before disappearing into nothingness. In the distance an owl hooted.

Kaden walked to the edge of the property and leaned against the wrought-iron fence.

"I've always wanted to come to New Orleans," the teen murmured. "So much history here." He shrugged his shoulders. "Too bad I haven't had a chance to really see any of it."

Declan opened the gate. "Let's take a walk."

He felt the pop of energy in his protection charm as he slipped through and waited while Kaden did the same. He'd woven their signatures deep into the spell. The protection ward only allowed those Declan wished to enter or leave.

The two of them walked for several moments in silence, Kaden having no trouble matching his strides to Declan's long gait. There was no one out. Not one trace of otherworld, but Declan knew that meant shit. He constantly scanned the area for any anomalies. A demon could appear from nowhere in an instant and if something happened to Kaden, it would totally be on him.

He probably should have stayed back at the house and yet—he glanced at Kaden—he felt sorry for the kid.

As it was, Kaden gravitated toward the cemetery. Figures. The two of them stopped just outside the wall. Declan sensed the spirits that wandered just beyond and looked at the teenager.

"Do you feel them?" he asked quietly.

The boy shifted his feet but kept his gaze focused in front of them. "I know there's something there. I can feel energy." He looked at Declan. "Some of it feels sad but most of it feels angry." He looked away again. "Are they spirits?"

Declan nodded. "Souls left behind for various reasons. Some have been here for centuries." He paused for a second. "How have you dealt with your magick? Who has been your teacher?"

"Myself."

His answer surprised Declan. "But the charms you wove, the protection wards I found were intricate. Well developed. Are you telling me you learned all that on your own?"

Kaden glanced at him as if he had two heads. "Dude, there's this thing called the Internet? You can freaking learn anything you want."

Declan didn't quite know what to say to that.

Kaden started forward and he was left to follow behind. They slid between the darkened rows, the air around them heavy with early-morning freshness. It was damp, cold, but the teenager seemed impervious to it.

He watched the boy as they slipped farther inside the cemetery. Kaden had never been here before and yet he showed no fear. He walked with confidence but paid attention. The boy was smart—had leadership qualities. From what Declan could tell, he'd mastered skills that took many sorcerers years to accomplish. With tutors.

Shit, the mark of seven. Declan wished he knew which way Kaden's tendencies were going to swing.

A crow appeared overhead, its nasty cry cutting through the silence with the subtlety of a jackhammer. Declan watched as it flapped its wings and settled upon a large mausoleum. The DeLacrux mausoleum.

"Hey, this is Ana's family, isn't it?"

Declan nodded. He climbed the steps once more but this time took a few minutes to study the building. It was impressive and by the looks of it, one of the oldest in the cemetery. He crossed to the large double doors. There were names etched along the side but it was the last one that caught his attention. Jean-Charles DeLacrux.

His gut tightened. Who the hell was this guy? Frustration rifled through him and the energy that sat at the tips of his fingers burned hot. He'd thought at first maybe a lover, and that was bad enough. Hell, the thought of Ana with anyone else drove him fucking crazy. When they'd worked together at PATU and she'd carried on an affair with Diego that lasted several years, they'd been some of the hardest he'd endured.

But what if this stranger was in fact tied to her on a level that transcended that? What if the dude was her mate? Her husband? And if so, where the hell was he?

He turned abruptly and swore.

Kaden was gone.

Overhead the crow cawed loudly as if to say, *Dumb ass*. It continued to screech at Declan as he started down the steps. His hand shot out and a bolt of energy quieted the bird. Permanently.

He didn't bother shouting out the teen's name. It wouldn't do any good. It would just alert Kaden to his whereabouts, and anyone else lingering in the cemetery of their presence.

Declan closed his eyes and concentrated. There was nothing there. Weird, but he couldn't sense the boy. Where the hell was he?

Alarmed, he took off, senses on high alert as he passed through the rows in silence. He knew Kaden couldn't have gone far. Jean-Charles had distracted him for only a moment.

As he trod deeper into the cemetery he noticed the fog along the ground was thicker. It clung to everything it touched, like ghostly tentacles. Unease tasted like crap and Declan stopped, listening carefully as he pulled up the power that lay inside him.

It thrummed heavily in his chest. He moved forward once more, silently. Something was out there. He could feel it.

The lost souls that wandered amongst the tombs followed in his wake. The wind picked up as he neared the far corner. Here the tombs were run-down, sadly neglected. Through the gloom he saw shadows moving and his power gathered, sensing an imminent threat.

The shadows melted into gray, with beams of light emanating from deep inside. Crackles of energy shot out from them and he clenched his teeth as they rolled across his flesh.

He knew them.

Declan broke into a run, his body feeding on the juiced-up adrenaline that flooded his cells. He jumped over the toppled remains of a tombstone and as if the Red Sea had parted in front of him, the fog was suddenly gone. He paused, and the only sounds he heard clearly were his heart beating like crazy inside his chest and the tortured breaths that fell from his lips.

Kaden was several feet away, legs spread, chin raised in defiance, staring ahead. A man sat upon the crumbled remains of a tomb, and it was he who drew Declan's attention.

The eyes that stared at Declan were not amused. The body was in repose, as if relaxed, yet the man was anything but. He was on the hunt, his power emanating off him in waves.

Declan flexed his hands and cracked his neck. "Kaden, move away." His tone brooked no argument, and surprisingly the teenager listened. Declan waited until Kaden was safely out of reach before he looked up and spoke.

"I thought you were on assignment in Antarctica."

The intruder jumped down and flashed a smile. He was tall, his dark hair worn short, military-style, and he was dressed in faded denim, big-ass boots, with *Mötley Crüe* emblazoned on his black T-shirt. "I was." He offered no further explanation.

"Who are you?" Kaden stepped beside Declan.

The stranger's eyes narrowed as he looked at the teen. He rolled his shoulders, cocked his head to the side, and smiled. "I think the question is . . . who are *you*?" He paused and glanced at Declan. "I was in the area and thought I'd check on my old friend."

Declan's fingers sizzled with energy and his limbs hung loose, at the ready. *Yeah, because we're so tight.*

"The name's Cale," he continued, though the smile left his face as he winked at Kaden. "I'm one of the Seraph."

CHAPTER 10

"Kaden, you need to go home, *now*."

Declan moved in front of the boy and faced Cale with a snarl. "Who'd you manage to piss off? Seems to me coming after an operative already on assignment is grunt work."

"Nobody sent me. Bill is with Azaiel as you know." Cale held his hands out, palms up. "I'm here on my own." Cale's eyes were focused behind him and Declan clenched his teeth. He was going to have to have a long chat with Kaden about orders.

And the need to obey them.

"Cross my heart." Cale winked, but when he turned his gaze back to Declan they were dead serious. "The underworld is closing ranks and some of the baddies have suddenly gone topside. They seem to be on the hunt for something." He pointed toward the teenager. "You have any idea what that might be?"

"I have no clue."

"Bullshit, O'Hara." Cale walked toward them. "Word is they're collecting"—he paused and his gaze slid toward Kaden—"*something*. You care to elaborate on that?"

"Son of a bitch," Declan swore. The game had just changed again. How in the hell was he going to get the large warrior off his back? He eyed Cale closely. "What's your interest in this?"

"Something big is going down. Bill is locked away at council with the rest of the Seraphim so that means we're on our own. If you want my help you'd best spill."

"How did you know I was in New Orleans?" Declan shot back, not willing to give in just yet.

"I didn't. Whispers of shit hitting the fan in the Big Easy are why I'm here. I thought I'd check it out." He shrugged his shoulders. "I caught your scent several hours ago and followed you back from the Voodoo Lounge. Your wards are strong, they prevented me entrance to the house."

Declan clenched his hands together tightly. He had a decision to make. Cale was one of the oldest of the Seraph, at least that's what he'd been told. Truthfully he had no clue what the hell he was, but next to Bill, he was the go-to guy. He had a reputation for being a cold son of a bitch, but he was fair.

His gut told him that Cale could be trusted. His mind told him he'd be a fool to chance it.

"Do not start a war between us, sorcerer. It cannot end well for either one of us."

A muscle worked its way sharply across Declan's jaw. Fuck, he hated being put on the spot.

"They're collecting the mark of seven."

Kaden moved in closer to him and his chest tightened. The boy had been on his own for so long and yet was willing to trust a total stranger.

Cale's eyes widened. It was obvious he was surprised. "Do the Seraphim know?"

Declan nodded. "It's why I was sent here."

Cale studied him in silence and when he finally spoke, his voice was subdued. "They will destroy them. The Seraphim will never let the mark of seven come together. They'll never chance something coming to fruition that they don't fully understand." He nodded at the teen. "He is one?"

"The fifth mark," Declan answered quietly, though the tingle of power still burned at the edges of his fingers. He'd have no problem letting it fly if Cale made one wrong move.

"I'm like right here, ya know?" Kaden stepped forward, his face twisted in anger. "Don't talk about me like I'm a moron. Like I don't understand what's going on."

Cale ignored his outburst. "Bill sent you?" At Declan's nod he continued, "And you would defy him?"

"Bill gave the boy a protector. He doesn't want the council to get their hands on him, either."

"A protector?"

"A vampire."

Cale's eyes narrowed but he remained silent.

"It's the right thing to do. I will not hand him over to certain death." Declan widened his stance and drew his shoulders square.

Cale frowned. "Death will follow him. You know this." His eyes strayed back to the teenager. "But I agree. It seems cruel to destroy something before it's had a chance to mature. To shine." He flashed a wicked smile. "Besides, if the mark of seven turn to the dark side we can always take them down later. There is no expiration date when someone has been marked by the Seraphim."

Declan turned to the teen. "It's nearly sunrise. We need to get you back before Ana freaks."

"Ana is the vampire?"

It was Kaden who answered. "So what are you exactly?"

"That, my friend, is a question for another day." Cale looked at Declan. "You got a plan?"

"We've snagged us a necromancer and she's tied to Samael."

"Samael?" Cale laughed softly. "Son of a bitch. He's topside?"

"He's not made an official appearance yet but he's close

by. We're hoping the woman will be able to point us in the right direction. Ransome has her at the Voodoo Lounge."

Cale snorted. "So you don't really have a plan." It was a statement.

"Nope," Declan answered.

"Excellent." Cale smiled and started forward. "I'm hungry. You guys have eggs?"

The first rays of light were just beginning to ride the horizon when they returned to the mansion. They stopped in front of the gate and Declan glanced at Kaden. "His body signatures need to be woven into the spell or he can't cross. Have you ever done that?"

Kaden shook his head. "No."

"You wanna try?"

Kaden hunched his shoulders forward and stuck his hands in his pockets. "Sure."

Declan glanced at Cale. The Seraph watched the boy closely. He turned back to Kaden. "All right. You need to visualize his energy."

"How do I do that?"

"Concentrate. Open up your mind." The teen closed his eyes and his hands fell from the pockets of his jeans as his body relaxed. "Feel it, every single nuance that makes him different from you, from me, from Ana. Can you see it? In your mind?"

Kaden nodded and the boy's fingers shook as his power unfurled. "This is so freaking cool," the teenager whispered.

"Yeah, you won't be finding this shit on the Internet." Declan smiled and moved closer to the teenager. "Now once you have his signatures memorized you need to draw them into the charm. Layer them in amongst the magick."

Declan watched in silence as Kaden's hands drew intricate designs into the air. Energy flew from his fingers, lighting up his work briefly before it disappeared.

He glanced at Cale and found the man watching him.

Their eyes connected and Declan's jaw clamped down tightly. He would not let anyone harm the teen. That was both his promise and his mission.

"I think it's done." Kaden's eyes flew open and the excitement that shone from within them was contagious. His cheeks were flush and his breaths were ragged.

"Are you sure?"

At Kaden's nod both he and the teen walked through the gate and turned to face Cale. "You coming?" he asked as the Seraph hesitated.

"You sure he's got it right? What happens if he screwed up?"

"Your ass will be fried," Declan answered.

Cale arched a brow. "Good to know." He then stepped through the protection charm with ease. He looked at Kaden and nodded. "You're a fast learner."

The teen seemed a little embarrassed. "Thanks," he mumbled, and turned, his hands once more shoved into the front pockets of his jeans. He shuffled his way down the path that led to the porch.

"The boy is impressive."

Declan nodded. "He's definitely special."

"He has a darkness inside that troubles me."

Declan glanced at the warrior as they started down the path. "What do you mean?" He'd not sensed anything out of the ordinary.

They stepped onto the porch and slipped into the house. Cale paused and lowered his voice. "I can see the purity of his soul but it's surrounded by poison, tinged with the color of blood."

An ominous feeling washed over Declan at the Seraph's words.

"Only time will tell if he defeats the parasite that is slowly growing inside of him."

"None of us are pure of heart. Not even you." Declan

unclenched his hands as his eyes followed Kaden down the hall to the back kitchen.

"Agreed," Cale said as he walked by Declan, "which is why he lives."

Declan ran his hands over his face wearily. Goddamn but he needed some shuteye. He eyed the small settee and blanket he'd abandoned earlier. Fuck it, he thought. A few hours' sleep would do him good. He wasn't Cale's bitch. The dude could make his own breakfast.

From two stories up Ana listened as Declan settled himself onto the settee once more. It had taken everything inside her to resist following him and Kaden from the house earlier, but she trusted the sorcerer. She knew he'd never hurt a child.

The newcomer they'd brought back, however? That was a different story. He frightened her. His energy was different. It was powerful, in the way an ancient was. Their energy was always more subtle. More dangerous.

She jumped from her bed and crossed to the largest window in the attic. Outside, the sun was just beginning to make her way upward and below, the rays only managed to emphasize how tired and neglected her estate had become.

Totally fit the owner.

She moved away from the window, deciding if she didn't look at it she didn't have to think about it. Ana quickly changed into clean clothes, freshened up, and then slid down the stairs in silence.

Nico greeted her on the second level. The jaguar warrior was unshaven, dressed in a T-shirt and jeans, his feet bare. She had to admit the Mohawk, while unconventional, somehow suited him. The nose ring? That she could do without.

"Where were you at last night?" Nico's voice was gruff, as if ill used. She knew from experience the jaguar was a man of few words.

She led the way down the stairs and kept her voice low,

though she knew if Declan wanted to listen in, he'd have no problem. "I had to feed."

Nico grunted at her answer and she paused at the bottom of the stairs, creeping forward softly. She glanced into the parlor, and though it appeared that Declan was fast asleep, she couldn't be sure. His face looked younger in repose, the lines softer.

An overwhelming urge to touch him, to trace the softness of his mouth tugged at her. As always the hunger she felt for him was there. She turned away, resentful, and headed toward the kitchen.

The nauseating scent of eggs hit her before she entered the room. Kaden and a stranger sat at her table, busily shoving the disgusting crap into their mouths. Nico leaned against the counter, his face stony, his eyes narrowed as he gazed at the two of them.

The tall, imposing man at her kitchen table concerned her. She couldn't get a read on him.

"Who the hell are you?" Ana asked bluntly.

She crossed to the fridge and grabbed a bag of blood. She felt his gaze on her as she threw the bag into the microwave and pressed the required buttons. Rationally, she knew that if Declan trusted him so should she, but there was something about this man that put her on edge. He made her uneasy, and for a vampire that was saying something.

She glanced at Nico once more. The jaguar gripped a coffee cup in his hands; his knuckles were white and his eyes were round balls of anger.

"The name's Cale."

She swallowed and turned. He was one hell of an attractive man, she'd give him that. Dressed the way she liked, jeans and leather. He was all male, rugged and ripped, with golden eyes and a wicked smile. The man oozed charisma and power.

He was definitely dangerous.

She grabbed her blood and poured herself a drink. Nico continued to watch in silence. He was definitely not in his happy place.

She took a long sip. "I guess what I meant was, what the hell are you?"

Cale finished his plate, pushed it away, and stood. Ana tried not to flinch but the man was freaking enormous. He was tall, with broad shoulders and powerful limbs. Her muscles tightened and she put her glass down carefully.

She had an *aha* moment. One that said the shit was gonna hit the fan.

"I am Seraph." His voice was like silk.

She glanced up at Nico, eyes wide as her fangs broke skin.

What the hell? The shit was definitely gonna be flying. Her fingers were clawlike weapons and she attacked with a vicious cry.

Her small body flew through the air and she hit him hard. Everything faded from the palette that was her world. The dull gray walls, worn linoleum no longer existed. Only this man. This *enemy*.

The two of them tumbled to the floor, her fingers digging into the soft flesh of his neck as she squeezed with all her might.

His arms went around her body and they crashed into the pantry. She barely avoided the cans that tumbled out, though the stranger wasn't so lucky. She smiled viciously as several large ones cracked his skull on their way down. To think that Declan had let a Seraph warrior into her house was unbelievable.

She'd deal with him later.

Vaguely, Ana was aware that Kaden was shouting at her, but the red haze that floated in front of her eyes left no room for anything besides the need to inflict pain. *A lot of it.*

She hissed and opened wide. She would kill the bastard and ask questions later.

She managed to get close. Her fangs were a whisper away from breaking skin when his large hands sank into the thick hair at her nape. His fingers closed around her head, and she knew in that moment if he wanted, he'd have no problem crushing her skull.

She lay on top of him, chest heaving, her body aching with the need to act. The Seraph held her for what seemed like forever, and she wanted to spit in his face at the smile that slowly spread across his face. Didn't matter that the dude was Hollywood handsome; a broken nose would go a long way in making her feel so much better.

"So"—his smile widened—"you're the little vampire."

Her eyes narrowed and she hissed. "Why are you here?"

"Why are you?" he countered.

She tried to shift her body but the bastard held her tight, and as she wiggled her ass, his smile widened. Ana's frustration boiled over and she swore loudly, a long string of profanities spewing forth that was impressive in its diversity.

"I won't let you hurt him," she managed to get out.

He cracked a smile and her fury increased tenfold.

She stilled, her mind making calculations as she stared back at him. Her fangs had retracted but if she could get close enough somehow and latch on, she might have a fighting chance of killing him.

"You could try." He whispered as if he knew what she was thinking, "But I'm not so sure the end game would turn out the way you expected."

His right hand loosened from her skull and slowly slid down her back.

"No?" She was breathing hard. "I'm thinking I'd enjoy draining you."

"I'm sure you would." His hand continued downward and he whispered, "I'm sure *I* would."

Ana let her fangs slide out once more. His hand was now on her hip. "You should know," she began, "I won't be responsible for what happens if you don't remove your hand from my ass."

His voice dropped to a whisper. "Promise?" He laughed softly, and that only infuriated her more. "And what exactly is going to happen?"

"I can't say for sure but I can pretty much guarantee it will hurt like hell."

Declan's words slid between them and Ana felt the man beneath her still. He shifted, looked behind her, and grinned, though he kept his grip tight on her body. "O'Hara, why you going and spoiling all my fun?"

"Take your hands off her or I *will* start a war." Declan was dead serious. The room flooded with dark energy. It slithered along Ana's body, electrifying her cells in a way that was wrong. And yet so right it was shameful.

The man beneath her tensed, his eyes darkened. He didn't like being threatened. Ana hissed at him and as his arms loosened, she pushed away, rolled to the side, and was on her feet in seconds.

"Why the hell is he here?" She turned her fury and general frustration on Declan. "A Seraph? Are you kidding me?"

Nico pushed away from the counter. "You boys duke it out. I need to run." Ana watched as the jaguar warrior headed for the back door and yanked it open. His hands were already at the waistband of his jeans but he paused, and his eyes were cold as he glanced toward the Seraph warrior. "I've pledged my allegiance to this boy. Do not think to harm him or I will hunt you."

Ana turned back to Declan, ignoring the tall man to her right. "Are you going to explain?"

Declan's eyes flickered past hers and settled upon the intruder. "His name is Cale. He's one of the Seraph, same as I."

She turned and kept her barely controlled anger under wraps as she studied him.

"And he's here because?" she asked Declan, though her eyes never left the stranger.

Cale ignored the question, but smiled widely and winked at her. "Seriously? Your"—he made quotation marks with his fingers—"save the mark of seven kiddies is an exclusive club? What do I need, a password?"

"I don't want you here," Ana spat. "I don't trust you."

Cale's demeanor changed instantly. The warmth fled his eyes and his voice dropped. The man was scary powerful, and a chill raced along Ana's flesh.

"I'm not promising we can accomplish what it is you intend to do. The hounds of Hell themselves will come after him"—he pointed toward the teenager—"and they'll bring everything that they've got. The destruction they will wreak, the havoc that they'll commence will be beyond anything you can comprehend. The mark of seven is the ultimate weapon and one that begs the question . . ." His voice trailed off as he turned his attention onto Kaden.

Kaden faced the Seraph and spoke clearly. "What's that exactly?"

"Well, the obvious, my friend." Cale shook his head. "There are two sides to this scenario and as of now we have no clue which side you'll land on." He nodded toward Declan. "The sorcerer and the vampire are willing to lay their lives on the line for you. That tells me they believe you'll land somewhere in the middle." He arched a brow. "The middle is good."

Cale moved away and Ana was glad to have a bit of distance between them. She exhaled softly. Declan moved closer to her and they both faced the Seraph together.

"I'm not convinced that will be the outcome, however, I'm willing to see how this plays out."

Kaden's face whitened and Ana's heart broke at the sight of him trying to be so brave. She wanted to rush to his side and take him into her arms, but he was no child and she knew he needed to stand on his own.

"And what if you . . . what if I . . ." Kaden didn't finish his sentence but there was no need, Cale was more than willing to do it for him.

His voice was sharp, his intention clear. "I will end you."

Declan was barely able to hold Ana back. Her rage and frustration erupted into a guttural scream. Cale's parting shot as he disappeared down the hall only served to fan the flame.

"I'll meet you at the Lounge once the vampire has had time to cool off."

It took nearly the entire day for the vampire to "cool off."

CHAPTER 11

The afternoon was overcast. It fit the general mood at the DeLacrux mansion, and it was a somber bunch that left for Ransome's place several hours later.

They decided to let Kaden come along. The teen desperately wanted to have a hand in controlling his destiny, and Ana didn't have the heart to keep saying no to him. Besides, though the protection wards put in place were strong, she still wasn't one hundred percent sold they'd hold against Samael should he decide to make an appearance.

And he was close by. She could feel it.

Benny waved the four of them in, Nico, Declan, Ana, and Kaden. It was early Sunday evening, and the crowd was sparse. A blues band was jamming, the sad melodic tone of the female singer perfect. She was all kinds of smoky haze and secrets. Ana found her voice soothing and paused to listen. Declan stopped but she waved him on, and he followed Nico to the upper level. She felt the weight of his stare as he gazed down at her, but Ana kept her eyes focused on the singer and eventually Declan disappeared into Ransome's office.

She needed a few minutes to be away from him. The past had come rushing back at her with the ferocity of a crazed bitch. Being here at the lounge did nothing to alleviate her stress. She could close her eyes and literally transport back in time. The smells and sounds were exactly the same. All that was missing was Jean-Charles.

"Glad to see you back."

Asher stood less than a foot behind her. She chose to ignore the fact that the werewolf had just snuck up on her like she was a newbie operative. If she didn't pull herself together she was going to end up on the wrong end of a stake. *Again.*

He took the last step until he was abreast of her, looked down his arrogant nose, and grinned. It was the kind of smile that was in abundance these days in the Big Easy. One that was pasted to his mouth but avoided his eyes altogether. The two shared a history that was bathed in blood, and the wolf's animosity was returned tenfold.

"You're full of crap," she said, her eyes returning to the band as they slid into a new song.

The werewolf shrugged. "I thought I'd make an attempt to be polite but if we're not posturing, if we're truly showing our feelings . . ." He paused and she glanced up at him. "Well then, let's try this again, shall we?" The tips of his teeth were visible, their sharp ends exaggerated as he spoke. "I'm so glad to see you back, Ana, though I'd like it much better if you were flat on the floor with a stake shoved through that cold bitch heart of yours."

She smiled. "That's much better, Asher."

The two stood side by side for several more minutes. She knew the werewolf wanted something. There was no other reason for him to be there but she chose to ignore the obvious and instead opened herself up to the music. The hypnotic rhythm of the bass pulled at her and she wished she could close her eyes and get lost in the melody.

On the dance floor a couple slid against each other, their limbs entwined, their bodies touching. It was obvious they were lovers. They moved to the music, slowly swaying in a sensual display that left an ache inside Ana.

She turned abruptly. There was no sense thinking about such things. She'd never have what that couple had—she'd never belong to anyone. Ana glanced upstairs and sighed.

No matter how much she wanted it.

"Interesting company you're keeping these days," the wolf whispered as she stepped around him.

"Meaning?"

"A sorcerer? A shifter? Where does Ransome fit in all of this?"

"Why do you care?"

"I don't give a shit about you, but Ransome is the head of my pack, and if anything happened to him—"

Ana laughed outright. "If Ransome bites it, you think you're the one to step in and replace him as alpha?" The wolf's face darkened and a growl sounded from deep in his chest. "Are you kidding?" she continued. "An alpha needs something that you don't have."

"And what would that be?" Asher's mouth twitched into a grimace.

Ana pushed past him but stopped long enough to whisper, "Balls," before heading toward the stairs. She smiled at the outraged curse that flew from the werewolf's mouth. Asher LaPierre was a weak, selfish bastard who had not one shred of leadership in his entire body. The wolf was seriously delusional if he thought to challenge for alpha.

The office door was closed and Ana pushed it open without knocking. Kaden and Nico stood near the window. The view was nothing more than a brick wall, but they sure as hell seemed interested in something.

Declan followed the line of her gaze. "Kaden's visualizing the charms Ransome has in place. He's getting quite good at it. I think if given the time he'd be able to break them."

"Where's Ransome and the redhead?" She asked quickly. She wanted this business done.

Declan nodded toward another door located at the rear

of the office. "He went to get her. He had her stashed at his place."

Ana's eyes narrowed. "Where is the bastard Seraph?"

"Cale hasn't arrived yet. Apparently he had other business to attend to but will be here soon. Promise me you'll play nice." His answer was tight-lipped. "I know you don't trust him but he's an asset we need to utilize."

The door opened and they turned as the werewolf strode into the room. At his side was the necromancer, Francesca. She was not happy, that was obvious. She grimaced as her gaze swept the room, and her face darkened even more. Her hands dangled at her side and Ana noted the iron bands that covered her wrists. The skin beneath was raw, chafed. They were an effective preventive to using the dark arts, and with the woman in question, much needed.

The redhead was a powerful necromancer, especially for someone so young. The ghouls she'd raised and sent after Kaden were out of the ordinary. They'd been strong, fast, and vicious. She'd been feeding from something dark and there was no way she could be trusted.

Ransome stopped and nodded toward a leather chair in front of his desk.

"I'd rather stand, if that's all right with you." The girl's voice was husky, as if ill used.

"Suit yourself." Ransome shrugged and moved toward his liquor supply. "Anyone want a drink?" The wolf seemed edgy, and Ana watched him closely as he poured himself a generous amount of whiskey.

She moved toward the woman and took a moment to study her. She was attractive, slender, with long crimson hair, creamy skin, and a figure that was almost boyish. Dark circles bruised the flesh beneath her eyes and she was still dressed in the clothes she'd worn the night before.

"Nice tats," Ana said. The woman had intricate markings that encircled her neck.

Francesca remained stone-faced and kept her eyes trained ahead, focused on the trashy velvet paintings that decorated the walls of Ransome's office.

Declan moved closer. "Those aren't tattoos," he murmured. Ana watched the woman flinch, but she recovered quickly and remained silent.

The sorcerer had everyone's attention now. Francesca's face was pale, her lips pressed tight together.

"What are they?" Ransome asked as he, too, moved toward Ana and the necromancer.

Declan glanced at Ana. Something was up.

"You're enslaved," he said to the woman.

Francesca's bottom lip trembled and Ana was certain her eyes glistened with unshed tears. A crack in the lady's facade.

"What the hell is it? What do you mean?" Ana whispered.

Francesca opened her mouth to speak but the markings along her neck began to move. As they slid along her flesh a gasp of pain escaped her and she bit her lip hard. She recovered quickly and remained still as blood started to seep from the tattoo.

"It's a demonic slave collar." Declan's face was shrouded in something akin to pity. "I've seen them before."

Another groan escaped Francesca, and Ana took a step back. The scent of her blood was wonderful, full of power and darkness.

"Can't you do anything?" Ransome blurted, and Ana looked at the wolf in surprise. Did they really care that she was in pain? The woman had sent a pack of ghouls after Kaden. If it was up to Ana the lady would rot in Hell.

Declan shook his head. "No, there's nothing I can do. Only the demon who put it there can remove it and I'm guessing that would be Samael."

The woman's eyes widened and then she exhaled slowly. Several seconds later the markings stopped moving and the blood disappeared from her skin, like water evaporating.

"Are you the demon lord's bitch?" Nico moved toward them, his tall body humming with predatory grace. Ana sensed his animal scratching below the surface and she knew it wouldn't take much to set the warrior off.

Francesca remained quiet though her hands were now trembling.

"What does he want with Kaden?" Ana asked, deciding the most direct approach was the best. If it didn't work they could always use torture. That usually did the trick.

Ana took two steps until she was in the woman's face. She pointed toward the teenager, who was now watching the entire scene unfold with rabid interest. "That is who your ghouls were after the other night. He's a child. You would hand him over to someone like Samael?"

Francesca met her gaze full-on and yet she remained silent. The shimmer of tears still clung to the corners but she wasn't giving anything up. Her attitude enraged Ana, and Ana's fangs slid out.

That got the woman's attention.

"I'm not afraid of you." Francesca whispered. "You are nothing compared to what waits for me if I fail."

Ana's features shifted subtly, for just a second, but it was long enough for the necromancer to catch a glimpse of her true self—the one who could drink her dry with no qualms. Ana hissed and walked away.

"I hate to break it to you, sweets, but from where I'm standing, seems as if you've already failed. Big-time." Ransome took another long draw from his tumbler and set the empty glass down on his desk. He looked at Francesca. "You think your visitor last night was from the welcome wagon? You're a smart woman, Francesca, figure it out."

"Don't call me that." The words were uttered rapidly and the woman's eyes slid away as she once more gazed at the ground.

"What do you want us to call you?" Ransome moved

closer and Ana stepped back. She watched the werewolf closely, and though she could tell he was still edgy, he seemed to be focused.

"Let's skip the whole name thing because I really don't give a shit what we call her." Nico looked at all of them. "Let's keep this simple, shall we?" The warrior's skin shifted and blurred as he snarled at Francesca. "Tell us where the fucker Samael is and we won't kill you."

Francesca faced the jaguar warrior, and Ana was impressed at the balls it took for her to defy the huge warrior. "Don't threaten me, shifter. I cannot tell you where the demon is. As for the other . . ." Her words drifted into a whisper, though Ana had no trouble understanding them. "I'm already dead."

Silence filled Ransome's office.

"You said you couldn't tell us where Samael is," Declan stated, "not that you wouldn't. What did you mean by that? What does he hold over you?"

Francesca's bottom lip trembled once more. The woman was so young. How in the hell had she managed to insert herself into a war between the Seraph and a demon lord?

The necromancer straightened her shoulders and gazed straight into Declan's eyes. "I will not give him up."

"But you do share a connection to him. The collar belongs to Samael, correct?"

Francesca swallowed thickly and nodded.

"Why did it move?" Kaden's young voice grabbed her attention and Francesca glanced toward the teenager. The sorrow and pain that filled her eyes in that moment shocked Ana.

"It's a reminder of what I've lost, of what I have to gain if I'm smart."

"Does it hurt a lot?" Kaden looked at Declan. "Are you sure you can't, like, do some weird mojo stuff and get rid of it?"

Declan shook his head. "No, the only one who can remove it is Samael. Once you've been enslaved by a demon, your ass is pretty much toast."

Ana stared at Francesca. She had a hard decision to make. The woman before her was the only link she had to Samael and even though it appeared she was more or less being forced to do his dirty work, Ana had to push that from her mind.

She let her fangs slide out and hissed at Francesca. "You will tell us the location of Samael or—"

"Let me try."

Ana looked at Kaden in surprise. The teenager's eyes were focused on the necromancer but he glanced to her quickly. "Please, Ana I can help."

The room was quiet as everyone's focus shifted from Francesca to Kaden. He ignored them all and moved to within a few inches of the redhead. Ana took a few steps back to give him room and shot a puzzled look toward Declan.

The sorcerer's lips were thinned and she could tell Declan didn't like Kaden anywhere near the woman. Ana had no idea what Kaden was going to do but the teenager seemed sincere. Sure of himself.

"If you touch him I *will* make you regret it," Ana said from between clenched teeth. Her fangs had retracted but she stood with her feet spread, her arms at the ready.

Francesca made a gurgling noise and held her iron-clad wrists aloft. "No worries there," she muttered before glancing toward Kaden.

"You won't feel a thing, I promise," he said softly, his manner grave. "Um, you said that he'll punish you if you speak. If you tell us the thing that he doesn't want us to know, right?"

What the hell was he getting at? Ana frowned. She had no idea where the teenager was going with this or what he planned on doing.

Francesca nodded but remained silent.

Kaden shrugged his shoulders. "Don't worry. You won't have to say a word."

He moved until his body was nearly touching Francesca's and then raised his hands. Energy sizzled along Kaden's limbs, crackling into the air as he held his fingertips near her head. He never touched her; didn't make a sound, and the silence that engulfed them echoed so heavily in Ana's ears that she winced.

A chill ran along Ana's body as she watched the teenager, and goose bumps spread along her arms. Kaden's eyes were closed, his face a mask of concentration. He looked well beyond his sixteen years, and not for the first time, Ana wondered about the secrets he held inside.

A breeze drifted from out of nowhere, lifting long tendrils of red hair to dance in the air. Francesca's hands came up but Kaden flicked his wrist and she was unable to move. Ana looked at Declan in surprise and she saw the same mirrored in his face. The boy was powerful and had layers to him that he'd not shared.

Long moments passed as Kaden stood before the woman, his young body thrumming with power. When he turned abruptly Ana exhaled, not knowing her breath had become trapped until it fell from her in a rush. The teenager's mouth was pinched, his eyes darkened, and perspiration lined his forehead. He was breathing rapidly and with some effort slowed his breaths as he stepped away from Francesca.

He took a few seconds and then spoke. His voice was quiet, calm. "The demon lord is in a place of darkness. It's cold, damp but there are flashes of light, whispers of voices." Kaden glanced at Ana. "There's loud music, wetness, and pain." Kaden glanced around the room. "There's a lot of suffering and so much fear." He shook his head and winced. "He's not alone. There's someone else hidden beyond the darkness. I couldn't see what it was, but I could *feel* someone or something. There are two more. They're like asleep but not asleep if that makes sense." Kaden shook his head as if trying to get rid of the images in his mind. "I can't explain it any other way."

Kaden took a few steps. He rubbed the back of his head as if trying to gather his thoughts before he eyed Declan. "They have tattoos like mine, a boy and girl. They're different—the tattoos—the center is not the same. One has a symbol that looks like lightning and other has scales, like the scales of justice."

"Shit, it sounds like he's already got his hands on two of the marks." Ransome slammed his empty glass down and Francesca jumped. "This is not good, boys." He grabbed the whiskey decanter and proceeded to pour himself another glass. "Not good at all."

"What of the girl? Is she all right?" Francesca asked as a tear slid down her cheek. Ana had to strain to hear her words but the pain that sat upon her face was awful. This young teenager meant something to the necromancer.

"She's asleep, too." He lowered his gaze. "Her hair is the same color as yours."

"Who is she?" Declan asked, moving closer to Ana's side as he did so.

"Francesca's sister," Kaden answered quietly. "I think," he added quickly. "I mean she looks an awful lot like you."

Francesca didn't say a word. Her face went blank and her gaze fell to the floor.

"How the hell do you know this stuff?" Nico asked, his face as dark as his thoughts. "If you ever pull that kind of crap with me I'll kick your ass but good." He tossed a look at Ana. "I don't care who the hell you are."

"He's the fifth mark." Declan answered. "His gift is sight."

Kaden nodded. "The demon Samael is linked to Francesca. I tapped into their bond. The images aren't clear and sometimes they're not quite right. Like, he might not be there right now. What I just sensed could be days old."

"None of this means squat if we can't find Samael." Ransome eyed the teen. "You nail down a location while you were trespassing in her brain?"

Kaden shook his head. "No." He glanced at Ana. "Sorry."

"It's all right—" Her words were cut off as the door to the office swung open, letting in loud music, voices, and the general party atmosphere from below.

"No worries, kids. I know where the demon is." Cale strode into the room, crossed to the sidebar, and eyed the selection of bottles on the wall. "You got any scotch?" He asked the werewolf. "I prefer single malt, but at the moment anything will do."

"Who the hell are you?" Ransome growled as he took a step toward the newcomer.

"He's one of us," Declan answered. "A Seraph warrior."

The wolf glared at him and nodded. "Help yourself, the glasses are below."

Cale grabbed the bottle. "I've no time for social grace tonight and do apologize, for I won't be in need of a glass."

Ana saw the flash of anger that crossed Ransome's face. She turned to Cale. "You said you knew where the demon lord is? Care to elaborate?"

The Seraph took a long swig from the bottle and then set it back down. His gaze swept over all of them. Ana had a bad feeling she wasn't going to like his answer.

He nodded toward the door. "He's downstairs."

CHAPTER 12

"Son of a mother—" Declan stared at the Seraph in surprise. "Samael is here?" he repeated.

Cale nodded once more and cocked his head toward the door. "I followed him in not more than five minutes ago."

"You followed him in and did nothing?" Declan was incensed.

Cale smiled at the sorcerer though the tone of his voice was frosty. "You forget to whom you are speaking, O'Hara. I'm not stupid and the demon lord is not alone."

"Well what are we waiting for?" Nico's voice erupted from the other side of the room. "Let's get go get him. Finish this."

"Hold on a second. I'll not have my establishment leveled because you want to go ape-shit and attack without thought." Ransome spoke up before turning to Cale. "What the hell is he doing down there?"

"Shots at the bar." Cale shrugged his shoulders. "It seems Samael enjoys his tequila almost as much as I like my scotch."

"I don't understand. We should have had some warning. How could we not *feel* him? Not *know* he was nearby?" Ana asked. It was obvious she didn't trust Cale.

"That *is* strange." Declan watched the Seraph closely. He,

too, was wondering the same things. "Did he leave his chaos ring at home?"

Cale's eyes narrowed, but his voice remained neutral. "He's a demon lord. If he wants to travel incognito, he will." Cale smiled. "I do it all the time."

"We need to get Kaden to safety." Ana flew to the teen's side. "Is there another way out of here?"

Ransome nodded. "My place, the loft above the club." He pointed toward the door he'd arrived from earlier. "It's through there."

Ana looked at Declan. The fear he saw in her eyes touched him deeply. If he could never see that look on her face again he'd be a happy man.

"We can't let Samael get to him," Ana whispered.

Declan walked to her and stared down into eyes. "Nothing will happen to the boy." She was trembling. Her face, so pale already, looked ashen. Ana DeLacrux was a fearless, tough operative. To see her in such a vulnerable state did something to his insides. It twisted them into all kinds of want and need and filled him with a desire to protect what was his.

His hand grazed the coolness of her cheeks. *She was his.* Ana might not know it yet but as he stood there in front of her, he made a vow to make her realize the absolute truth. One day.

Her eyes deepened into liquid navy and glistened like glass. She moved her head slightly, as if she wanted to rest her cheek in his palm but then jerked back and stepped away.

The moment was gone.

No matter. He'd get it back if it took him until the end of eternity, but first things first.

"Take Kaden and the girl. Get them to the mansion and we'll be along shortly." Declan glanced at Nico. "You go with Ana. Make sure they get there safely." He then nodded to the others. "I'm feeling thirsty, boys. I think it's about time Ransome buys us a round."

His gaze settled onto Kaden. "You listen to Ana. This isn't a game." The boy nodded. He knew how serious the situation was.

Ana pushed Francesca toward the door and then her eyes met his once more. She raised her chin. "Take care of yourself, O'Hara." She opened her mouth once more, but then closed it before speaking. He watched as she slipped through the door, Francesca and Kaden ahead of her.

Nico paused before following her through. "I expect to see you sons of bitches later."

The door closed behind the jaguar warrior and Declan exhaled. "All right, let's do this." He pulled up the power that lay inside his chest. It thrummed against the walls of his heart and pushed its way out. His hands were held loose at his side, languid almost, but the utter carelessness of their posture was a lie. Declan O'Hara was ready to wage war and as he stepped out of the office into the heated air of the club, he smiled.

It was about time. He felt as if he'd been standing still for the past few weeks.

The three of them stood above the mezzanine and their gaze swept the now-full room below. The band was gearing up for another set and as the house lights dimmed and the crowd erupted into a noisy welcome back, three men at the bar grabbed Declan's attention.

He focused and ripped back the layers of reality that clung to them. It was difficult to see past the veil but after several moments their true countenance was revealed.

The tall man in the center was Samael. Him Declan knew on sight. As the demon lord of chaos, the bastard was well-known throughout the underworld and when Declan had been imprisoned below, deep within the bowels of Hell, he'd seen him on several occasions.

His features were hidden, deep in shadow, but Declan felt the intensity of his stare as Samael glanced upward. He held a shot glass aloft, tossed back the liquid, and then turned to the bartender. Sarah dutifully filled the glass before administering the same care to the other two men.

They were not demon lords, rather bodyguards, but that didn't lessen the threat any.

Declan took a step down. "You think there's a chance the bastard is drunk? 'Cause I'm thinking that wouldn't be a bad thing."

Cale snorted. "Not likely."

"Not that it matters," Declan answered as he cleared the last stair. He flexed his hands, reveled in the energy that sizzled along his limbs.

Ransome slipped between the two of them. "I want those three goons out of my place." He glared at Declan. "And if anything gets broken I'm holding you totally fucking responsible."

"Shit, Ransome. That's a tall order. When's the last time you kicked someone's ass without anything getting broken?" Declan asked.

The werewolf growled and nodded toward the bar. "Ladies first," he said. Declan didn't bother to answer. His mind shifted gears and he concentrated on the task at hand.

The bar was full of people. All sorts of beings, human, shifter, vampire, and aside from the three at the bar, he caught the unmistakable scent of demon. He let his gaze run over the heaving crowd on the dance floor. Bodies were entwined, limbs pressed against secret places as they swayed to the hypnotic beat of the music. There were several demons in the midst, but they seemed oblivious to the fact that one of their own, a demon lord no less, was present.

"You think it's a trap?" he said to Cale as the tall warrior stepped beside him. A blonde danced by and tried to grab the Seraph's hand, but Cale smiled and let her pass.

"I think that it's unusual for a demon lord to come top-side and visit a bar inhabited by Seraph." Cale's voice hardened. "If he wanted to snatch the boy he'd have gone for it, not walked in here like a tourist." Cale frowned. "There's a reason behind his actions."

"Let's see what the bastard wants." Declan pushed forward. He smelled the darkness that surrounded Samael. It was sweet, *sickly sweet*, and he swallowed as it caressed his flesh. Like a drug, the dark side called to him constantly and it was a struggle to resist the pull.

Working for the Seraph did nothing to alleviate the need that gnawed at him. No one knew of the darkness he'd fed from when he'd been imprisoned in the Hell realm, not even Bill. Surely if the elf had known, he'd never have offered him asylum.

Declan clenched his teeth together. He needed to be strong for Ana and Kaden.

He led the way, the three of them sliding through the crowd with ease. His eyes never left Samael, and as they came abreast of the demon lord, he nodded. A wicked smile broke upon Declan's face, and the two demons flanking Samael, snarled at his audacity. They were from a class of lower demon, grunts really, and that surprised Declan.

The demon lord wore dark glasses, large aviator frames that hid what Declan knew were freaky-ass eyes. They would have outed him immediately. Samael was tall, his powerful frame clothed in the requisite denim and leather. His closely cropped hair was jet black and the tattoo along the side of his neck glistened underneath the lights from the bar.

Declan eyed it warily. The dragon tattoo was no ordinary etching. It was alive and could be commanded at will. Such was the power of a demon lord.

"Gentlemen." Samael's voice was deep. He smiled. "Can I buy you boys a drink? Unfortunately, there's no more tequila. I've tapped out their supply."

Declan had no time for games. "Cut the crap, Sammy. We're not drinking buddies. What the fuck are you doing here?"

Samael laughed softly. Declan wasn't fooled. He knew the demon lord was a stickler for respect and he'd just dissed him. Big-time. "Always so abrasive, sorcerer. I see you haven't changed much since last I saw you." He leaned forward. "On your knees, I think it was. Or between Lilith's legs?" He shrugged. "I can't remember."

Declan's fists clenched and he took a step forward, but Cale's hand on his arm stopped him. "Take care," the Seraph whispered. "Don't let him bait you."

Declan glared at the demon, his hands tingling as the darkness inside began to pulsate, feeding from the energy that sizzled around them. He took a moment. Pushed it back. He needed to keep a clear head.

"Look, can we take this outside?" Ransome took a step forward. "Seriously, guys, I'd like to keep the Lounge in one piece if at all possible."

Samael glanced at the wolf. "What makes you think things will get messy?"

Ransome growled. His skin blurred momentarily and the wolf shifted beneath.

"Oh, it's gonna get messy," Ransome retorted. "Trust me."

Samael ignored the wolf and turned his attention to Cale. "It's been a long time, brother."

Brother? An odd word choice.

Declan's eyes narrowed as he studied the Seraph. The warrior looked relaxed, yet a muscle that flickered across his jaw told a different story altogether.

"Several centuries at least." Cale nodded toward Sarah. "A double shot of scotch, neat."

"You still wiping the asses of the Seraphim?" Samael grinned. "What of Cracker? Is he still playing human with his beloved jaguar warriors?"

Declan's eyes widened. Son of a bitch. He'd always known Cracker was different.

Cale ignored the question, grabbed his drink from the bartender, and knocked it back. He waited for a refill and then spoke, his voice falling in layers. The words were in a foreign tongue, ancient speak that Declan had only heard the Seraphim use before.

The whole thing was weird and had him looking at both Cale and Samael in a new light. The two continued to converse, and Ransome made a sound of disgust.

"What the hell's going on?" the wolf asked darkly.

Impatience flared inside him and Declan flexed his fingers, letting a ripple of energy fly. The two goons on either side of Samael straightened and he caught sight of their serrated teeth as they turned their attention to him.

"Look, this isn't some fucking Boy Scout meeting. Why are you here, Samael?" Declan had learned the hard way that sometimes the direct approach was best. Even if it meant an ass kicking was in his immediate future.

Samael turned from Cale and swept the dark glasses from his face as he gazed at Declan. His eyes swirled bloodred, their glow eerie in the dimly lit bar.

"I'm looking for something, truth be told."

"No shit," Declan answered. "Aren't we all."

Samael's eyes narrowed. "The problem being, it seems you have that which I seek."

Declan studied the demon closely. He was too calm.

"What's really going on, Samael?" Cale tossed his empty glass back on the bar. "We both know if you wanted your hands on the fifth mark, you'd have snagged him for yourself days ago."

Samael straightened and pushed away from the bar. He glanced at his companions and spoke tersely. "Leave us."

Declan watched in silence as the demons turned on their heel and disappeared into the crowd.

"Is there someplace we can converse in private?" Samael asked as he slid the aviator glasses back into place. "This doesn't concern you, wolf."

Ransome growled and took a step forward, his canines flashing white as he bared his teeth.

"Think hard about your next move, shifter," Samael taunted. His voice deepened as a whisper of power swept over them. "I won't hesitate to cut you down."

Ransome's body trembled with suppressed rage, but he held still as Declan stepped beside him. The sorcerer leaned over. "He's not worth it, LaPierre."

Ransome's lips pulled back into a feral grin as he sneered. "I'll leave you to your privacy but I expect you gone from my place when I return."

Declan watched the tall wolf disappear into the crowd. Ransome was pissed but he'd get over it.

He turned back to the demon. "Spill. What's got your panties in a knot?" He glanced at Cale but the Seraph's face was like stone—no emotion. Something was way off.

Samael shook his head. "Ever the joker. One of these days your tongue will be the end of you." He grabbed a bowl of beer nuts off the bar and shoved a handful into his mouth as his gaze swept the room. "They're so unaware, these humans, so fragile," he murmured. "I suppose it adds to their charm. However, it will not serve them well in the coming days." Samael carefully set the bowl back onto the counter. "I had two of the seven marks in my possession."

Silence followed his words. *Had? As in no longer?*

"Where are they?" Declan asked, his voice dangerously low. He let a few sparks of energy fly from his fingers as he took a step toward Samael. The power circling his gut burned with a harshness that set his teeth on edge.

"I no longer have them."

"What the hell does that mean?" Cale asked as he, too, stepped forward.

Samael sat on the closest bar stool and grabbed another handful of nuts. He tossed a few into his mouth. "They are with Lilith."

Declan exploded as his anger took over. The air around them shimmered and the floor beneath their feet shook.

"You handed off two innocent children to Lilith?" *Un-fucking-believable.*

He snarled and raised his hands, ignoring the pain that lashed across them as the heat of his power erupted in a flash of red-hot energy. He would fucking pulverize the bastard.

"You shall move back, sorcerer, or I will not be responsible for the lives of those around you." The demon spoke calmly.

Declan hissed. He knew Samael's threat was real. Behind the bar, Sarah stood still and straight as a pen, though the terror in her eyes told the truth. She began to move, her arms awkward as they fumbled beneath the bar.

She raised her hands slightly and Declan cursed. A gun was held tightly within her grip, the barrel aimed directly at her heart. All around them the noise got louder—the band, the voices—and the air was thicker, hotter, filled with a dark desire that he could taste. It was the taste of wanton abandon, and to the humans and otherworld alike, it was like candy.

He glared at the demon. The fucker had definitely pulled out his chaos ring.

Cale's hand on his arm brought him back from the edge and Declan slowly let out a tortured breath as he regained control. "Hear him out," Cale whispered.

"No more games, Sammy." Declan couldn't resist one more taunt and glared at the bastard.

Samael removed his glasses once more and hissed. "If you weren't so valuable to me I'd take great pleasure in cutting your heart from your chest and feeding it to my pet."

Declan watched as the tattoo moved along the side of Samael's neck. It shifted and for a moment was out of focus, until it settled once more into the bed of vibrant color that adorned the demon's flesh.

"What is that you want?" Cale asked.

Samael set the bowl of nuts back onto the counter and then spoke. "My hands are tied. I can help no longer."

"What the hell does that mean?" Declan was close to losing it. He hated games. "You're talking in riddles. Why are you really here?"

The demon lord stood and placed the aviators once more over his eyes. "I came to make a deal."

"Your deals are never what they seem, brother." Cale's words were so low Declan was barely able to catch them.

"This one is quite simple. I'll provide safe passage to the underworld and you"—he pointed to Declan—"will retrieve the children from Lilith's clutches. Get them to safe haven."

"You're full of shit," Declan snarled. "Two nights ago you had a band of fucking ghouls on Ana's doorstep and they were after Kaden. None of this is making sense."

"Two nights ago I still had possession of the other two." Samael shook his head. "The game has changed. I no longer have them."

"How the hell did that bitch get her hands on them? Are they still alive?" Declan was breathing hard, his anger palpable.

"The details aren't important, but trust me. They live. They're no good to her dead." Samael's brows furled and his mouth tightened. "I will do whatever it takes to make sure Lilith never gets her hands on the mark of seven."

"Just as the Seraphim can never have them," Cale added.

Samael nodded. "Seems we are on the same page, brother." The demon turned to Declan. "Believe what you will but know you have until tomorrow evening to give me your answer."

"Or what?" Declan asked, his voice tight. "I don't like being pushed into a corner." And yet it was so much more than that. The thought of diving into the pit of darkness below, of seeing Lilith again, filled him with dread. No one knew of his torture at her hands, though he suspected Samael had an idea.

The demon shrugged his shoulders and moved away. The air around him blurred and his image wavered until he disappeared altogether, yet his words echoed inside Declan's head.

"Do this, sorcerer, or I *will* kill the children and make it my mission to hunt down the rest until they are no more." Soft laughter echoed eerily in his brain.

"And then I will take your vampire."

CHAPTER 13

t was hours later when he returned. Ana knew the moment Declan stepped foot inside her home because the energy in the air shifted. She drew a deep breath and rose from the kitchen table.

She and Nico had made it back to the mansion without incident, but as the night wore on and Declan remained absent, she'd begun to worry. It had taken every ounce of control she had to stay and not rush back to the Lounge. But with Kaden to watch over and the woman Francesca as well, she knew she needed to be vigilant and stay put.

Declan was one of the Seraph now as well as a powerful sorcerer. He could look after himself. Yet her mind ran through all sorts of scenarios, each of them ending with her sorcerer dead or gravely injured.

It had been years since she'd worried so, and anger pinched her cheeks red as she listened to his slow gait. He walked as if he had all the time in the world. Not a care to bother him. He paused, just beyond the doorway, and for a second she thought he'd turn and leave her.

She bit her lip and considered slipping out the back. Did she really want to face him when she was a vulnerable mess? On one hand she wanted to bitch slap him for worrying her, but on the other . . . she didn't want to dwell on the things she craved.

Ana knew she'd be better off alone in her room or out hunting. Even now the hunger inside was making noise. She'd ingested nearly a decanter and a half of blood and yet it did nothing to quench her thirst.

With Declan back she could breathe easier. He would keep her charges safe. Decision made, she was at the door in less than a second, her hand on the knob.

"Don't leave."

He sounded weary. She stared out into the darkness beyond the windowpane. It had rained again. She smelled the dampness of it, saw the glistening drops that clung to his hair and sat upon his skin as she gazed at his reflection.

An image of her tongue slowly licking them away flashed before her eyes and her mouth went dry.

Ana heard his heart beating steadily. The rhythm called to her like no other and she shuddered as she closed her eyes and prayed for strength.

"I need to hunt," she said carefully. "I've been waiting for hours." Accusation rang in her words. Her hand closed around the doorknob once more and she was about to yank it open when he spoke, so softly she barely heard his words.

"Don't go."

Ana stared down at her feet, afraid to glance into the window and see his face. She didn't know what the hell was going on. What had changed?

The room became a vacuum, as if everything had been sucked into a void leaving only the two of them and the slow ticking of the clock. Each second that passed by sounded loudly in her ear. *Tick tock, tick tock.*

Her fingers gripped the knob and she twisted it. "I can't stay. I need . . ." She gave a mental shake as once more she envisioned her mouth upon his flesh. "I need something you can't give me."

He was there, just behind her.

"Don't go," he whispered again. His voice was rough and there was a new depth to it that sent shivers rushing across her skin.

Ana stared at her hands. Her knuckles were white, a testament to how tightly she gripped the handle, and she relaxed her hold a bit. Slowly her gaze rose until she once more stared out into the darkness beyond. The moon was incognito, fog was a constant, and everything glistened with a wet sheen.

If she was smart she'd disappear into the velvet blackness and forget about Declan O'Hara.

Don't do it. The whisper slid through her mind even as her gaze traveled upward. She met his eyes in the reflected glass. It was like a physical touch and she licked her lips nervously as he moved closer still.

The heat of him was at her back and she dragged a long, torturous breath into her lungs.

His hands fell to her shoulders and she let him turn her body until she faced him fully. Ana stared up into his dark eyes, and it felt like everything inside her was falling away. She couldn't describe it any other way.

He was beautiful and her hand reached for his cheek. She frowned as he rested into her palm. There was pain, deep within the recesses of his eyes.

Declan had always been so adept at hiding his true self that to catch a glimpse of something real was somehow sacred. It scared her. She let her gaze fall, suddenly uncomfortable. She didn't want to see into his soul. That was much too intimate, something they could never be.

Intimate.

"What happened?" she whispered.

"Shhh," he answered. "No words."

Ana shuddered at the intensity within him. He seemed lost somehow. "What is this, Declan?" she asked, glancing up.

His eyes never left hers and for a moment there was silence. She sensed his struggle and fought the urge to clasp him to her breast, to hold him tight.

His hand crept up until he cradled hers within his large grasp, and he held her firm against his cheek. She felt the rough stubble on his skin and her eyes drifted away from his, traveling over the planes of his face before settling on his lips.

Her breaths fell faster as she eyed his mouth. So strong and firm.

Ana looked away. Her control was thin at best.

His arms slid around her waist and Declan pulled her flush against his body. Her first instinct was to resist but something held her still. Was it his need?

Or her own?

She felt every inch of his hard frame and as she laid her head upon his chest, the beat of his heart called to her.

"This," he whispered into her hair, "this is what I need."

Ana exhaled slowly and relaxed a bit. She listened to his even breaths and relished the warmth of his skin. She bit her lip when he lowered his head, and as he nuzzled the hollow between her neck and shoulder, she couldn't help the groan that escaped.

"Declan, I don't—"

"Shhh," he interrupted. "No words. I just need to feel something real tonight, nothing more." His lips brushed along her neck once more. "I want to hold you."

Declan straightened and arched away, his dark eyes piercing as he stared down at her. "Let me hold you."

Ana's breath hitched. Shadows played across his face and when he bent low she froze. The need that sat in the pit of her belly burned hard. The tips of her fangs broke skin, and sweat beaded along her forehead.

If he kissed her now there was no telling what she'd do. She ached for the taste of his blood, for the touch of his soul.

She should turn away.

If she was a good girl she would, but Ana remained still, her body gripped with the seductive pull of bloodlust. His hands slowly spread across her lower back, and without warning he hoisted her into his arms.

He paused and hugged her to him as if she were breakable. The gentle rise and fall of his chest rocked her, and inside, buried deep within her soul, she heard a cry. It was a sad lament for what would never be.

And in spite of the fact that it was all kinds of wrong, Ana ignored the cry and the urge to break from him. Instead her arms clung to his shoulders and she relaxed against his body as he carried her from the kitchen.

Swiftly his long legs strode down the hall and he took the stairs two at a time, showing no effort as he climbed yet again to the next level. Declan walked with purpose toward the end of the landing, as if he knew where her lair was. He waved his hand and the door opened, allowing him passage into her secret world.

One she'd not shared with anyone since Jean-Charles.

The loft was large and bare of furniture. It smelled of paint, oils and canvas. There were a few rugs tossed about the wood floor, a large cupboard to the right, and several paintings hidden in the far corner. An easel stood with a clean canvas resting upon it.

Underneath the tall window was her bed and it was there that Declan stopped. Gently he lowered her onto her back, his hands quickly removing her boots before he did the same to his own.

Ana turned onto her side, her mind a whirl of confusion. There'd been no words between them, no talk of what the night would bring.

She should order him to leave. If she was stronger she would.

Instead, Ana watched the shadows on the wall disappear as Declan closed the wooden shutters that dressed the window. And then the bed sank as he slipped behind her, his arms going around her midsection to pull her in tight to him once more.

She reveled in the warmth of his breath and the safeness of his embrace. Her small body tucked into the curve of his as if it was meant to be. How many times had she visualized this very thing? It was heartbreakingly perfect. *Heartbreakingly wrong.* The words whispered around the corners of her mind, bringing with it fear and the fury of her hunger.

It was the hunger that scared her more than anything. She knew in that moment that her thirst would plague her until the end of her days. He was the only one to quench it.

Declan's arms tightened as if he knew she was about to bolt. "Just one night. That's all I ask."

Ana frowned. He sounded different. Troubled. Something was off.

"What happened tonight?" she whispered.

A long silence followed her question and his breathing slowed. Declan held her so gently, his head nestled into the crook of her neck, that after several moments she thought maybe he'd not heard her.

"Declan?" she whispered, not understanding any of this. "Are you sure you're all right?"

After a few moments he spoke. "Fate," he said simply.

"What?" She tried to turn, to look into his eyes, but he held tight. Declan was definitely hiding something.

"Fate happened tonight."

"I don't understand."

"No more words," he murmured, "just let me hold you."

So many questions crowded her mind, yet Ana remained silent. She would honor his wish and leave it alone—for now.

She tried to relax but her hunger was biting. It clawed at her something fierce. She stared into the darkness and thought about puppies and rainbows. Eventually the hunger abated.

Ana closed her eyes, settled into his embrace, determined to enjoy this moment for what it was, a slice of Heaven that would end as soon as the sun rose.

Declan woke abruptly and was immediately aware of the fact that he held Ana tight to his body. She felt amazing in his arms and he groaned softly as he shifted. Her small form fit perfectly against him, her ass especially exquisite, and his cock swelled at the thought.

She was asleep. The gentle rise and fall of her chest, the way her head lay to the side leaving her neck exposed and vulnerable, told him so. His arms tightened and he lowered his face, drank in the scent of her as his mouth graced the pale skin along her neck.

If he could stay like this and never let her go, he'd die a happy man. Yet Declan felt the weight of his cold, hard reality. It was heavy. It sucked. He was going back in.

Back to Hell.

There'd never been a question he wouldn't accept the gauntlet thrown by Samael. How could he not? There was no other who stood half a chance of getting to the children. Cale was unacceptable. His light was too pure, his link to the Seraphim too strong. He'd be outed before he got anywhere near the children.

He'd not fed from the darkness as Declan had.

Declan felt it—Lilith's cold, seductive power circling through his veins. It was a craving and it ate at him constantly. When Declan had first broken free from the underworld it had been bad. He'd been like a junkie jonesing for his next fix. Yet he'd struggled through, thinking that once he'd accomplished the mission, returned Azaiel to the Seraphim, it would be over. Bill would return the damaged half of his soul and all would be well.

What a joke that had been. His soul had been restored but the hunger for something more, something dark, was always with him. Turned out, he was as bad a seed as his father, Cormac. Maybe worse.

He was a warrior of the light, a Seraph, and served a higher order, but his soul was stained and perhaps beyond cleansing.

Fucking Lilith.

She'd gone after him like a bitch in heat the moment he'd arrived in Hell and pounced upon his weakness, his desire to be free. It was a bitter pill to swallow, but Declan knew in the end, there was no one to blame but himself.

He sighed and shifted once more as his thoughts turned to the woman he held. She was so small, fragile almost, and yet he knew how fierce she was. He loved that about her, the contradiction.

"Do you know how much I want you?" he whispered. "How much I regret the things that will never be?" Was it only a few nights earlier he'd envisioned a future with Ana at his side?

Fate was a bitch and for him her name was Lilith. He had to face the fact that his chances of escaping her clutches a second time were not great.

Declan smiled wryly as he cradled Ana to him. He knew she desired him. That had been plenty obvious when he'd kissed her a few nights back. Christ, but he wanted more, and yet just holding her was almost enough. The demons inside were at rest.

The sound of her breaths lulled him momentarily and he glanced at the awakening shadows that licked along the edges of the wall. Outside the moon had given way to the first rays of sunlight. Though he'd closed the shutters hours earlier, brightness still found its way in.

The loft was large and he found his gaze centered on several large canvases that were seemingly tossed into the far corner. An easel and paint supplies were scattered along the floor.

Ana was an artist. That was something he'd not known.

Declan glanced down at her and shook his head. There was much about her that remained a mystery. If only he had more time. If only she'd let him in.

He grabbed an errant strand of auburn hair that lay against her pale cheek. Slowly he twisted it around his finger and then bent low, inhaling the richness of her scent. God damn but the woman smelled like every fantasy he'd ever had. She was exquisite spice and her hair was like silken sheets of sin.

She moaned softly and he froze. There was no way he was ruining this moment. Declan knew that as soon as she woke she'd bolt. He considered using a charm to keep her lulled into sleep, but dismissed the thought just as fast.

She'd kick his ass if he ever attempted something like that.

His gaze fell to the soft swell of her cheek, the full lips, and the small chin. She moved and he could not help the groan that escaped as her butt settled deeper into his body. Her softness was pressed tight to his aching cock, and Declan tried to shift once more, but it was no use.

Jesus fucking hell. This was not good.

His arms tightened around her and his hand fell to her small breasts. He felt her nipples beneath the cotton. They were hard, puckered. His thumb massaged the hardened peaks with a controlled precision that belied the madness inside him.

Her softness swelled beneath his touch. She sighed and turned slightly, snuggling into the crook of his arms even more. Her long lashes swept downward but the eyes remained closed, her breaths even.

With regret he withdrew his hand. Who the hell was he kidding? Nothing good could come of this, and what was the point in torturing himself with something he'd never be able to claim?

Declan fell back against the pillow instead, taking Ana along with him so that she lay on top of his chest, her cheek turned toward his shoulder.

"But this feels so right," he whispered.

The shadows on the wall now mingled with streams of light. They caught his gaze and mesmerized him, lulling him into a sense of peace he knew was false.

"I'll take it," he murmured to himself, even if it was only a taste. He closed his eyes and relaxed, content to *just be* with Ana.

Outside, the clatter of a bike chain echoed sharply and the methodical thwack of newspapers hitting pavement could be heard. Down the way the neighbor's sprinkler system engaged and a dog barked as it was let outside.

The humans that dwelled in the Big Easy had no fucking clue what lived beyond their vision. No idea that the struggle between darkness and light was a constant battle and if he lost, the consequence would be deadly.

A sliver of energy rippled over his flesh and pulled Declan from his thoughts. He stilled, letting the quiet wash over him as he listened. Ana's breathing had changed. She was awake.

She moved against him, slowly, sensually. The exquisite feel was torture and he hissed as she wiggled and pulled herself upward, along his torso. His eyes slid open and he stared up into her face.

The expression that graced her features was unlike any he'd seen before. Her eyes were round balls of navy and hung huge in her pale face. The skin of her cheeks was tight and her lips held the barest hint of pink to them. Slowly his gaze moved lower until they rested upon the fangs that glistened in the early gloom.

A groan escaped from between her lips.

He knew what she wanted. Ana was hungry.

What would it feel like? If he let her feed from him?

His hands crept around her shoulders and he pulled her

to him, so close that he could see the tinge of red mirrored within the depths of her eyes. She licked her lips, and the thin veins that ran beneath her skin sharpened, like tiny spider legs.

"Do it," he whispered.

Ana hesitated, shaking her head, her eyes never leaving the pulse that beat at his neck. She began to pant; her veins were more pronounced. "Don't look at me." Ana turned away. "I don't want you to see me like this." Her words ended on a sob, and a chunk of his heart broke away.

How could he make her understand? He wanted to see her in every way imaginable. Down to the dirty. The real Ana. Nothing less would do.

Declan was on fire with the need to connect to the woman on a level he'd never dreamed possible. Fuck the consequence. There would never be another time and place for this.

His right hand slid into the silky hair at her nape and he pulled her closer still, and though she resisted, he eventually forced her to look at him once more. She was magnificent, fangs and all.

"I want you, Ana." He shuddered as she moved against him.

A groan escaped from her once more and then she bent toward him. "I'm so hungry for you. I've never been this hungry." Her eyes were luminous as she looked down at him. "For anyone."

The warmth of her breath caressed his neck and he tensed as she hovered above him. A strangled noise erupted from her chest as she flicked her tongue along his flesh, but it was nothing compared to the cry of need that rifled through his mind.

The world fell away until there was nothing but Ana.

"Do it," he whispered once more, his tone urgent, his voice harsh. *Commanding.*

"I don't . . ." she began, "I can't . . ."

"You will." He stared up into her eyes. They were now completely black. "I've waited years for this." His hand circled the roundness of her ass and he pulled her into his erection. "You will not deny me."

Ana stared down at him for several moments, her chest heaving, fangs fully extended. Something flickered in her eyes and she hissed, her breath escaping in a rush. She clasped his shoulders and sank her fangs deep into his neck.

CHAPTER 14

The rush of his blood across her tongue, the taste of his sweetness, and the feel of him beneath her were nearly too much for Ana. Bloodlust hit her hard, and it took everything inside her to pull back.

She couldn't do this. She wasn't strong enough. In her lifespan of nearly three hundred years she'd fed from all kinds of humans. Men, women, and yes, even children. None of them had taken her to the edge, to that point where she was in danger of losing herself—her mind, her soul.

Until Declan.

She'd known it would be like this. His essence was beyond what she'd even thought possible and she'd taken just a nibble. He would be the drug she'd forever be slave to.

Ana licked her lips, savoring his taste as she pulled away and stared down at him. She was straddling his body, his hardness firm between her legs.

His dark eyes gazed up at her. "That's not enough," he whispered hoarsely. "I want more." He moved and she felt dampness between the folds of her sex as he did so. "I want to connect with you in the way of your people."

She ground her center against him, the action a reflex, and hissed as her clitoris swelled with need. A whimper fell from her lips and for a moment she had no clue what to do.

The urge to feed was a relentless ache but the desire that now coursed through her was equally as strong. Ana felt as if she were coming apart and the only person who could put her back together was Declan.

No man she'd ever been with had reduced her to such a puddle of need. And she'd had only a taste.

Declan's hands dug into her ass and he shifted until he sat against the headboard, with her body snug between his legs. His dark eyes never left hers. His right hand slipped behind her neck, while the other was firm against her backside.

Slowly he pulled her forward until her mouth was but inches from his flesh. "Take from me," he whispered.

Ana's eyes were riveted to the frantic beat of his pulse, and the drops of blood that lay against his neck. Her fangs ached, her gut twisted.

"Declan, you don't know what you ask." Her voice was just above a whisper. Thoughts of the past hit her briefly and she winced. Jean-Charles, his dead lover, Diego . . . all of it became a mishmash of memories and yet they faded fast, overpowered by the sound of Declan's heartbeat.

"I want you," he said simply, and she felt something inside her break as she stared into his eyes. "I always have, and right now"—his hands roved the curve of her back before settling along her hip—"it's our time." His eyes darkened. "We might never have it again."

Desire was a traitorous bitch and the heat of it ran along her skin until she was trembling. She hissed and forced her fangs to retract.

Nothing would ever satisfy the hunger inside except to claim the man beneath her. To drink his blood and tap into his soul. To imprint her essence upon his own.

She stared at him in silence, his words echoing into her brain. The energy around him was dark and a shiver rolled over her. Something wicked was heading his way. She could feel it.

Ana let out a long, shuddering breath and reached for her T-shirt. Slowly she peeled it back until her breasts were laid bare to him. His gaze didn't leave her face as his cock swelled beneath her, and she smiled as a groan escaped his lips.

She tossed the shirt onto the floor. She would not bond with him. She would never claim him as her own. The hunger she felt would never abate and she knew after this morning that it would only increase.

And yet, for him, Ana would do this. She would give him what he wanted, but she'd do it on her own terms.

Slowly she rose and stood above him on the bed. He was breathing heavily, his face a mask of heated want. With deft fingers Ana undid her jeans and tugged them off, throwing them onto the floor with her shirt.

She didn't wear underwear and smiled to herself as he hissed sharply. His eyes were now glued to the aching folds between her legs. Slowly she widened her stance, allowing him a peek at her most private area.

She was wet, throbbing, and her hand inched downward. His breath hitched at the back of his throat as her fingers flicked along the outer edges of her lips.

"You're fucking killing me." He shifted his weight on the bed. "Christ, but you're more beautiful than I imagined," he said hoarsely, "and trust me, I've imagined you plenty times."

Ana took a step forward and sank down. She straddled him and pushed herself onto the straining bulge in his jeans. The friction against her wetness was electrifying and she growled as his hands once more claimed the soft roundness of her breasts.

His mouth soon followed and his tongue licked her nipple, long, torturous strokes, and then he opened fully, taking the engorged peak into his mouth. His free hand traveled lower and joined hers and she hissed with anticipation.

Without pause he sank two long fingers deep into her body, his thumb massaging her clitoris as his mouth continued to pull hard at her breasts.

Ana knew Declan's touch would be magical, but they'd barely started and she was already coming undone.

She looked down from eyes half closed and the sight of her milky flesh against his hard, clothed body was more erotic than anything she'd ever seen. His dark head suckling at her breast was something she'd take to the grave.

He tore his mouth away.

"Don't stop," she whispered.

"Stop?" Declan laughed, and her belly turned over at the sound. It was full of naughty and dark promises. He stared directly into her eyes and shifted his body so that there was room between them. She gasped as his fingers continued to massage deep within her. The gasp soon turned into a loud groan as a series of vibrations erupted along the walls of her channel. They burned hot and then cold, traveling all the way to her womb and back again like an electrical conduit from his fingers.

"Jesus, Declan, what was that?" She barely got her words out before the sensation started once more and she bit her lip as he held her gaze.

"Hold on." His voice was rough and he was breathing heavily as the pulses started once more. "I'm not done." Her womb contracted and she stifled a scream as their intensity increased. What the hell was he doing to her?

His fingers spread their magical sensations once more but this time the vibrations and pulses burned hotter as they traveled back. She was slick and tight and when the pulse burst through and erupted along her clitoris she fell forward.

She cried out as an orgasm ripped through her, hot, heavy, and fast.

He kissed the side of her neck. "I have many secrets to share with you, sweets."

His hands were on each side of her face now and slowly her eyes focused. His irises were black, his breaths ragged.

"I want to see you," she breathed against his lips, and she thought she heard him sigh as she opened beneath him. His mouth was hot and she plundered it mercilessly. Her tongue danced along his warmth, and the taste of him was like no other.

Her hands fell to his shirt and she tugged at the fabric frantically. "I want to see you," she said again, this time with a firmness that brought his head up. She felt the beast, her true nature, shifting beneath her skin and averted her gaze. Her fangs were itching to break skin but she concentrated and pushed them back.

She fell backward and rested on him. They stared at each other in silence and in that moment something changed. Ana didn't know if she could put her finger on what it was exactly but she felt a connection that she'd never felt before.

Like she'd finally come home.

Carefully he pulled his shirt over his head, leaving bare the marred flesh beneath his left pectoral. The skin was a macabre design of precise scars. She swallowed thickly and looked into his eyes.

Ana knew they were from his time in Hell—he'd had half his soul taken from him. She moved forward and gently kissed each and every scar, her lips trailing along the rough edges. An ache formed in her heart for all that he'd been through. She wanted to make him forget even if it was for only this one moment.

Declan was breathing erratically and her hands fell to the waistband of his jeans. Carefully she undid the snap and he moved so that she could tug his pants down. She threw them to the floor and then allowed herself to gaze upon the most beautiful man in the world.

Shadows fell across his face, bands of darkness that left his mouth and chin open to her eyes. Rough stubble darkened his skin and she knew his beard was heavy. This was no boy before her, but a male in his prime. Declan's shoulders were wide, his frame powerful, and yet he was built like an athlete, long-limbed, toned, and hard.

Her eyes moved lower, past impressive abs, and she followed the dark line of hair that pointed toward his straining cock. Her mouth went dry at the sight and she licked her lips as a groan escaped from him.

"I've wanted you for so long," he whispered, and then his hands were on her shoulders as he pulled her against him roughly. Declan kissed her, long and hard, his tongue tasting every inch of her mouth. His hands were all over her body, running up her back until he buried them deep within her hair.

She could stay like this forever with only his body and warmth to blanket her skin.

His hardness was flush against her belly and her hand closed around the tip of his cock as he continued to kiss her. His passion bordered on fever and she knew if she let him, he'd eat her soul, claim her heart.

As she massaged the soft underside of his cock, he groaned into her mouth.

"Slow down, babe," Declan said hoarsely. "I need for this to last longer than two minutes."

Her clitoris began to throb and pulse once more. She gyrated against him, small whimpers falling from her throat. A fire burned inside her, hot and demanding, but it was the other, the darker sensation that scared her. It was the need to claim to him, to drink from him and make him hers.

Could she stop in time? Pain lanced across her gut and she shook her head. Ana broke the kiss and stared into his eyes, uncertain. "I don't want to hurt you," she whispered.

Declan groaned. "Honey, the kinda hurt you're doling out is exactly what I want." His hands slid to her ass and he pressed his cock against her wetness. "What I've been dreaming about for years."

"You don't understand." Her words ended with a strangled sound as his mouth closed once more around her
nipple. He suckled, taking long, hard pulls from her, and
each time he did, she felt a reaction deep within her womb.
Ana's breaths were coming fast and hard. "I feel like I'm
coming apart," she said hoarsely, "as if I have no control. It
scares me."

His fingers dug into her flesh. Declan shifted his body,
and his eyes were piercing as he smiled at her. "Don't worry."
He lifted her as if she were no more than a doll. "I have no
problem taking control." And then he thrust upward, pulling
her down onto his hardness at the same time.

An animalistic sound fell from her lips. The feel of him
inside her was unlike anything she'd imagined. Declan
filled her completely, his long, powerful stroke bating the
fire inside immediately. She looked at him in surprise. Sweat
lined the ridges of his mouth and Ana bent forward, licking
at him, grinding against him as she did so.

The fiery need that rippled inside was instant and her
fangs broke skin as desire swept over her. All thoughts of
consequence fled as her true nature rose to the surface.

She wanted him. In every way possible.

"Holy Christ but you feel sweet," Declan whispered into
her ear.

Her hands dug into his shoulders and she moved, letting
his cock slide along her channel in slow, torturous strokes.
He was large and each pass touched nerve endings with a
friction that had her insides quaking. She groaned loudly
as he increased the rhythm of his thrusts, each time going
deeper until she didn't think she could take it anymore.

They moved together for several long minutes. The only
sound to break the silence was the soft moans she couldn't
hold back as he held her firm and moved her up and down.
She tried to go faster but he wouldn't let her. The need inside
her was such that she began to whimper.

"Not yet, babe. I want this to last as long as we can make it." His voice was terse, his breathing heavy. "I *need* this."

Her nails had dug into his shoulders so hard that they'd drawn blood. The scent rose into the air and Ana hissed, closed her eyes. The smell of him, feel of him—the taste of him was too much. There was no way in hell she'd be able to hold back.

Panic set in and she tried to move away but Declan was strong. He growled loudly, slipped from inside her, and flipped her so that she was now beneath him.

He positioned himself between her legs and thrust into her once more. Ana screamed at the force of it and her legs wrapped around his hips. She closed her eyes as he thrust faster, harder, and the sounds of his flesh slapping against hers excited her like nothing before.

The smell of his blood mingled with the scent of sex permeated everything around her. Ana's fangs broke free and she was too weak to do anything but allow them freedom.

She looked up at Declan, and the raw passion in his eyes undid her. She clenched tight against him, her legs locking behind his hips as an orgasm shuddered through her.

Ana writhed beneath him as a guttural cry fell from his lips, and she clutched at his shoulders, pulling him down to her. Declan's right hand held her ass tight to him as his orgasm erupted and she opened her mouth, welcoming the intensity of her own release as it washed through her.

Her fangs ached and she was inches from his neck. Her thoughts were scattered but one thing stood out with clarity. The need to complete the act. To take his blood and make him hers.

"Do it." Declan's cry was hoarse and she scraped her teeth along his flesh, inhaling the scent of him as her body continued to rock with the most incredible orgasm she'd ever had.

Yet it wasn't enough. Her belly clenched almost immediately and a hunger like nothing she'd ever experienced before hit hard. The urge to feed from Declan was painful. It erased the pleasure that thrummed through her body in less time than it had taken to fall into bed.

Dark thoughts crowded her mind and she shook her head, crying out as she tried to push him away. She could not feed from him. Ana knew she'd never be able to stop with just a taste.

His other hand was at her head, urging her forward. "Do it," he commanded.

Ana stared at the flesh before her. His heartbeat pounded inside her head, a melody so beautiful it hurt. Her mouth watered, her fangs ached, but she whispered, "No."

Declan moved so that he could look at her and shame scorched her cheeks as his eyes lingered on her fangs. She knew her face was in the throes of bloodlust and she wanted to look away, but couldn't. Declan needed to see what she really was.

What he should be afraid of.

His breaths fell in short, fast bursts and slowly the passion fled, leaving a blank, cold look upon his face. He was still inside her and yet the space between them seemed infinite.

Declan withdrew and turned from her, his shoulders hunched forward. She ached for him and when he stood, hands clenched at his side, her hand reached for him but then she let it fall. He scooped up his pants from the floor and she hugged herself, suddenly cold.

He turned his head and she gazed upon his profile. The light filtering in from outside bathed him in an eerie glow. Her heart ached because she knew he was confused, that he would take her refusal to feed from him as rejection. And why would he think otherwise?

The only way to guarantee his safety was to steer clear. She'd already crossed the line today, hell, she'd fucking leapt over it, and now she'd have to deal with the consequence.

"You feed from humans all the time. Press that hot body of yours against strange men, and yet you won't drink from me."

Ana heard the accusation in his words and though she didn't trust herself to speak, she managed to blurt, "That's different."

He turned then, his anger palpable. Vibrations rippled along the floor. They crept up the bedposts and rattled the shutters that covered her windows.

"Why is it different?"

"I need blood to live, Declan. They're a food source. Nothing more."

He arched a brow. "Did you take from Diego?"

Ana's belly dropped and she felt faint. Diego was a name that would haunt her forever it seemed. Diego Castille, her former lover and the man she'd fancied herself in love with when she'd worked at PATU.

"When you had sex with him . . . did you feed from Diego?" Bitterness hung in the air and she swallowed heavily. She couldn't lie.

"Yes." *But I didn't bond with him. I didn't give him my blood. There was no fear of consequence. I never wanted him the way I want you.*

Declan stared down at her, his dark eyes fathomless and cold. His chest rose and fell as he fought for control, yet he remained silent. Slowly he pulled on his jeans and left without another word.

Sadness welled in her heart and Ana fought the tears that stung the corner of her eyes. She slipped from the bed and grabbed his T-shirt. It still held his warmth and she hugged it close to her body. Eventually she pulled the shirt over her head and fell back onto the mattress. His scent was all around her—on her body, his shirt, and her sheets. She inhaled it and closed her eyes as she savored his unique signature.

Ana didn't regret one moment she'd shared with Declan. She was selfish enough to admit that, though the hunger he'd awakened would curse her until the end of days.

Outside the sun was nearly full in the sky. A new day dawned for the residents of New Orleans. Ana snuggled deeper into the bed, hating the emptiness that sat in her gut. There would be no promise of new beginnings for her.

They'd died the minute Declan had claimed her heart.

CHAPTER 15

"Y ou want another?"

The question turned his head and Declan nodded. Sarah grabbed a bottle of whiskey and freely poured him a triple. The liquid burned as it went down but he savored the sensation and glanced around the room.

It was late afternoon and the Voodoo Lounge was quiet. His ass had been parked at the bar for a few hours and the landscape hadn't changed much. Ransome wasn't in yet. Apparently he'd taken a drive out to Bon Terre, the town where he came from, to attend to some pack business.

"You got woman troubles?"

Declan downed the remaining liquid and set his glass on the bar. "Excuse me?"

Sarah wiped the counter with careful precision. Her hair was held tight in two ponytails, the faded blond shot through with gray. Though the bar was supposed to be smoke-free, a cigarette dangled from her lips. She took a long drag and blew out a fine line of gray.

"The only thing that drives a man like you to my bar on a perfectly beautiful afternoon"—her eyes narrowed—"is woman troubles."

"Yeah, well, maybe I like the ambience."

"The what?" Sarah poured herself a drink and leaned

toward him. Apparently the bartenders Ransome hired had free rein with his stock.

"I don't much care for big words."

There was something about her that he liked; her simple attitude and no-bullshit way of speaking, for one. Declan smiled at the woman. "I had nowhere else to go."

"Ah, I see." Sarah butted her cigarette and threw a towel over her shoulder. "The lady you were with last night, she part of your troubles?"

Declan's face immediately darkened.

Sarah nodded. "I knew it." She leaned forward. "A piece of advice?"

Declan stared at her but remained silent. Down the way, the only other occupant of the bar shouted for a beer. Sarah turned and yelled at him, "Hold up, I'll be there in a second."

"Not the best way to garner tips," Declan murmured.

She shrugged her shoulders and smiled. "He's a regular. A two-bit shifter from Florida who only tips the first hour his butt is at my bar." She glanced toward the glowering male. "He's been here longer than you, so trust me, he can wait."

Declan indicated he wanted another drink. Sarah dutifully filled his glass and then narrowed her gaze on him. "She's a vampire."

He eyed the amber liquid. What the hell was the woman getting at?

"Your lady friend."

No shit.

"I'd rather not discuss Ana." A muscle tightened along his jaw as he held the glass between his fingers.

Sarah shrugged her shoulders. "They're bad news is all I'm saying."

"You don't sound like a fan."

"I'm not," she retorted. Sarah turned and grabbed a cold beer from the cooler. She glanced back at him before heading toward the shifter at the end of the bar. "Trust me." She arched a brow. "You stay away from her and you'll be a happier man."

It's too late for that.

Declan remained silent and stared down into his drink. Way too fucking late. He was still angry, frustrated, and if he wanted to be brutally honest, he'd admit that a whole lotta hurt was mixed into the equation as well.

He'd fantasized for so long about what it would be like to have her. To hold her sweet body in his hands and make her sigh with pleasure. He wanted to connect with the woman on a level that was sacred. He wanted to be that guy who stood above all the others. The one she wanted for keeps.

Declan clenched his teeth and turned away from the bar. The connection he'd craved hadn't happened.

He felt empty, cheated, and pissed off.

Why couldn't she be like any other lay? A quick fuck, no need for conversation, and move on to the next. He'd thought that if he could have her, even just once, *maybe* the raw need he felt every time he looked at her or thought about her would go away. Instead, it burned hotter, meaner, and Declan knew it would never abate.

He ran his hand through his hair as his gaze traveled the room. Tonight he was heading back to Hell. *Back to Lilith.* He needed to focus and yet all he could think about was Ana.

A sliver of energy rippled along the air, a soft whisper of darkness. He turned toward the door. Benny stood aside as Cale strode in, followed by Samael. They were early.

Declan squared his shoulders. He was fucked. There was no way around it.

He watched the two men as they advanced through the crowd. The demon's eyes were hidden once more behind large aviators, while Cale's piercing gaze zoomed in on Declan immediately. Cale said something to Samael and the demon nodded; a flash of white cutting through the dim as he smiled.

It was odd, the way the two men were so comfortable together considering they were in effect sworn enemies. Declan settled back onto the bar stool. It was only another layer to an already bizarre set of circumstance.

"I'm impressed with your enthusiasm." Samael grabbed the stool to Declan's left and sat. "I didn't think you'd show until midnight." The demon twirled around until he faced the room and he leaned back, elbows on the bar. Samael looked totally relaxed. Declan glanced at Cale. The Seraph's face was blank, his eyes flat.

The demon ordered three shots of tequila and remained silent as Sarah quickly grabbed the glasses. Her eyes were shooting bullets at Samael. She was no doubt still pissed over his treatment of her the night before. Yet money talked in the Big Easy and she quickly pocketed the fifty spot he threw on the bar.

She handed them each their glass and leaned toward Declan. "I hate to tell you this but you're challenged when it comes to choosing women"—she nodded toward Samael— "*and* the company you keep. He makes your vampire look like a pussycat."

She didn't know shit about Ana, but Declan smiled. "Agreed."

"Just leave the bottle, darling." Samael tossed an additional wad of cash onto the bar and Sarah grabbed it quick. She left the bottle where it stood, threw a disgusted look at the demon, and moved away.

The shifter at the end of the bar nearly toppled his bar stool in a mad effort to leave. Declan watched him go. He might be a shitty tipper but he sure as hell had some smarts.

"Is the boy with Ana?" Cale asked as he sat down on the other side of Declan.

Declan nodded. Nico was privy to the situation, and though he didn't like what was going down, the jaguar's first priority was Kaden. Declan trusted that the boy would be safe. He'd strengthened his wards around the mansion ten-fold and had a long conversation with Kaden. He was confident the teen knew how precarious, how *dangerous*, his situation was.

As for Ana, he'd woven a little extra charm into the protection spells. It wasn't foolproof, but hopefully was enough to contain the vampire for the evening. Before he took the trip down below he'd make sure Ransome was in the loop. He wanted the wolf patrols doubled.

"He's good." Declan glanced at the Seraph. "I've got everything covered."

"What of my necromancer?" Samael asked.

"She's not yours anymore," Declan answered. Francesca was locked away in Ana's mansion. She'd been near catatonic and hadn't said a word since the night before.

Declan glared at the demon and allowed a surge of power to exit his hands. The glasses on the bar shook slightly as an invisible conduit of energy erupted across the surface. It narrowly missed the demon's elbows as he rested them there, though his bottle of tequila wasn't so fortunate. The bottle toppled over and crashed to the ground.

"Your parlor shenanigans are growing tiresome, sorcerer. I suggest you stop." Samael looked straight ahead but the tightness of his mouth indicated he was not impressed.

Declan's hands burned hot. He clenched them tightly and considered smashing them into Samael's face. "You're right," Declan said, his tone conversational. "Parlor tricks are for amateurs and that's something I haven't been for decades. You should tread lightly, demon, because Lilith taught me well"—his voice lowered—"and it was from her fountain of depravity that I fed for months."

Samael laughed. "I hope you're thirsty, because a steady diet of Lilith is what you'll be surviving on if you fail."

"Enough!"

Both Declan and Samael glanced at Cale in surprise. The

Seraph stood with legs spread and arms across his chest. He was decked out in requisite black, his face tense, his manner grave. A tall, skinny human sidled up to the bar, totally unaware of the company that surrounded him.

"Dude." His voice was raspy as if ill used, and his dead, watery eyes told a tale of illicit substances. "You know where I can score some—"

"Leave at once," Cale ordered. The stranger froze and gave his head a shake before turning around without another word.

"Hey, buddy," Sarah inserted, "this is a *bar* and we make *money* selling alcohol."

Declan was impressed. The bartender had balls.

Cale tossed a look her way. "He was not looking for a drink and you will give us privacy."

Sarah's eyes narrowed but Declan nodded. "Just a couple of minutes," he said quietly.

"I gotta grab some bottles from the stockroom." Sarah glanced at the massive bouncer whose eyes were trained on the three of them from across the room. "Benny is a mean son of a bitch, just so you know." She slipped under the bar. "I hope you're gone when I get back."

As soon as Sarah was out of earshot Declan jumped from his stool, stretched his long limbs, and faced Samael. "Why are you really here?" he asked pointedly. This was all wrong. He was the fucking demon of chaos, yet not an ounce of his madness could be felt.

He was *behaving*. Hell, his brand of nastiness had been stronger in the preceding days.

The demon studied him for several seconds before removing his glasses. The strange eyes that looked at him were focused, serious. "I will not let Lilith gather the mark of seven."

"That doesn't answer my question." He glanced at Cale. "I'm willing to lay my ass on the line because I think it's the right thing to do. The mark of seven is not written in stone. These kids should have a chance to prove their worth without being manipulated by either the underworld or the Seraphim." He arched a brow. "You two, on the other hand, confuse me. Why is a demon lord holding hands with the Seraph?"

Declan watched Cale closely. The Seraph's features remained stony, though he saw worry in his eyes.

"Answer me," Declan said, "or I walk away and do this myself." A whisper of darkness slithered along his body. It was a caress of power and Declan loved the feel of it. He kept his hands loose at his side and glared at the demon.

"Look at you," Samael whispered as he twirled his empty glass along the bar top. "All take charge and no bullshit." He cocked his head to the side. "I see why Lilith took a fondness to you. You're so like your father, and according to my sources, she had her fill of him as well."

The fuse that had been burning the edge of his brain all day erupted and Declan flew at the demon. His hand went around Samael's neck before the demon had time to react.

In Declan's mind, words flew forth—black words, *charmed* words—that threatened to unleash a fury upon the demon that would hurt. Samael said nothing, though the light that shone from behind his eyes warned of retaliation.

Declan grunted and pressed his fingers into the demon's neck, hissing as a burn shot up his forearm. Skin moved beneath his fingers and he faltered.

Christ.

Too late he remembered the tattoo that marked the demon as lord and he cursed as intense pain ripped into his hand. The tattoo moved and Declan growled, spewing a torrent of foul words, his thoughts wild with the need to hurt.

He gathered as much strength as he could and just when he would have blasted Samael, he was pulled back and Cale stepped between the two of them.

The Seraph was furious. Beneath them the floor rumbled

and a few screams echoed into the near-empty room. Declan turned away, his chest heaving, full of repressed rage.

"Pull yourself together." Cale's words were harsh. "Or I will end this now."

Declan turned to Cale. "What is your connection to him?" He pointed to Samael and snarled, "I will not go back to that shithole until I know the truth."

Samael growled and put his glasses back in place. He kinked his neck and let the tattoo settle once more upon his flesh. Long seconds of silence followed.

Declan was aware that many eyes rested upon them and he forced himself to be calm. He saw Asher leaning over the mezzanine, Benny near the door, and Sarah as she slowly made her way back.

Samael nodded to the woman as she slid behind the bar, her eyes wary and hands full. He helped himself to one of the bottles that she clutched, threw some more bills onto the bar, and turned to Declan and Cale.

A blond woman approached them, a werewolf, one of Ransome's. She was all wild hair and large breasts, and sported an ass that was barely covered by the black leather skirt she wore.

She paid no attention to Cale or Declan and melted into Samael's side, her hand immediately disappearing beneath his jacket.

"I suggest you adjust the sorcerer's attitude. I'll meet you at the Gate before midnight." The demon shot a look of disgust his way before continuing in the ancient dialect of the Seraphim.

Declan glowered at them, hating that he had no clue what they were saying. The conversation was abrupt and he watched the demon melt into the darkness that clung to the edges of the club. The gawkers, mostly otherworld by this point, carried about their business as if nothing were out of the ordinary.

"You care to explain the mumbo-jumbo?" Declan asked, his frustration evident in the tone of his words. "And maybe tell me why you're getting into bed with the likes of him?"

Cale stared at Declan long and hard and then, decision made, spoke. "He is my brother."

"Pardon me?" Declan was incredulous—no—more like confused as all hell.

Cale turned. "Come. Let's take a walk. There's much you don't know."

As Declan followed the Seraph out of the Lounge, he had a feeling his life was once more taking a major turn. To the left.

Fuck.

Just when he'd learned to navigate the straight and narrow.

CHAPTER 16

Decatur was busy. It was early evening now, the air was crisp. Declan followed Cale in silence. There were many words inside him; he just didn't know what the hell to ask first.

The two men slipped through the throngs of tourists and a few minutes later ended up in front of Café du Monde. "I need a fix." The Seraph glanced his way. "You want one?"

Declan shook his head. "Not unless they've got Bailey's."

Cale winced. "You'd ruin such a delight with a cheap Irish cream?" He looked horrified at the idea and promptly ordered himself a large café au lait and a plate of beignets. Declan smelled the sweet chicory used to flavor the coffee, and the beignets were deep-fried and smothered in powdered sugar.

His stomach revolted at the sweet overkill and he moved away, back onto the sidewalk.

"Let's walk." Cale proceeded to down three large beignets as they headed toward the water and by the time they reached the edge of the Mississippi, the Seraph had finished every last crumb.

Cale took a long draw from his coffee cup and then spoke.

"Samael is my brother but not in the literal term. We're both part of a select group of warriors, from every class of being. Demon, Seraphim, nephilim, vampire, shifter, magick . . . even humans." Cale blew at the steam that hovered above his cup. "You name it, we've got it."

"And the purpose for this, ah, *group* is what exactly?" Declan watched several seagulls fly overhead, their sad cries riding the wind as they dipped and dove toward the muddy water.

"We're the last line of protection. We keep things in order." He paused. "We are *Guardians* . . . a League of Guardians."

"Seriously? Like the Justice League . . . or X-Men or . . ."

Cale shrugged. "We are what we are."

"That tells me nothing."

"Let me explain it to you this way. Our job is to make sure neither the underworld nor the upper realm become too powerful . . . yin-yang and all that. Without darkness there can be no light, the line between the two is delicate, like the thinnest weave of silk."

Declan let Cale's words sink in. "So you're not one of the Seraph. You're spying on them."

Cale frowned. "Spying? No, that's much too literal. I believe in the good and for the most part the Seraphim's agenda is above reproach. But I also know that absolute rule is not the answer. How many crimes have been committed because righteous thought believed the end justified the means?" He shook his head bitterly. "Too many."

"So you police the Seraphim."

Cale paused for a few moments, his brow furled. "I'm not sure *policing* is the correct term, either. We gather evidence and act upon it if need be, work in tandem with operatives who exist in every plane of existence."

Declan took a few moments to let Cale's words sink in. "So who polices you?"

A smile tugged the corner of Cale's mouth. "We answer to one of the original seven Seraphim—a true warrior who speaks directly to the highest power." Cale licked at the bits of sugar that remained on his fingers. "You've already met him."

Son of a bitch. Declan could see where this was going. "Bill." He found it ironic the little elf man had such power.

Cale nodded but remained silent.

Declan shook his head. The whole thing sounded bizarre. "I've seen Samael in action when I was imprisoned below in Club Lilith. He's no fucking hero."

Cale nailed him with a dark look. "You will not question the demon. Every day of his existence he treads a thin line as do we all." Cale looked away, his hands clenched to his side. "You think if the Seraphim find out of our existence they'd welcome us? Thank us for the many times we've driven them back from the brink of war with the underworld? From slaughtering entire peoples because they were pagan and did not believe in our higher power?"

Cale sighed. "Samael is a demon. Make no mistake that his true nature is volatile at best. His very core is fed by chaos but he swore allegiance to Askelon, or Bill as you know him, eons ago. He saw the need for control . . . for balance."

Declan digested the information. "So if anyone found out about your *affiliation* with this *secret* group you'd pretty much be toast."

"You're smarter than you look, O'Hara." Cale paused once more. Lines of tension crept over his features and there was no doubt as to the seriousness of the situation. "Our organization has been in operation for millennia. There are whispers of our existence, bands of information that twist in the wind only to disappear as we act upon them. There are those who would hunt us, but our identities remain dark, unknown. Even amongst ourselves all is not revealed. Our inner sanctum cannot be breached or all is lost."

Declan thought of Ana. "Is DeLacrux part of your gang?"

Cale shrugged. "I'm not sure what Bill's plans are for your lady."

Declan walked a bit, taking a few moments to digest all he'd heard. Abruptly he turned back to Cale. "Seems to me information about this exclusive club of yours isn't offered up freely. Why you including me in the loop? What's the catch?"

"For this to work, for you to successfully retrieve those kids, you need to know everything. Samael is involved. *Heavily.* His safety is paramount. He's much too valuable an operative in our organization to chance his safety."

"But my ass is expendable," Declan observed dryly.

"No offense."

"None taken."

Cale's mouth twitched but there was no humor in his eyes as he studied the sorcerer. "Consider this an initiation of sorts."

"You mean I don't get a free pass?"

"Your initiation will come fast and hard. Hell is not for the weak." Cale spoke quietly.

"That's a fucking understatement." Declan's bitterness couldn't be hidden. The physical pain doled out in the lower realm was impressive but it was the mind games that brought down the mightiest of warriors. Declan had barely hung on, and some nights only thoughts of Ana had gotten him through.

"Great." Declan arched a brow. "So how will I know I passed?"

Cale waited as a couple strolled by and turned. "That's easy."

"Yeah?" Declan fell into step beside the Seraph.

"Sure. You make it out alive. *That* means you've passed."

"Good to know," Declan murmured.

Cale's cell phone rang and he quickly dug it from the

pocket of his jeans. He didn't speak a word, just listened intently and then turned away from Decatur.

"Aren't we headed back to the Lounge?"

"No." Cale nodded toward a sleek black limo that was parked a few blocks away. "We're meeting Samael at the Gate."

"The Gate?"

"The Devil's Gate." They reached the car and a driver immediately stepped out, opening the door with a respectful greeting. Declan waited until they were inside to ask for a little elaboration.

"What the hell is the Devil's Gate?"

He sank into the soft leather and the interior was immediately flooded with the earthy tones of jazz. It was a whisper of smoke and whiskey. Declan relaxed as the sound infiltrated the small space.

Cale offered a cigar but Declan refused. He watched as the Seraph ran the thick stogie under his nose and then gripped it tight between his lips. "It's a location where it's safe for us to gather."

He was being evasive.

"In New Orleans?"

"No. A place called The Pines."

"Where's that exactly?" Declan's tone was sharp but he was getting fed up with playing twenty questions.

Cale rested his head back and whispered, "A long way from here."

They traveled to an airstrip on the outskirts of New Orleans, and it wasn't long before Declan was chilling in the cabin of one of the most luxurious jets he'd ever seen.

He placed a call to the Voodoo Lounge while waiting for the plane to taxi to the runway. Ransome picked up on the first ring.

"Where the hell are you?" the werewolf growled. He

sounded on edge and Declan sat a little straighter, his face set in a frown.

"I'm heading out of town for a bit." He had to make a decision. Include the werewolf in the details or leave him in the dark. "Not sure how long I'll be gone."

"For fuck sakes, O'Hara. I don't need this shit. You dump your crap at my door and then leave? What the hell is up with that?"

"Everything all right, LaPierre? You're sounding a little stressed."

The werewolf growled into the phone. "I'm fine. Hell, I'm fucking peachy." There was a pause. "There's been a challenge in my pack for alpha. On top of your shit it's just one more thing to deal with."

"Sorry to hear that."

"Whatever. Where you headed?"

Declan paused, exhaled slowly, and dove in. "I'm going to Hell."

"Buddy, I could have told you that, years ago."

Declan smiled at the wolf's sarcastic comment. "No, this is for real. I'm heading down to the shithole lower realm. They've got their hands on two of the seven marks."

There was a long pause as Ransome digested the information. "I hate to say it but that sucks freaking horse balls."

Declan smiled at the wolf's analogy. "I'd say no worries but who the hell am I kidding? I just . . . while I'm gone I need to know that Ana and the rest of my crew are safe. Can I count on you for some extra bodies to watch the DeLacrux mansion?"

"I've already sent a few more of my boys over. Don't worry, I'm still in charge. I'll head over myself later."

Declan was relieved to hear this. "I owe you."

"Yeah, I'm keeping track."

"Just so you know, Ana might be pissed when you see her so I'd stay the hell out of her way."

"Why? What have you done now?"

"I wove a spell into the wards that will make it impossible for her to slip through. It's for her protection." *And mine.* "Don't spill what's going on. I need to focus and not worry about her or the boy."

"What do I say when she asks where you are?"

"Tell her . . ." His voice trailed off as he glanced out the window into the darkness. He had no idea what the hell to say. "Tell her I'm sorry I wasn't enough." He paused. "I'll be in touch."

"That's the corniest fucking thing I've ever heard. Shit, if Ana grills me I'll make something up. Trust me. It's not in your best interest to let her know she's got you by the balls."

Declan's mouth pinched in anger. "My balls are secure, thanks. Forget I said anything."

"Whatever. Don't worry about the vampire. I'll have my boys double the patrols in and around the Garden District. They'll pay special attention to the DeLacrux mansion and I won't be far along." The wolf paused. "After I deal with Asher."

"Asher?" Declan's mouth thinned at the mention of the werewolf. He was no fan.

"Don't ask."

He didn't.

Five minutes later the plane was wheels up and Declan said good-bye to the Big Easy. Cale advised him to relax, catch a few zzzzz's, but there was no way in hell that was going to happen. He was wound tighter than a crackhead scrambling for a fix.

Declan sighed and tried to turn his brain off, yet he couldn't stop thinking of Ana. He was all twisted up inside, his emotions running the gamut of anger, need, despair, and if he was honest, hatred. Christ, to have the power she held.

Ana had made it more than clear she wasn't interested in

him. The sex had been beyond anything he'd imagined but he wanted to be more than fuck buddies. That was never going to happen. It was time he buried all thoughts of her and dealt with the reality of his here and now.

He was falling down the rabbit hole back to Hell where he'd have to deal with Lilith. Then there were the three teenagers who might or might not signal a coming apocalypse, and a bunch of others not accounted for.

Not exactly a Hallmark movie of the week.

If he wasn't careful it would be an epic disaster.

The plane landed three hours later on a desolate airstrip out in the middle of nowhere. The night was chilled, the moon low, and the quiet that greeted his ears disconcerting.

Declan walked toward a large SUV parked several feet away and turned in a full circle. He couldn't see beyond the ridge of darkness that blanketed the perimeter, and that made him nervous. He held his hands loose at his sides and watched as Cale exited the plane.

The tall Seraph strode his way and nodded behind him at the driver who waited patiently.

"Where the hell are we?" Declan said. "This place feels different to me, and in my world different ain't always good. In fact it very rarely is."

Cale paused at the side of the truck and glanced around. "Relax, we didn't land on Mars. We're actually pretty close to the Canadian-American border."

Declan grunted in answer.

"This entire area isn't so much different as it is special," Cale murmured.

"Special, huh?" Declan followed Cale into the vehicle. "I don't like special. I prefer normal, boring. Anything but otherworld would be just fucking wonderful right about now."

The truck roared into the night, its twin beams of lights illuminating a road that ran between heavily forested areas on either side. Though the moon was out, the darkness that clung to the trees seemed impenetrable. Declan felt caged in and didn't like it.

He kept his fingers loose, at the ready. The driver was human, which surprised Declan. He was young, maybe early twenties, and had the heavy guitars of Metallica cranked, "For Whom the Bell Tolls."

How fucking appropriate.

Declan was on a collision course to an end that was totally unclear. The sad, lonely bell of death might be ringing for him before the week was over. He sat back, closed his eyes, and let the hard rocking tunes energize his soul.

Ten minutes later the truck came to an abrupt halt and Declan sat up and looked out the window. They were parked in front of a large, rambling building, obviously a bar. Above the main doors a neon sign illuminated in red, THE DEVIL'S GATE. There were a couple of bikes parked out front, impressive Harleys from the looks of it, as well as an array of SUVs and beat-up cars.

This was interesting.

He hopped from the truck and stopped in his tracks. Heavy magick permeated the area. It clung to everything, rode the wind, and settled in his lungs as he inhaled the cool night air. It was different from anything he'd felt before. At first he couldn't put his finger on exactly what was different and then it hit him. The magick was organic. It was not something produced by a sorcerer's hands.

Declan glanced at Cale in surprise. "What is this place?"

Cale walked past him. "The Devil's Gate is located in a small town called The Pines." The Seraph paused at the top of the stairs and waited for Declan to follow suit. "It's not a place you'll find on any map."

"Not even Google? I find that hard to believe." His words were laced with sarcasm.

Cale ignored Declan's smart-ass comment. "The magick

that protects us is ancient and does not take kindly to intruders."

Declan didn't know what to say to that so he strode past the warrior and pushed open the door. He was hit by loud music, the smell of booze, fried foods, and an overload of otherworld beings that immediately set him on edge.

The room was low, long, and wide. The setup sucked for a bar with entertainment. The acoustics were not great and yet the heavy beat coming from the stage did the trick. The place was rocking.

Along the right a bar ran the length of the room, and at the moment it was packed. There were humans, shifters, vampires, and he sensed the subtle aroma of demon in the air.

Several shapes could be seen in the corners; the light that clung to their shoulders told Declan they were from the higher realm. He'd never seen such an eclectic gathering. Instead of the place making him feel relaxed, his gut tightened and he pulled hard on the magick within.

Cale walked in behind him and paused as a tall brunette appeared from the shadows.

"You're back." Her voice was husky. Declan looked at the woman with interest. She was one hell of a looker. Long legs, impressive rack, and a heart-shaped face that was milky white. Her eyes were huge round balls of chocolate and they looked at the Seraph with a hunger that was quickly hidden.

She was human.

"It's been months," she said softly.

Cale nodded to her. "Lily," and then walked past without another word.

Declan saw the hurt that crossed her features. It was quickly masked. She opened her mouth to speak and then closed it abruptly. She turned and disappeared once more into the shadows that clung to the corners.

"I didn't think you'd come, sorcerer."

Declan clenched his teeth and turned as Samael drifted over from the bar. The demon grinned at him. His tall frame was clothed in head-to-toe black, his arms were bare, and the tattooed dragon that lay upon his neck shimmered in the gloom.

"I hear there's one hell of a party going on at Club Lilith," Declan answered. "Wouldn't miss it for the world."

Samael handed him a glass. Declan arched a brow and accepted.

"Enjoy," the demon said silkily. "It might be a long time before you sample something so sweet."

Declan held the glass loosely in his hands and eyed the demon closely.

"The offer is only good once," Samael said, his tone changing slightly as he stared at the sorcerer.

Declan tossed back the amber liquid, enjoying the fire as it burned down his throat. The heat sizzled along his veins, spreading through his body rapidly, energizing his cells. He looked at the demon in surprise and was immediately suspicious.

"What the hell was in that?"

Samael took a step closer and removed the aviators that covered his eyes. The swirling liquid that lay behind them began to glow as the demon spoke. He was dead serious.

"A little extra something that will keep the taint of the human realm from your flesh, and cloak you in the scent of demon. You'll need it where you're going." The demon paused. Shadows fell across his face as his mouth tightened. "This will not be easy and we need those children safe."

Was that compassion Declan saw reflected in the depths of his eyes?

Samael threw his glasses back in place and shrugged his shoulders. "It isn't foolproof, but it's all I got. If you don't succeed, Lilith will never let you go. You know this." The demon stared at him for several long moments. "You ready?"

Declan glanced at Cale. The Seraph stood a few feet away. His face was dark, seriously intense. Christ, they looked like they were about to attend a funeral. *Yeah, mine.*

Declan squared his shoulders, ignored the lump of dread in his gut, and nodded.

Let the games begin.

CHAPTER 17

"Where is he?" Ana's voice rang shrilly and bordered on the insane but it was nothing compared to the anger that rippled beneath her flesh. She was hot from the force of it and that was saying a lot, considering her vamp skin was usually cool to the touch.

She turned her gaze to Nico, but the warrior was silent.

Kaden shrugged his shoulders and mumbled, "Not sure." She caught the nervous glance he tossed toward the jaguar shifter.

They were lounging in the kitchen like it was a fucking Sunday afternoon. Coffee and beignets from Du Monde had arrived as if by magic. The smell was making her ill and for that reason alone she wanted to rip someone's throat out.

Ana whirled around and hissed her frustration before letting loose an impressive torrent of curse words. She'd just come in from outside where she'd been trying to leave her estate for the past hour.

The property line had been charmed with extra stiff mojo, a bitch of an electric pulse that repelled her backward every time she tried to cross. There was no doubt as to who had put it there.

Declan.

To add insult to injury he was nowhere to be found and no

one was offering up any information. Something was going down, something big.

Ana shuddered as a wave of panic slid through her. The little bit of blood she'd drunk from Declan had already formed a tenuous link. He was in danger. She could *feel* it, and not knowing what was going on was killing her.

Quickly she crossed to the fridge and grabbed a bag of blood. She sliced it open with the sharp end of her fingernail and sucked it from the bag like an animal. No waiting. No manners.

Declan O'Hara had been pushing every single freakin' button she owned for so long that she should be able to handle it better.

Except she was ready to fall apart. Not good for a vamp to be off her game, not in this situation. She needed to focus. Try a different tactic.

Ana tossed the empty bag and wiped blood from the edges of her mouth.

"Where the fuck is he, Nico?"

The jaguar looked up from the table where he was fiddling with a cup of coffee. He rolled his shoulders and appeared relaxed, but she knew better. The cup was gripped too tightly and the smile upon his lips, too fake.

The warrior never smiled.

"It seems the game has changed." Nico's voice was low, his words controlled. "O'Hara is dealing with it."

Kaden made a weird sound but his eyes quickly fell from hers as she glared at them. "Has he sworn you all to secrecy? Are you really going to play that game with me?"

Silence greeted her words and it only fed her anger more. Her fangs slid out and her veins fattened to form spidery artwork along her face. Her strength lay just beneath the surface and for a second she envisioned her hands wrapped tightly around the jaguar's neck as she quickly snapped it.

It was insane, where her mind was going, but the loss of

control, the fear she felt for Declan was coloring everything in a dark, desperate palette.

Nico stared at her, his dark eyes hooded, lips open in challenge. "I don't play games."

"Then tell me where the hell O'Hara is. I don't need to remind you how delicate a situation we're in, and after last night I don't think Declan is in the right frame of mind to be running ops." She glared at the shifter. "Or to be keeping me in the dark. I'm not some sniveling, weak human."

"What happened last night?" Nico stood in one fluid movement, his six-foot-six frame dwarfing her petite form.

Ana's eyes widened and though she didn't answer, a knowing grimace flickered across the jaguar's face.

"Just fucking wonderful." The shifter eyed her, clearly pissed off. "I don't know the specifics, only that O'Hara is taking a trip below."

"Below?" The acrid taste of dread rose up from her gut, and Ana clenched her fists together tightly as she stared up at Nico.

The jaguar pointed toward the floor and nodded. "To Hell."

"Why would he . . ." Her voice trailed off as an image of his scarred, mutilated flesh flashed before her eyes.

"Apparently Lilith has the children."

The glass in Ana's hand shattered and she watched the small bits fly like diamonds across the floor. Droplets of blood marred their perfect jeweled form.

"He *can't* do this on his own. Is Cale helping him?" What if he was screwed up because she'd taken his blood? They'd had sex as well. Hell, they were halfway to bonding. What if he wasn't on his game?

Lilith was no run-of-the-mill demon. She was renowned for the darkness she wielded, a legendary princess of darkness who was as bloodthirsty as, if not more so than, her master, Lucifer.

I held up Lilith's whipping post for six months.

Nico shook his head. "Cale cannot enter the demon realm. His light would be like a beacon. He'd have no chance of survival."

The jaguar continued to speak but Ana didn't hear any of it. Her fear for Declan was fierce and her hands shook from the strength of it. She closed her eyes and concentrated, seeking him out, looking for the tenuous thread that joined them. The barest whisper of emotion was there and she grabbed it greedily.

Her sorcerer was resigned. Filled with hatred and fear. Could he sense her anguish as well?

A thousand thoughts slid through her mind but one stood out in stark relief. The need to get to Declan, kick his ass for pulling such a dumb-fuck move and then . . . then what? Kiss him silly with relief? Claim him as hers? Push him away again?

She groaned at the complexity of her situation and ran a tired hand across her brow. "Is it done already?" she asked, and the room fell to silence once more. Kaden's gaze slid away but Nico's hard stare held firm. The jaguar nodded and glanced toward the darkened windows.

"He met with Cale over an hour ago," Nico said.

"What of Samael?" she asked. "What is his part in all of this?"

"That I can't speak to," Nico admitted, "but all is not what it seems."

Ana's mind continued to work through a hundred scenarios. "And you're cool with him out there, alone?"

"No, I'm not cool with it." Nico's eyes narrowed and he ran his hands through the thick blue Mohawk that sat atop his head. "It was the only option."

Ana stepped around the mess on the floor and spat, "Yeah, well, that option stinks."

She stared out the window and watched the splatter of

rain against the glass. Her eyes slid shut and she smiled as the scent of earth, rain, and Declan assaulted her. She felt that, if she tried hard enough, she could feel his warmth against her skin.

She would do whatever it took to have that feeling again.

Long moments passed and eventually Nico left.

"Will he be all right?" Kaden asked. The teen had grabbed a broom from the pantry and was cleaning up her mess.

Ana grabbed a bag and together they had the floor clear of glass in no time. "I don't think so," she answered simply.

How the hell did Declan think he was going to sneak into the Hell realm and rescue two teenagers from the clutches of the underworld on his own? Was he insane? Did he care so little for his own life?

Guilt nibbled at her. Ana found herself staring into the dark once more. She'd hurt him the night before. She'd rejected him and knew it had cut deep.

How could it not? She felt the scars as if they'd been slashed into her own flesh. She'd sent him below as surely as if she'd stood behind and pushed him.

"I wish there was something we could do." Kaden threw the last remnants of debris into the bag and straightened.

Ana stared at the teen as a plan began to form. She needed to make things right. Needed for Declan to know how much he meant to her even if she could never have him.

Most of all she needed to know he would survive, and as far as she could tell, his chances of that were less than slim, unless he had help.

There was no way she'd let him do this on his own. It might not end well for either one of them, but at least they'd be together. For that chance she would risk her life. She glanced at Kaden. With Cale and Nico involved, she knew he'd be safe.

"Maybe we're not as helpless as we think," she murmured.

"What do you mean?"

Ana's brow furled and she bit her lip. "You need to get me out of here." Her words were low and they shook slightly as she stared at Kaden. She saw a flicker of fear in his eyes.

"Declan will freak, I . . ."

She pounced as his voice trailed into nothing. "*Can* you get me out of here? Are you strong enough to break through his charm?"

Kaden was silent and then nodded. "I think I can."

"Think?" she repeated. Ana glanced at the kitchen and then lowered her head until she was inches from the teenager. "I need more than *think*."

Kaden stared at her, his eyes intense. "Declan is strong but I've been practicing." He ran fingers through his hair. "Are you sure? If something happens to you . . ."

Ana put her hands on his shoulders. "If something happens to *him* I may as well run a stake through my heart. I hurt him last night." She shook her head. "I need to make him understand."

"I'll do my best."

"Thank you," she whispered.

"He'll be pissed."

"I know."

Kaden flashed a smile. "I'm cool with that."

"I need to find a way into the Hell realm," she murmured more to herself than to Kaden.

"What about the necromancer?" Kaden stood beside her now. "Wouldn't she have access or at least know how to get down there?" The teenager glanced up at her. "How *do* you get into the lower realm? Is there like a password or something?"

Ana shook her head. "No, a portal is needed and they're not easy to find." She stared at the boy thoughtfully. He was right. Francesca should have an inside line on the local portal.

"Wait here. I'll be back."

She ran through the hall and was up the stairs before Kaden had even digested her words.

Nico had shifted and run off the moment he'd left the kitchen. Seemed Declan's wards were meant only for her and the boy. Jaguar warriors didn't count.

Now would be her only chance.

Her feet glided across the floorboards in silence and quickly she opened the last door on her left and slipped inside. The room was in darkness save for the soft glow of a nightlight that had been left on. Ana felt the heavy vibration of magick that caressed every corner of the room. There was no way the necromancer would be able to call any of her ghoulie friends for help.

Francesca stood near the window, gazing out into the night. Ana cleared her throat. The young woman's arms were wrapped around her body as if seeking whatever form of comfort she could. Her head turned to the side and her profile was illuminated.

Ana's eyes strayed to the intricate tattoo that graced the delicate lines of her neck. The colors were vibrant.

Francesca didn't say a word, not even when Ana took the last few steps until she was beside the woman. Fear, pain, and anger radiated from within her frail body. Ana could taste it. She would use it.

"Your sister is being held in the lower realm." The necromancer flinched as her words sliced through the silence, but remained tight-lipped.

Ana was fine with that. She had no problem doing the talking.

"Here's what's going to happen. I'm going to get the two of us out of here and you're going to get me to a portal that leads to the underworld."

Francesca turned and their eyes locked. Ana saw distrust, but it was overshadowed by something else . . . interest? Good. She was halfway there.

"I'm assuming you have the scoop on the location of the nearest elevator to Hell?" She watched, eyes narrowed, as the necromancer turned and stared out the window once more.

Ana let her fangs slide out and hissed.

"There's no need for intimidation," the girl said. "I'll do it but I want something in return."

"Yes?" Ana prompted, trying not to sound too impatient, but the urge to act was making her antsy.

The redhead whirled around and squared her shoulders. The jingling of a chain echoed between them and Ana glanced at the heavy rope that had been shackled to her left leg. It was made of iron and was more than adequate as an aid in keeping the necromancer confined.

Francesca pointed to the tattooed collar on her neck. "My life is bound to Samael. I'll have to deal with the consequence for the rest of my days, but Alex is innocent. The taint of otherworld hasn't touched her, not really. The only reason Samael was able to get his hands on my sister was because I was fooling with dark arts, trying to impress a stupid date if you can believe it."

Francesca exhaled slowly and her lower lip trembled. "Promise me you'll get her out, *alive*."

Ana nodded. "I'll do my best but there are no guarantees." Her gaze drifted over the young woman. "What will he do when he finds you?"

Francesca's hand drifted to the tattooed collar against her neck. She started to walk toward the door. "I suppose he'll fry my ass, and I'm fine with that as long as Alex is safe." She reached the end of the chain and glanced down. "You able to get me out of here?"

Ana easily snapped the iron rope into two pieces and then pried the anklet loose.

The vampire led the way toward the kitchen and felt a moment of unease when she was greeted by an empty room.

But the door was ajar and she slipped out into the dark, Francesca close on her heels.

An owl hooted in the distance and the feel of rain against her skin was welcome. Funny. She hated the rain. "Over there." She pointed toward the far corner of her property. Ana saw a slash of white through the gloom—his white cotton T-shirt. Kaden was there.

The two women jogged through the overgrown grass and around the large trees that littered her yard. They stopped a few feet from the teenager and Ana touched a finger to her lips, indicating silence as they watched the boy.

Kaden drew intricate charms into the air. They fell from his fingers, thin webs of silken magick that shimmered for a few seconds before disappearing. Soft words fell from his lips and Ana frowned as she listened. They were strange, melodic words she'd never heard before.

His arms were spread and she took another step closer. The weight of his power filled the air and she shook her head in amazement as the wards Declan had placed around her home began to glow.

Holy shit, the kid was going to get it done.

A soft grunt fell from Kaden and he stumbled to the right. Ana would have grabbed him, but he quickly righted himself and whispered, "No."

She stood back and let him continue.

A low-grade hissing stirred in the wind and small spidery cracks formed in the air, glowing red hot before vanishing once more. Kaden was breathing heavily but walked toward the edge of the property, hands outstretched, strange words still falling from his lips.

The invisible prison walls sparked in several successive showers of energy and a breeze swept along the ground. Rain pressed against her skin from the force of it, little bullets of wetness that stung.

Kaden held his hands high; macabre shadows danced between the sheets of rain as his fingers illuminated in short, bright bursts. Ana glanced back at the house, but it lay in darkness. Francesca stared past her at the teenager, and Ana watched her eyes widen.

A slight pop fizzled into the night. Ana turned just as the entire length of her property shimmered like glass. Luminescent cracks formed and then darkness claimed all of it.

She took a hesitant step, and then another until she was inches from Kaden. His tall, lean, frame trembled but he looked at her, a grin wiping the strain from his face.

"I did it." He pointed and cocked his head. "You feel like taking a walk in the rain?"

Ana bit her lip and winced as she approached the property line and carefully pushed her hand forward. Her fingertips slid through a layer of energy but there was nothing left to repel her.

Kaden had defeated Declan's powerful mojo. Damn.

She touched his cheek. "You need to shore these up again and stay in the house. Can you do that?"

Kaden shook his head. "I'm coming with you."

"No!" Ana shook her head. "Definitely not. You're going to stay behind and not breathe a word to anybody. When they realize Francesca and I are missing, shit is going to fly. I need you to keep a cool head, understand?"

He opened his mouth but Ana interrupted, her voice softer. "Kaden, I can't do this if I'm worrying about you. I need to know you're safe. If you're here with Nico and Ransome's boys I won't worry, but you have to promise me you'll stay, or I can't help Declan. I won't leave you unprotected."

Kaden was silent, his face dark.

"I mean it," she reiterated. "This isn't a game. It's life and death, and your butt is on the chopping block, are we clear?"

"Yeah, I get it." His tone was belligerent, but she knew he'd listen. "Just . . ."

Ana pulled him close into a quick tight hug. "What?"

Kaden moved away, hunched his shoulders forward. "Come back."

She kissed him on the forehead, smiled at his blush. "Stay safe and I'll be back. Do not leave Nico's side, understand?"

A whisper of energy sizzled along the air. They were no longer alone. "Ransome's wolves are making their rounds." She looked toward Francesca. "We need to hightail it. Where are we going?"

The necromancer's face tightened. "The Grease Pit."

Ana raised an eyebrow. "What's that exactly?"

Francesca moved past her. "A diner near the Quarter."

"A diner?" she repeated in disbelief.

"The dude I was trying to impress last week? He owns it." Francesca scowled.

"I find it hard to believe a portal to the underworld exists in a diner."

Francesca shrugged. "Believe what you will, but the demon lord comes back week after week."

"Any particular reason?" Ana shook her head as the two women slid into the night.

"Samael likes the poutine."

CHAPTER 18

The Grease Pit lived up to its name. It was a hole in the wall and if you weren't looking for it specifically, you'd never find it. Yet early evening found the place full. There were several booths to their right, a smattering of tables in the middle of the space, and a long counter running the length of the room.

Ana's first impression was dull. Gray. There was no color to dress the dingy walls.

She spied an overly large man stuffing a shitload of syrup-soaked pancakes into his mouth. She grimaced. Ambience was at the low end of the priority list in this place. What kind of establishment served breakfast crap at dinnertime?

Ana followed Francesca inside. She wasn't sure what she abhorred more, the sickly sweet smell of sugar from the pastry rack to her left or the heavy scent of greasy bacon.

She took a second, her gaze sweeping the entire area, but there were no otherworld creatures present. In fact, there was nothing whatsoever that indicated the place was anything more than a greasy spoon.

All the stools at the counter were occupied save for the last one on the left. Francesca leaned against it and Ana slid in beside her.

The necromancer was shivering. Light rain had soaked

them both, though Ana welcomed the coolness of it against her skin. One of the perks of being vampire. The ability to regulate your body temp to whatever the hell was in play.

A young teenaged couple caught Ana's eye and she watched them kiss and play footsies underneath the table as they waited for their food. She thought of Kaden. What did his future hold? A girlfriend? Date nights? A lover?

Heartache and pain?

"So why are you risking your life for these kids?"

Ana turned at Francesca's soft question. "It's what I do. What I was brought back for . . . the saving of children or whoever else is in trouble."

"Brought back?" Francesca's brows furled.

"It's a long story," Ana murmured.

"Kaden means a lot to you." An astute observation.

Ana bit her lip. "He does." She nodded. "At first he was just a boy I was asked to protect but . . ."

"But?" Francesca prodded.

She shrugged. "He's special and he's alone and he's had a shitty go of it. If I ever had a son, I'd want him to be like Kaden."

Like Declan. Ana's heart constricted at the thought. Kaden reminded her of the man she loved . . . and of a child that would never be.

Declan owned her heart and since he was not vampire she would never know the joy of holding her own child. Vampires could not reproduce with anyone other than their own kind.

"What's the deal with you and the sorcerer?"

Ana was getting annoyed. She hated questions. "I'm not looking for a heart-to-heart girlie talk. There is no deal. Declan is nothing more than a complication and I—"

"Holy crap. What the hell is that on your neck?"

Ana was thankful for the interruption and turned to the waitress behind the counter. She was young, most likely close to Francesca's age. Bright pink lipstick was slapped onto overly ripe lips, and her breasts nearly fell from the too-small tank top she wore.

Francesca's hand fell to Samael's slave collar, her fingers running along the skin nervously. "It's a tattoo."

"I can see that," the girl replied. "You look like shit."

"Thanks for pointing that out," the necromancer murmured. "Jake around?"

The waitress's eyes narrowed and she nodded toward the kitchen. "He's in the back, why?"

"No reason, I just . . ."

Ana surmised by the stain of red that flushed Francesca's cheeks this Jake was the man she'd been trying to impress when she'd inadvertently summoned Samael.

"I just," the necromancer continued, "forgot my bag in his office the last time I was here."

"Ah huh." The waitress frowned.

"Um, there's no need to bother Jake. I could just grab it and go." Francesca's voice held a hint of nervousness as she fingered a napkin.

"We're not supposed to let anyone back there."

"I promise I'll be quick," Francesca said. "I don't think I can see him right now. Things didn't . . . the last time I saw him . . ."

"I warned you he was a douche bag." The waitress's voice softened. "It's probably locked though, but you can try."

Ana followed Francesca to the back of the diner, past the booths and into a darkened hall that led to the restrooms. They walked to the end and turned left, quickly sliding past the kitchen area. A set of doors led them into a stockroom.

"Through here." Francesca pointed toward the far corner. The door was locked but Ana had no problem crushing the handle and within seconds they were safely ensconced within Jake's office.

The walls were filled with photos of women in various

stages of dress and an impressive array of Harleys. Great. The man liked tits and bikes. A real winner. Ana made a face and turned to Francesca.

"Don't even go there," the necromancer mumbled.

A desk stood in the corner, overflowing with papers; a dingy window graced the opposite wall. It was the sorriest-looking space she'd seen in a long while and Ana frowned as she glanced at Francesca.

"A portal to the underworld exists here?"

"Open up your mind, Ana. Feel the subtle vibrations that color the air."

Ana shrugged. "I'm a vampire, not psychic. Sensitivity isn't one of my strong suits."

"You don't say," Francesca shot back. "Give me a few minutes. The stupid thing moves around and I need to concentrate in order to find it."

"What do you mean it moves around?"

Francesca remained silent, closed her eyes, and held her hands out, palms up. Her long fingers moved slowly as she turned in a circle. Ana watched her closely. The whole thing stank of weird mojo but she couldn't deny the tremulous waves of energy that lapped at her body.

The necromancer continued to mumble a bunch of words Ana didn't understand and she stood back as a low-grade humming started.

Francesca crossed to the desk and ran her hands along the surface, inches above the mess of papers. Her fingers slid over a laptop, a couple of picture frames before she grabbed hold of a paperweight, which incidentally wasn't being used to its full advantage.

Several mountains of bills fluttered to the floor as Ana continued to watch. That couldn't be the portal, could it? Francesca swore and tossed the paperweight back onto the desk.

Guess not.

The humming continued to build in strength as the red-head chanted loudly. The sensation was uncomfortable and Ana shook her head, trying to relieve the pressure in her ears.

Pain hit her in the chest suddenly, and she nearly fell to her knees. The air was sucked from her lungs and she clutched at her chest. She felt empty, bereft. *He was gone.*

Ana's eyes flew open. "You have to hurry. He's there . . . in Hell."

The necromancer stopped suddenly. Ana held her breath as the woman crossed to the far wall, her hands still outstretched. She stopped in front of an elaborate portrait of a classic Harley. It dominated the wall, was heavily framed in gilt. Francesca's hands ran along the seams of the picture.

"This is it," she whispered.

"You've got to be joking," Ana replied as she stepped beside her.

Francesca grabbed her hand and Ana hissed as a shot of energy slid through her body. "Feel this," the woman whispered.

Heat ran up her arm. It was painful and Ana yanked her hand from Francesca's. Nervous energy barreled through her gut and her breaths fell in short, quick bursts.

"How do we do this?" she asked softly as she eyed the Harley. The painting had taken on a tinge of green as if backlit with a wash of light.

"Once I open it, you won't have a lot of time. You get close enough and it'll suck you in."

"Just like that?"

Francesca nodded. "Just like that."

Ana glanced at the large frame and loosened her stance. "Okay then."

"Have you ever been below?" Francesca asked carefully. Sweat beaded along her forehead and her skin looked sickly.

Her hands were still palm out. The thread of energy that ran from the tips of her fingers was now visible to Ana.

The vampire shook her head. "No."

"I've seen glimpses." She looked away quickly. "Since I've been linked to Samael, that is. He's shown me things I don't understand." Francesca shook her head slowly. "It's not at all what I expected it to be."

The tension in Ana's belly was becoming more pronounced by the second. "Can we get on with it?"

The painting pulsated, widening and then thinning back and forth like a rubber band. Francesca looked scared. Ana gritted her teeth. That so didn't bode well for her.

"When you get down there you need to find a place called Club Doom. That's where I saw Samael."

Ana looked at the necromancer in surprise. A club?

The humming vibrated into a loud shriek that swept through the room as the picture elongated. The glow was now a fiery red, the heat of it slammed against her skin. She wondered briefly if it would burn—if her vampire body could even withstand the heat.

No matter. There was no choice. She took a step forward and then another until she was inches from the portal.

Ana glanced at Francesca and the two women stared at each other for several seconds. "Be safe and bring my sister back," the necromancer whispered.

The vampire nodded. Francesca widened her stance and closed her eyes. Ana watched as a dark hole appeared in the middle of the glowing portrait. It shimmered and within seconds enveloped the entire frame.

"Now." Francesca's voice was hoarse, urgent.

Ana did not hesitate. She clenched her hands together and stepped forward. Searing heat flickered along her flesh and for one brief moment such terror and fear clogged her mind that she was sure she screamed.

Then she was falling and there was nothing but darkness.

The smell of sulfur was Ana's first impression of Hell. It was subtle, not nearly as overpowering as she'd expected, but it was there, tingling along her nasal passages.

She was on her stomach, facedown, cheek resting against a hard, flat surface. It was damp, cold. Sounds echoed in her ear—voices, conversations, and the loud thrum of music.

Her body ached and she rolled over. Slowly her eyes opened, and it took a few seconds for them to focus. She was in an alley, a narrow chasm between two large buildings.

Ana sat up and groaned. Her head was thick, her mouth fuzzy. Fog rolled in from the opening of the alley, slithering along the ground like long, clawlike fingers. Edges of gray mist sparkled, shot through with a weird green color. She pushed herself to her knees and rose.

A small squeak made her jump and nearly fall back again as she looked to the side. Two beady eyes glowed bright in the dark as a small animal sniffed at her toes and then scrambled off.

She relaxed a bit. Who knew rats existed in Hell?

Her body felt weird, off center, like her equilibrium was all screwed up. Ana inhaled a huge gulp of air and took a few cautious steps forward. The walls on either side of her were brick, and in fact the alley looked no different from any you'd find in the human realm.

Where the hell was the fire? The brimstone? The bloody pits of Hell?

She crept forward, not liking the way the fog caressed her booted legs as she did so. It felt alive somehow, as if there was a presence within the mist.

Ana reached the edge of the alley and froze as a shadow passed in front of her. It stopped, solidified into a shape that while not humanlike, was close enough. It was an ethereal being, spectral in nature, and drifted a few inches above the ground, its feet hidden within the fog. She couldn't tell if it was male or female. The damn thing reminded her of the shades she'd encountered in Vegas.

Its eyes were hollowed out, dark holes that stared at her in silence. Ana wasn't sure how long they were frozen, staring at each other, not saying a word, but suddenly the specter moved, glancing behind it before disappearing from view.

Something echoed just beyond the range of her vision. It bounced along the brick walls and faded quickly. And then sounded again.

She realized it was the steady, even gait of a footfall.

Someone was out there—someone who didn't float upon the air, but had legs. Which meant there was substance to it.

Ana loosened her hands, rolled her shoulders, and let her fangs slide out. She melted into the shadows, lifted her arms, and rose into the air. Her fingers dug into the brick and her boots gripped the wall tightly as she clung to the side like a spider.

She was nearly twenty feet from the ground and watched the opening carefully as the footsteps got closer. She held her breath and waited.

Something stopped just outside the alley. It was tall, with massive shoulders that were covered with long, sharp spikes. Because it was dark, Ana couldn't tell if the spikes protruded from flesh or were part of his clothing.

It took another step, its large frame moving into a beam of light, and her eyes widened at the sight. He was a demon; the fiery eyes pretty much sealed that deal. His nostrils flared and his massive head rotated slowly as he perused the darkened alley.

Ana was so engrossed in watching the demon that when a tickle crept up her arm she nearly fell. The freaking neighborhood rat crawled beside her, its beastly eyes glowing with feral delight as it eyed her up.

Its nose twitched, its teeth chomped madly, their razorlike ends glistening in what little light there was.

Ana gripped the brick tightly with her right hand as her left shot out, her fingers closing around the little bastard's neck with lethal precision. In one quick move she snapped its neck, taking care not to do too much damage. She didn't want the scent of blood in the air.

She froze as a splash of water signaled the demon had taken at least one step farther into the alley. Ana turned her head slowly, carefully remaining as still as possible as the demon stared up into the darkness, his eyes trained on the exact spot where she was.

Jesus fuck, if he spied her, her sojourn into the underworld might be brief. And painful.

The demon took another step until the dark shadows from below hid most of his face. Ana gritted her teeth as she stared down at him, a lifeless rat held tight in her left hand.

She heard him grunt. Her muscles bunched in anticipation as adrenaline flooded her small frame. She gripped the rat tightly. It was the only weapon available to her and if needed, she'd use it, hope for the element of surprise. Pretty pathetic but there was nothing else.

A voice drew the demon's attention and she held her breath as he turned. The words spoken were guttural, too low for Ana to hear properly, however she thought she heard *doom*. Her ears perked in interest.

Ana couldn't see who or rather *what* spoke and remained still as the two conversed. The conversation lasted for all of ten seconds and then the demon glanced her way once more. Its chest rattled loudly with each breath it took and then he turned abruptly. He followed the voice out of the alley and left her alone with the dead rat.

She tossed the carcass behind her and dropped to the floor before creeping forward once more. Slowly she turned the corner and couldn't believe what she saw. In her wildest imaginings she'd never envisioned Hell like this.

It looked like a typical city street. One from the shit-ass

part of town to be sure, but a street nonetheless. Refuse blew down the sidewalk, dancing in the warm air that ruffled her hair. Shops lined the street; however, none appeared to be open, and most looked abandoned, with broken windows or boarded-up facades.

The strange mist that clung to her boots and slithered along her jean-clad legs was everywhere. Above her, darkness ruled a sky that ripped open with slashes of red. They slid across the vast space, disappearing and then reappearing like ribbons of scarlet. There were no stars, no moon.

Ana shivered and took a step. She glanced to her left, kept to the shadows, and darted along, her small frame nothing more than a blur as she sped forward, following the scent of the demon.

Less than a minute later she stared up at another large brick building. It was nondescript, save for the garish neon sign above it.

Club Doom.

Ana hesitated. She knew in any other circumstance, she'd wait for backup. That running headlong into a situation without knowing the details was stupid.

Yet what other choice did she have? There was no backup plan, no fucking unit at her command. She was it.

A tall woman strolled along the opposite sidewalk, bopping her head in time to the beat that fell from the windows above. She was dressed in vintage clothing, Victorian from the looks of it. Her small waist was cinched tightly with a corset, though the boots that peeked from under her long skirt didn't exactly complement the dress; they looked military and were covered in mud.

The woman paused and her head swiveled around slowly. Ana's face widened in horror. The eye sockets were empty, the lips blackened and thin. She thought she saw maggots twisting in the corners. The woman turned, opened the door, and passed through.

Ana didn't hesitate and was there in a second, her fingers clutching the edge of the door, preventing it from shutting. The music was loud, aggressive, and the swell of voices rose sharply.

Ana yanked on the door and entered Club Doom.

CHAPTER 19

Declan downed a shot of Brimstone Fire and slammed the glass onto the bar. He'd been sitting in the shadows for hours but the frenetic energy that sizzled in the air had finally lured him out.

The music was loud, heavy. He glanced at the stage in wonder. Derrak Dragon had OD'd nearly a decade ago, heroin being the culprit. He'd fronted one of the most memorable punk rock acts in the world.

Now he performed six nights a week in Hell. Un-fucking-believable.

The bartender grunted and Declan indicated another shot was in order. He turned, leaned against the bar, and perused the chaotic scene before him. The place was packed, full of the souls of the damned, demons of all ranks, and a smattering of otherworld beings that for whatever reason had ended up in District One, top surface, Hell.

Hundreds of bodies writhed and moved to the aggressive beat, feeding off the darkness that permeated the air. Several couples were having sex, their bodies rocking together, uncaring of where they were—only interested in the pleasure of the moment.

He downed his second shot and hissed as the fire wove into his gut. A tall, leggy blonde broke from the crowd and

walked toward him. She was demon; her eyes burned a vibrant orange as she smiled at him. Her voluptuous body was
draped head-to-toe in black leather, though the corset she
wore left her breasts bare.

She was hot. In a deranged sort of way.

She sidled up alongside him and ordered a drink from
the bartender.

"You're new." Her voice was husky, held a slight accent.

Declan nodded. The potion Samael had offered him
masked his true signature, and to anyone here he appeared
to be just another demon.

"Where you from?" she asked casually.

"District Three." His answer was abrupt.

She snorted, tossed her drink back, and carefully wiped
the excess from around her mouth. "Well, you're on holiday
then."

District Three was one level above the pit. It was without
a doubt the shithole of Hell and had been his home for the
six months he'd been held by Lilith.

"I've never been," she said, her thigh touching his as she
leaned against the bar. "I've heard it's . . ."

"Hot?"

She laughed and cocked her head. "Among other things."

Declan smiled. He figured she was from the upper ech-
elon of the demon world, the ruling class. They never ventured below.

It was always Friday night in Hell and she was looking
for some fun. Her hand was now on his thigh. Apparently he
was on the menu.

Declan shifted slightly, turned to order another drink, and
her hand fell away. He was looking for a way into District
Three and didn't want to offend anyone. For all he knew, she
could be his ticket back to Lilith.

She leaned over the bar, her breasts inches from him, and

licked her lips. "Have your drink and let's dance." Her hips moved in a sensuous motion, slowly gyrating as she smiled at him.

The bartender shoved a glass his way and Declan grabbed it, welcoming the coldness of the brew it held. He took a sip and stilled as a familiar scent wafted in the air, teasing his nostrils.

There was no way . . .

Slowly he turned, ignoring the blonde beside him. The band was cresting a wave of hard-ass melody and the crowd was jumping, writhing to the madness. His gaze swept the entire room and didn't stop until he spied her.

Son of a fucking bitch.

Ana.

What the hell was she doing here?

Anger crashed through him and he slammed his glass down. Already he saw several demons and otherworld creatures sniffing madly, wanting to find the source of this new odor.

She was in Hell for fuck sakes. Did she think her unique vampire signature would go unnoticed?

She looked up then and their eyes met. It was like a physical hit to his gut and he clenched his hands together tightly. She was frozen, a graceful gazelle about to be slaughtered.

He needed to act fast.

Declan pushed away from the bar, his long legs eating up the distance to her as he dove through the crowd, ignoring the noise, the insanity that surrounded him.

He didn't take his eyes from hers. She moved into the shadows along the wall and when he stood in front of her, he had to take a moment, afraid to speak.

"Are you fucking nuts?" he whispered harshly, moving forward once more, crowding her small frame against the wall.

"Apparently not as crazy as you," she hissed. "What the hell are you thinking? Going after the kids by yourself—"

His hand shot out and he gripped her chin between his fingers, effectively silencing her. She struggled, but something in his eyes held her still and she relaxed.

Declan couldn't articulate the absolute rage he felt. She was as good as dead if he didn't do something quickly. He leaned down, his dark eyes intense, and when he spoke there was no doubt as to the severity of the situation.

"This place is full of demons and every kind of otherworld creature you can imagine. Right now your sweet-ass scent is circulating and it will be both of our butts served up and thrown into the pit unless we mask it."

Her nostrils flared. Her eyes widened.

"You will feed from me, *now*."

"I won't," she whispered hoarsely, "I can't."

His lips were inches from hers. He saw the fear in her eyes and how she quickly covered it.

"You will. It's the only way. My blood is filled with a serum Samael supplied. It masks my true signature. If we get enough of it into you, I might have a chance at getting you out of here alive."

She opened her mouth but he gripped her harder, until a whimper of pain fell between them.

"There is no other choice, Ana. If you want those children safe you need to listen to me. This is my turf, you understand?" he snarled.

"There has to be another way."

"I know my blood repels you but you should have thought of that before you came here." He was livid. "There is no alternative."

Ana's eyes were shadowed, her voice subdued. "Your blood doesn't repel me. It sings to me in a way that's wrong." She shuddered. "And I'm afraid . . ."

"What are you afraid of?"

She looked up at him and he was stunned at the emotion in her eyes. His vampire's facade was slowly cracking.

"I'm afraid I won't be able to stop."

He pulled her in, held her head against his neck, and whispered urgently. "I trust you."

Her breath slid across his skin and he braced his body against the wall with his left hand. They were shielded from the crowd behind him, his frame covering hers effectively. His fear for her was making him crazy.

"Now," he hissed.

Her mouth was against his throat, her body crushed to his, and when he felt the scrape of her teeth just over his jugular, his body hardened, more than ready.

She broke skin and sank her fangs deep into his flesh.

Instantly the connection was made and he leaned against her, eyes closed as she began to suckle. He heard her groan and then felt the pull as she started to take long draws.

It was the most exquisite sensation he'd ever experienced, an erotic high that was instant.

His cock hardened, his body was on fire with need, and his mind was filled with images of the two of them together. Her small, naked form above him, riding him, letting him fill her in a way he'd never thought possible.

Declan ground his hardness against hers and felt like he was spinning out of control. He wanted to crawl inside her, to hold her and make love to her. He heard the beating of his heart, loud inside his head, and then it was joined with another.

Ana's.

She broke away with a cry, but he held on savagely. "It's not enough," he managed to spit out.

"I can't . . ."

Brutally he forced her head against his flesh and again she fed, this time with an aggressive abandon that made his head swim. His legs sagged and if not for the wall, surely he would have fallen. It seemed to go on forever, but in fact must have been only a few minutes. His body was cold, yet inside he was on fire.

She wrenched away and he stared down at her. Ana's eyes were huge pools of licorice, her fangs were distended, and his blood lay upon her mouth.

He stared at the crimson stain for several seconds. He found the sight fascinating and bent down to gently sweep his lips across hers. He was breathing heavily and rested his forehead against her cheek.

Christ but his head was spinning. His senses were on overload, and the joy, the sheer fucking thrill he felt at finally connecting with the vampire, was overwhelming.

"Oh my God, are you all right?" she asked quickly, her fingers flying over his face. "If I hurt you . . ."

"I'm good. Just need a second."

He was, in fact, weak as hell.

He took a few more moments and then slowly turned. They were still deep in the shadows that clung to the corners, and he saw the blonde he'd left at the bar looking his way. His gaze swept the room; no one else paid them any mind.

He inhaled Ana's scent and felt relief. Her sweetness was no longer. She smelled like any other demon in the place.

"We need to go." His voice was hoarse. The room was now spinning. If shit was gonna start flying there was no way he'd be able to defend her.

He tensed, expecting her to challenge him, and was surprised when she acquiesced. "Where?"

His arms went around her shoulder and they started toward the door. "Anywhere but here," he said roughly.

They were nearly to the exit when the blond demon appeared, her eyes curious and maybe a little suspicious.

"Who's your friend?" she asked. "She on vacation from District Three as well?"

Declan nodded, his voice curt as he dismissed her. "She's mine." He turned toward the door.

"Sure you don't wanna share?" The blonde stared at Ana, her serrated teeth glinting through the dark.

Ana hissed, "I don't share what belongs to me."

The demon smiled. "Honey, if you leave premium candy like that lying around"—she nodded toward Declan—"someone will come along and lick it."

"I need to go," he whispered. Darkness skirted the edges of his vision and Declan feared he'd pass out. He pulled on the vampire, a wave of relief washing through him as she hurried along to follow.

He reached for the door, afraid to look back, and when he yanked it open, felt the cool air caress his face, Declan groaned.

They slipped outside, his heavy weight leaning on Ana for support.

"Shit! Declan, I didn't want to do that!" She sounded frantic as she whirled around. Dizziness washed over him and he took a second to center himself.

"I need to get out of here," he said, grabbing her hand as he started up the street.

"You don't understand. What the hell have I done?"

He heard a dirge of loud music erupt from behind them and knew they were no longer alone. "Now." His tone was urgent and she was quiet as they made their way up the street.

Declan fought the urge to break out into a full-on run, but he knew that would be like painting a bull's-eye on his ass. Besides, the dizziness that had settled inside his head wasn't going anywhere. In fact it was making it extremely difficult to concentrate.

They crossed the street several blocks down. Declan gritted his teeth, his gaze carefully sweeping the perimeter around them. He glanced to the right, felt relief when he spied the large clock tower. They were close.

"This way," he murmured, tugging Ana along. He was now stumbling like a drunkard.

Ana gripped his hand, her nails digging into his skin. Her anxiety pressed on him and he shakily swept his hand along her cheek.

"We'll be fine." He winced as another wave of dizziness washed over him. "It's not much further."

"Declan, if I've hurt you I'll never forgive myself."

He stilled, his breath hitching in his chest. Ana turned. She heard it, too. Footsteps echoing in the dark.

He started to jog and as they approached the clock tower, the strange gray mist swirled faster, thicker until they were able to disappear inside it.

"Where are we going?" she asked hurriedly.

"There's a place we can crash, next to the tower."

His head felt like it was going to explode, and the relief Declan felt when he spied the run-down hotel, Soul Sucker, nearly brought him down. The building rose thirteen stories into the air, though the last several weren't visible due to the thick mist.

"This way." He pulled Ana along with him and tried to keep it together as they slipped inside.

The lobby was large. An enormous chandelier hung from the ceiling, teetering dangerously as it swayed back and forth. There was no reason, no breeze to help it along, it just did.

A grand piano sat upon a pedestal to their right; sitting at it, a demon. A melody fell from his fingers—the tune was off, the notes harsh.

Good to see some things never changed.

Declan carefully paced himself and the two of them walked to the front desk. A tall, thin ghost of a man stared at them in silence.

"We need a room." Declan nodded curtly. Sweat beaded his forehead, his belly was shifting uncomfortably. He was going to pass out. He just needed to hold on.

He reached into his pockets and withdrew a thin, metallic card. A gift from Samael.

The clerk grabbed it, long, wraithlike fingers caressing it greedily. He passed it through a device to his right, grunted, and handed Declan a key card.

"Ten-twenty," the clerk announced. His voice was like gravel underfoot.

Declan heard the door open behind them. He pocketed both cards and turned toward the elevators. Ana was silent at his side, her arm wrapped around his waist, and he was grateful for the support.

They slipped inside the elevator, footsteps echoing behind them, and as the doors slid shut Declan sagged against the walls, listening to the echo of footsteps fade.

They rode the lift to the tenth floor in silence. He barely had enough energy to hold on. When the doors slid open, it was Ana who helped him out. She fished the card from the front pocket of his jeans and led him toward the end of the long hall.

She opened the door, and by this time his head was spinning so badly, the groan that escaped his mouth sounded like a pathetic wail.

"Here," she whispered, and helped him toward the bed.

"Don't leave." Damn, he sounded weak. Her eyes wavered above him. The mattress at his back afforded some relief.

"I'm not going anywhere." Her hand was on his cheek. "Oh, Declan, what have I done?"

He tried to smile, but grimaced instead as his gut rolled. He opened his mouth, but no words came. The haze that lingered along the edge of his vision swept across him like a curtain.

He closed his eyes and slipped away.

CHAPTER 20

Ana stared at Declan in disbelief.

She'd taken too much.

Her fingers were shaking, *badly*, as she traced them over the planes of his face. Declan's breaths were shallow and she bit her lip as she looked down at him.

She'd not been strong enough.

The taste of him was still fresh in her mouth. Never had she felt so exhilarated. So alive . . . and so scared.

Never.

A sob escaped her and she rose from the bed. She began to pace, her eyes never leaving Declan's ashen form. He looked like shit.

She flew to the bed, pressed her finger against the pulse at his neck, and swore savagely. It was weakening.

Hell yeah, she'd taken too much.

A ragged breath slipped from between her lips. If she didn't do something he'd die.

She glanced around the room. Dingy walls, threadbare carpet, rickety furniture, and a television that was missing its screen. By the time her gaze returned to the man beside her, a decision had been made.

Her blood was his only chance.

Ana didn't think about the consequence. What was the point?

If he didn't take her blood he'd die. *The man she loved would die.*

The word whispered through her mind like a secret—*love*—and brought with it a certain clarity she'd not had before. She had history with this man. Infuriating, exhilarating, and painful history.

She thought of the night before and what it had felt like to have him inside her. To hold him close and breathe in his spirit.

She loved Declan O'Hara. *Had* loved the man for years. She would do anything for him, even this. She had to believe he'd be strong enough to take the change. Other than her brother's lover, Cerise, she didn't know another who'd been turned.

Ana slipped her leather coat from her body, leaving her arms bare. She settled onto the bed beside Declan, leaned over him, and swept her mouth across his.

He moaned, his eyes fluttered, but they remained closed.

She didn't have much time.

She thought of Jean-Charles and his lover's tragic end, but then quickly pushed it aside. She had no choice, and now neither did Declan. She would turn him.

It was the only way. She'd deal with the consequence later. If he ended up a raving lunatic because of the change, that would be on her.

But she'd rather try than watch him die.

Her fangs broke skin once more and she sank them deep into her wrist. Almost immediately, bright red, life-giving blood formed along the puncture wounds. Ana gripped Declan's head. "You need to feed."

She held her wrist against his mouth, coaxing his lips open, forcing her blood onto his tongue. He moaned and turned from her. Nearly a minute went by and though her shoulders filled with tension, she pressed forward. He needed to drink.

"Take from me, now," she commanded.

Declan groaned against her skin. His beautiful dark eyes stared up at her. She saw confusion and lowered her mouth to his. She swept her lips across him, tasted her own blood, and whispered, "Please."

He murmured something that was unintelligible, his fingers tightened upon her wrist, and then he latched on.

In all of her three hundred years, Ana had never let anyone feed from her. Never. She was unprepared for the assault of emotion, of want and need that pounded through her.

She hissed loudly as he pulled from her; each suckle was exquisite, pain-filled ecstasy. She couldn't take her eyes from Declan as he continued to feed and forge a connection. Time stilled. She didn't want the sensations to end. The feeling. The need. The desire.

Her chest was heaving and she leaned closer. "Take more."

Their eyes held and as he continued to feed, her body became languid. Slowly she slid alongside him, her arm held tight to his mouth.

She felt his warmth, the steady beat of his heart as she laid her head against his chest. There was a rightness in what she'd done and how she felt. It filled her with a glow that was not sexual, but one of completion, or rather, near completion.

She closed her eyes and smiled at the ironic thought.

She was in Hell. In the space of less than an hour she'd fed from Declan and let him take her blood. He would live; however, his fate was cloudy. If he survived the change he would be vampire. He would live and yet . . .

Ana was royalty. A direct descendant of the queen. Would

Isobel accept what she'd done and forgive her? Would she let Declan live if Ana promised not to complete the bonding ritual?

She groaned, confused and fearful. Now that she'd tasted him, let him drink from her, she couldn't envision a future without Declan by her side. And yet how could she be with him unless they were bonded to each other?

Ana was not that strong. This she knew.

The queen might show leniency for his turning, if Ana begged forgiveness, but she'd never allow one of royalty to bond with someone not of their race. Declan could never belong to her in the way that was forbidden.

Ana had broken every single rule that her people held sacred. If the queen ordered his death, she'd never survive it.

Carefully she pulled her arm away and slid into Declan's embrace. She had no clue what the next few hours would bring. She only knew that at this moment, in this place, peace was the man beside her.

She rested her head into the crook of his neck and closed her eyes. Her mind slowed and eventually she drifted into sleep.

Fire ran through his veins, lapping at his insides and tingling along his nerves.

What the hell?

Declan's eyes flew open. He was immediately assaulted with a host of sensations, smells, and sound. The soft body pressed against his chest was a welcome weight, the feel of her so right. He shifted, held her like a breakable, and the glow left him as his thoughts darkened.

Ana. Here with him. In fucking Hell.

Was she crazy? His mind ran through images in quick succession. Club Doom. Ana. Blood. Pain.

He swallowed thickly, his tongue aflame with the taste of a metallic substance. It was blood—Ana's blood. His power coiled hard in his gut and he felt something new inside him. An added strength.

He hissed sharply. Ana's scent was all over him, her taste was *in* him. It was intoxicating, vibrant, alluring. He closed his eyes and fought the overwhelming emotion that pummeled him.

Was he vampire? Had they really done the deed? Shouldn't he be sick? Or deranged? He'd wanted her to take his blood, to have a connection to him that she'd never had with another.

But this was something else entirely. He'd never thought of taking from her. Of becoming *like* her . . . a vampire.

Declan shifted once more, his gaze wandering the room they'd escaped to. Outside, the wind continued to howl as a storm rolled across District One. Long tendrils of fog slithered across the window.

He couldn't see shit.

The children were out there. He groaned and relaxed into the mattress. He was having trouble focusing.

Christ, he thought he had it bad before, but now? Now that he'd tasted her, now that she'd taken from him, the feelings and emotions were much more intense.

Her long hair spilled across his chest and carefully he pushed the silken strands back. He wanted to see her. To touch her. To taste her.

Her pale skin shone smooth alabaster. It glistened in the dim glow. Carefully he traced the curve of her cheek, his fingers light. He didn't want to wake her. He wanted to savor the moment. He knew the fragile world that existed around him could shatter at any moment. In fact, it most likely would.

Silent treasures like this would be scarce. Lilith waited, with her doe-eyed smile, silken limbs, heart full of maggots, and touch of evil. His belly clenched at the thought and he angrily shoved it aside.

He wanted one more moment, one more chance at peace before plunging headlong into the fire that was District Three.

Ana moved. His body, already hard, thickened painfully with need. He held her close, his mouth nuzzling the small space between her ear and the crook of her neck.

She squirmed slightly and he smiled, his nostrils flaring as he breathed in her unique signature. Had it always been so sharp? Intoxicating?

His lips moved along her jaw and when her eyes fluttered open, he paused, a whisper away from her mouth.

"Declan," she said softly, hesitantly. "Are you all right? I'm so sorry, I thought . . . I couldn't let you . . ." She paused and exhaled. "I had to give you my blood or you would have died." He pressed a finger to her lips.

"I don't want to hear it."

Her eyes widened, the solid blue depths glistening. He slipped his finger inside her mouth; his breath hitched at the warm wetness he found. An overwhelming need rushed through him and for a second his vision blurred. When he spoke again his voice was rough and it took a hell of a lot of effort to maintain control.

"Thinking wastes time. Breeds regret."

His eyes dropped. He opened his mouth and took hers, plunging his tongue inside as his hand slid down her body to rest on her ass. She was perfect. Every line of her body was perfect and meant for him.

Declan groaned into her mouth, hissed with pleasure when he heard her answering moan. She was all kinds of wet warmth and his tongue tasted every inch of her mouth.

Wicked hot passion thrummed through him, lapping at his soul and setting his flesh on fire with an all-consuming need. A hunger that was relentless.

His world narrowed into the space of one small, hot lady. He was fine with that. An infinite universe was overrated.

Declan came up for air, his tongue tracing the soft curve of her jaw, but Ana began to struggle, to push at him. The hunger inside gnawed hard, the line of black that rode the edge of his sanity was growing in strength.

"Declan, stop." She wrenched her mouth from his and threw her head back. She pushed against his chest. "Now."

He was breathing hard, shook his head as a curtain of black threatened. His muscles were tight, his chest on fire, and his mind was going places they shouldn't. Blood, darkness, pain, and pleasure.

The palette had been set. He wanted more.

"You need to understand what happened."

Ana sat up, ran her hands through the disheveled waves that rested against her cheek. Her chest heaved, her pale cheeks now held a blush of rose.

"What I did to you." She bit her lip. "What it means . . ."

"Why are you fighting this?" Declan's words were like whiplash, slicing through the air as his anger rose. "You've been fighting me for years."

Why the hell did she have all the power? He hated that he wanted her so badly it physically hurt.

A guttural sound escaped her lips. "You don't understand."

"No, I don't. So why don't you fucking explain it to me?" He nodded toward the room. "You might want to hurry it up. I'm not sure how much time we have and there are things to be done."

"Things?"

Her mouth was open. He saw the tip of her tongue, the edge of her fangs. He knew she was as aroused as he. His gaze wandered over the tight tank top she wore. Her nipples were plainly visible, erect with need. He bent toward her, grabbed her to him, his thumb immediately teasing the hard nub mercilessly.

His dark eyes sought hers. "By the time I'm done with

you, every single bone in your body will belong to me." He slid her shirt up slowly and took her turgid nipple deep into his mouth. He smiled wickedly as she whimpered, the sound exciting him, and he sucked harder as she writhed against him.

"Oh God, Declan."

He released her nipple from his mouth, blew hot air onto the wet flesh, and grabbed her chin so that she could look nowhere but into his eyes. "You belong to me. You know this."

"Declan," she whispered. He saw pain in her eyes and it pissed him off. "We need to talk about what happened. You are vampire now. I'm sure that's not something you've aspired to."

"What's the issue?" His words were gentle, but the harsh need inside was rubbing him raw. He felt like he was going to break apart, like he was holding on with the thinnest of control.

"The issue?" She laughed, a hysterical bubble that echoed into the silence. "It's bad enough the only way I could save you was to give you my blood. You are vampire and I'm sorry for that but if we do this . . ." Her eyes locked onto his and he was startled at the change in them. No longer were they blue, but they'd morphed into solid black. "If we do this," she began again, "if we make love I won't be strong enough to stop the bonding process. If I bond with you your fate is sealed. We can't take it back."

"I'm fine with that. I'm not interested in anything before now."

"You know nothing of my world." The way she bit her lip was going to drive him fucking crazy. "It's forbidden to make a vampire. Our queen banished the practice over two hundred years ago."

Declan snorted. "That's bullshit. I know several vampires and at least three of them have humans they've turned."

Anger tingled along his flesh. It was true. He'd never

taken the time to learn of the intricacies of the vampire world. But then again, vampires pretty much kept to themselves. They didn't socialize a whole hell of a lot.

Her eyes flashed and she hissed, exposing her fangs. "They were probably turned before her edict. Vampires have several levels, a hierarchy of sorts. I am a direct descendant of the queen and per her edict, the line must remain pure. She might overlook the occasional incident with her subjects, but royalty is something different. It's always been forbidden. Our bloodlines must remain pure, untouched by outsiders." She shook her head. "I don't agree with it, but it is the way of our people. Plus I'm already betrothed."

His eyes narrowed. "Betrothed, as in fiancé?"

Ana nodded. "Aleksander . . . it was arranged a long time ago."

His anger tripled and he could barely speak. "Where is he?"

She shrugged. "I don't know. He's ancient, a Viking. He came to America, took one look at me, and left."

The fucker must be deranged. "So that's good."

"No, it's complicated. Unless my queen breaks the betrothal, neither one of us can move on. She'll never do that for someone who is forbidden."

"I don't care." He didn't. With everything going on in his world right now, he didn't give a flying fuck about some vampire queen he'd never met or a dumb-ass Viking with no last name.

His voice lowered, his eyes darkened. "I will have you, Ana. All of you." His fingers glowed with heat as he pulled on the magick inside. "What's done is done."

"There'll be no turning back. Right now there might be a chance for you. If I explain to council that I gave my blood to save you, that I turned you because there was no choice, they might let it go. There have been exceptions over the years, but if we bond . . ."

He ran his fingers along her bare shoulders, smiled as she shuddered against his touch. "If we have sex?" His whisper was barely audible.

"We've exchanged blood, Declan. If we have sex, if we *bond* while having sex, then we're forever linked. You will become my fledgling. I don't think you can appreciate what that means."

He arched a brow and carefully tugged at the edge of her shirt. "Take this off."

She was breathing heavily. The thin veins beneath her flesh were pronounced and he saw the tips of her fangs. His cock hardened, straining against his pants, and a wave of desire rolled over him.

"Now," he commanded harshly.

"Declan," she whispered, "council will hunt you down. They will end you."

His fingers arced forward and with one motion, her shirt was sliced evenly. He pushed her down into the mattress, his hands claiming the roundness that was now exposed.

She gasped but did not push him away.

"I spent six months in the bowels of District Three. Anything Lilith threw at me, I took. I did things that you can't imagine. Things that would disgust you." He felt like his throat was going to close. "A hundred vampires will not keep me from the one thing I desire above all else."

His free hand tugged on the waistband of her jeans, his fingers dug into the softness that was there. "I'm done playing games, Ana." He lowered himself until his mouth was inches from hers. "I will have you, *all of you.* Your body, your soul, and your mind." Declan pulled her jeans lower. "I'll love you now, here in this place, and there is no one who will stop me."

CHAPTER 21

Ana stared up at Declan. He'd rolled from the bed and now stood. The lines of his face were half hidden, shadows caressing the planes of his left cheek and mouth. Yet his eyes remained clear, intense, and in that moment, she felt an answering cry. An acknowledgment of need.

Everything drifted away—the doubt, the pain, the longing she'd been fighting for years.

She could have stopped him. Her power lay coiled, at the ready, and yet she remained still.

He pulled her jeans down her legs and she watched, her gaze hooded as he tossed her boots to the floor. He grabbed the remnants of her shirt and it, too, joined the pile. Within seconds she was naked, every inch of her flesh on display.

For a long moment Declan stared at her, his gaze roving her curves, his eyes tinged with crimson. Her mouth watered and the little voice that nagged from the corner of her mind, the one that shouted, *No*, was silenced. Maybe forever.

Carefully he reached for her, his hand caressing the heaviness of her breasts. They swelled beneath his touch and she couldn't help the groan that escaped when he bent forward and scraped his teeth along the edge of her nipple.

Tiny shards of pleasure radiated outward and when his mouth opened fully, and his warm, wet tongue closed over her nipple, she surrendered. Every tense, hard piece of reasoning inside her melted into nothing but raw need.

Her hands found their way into the thick hair atop his head, and her nails dug in as she thrust herself at him. The feel of his stubble on the sensitive peaks electrified and each time he tugged, sucked at her breast, an answering pull erupted, deep within her belly.

It grew, spread fire through her veins. She was hot, her insides burning, and with a growl she yanked his head up until she could finally claim his mouth with her own.

Their eyes caught and held. She opened for him, her eyes never leaving his as her mouth fed, tugged, and sucked from him. She watched his eyes widen, darken as her tongue tasted and stroked. She saw her passion, her *need* reflected in the depths of his eyes and when he groaned into her, when she ate his desire, she nearly came undone.

His hand slipped down her body, past the curve of her hip and lower belly until his fingers found the wetness between her legs. She groaned, spread her thighs wider, and hissed sharply when he skirted the edge of her swollen clitoris.

"Jesus, Declan," she moaned into his mouth.

He made another pass, this time his fingers lingering, caressing her slick folds, as his tongue stroked the inside of her mouth.

Pressure built inside and it was too fast. Her fangs ached. She broke from him, her chest heaving.

"It's my turn," she whispered, loving the way his eyes flattened to an opaque black as she ran her tongue along her swollen lips. He looked like a predator. Dangerous.

Ana pushed him back and he slipped off the bed. His long, lean form moved with the grace of an animal, and he turned to face her, his hands raking through his hair as his eyes rolled over her nakedness.

Carefully she pushed her hair out of the way as she rose to her knees and reached for him. "Take your shirt off."

Declan looked down at her, the corners of his mouth lifted into a smile as he shed his T-shirt. Ana gazed upon the taut, defined muscles of his chest. She ached at the sight of his scars and bent forward, ignoring the hiss that escaped from him as she kissed the marred flesh.

She would kill the animal that had marked her man.

His arms would have gathered her close, but she whispered, her voice barely audible, "Be still."

The command was firm and the hint of compulsion she added was enough. Declan's arms stayed at his side, though the fists were clenched, the veins along his forearms thick with tension.

She smiled and tugged on the snap of his jeans. He was hard and ready. Her mouth went dry at the sight of him as she freed him from his clothes. Slowly her fingers traced the defined muscle of his abs. She shivered beneath his flesh and bit her lips as he sucked in a harsh breath.

Her hands slipped lower and when she grasped his straining cock within her grip, the guttural sound that fell from his lips made her mouth go dry.

"Holy Christ, Ana." He was hoarse. She gazed up at him, a thrill rushing through her as they connected. There was a glitter to his eyes, a feverish tinge that she knew well.

Slowly she stroked him, her gaze not leaving his. She saw tiny lines begin to spread under his flesh and she felt his hunger. Her fangs ached. He groaned beneath her ministrations and she relished the velvety hardness that she held.

Her tongue darted out and she licked her lips as his hands crept into her hair. She arched a brow.

"I didn't give the command for you to move."

"No." His fingers clutched at her. "You didn't."

His voice was thick, odd-sounding. Ana knew they'd just leapt over the cliff. There was no going back. Declan was on the cusp. Blood and sex would seal the deal.

She opened her mouth and took him deep within.

A strangled sound erupted from him as her right hand gripped the hard roundness of his ass. She held him as tightly as he held her, her left hand gripped tight to the base of his cock. The moans that continued to fall from his lips as her tongue swirled and stroked his hardness excited her as nothing had ever done before.

She loved the taste of him, the feel of him straining inside her mouth. Ana whimpered, her hips slowly moving as the pressure between her legs pulsed, throbbed.

Her fingers massaged him, her mouth and tongue worked feverishly. Her only thought was to give him as much pleasure as she could. There was nothing else.

"You need to stop," he whispered hoarsely. He tugged on her scalp—none too gently— and she pulled one more time, long and hard. She smiled up at him when he swore loudly.

"Ana, you need to stop."

The long, hard, length of him sprang from her mouth, the wet sheen of his taut skin glistening.

His hands slid to her shoulders and he pulled her up toward him. Her body was now officially on fire, her nipples ached where they touched his flesh. He stared into her eyes, his soul bared to her, and Ana was humbled by the man before her.

"I want everything." His eyes were still flat, but they'd morphed into full-on black. "Every part of your body, your mind, your soul." His fingers gripped her shoulders hard. "Do you understand? If we have but one night together, I want it all."

"Are you sure?" Ana's eyes swept downward as a tingle of confusion rolled over her. What was she doing?

He grabbed her chin and claimed her lips in a kiss that made her head spin. It was both gentle and aggressive, and she stilled when her tongue scraped over the unmistakable feel of a fanged tooth.

She wrenched her head from him. "You've already been

turned. Your life is no longer what it was. There will be no sunlight, no warmth on your skin . . . only darkness, and for that I'm sorry," she managed to get out. Her chest was heaving so badly she could barely breathe. "But if you belong to me and I to you, all bets are off. You'll be hunted till the end of days."

Declan's finger traced the lines of her mouth. "Then we'll be running together."

Ana saw the tips of his newly formed fangs peek through his mouth and an answering hunger erupted inside her.

He lifted her from the bed, his mouth claiming hers once more. She tasted blood and realized he'd cut her. The scent rose in the air, mingled with the musky smell of her arousal.

Dark thoughts crowded her brain and the world tilted precariously, the canvas turning red as her bloodlust stirred.

His hands on her body stirred the passion inside. Liquid pooled, slid along her inner thighs, and knew that she was ready. That she ached for him to fill her completely.

"I can't take this, Declan." Her voice was low, aggressive, and she nipped at him, her fangs grazing along his collarbone. He turned her body and threw her onto the bed.

And then he was there, his long, torso covering hers. His hand slipped beneath her belly and he drew her hips into the air. She was on all fours, panting, and she growled when his mouth licked along the small of her back.

Ana spread her legs in anticipation, moaning when his hand found its way to her heated core. He plunged long fingers inside. She was swollen, wet with need, and when his mouth hovered above her other opening, she stilled.

He wouldn't . . .

He blew upon her, a warm breath that sent tingles racing across her flesh. She felt pressure there and stilled as he began to massage, to play and tease.

Erotic sensations attacked her from every angle. He nuzzled, nipped her flesh, while both of his hands worked her into a frenzied mess.

The fingers between her legs, inside her slickness, began to pulse. His energy sizzled, erupting along her channel and spreading fire in their wake. Her nerves were already raw and her muscles bunched as an orgasm ripped through her. The release was immediate and she cried out.

"Sweet Jesus, what the hell are you doing to me?"

Her knees nearly buckled and she heard him laugh softly. "Jesus has nothing to do with it." Several shots of energy fell from his fingers once more and she bit her tongue, eating the groan that sat at the back of her throat. Declan bent lower and his breath caressed the side of her neck. When he spoke, his voice blurred, as if amplified. He was so close to the edge and she was right there with him. "Once you've had a man of magick, there is nothing else."

His hardness rested against her and she knew he was near the edge.

Silence filled the room. The only sound she could hear was her ragged breaths. She throbbed, *everywhere*, and her fangs ached as she rolled her head. He kissed his way down her back once more, his hands gripping her hips tightly. The edge of his cock teased the slick center between her legs and she gritted her teeth in anticipation.

She stopped breathing, frozen with a need so raw, it was painful. "Now, Declan, don't make me beg."

The long, hard length of him slid inside her. Her walls stretched, gripping him tightly as he started to move slowly. It was torture, the way he held her and withdrew, taking his time before plunging inside once more.

"Ah, Ana, you wreck me like nothing before." She felt his heated skin, heard the slap of flesh against flesh, and reveled in the hardness that scraped every nerve inside her, leaving exquisite shots of pleasure in its wake.

Her hips answered in kind and they rocked together, two bodies melting into one. As Declan increased the rhythm, his strokes bolder, harder, the pressure built down below and small guttural sounds fell from her lips as another crest threatened to spill.

Ana arched her back and pushed upward, loving his touch as Declan's hands fled her hips, and gripped her breasts to hold her in place.

"I've never felt this before." His voice was rough, soaked in passion.

Declan's words trailed into silence but Ana paid no heed. Her eyes were now bloodred and she hissed as the burning desire inside of her thrummed against her soul, tore at her heart.

She heard him swear, cried out as he pounded into her flesh, and when he leaned into her, when their bodies reached that perfect plateau, his teeth scraped along her shoulder, grazing the curve of her neck.

There was no coherent thought. Only the need to connect, *to bond*. To feed.

"Now, Declan!" she shouted his name and began to mew as her orgasm ripped through her. When he broke skin, the pain was exquisite, intense. As he began to feed from her, to draw her essence into his body, her insides liquefied.

His cock expanded, filling her tightness to the max, and he roared loudly, releasing his passion as he drew her blood into his mouth.

Together they rocked, bodies still joined, and Ana brushed her mouth against his hand. She licked his wrist, hissed, and then plunged her fangs into his warmth.

Her mind exploded. His taste, his emotions, his soul—all of it combined to create the perfect storm of need and desire.

She wasn't sure how long they stayed like that, their bodies joined together, their minds and hearts now bonded.

She only knew that for the first time in her life, she felt complete. Satiated.

Carefully Declan withdrew, but his arms never left her. Slowly he turned her and for a few moments she couldn't look up at him. She was too afraid there'd be regret in his eyes.

Gently his fingers slid along her jaw and eventually she gathered enough courage to gaze up at him.

She saw drops of her blood against his skin and wiped them away. He didn't say a word, just stared at her.

"Declan, I . . ."

His finger closed her mouth and he pulled her into his embrace. Slowly they sank into the mattress and she smiled tremulously into the darkness.

"I love you, Ana." His mouth was at her ear and she shuddered against his breath. "Remember that."

A tingle of energy slipped over her, an awareness that all was not right. She kicked her legs and would have bolted, but his hands were sliding across her forehead. The world tilted, for just a second.

And then sleep claimed her.

How long she was under the spell of Sandman wasn't clear. But when Ana finally dragged her mind from the clutches of darkness, one thing was apparent.

Declan was gone.

Son of a bitch!

She flew to the door but was repelled backward as electric energy erupted up her fingers, singeing her flesh.

Ana cursed loudly, several times over, and stood mouth tight, eyes grim. What was he thinking? He *needed* her help.

Declan O'Hara was a fool if he thought to keep her contained. They were now bonded, for better or worse, and he obviously didn't know how deep those strings pulled.

She quickly gathered her clothes, her mind working feverishly, because she would find her way out. There would be hell to pay.

She clenched her hands together, considering where they were . . . How fucking appropriate.

CHAPTER 22

Club Doom was as frenetic and wild as it had been several hours earlier when Declan had first arrived in Hell.

He shoved his way to the bar, ordered a shot, and tossed it back, welcoming the burn as the blood red liquid slid down his throat. His senses were hyper, his body tingled, and a weird sensation settled inside him. It was the blood. Ana's blood.

His heart sped up at the thought of her. What they'd just shared was indescribable. It wasn't just the sex. It was something much deeper. Ana DeLacrux belonged to him. She existed *inside* him.

He clenched his teeth tightly. He would do whatever it took to make sure they both made it out of the Hell realm with the children in tow. A smile tugged at his mouth. She was gonna be pissed when the sleep charm wore off. But she'd be safe.

In the meantime he needed to track down a certain demon.

"Back already?"

Declan tensed, cleared all emotion from his mind, and turned. The blond demon from hours earlier stared at him, an elegant eyebrow arched in question.

He smiled. "You complaining?"

She slid beside him. "No, not at all." Her nostrils flared and his gut tightened as her eyes narrowed. "I can smell her on you. She's different, that one. I can't put my finger on it but—"

Declan cut in before she could continue and hoped like hell the panic he felt was invisible. "I'm looking for someone."

"And I'm guessing that someone isn't me?" She pouted.

"No." He nodded to the crowd behind her. "A demon by the name of Seth. I've been told he hangs here." The name was one he'd become familiar with during his forced stay in District Three. He knew that Lilith had no love for the demon and figured the feeling was mutual. Getting into District Three was nearly impossible, unless invited or thrown down.

He needed a way in. Like yesterday. Maybe Seth could provide access.

The demon's fingers stilled and wariness crept into her eyes. "What do you want with Seth?"

Declan smiled. "That's my business. Can you point me in the right direction or no?"

The demon chewed her lip, her eyes narrowed, and the smile that fell across her plump lips told Declan things were not going to be as easy as he'd like.

She ordered two drinks and shoved another into his hands. "I suppose that depends." She licked her lips and finished the drink in one gulp.

Declan nodded, tossed his glass back and stared down at her. "On what?"

Her hand was on his forearm before he could move, her hip pressed hard against his crotch. "On what's in it for me." Her breath was warm against his cheek and her razor-sharp teeth scraped along his mouth.

His anger flared and he grabbed her wrist tightly. He

grinned at her even as he spread fire along her flesh and lowered his mouth until it was inches from her ear.

"If you know where Seth is, I'd appreciate the information." He relaxed his grip slightly. "As for payment"—Declan's eyes went black—"I'll let you leave with your head still attached to your body."

She wrenched her hand from his and took a step back. "You're a piece of shit, asshole," she said angrily.

"I've been called worse."

She glared at him, licked her lips slowly as a tall demon with an impressive physique sidled up beside her, intent on getting to the bar. Her gaze shifted. In the background the music continued to pound, a heavy beat that thrummed loudly in his chest.

Declan's muscles were bunched into all sorts of tension. The need to move, to get things done had him sweaty and jumpy.

"When Seth is around he's holed up three blocks over. A nice little area of town called the Dunes, though it's the critters that hide in the shadows you need to be wary of."

She turned and grabbed the demon between the legs, before pushing the male back into the darkness that skirted the corners of the bar.

Declan watched them melt from view, turned to the madness that was Club Doom, and slipped through the crowd. Hundreds of bodies writhed and moaned, high on the dark undercurrent that slithered along the ground, fueled by demon drink and whatever nasty-ass shit was being sold in the corners.

And yet this was fucking paradise compared to where he was headed. Declan exited the club, inhaled the cool, wet air, and pulled the collar of his jacket up around his ears. He chanced a glance toward the tall clock tower. It was barely visible amidst the ever-swirling fog.

For the moment Ana was safe; it was up to him to finish the job and get her out. He peered into the darkness. The dunes. A shudder rushed over his flesh.

He disappeared into the shadows and missed the tall form that slipped into view.

Samael unclenched his hands and frowned. He stared into the back alley that Declan had just traversed. He itched to follow. To make sure things got done.

Instead he reached for the door and entered Club Doom, which in fact was *his*. It wasn't as quaint as the Grease Pit, there were no orders of poutine available, or humans to play with, but it did provide an endless bounty of darkness. And a good demon needed a certain amount of crap in his diet.

He paused, swept the dark aviators from his face, and took in the scene before him. It was full of every kind of demon imaginable and anything in between. Shades, vampires, shifters . . . anyone or anything sentenced to the fringes of Hell. His tall form moved with the grace of a much smaller being and he was aware of the interest he created, of the eyes that followed him.

And then slid away to avoid contact.

They were afraid of him. Of the power he represented. And they should be. Samael was a grand duke, a demon lord who commanded an impressive army of over one thousand legions of doom.

He made his way to the bar and tossed his leather coat at Jim, the bartender. The red demon had his favorite brew ready and he grabbed it, took a long swig, and leaned toward his trusted employee.

Time to test the waters, see if Declan was on track.

"Anything interesting happen while I was gone?" His voice was light, inquisitive.

Jim tapped a keg. "Not really. Some crap dude who

crawled up from District Three pissed Tasha off, but that's about it."

Samael sniffed the air and turned to the right. The shadows were particularly strong there but he knew bodies hid amongst them. He finished his beer, wiped his mouth, and turned.

"Pour me another. I'll be right back."

A shade passed in front of him, its ghostly smile etched in a permanent macabre greeting. He ignored it, pushed through it, in fact, and quickly made his way toward the shadows.

He let the darkness cover him, inhaled the magic of its scent as he felt its coolness caress his face. He saw them. Tasha's body pressed tight between the legs of a massive demon—green skin, brainless, and no doubt well hung—an apt plaything for her.

He watched them for several seconds as their bodies rocked in a raw, frenetic dance. He enjoyed their base display of the sex act and just when victory would have been theirs, when she moaned on the cusp of orgasm, he cleared his throat. The demon snarled, its eyes glowing a fiery red as it turned its massive head his way. The tongue that darted out fell limp, lolling to the side as it panted and moaned in an almost painful fashion.

Immediately it pushed Tasha from its body. "Sorry to offend, master, I had no idea she was yours."

"What the—" Tasha whirled around, breasts hanging freely, mouth pulled back in a menacing growl. The surprise on her face fled quickly as she stepped away from the demon and bowed her head. "Samael."

He nodded toward the demon and watched, amused at the speed the beast gained in its attempt to get away from him. He then turned to Tasha.

"I hear someone from District Three is trolling my club," Samael said lightly.

Tasha made a face, her fingers twirling around the hard nipples of her exposed breasts. It was a nervous gesture and one he would forgive. He could, after all, end her with the flick of his wrist.

She nodded, swallowed, and met his eyes. Score one for the demon whore. It was more than most of the patrons in his club could muster.

"I didn't get his name, but he's looking for, uh . . . Seth."

Samael's face remained blank and he said not a word, but turned toward the bar. Good. O'Hara was headed in the right direction. Seth would be able to provide a way to the District Three without Samael's interference. The less he was involved, the better.

"He had a woman here, too. Not sure about her." Tasha spoke quickly, and Samael paused, but didn't turn back.

"A woman? Another visitor from District Three?"

"I don't think so. The smell from below didn't cling to her, to him, either, now that I think of it."

Samael whirled around, his hands clutching the demon's head tight. He stared down into her wide, terrified eyes and smiled as he massaged her skull. "This won't hurt," he murmured, "*too much.*"

She moaned and shook as his fingers fed from the images in her mind. When he was done he settled her onto the low-slung bench and left her to the shadows.

Tasha wouldn't remember Declan or the green demon she'd been riding. His face was grim as he grabbed his beer from Jim and headed outside. She definitely wouldn't remember the vampire, Ana DeLacrux.

Samael walked with slow, precise steps through the darkened streets of District One. A storm had just blown in, he'd rode the tail end of it as he'd ascended from the human realm, and another threatened on the horizon. Such was the way of it here.

He exhaled twin shots of mist as the warm air from his

body mingled with the cold. Shrewdly his gaze swept the street. Declan would have stashed the vampire close by. He knew the sorcerer was attached to the woman. He'd made it a point to know everything about the man.

He snorted as he cut through the thick gloom. Feelings were for the weak.

Ahead he spied the watchtower and without breaking stride, turned toward it. His long legs ate up the distance in no time and he shook the excess moisture from his thick hair as he walked toward the front desk of the ramshackle hotel adjacent to the tower.

The Soul Sucker was a dump, as was ninety-five percent of District One, but he paid no heed to his surroundings. What did he care? His palatial estate was nothing like these ruins.

The clerk behind the desk stood straight when he spied Samael, and though he appeared calm, his thin shoulders shook slightly as they hunched forward.

"Master." His tone was flat though respectful.

Samael arched a brow. "Anyone check in tonight?" he asked casually. He smiled as the clerk swallowed thickly and nodded.

Silence fell between them and he leaned in close. "I'm not a mind reader"—he flexed his fingers—"though there are ways."

The tall man jumped, his Adam's apple bobbed in a fluttery motion as he cleared his throat. "Sorry, master. Yes, a couple came in, uh, I don't know about—"

"Number?" Samael bit in harshly.

The clerk's face was pinched as he pointed toward the elevator. "Ten-twenty."

Samael turned without another word. He ignored the elevator and took the stairs, enjoying the strenuous exercise as he jogged up them. He entered on the opposite end from where he needed to be. Garbage littered the corners, rats scurried about, and a few lost souls stared his way as he made his way down. They were derelicts. Souls that had managed to claw their way up from below, but sadly would never leave District One, which was basically Hell's version of purgatory.

He stopped in front of the last door on the left and removed his aviators. A thin sheen of energy slithered across the entire frame. It was magick, O'Hara's brand, no doubt. A ward of some sort.

He heard a crash followed by a cry of rage from inside. He smiled. Nothing like a little tension and anger to feed his soul.

Declan had obviously charmed the door so the vampire wouldn't be able to leave. That was good, because she could royally screw things up if allowed out. His full lips thinned into a grimace. Lilith would not win.

Could not win.

If she managed to gather the mark of seven then all was lost. The scales would be tipped so far to the left, the right side would never be able to recover. Life as he knew it would cease to exist.

He fucking liked things the way they were. Why else would he risk his life every day that he drew breath? Why else join with Bill and the rest?

He stilled as his heart flushed hot with anger. That Lilith had managed to take them from his man, Janus, must still be dealt with. The soul reaper had been in charge of teens. He'd turned up dead, the children were missing, and Lilith gloated from her dungeon below.

Someone had set her on the path to the children. Had the audacity to betray the demon of chaos. Samael clenched his hands tightly and growled. A rat scurrying at his feet bolted, startled as the sounds echoed down the hall. He snorted. They knew not what they tangled with.

He pressed his hand against the frame and hissed as pain

traveled along his arm. It was intense and left blisters in its wake. He smiled and turned away. He liked pain. It was one emotion that made him feel alive.

The vampire would not be going anywhere. One less thing for him to worry about.

Samael cracked his neck, rolled his shoulders, and was about to leave when a curse, bang, and shriek sounded once more—this time, accompanied by an incredible crash and the sound of glass breaking.

Bloody fuck! What the hell had she done?

He turned a thunderous eye toward the door and tweaked his shoulders once more as the tattoo along his neck shimmered.

"Sleep, my friend. I can handle a vampire. Especially one that comes in such a small, pretty package."

Samael didn't hesitate, issued nothing more than a grunt as he sent his booted foot straight through the door, splintering it in two sections. The energy that burned up his leg was fierce. He clenched his teeth and growled as he stepped through the ward, wincing slightly as the pain tripled before fading away.

He inhaled a quick, even breath. Sex was heavy in the air, as was the scent of blood. The room was small, dingy, and save for the gaping hole in the window, there was nothing but rumpled sheets showing the evidence of O'Hara's passion play.

Blinds banged loudly against the window frame as the wind whistled into the room. Samael crossed to the gaping hole and looked below. He was ten stories up and though it was quite a drop, he knew it was nothing for a vampire to navigate.

Question was . . . how the hell had she managed to break O'Hara's charm?

He stilled, nostrils flared, and heard the sharp pounding of feet on the cobbled streets below. She was on the run.

Samael laughed, low vibrations falling flat as he kicked out the rest of the glass and slid his large body through the opening. He stood atop the ledge, his gaze roving over his dominion below.

He took a step and fell into the night.

CHAPTER 23

Ana hit the ground running and didn't stop. Her lithe body flew down the darkened streets as she navigated through a maze she swore hadn't existed hours earlier. The wind howled in her ear and wet hair was slick against her skin. The rain was falling in sheets and she wiped excess from her eyes as she scanned the area ahead.

Unfortunately the rain made it next to impossible to follow Declan's scent. She would have to go deep, try a different approach. Was their bond solid enough for her to find him on a mental path?

Ana sent out a tentative bite, careful to keep it low-key, not wanting to attract any predators. But there was no answer.

She paused by the watchtower, surprised that she'd found her way back to pretty much where she'd started. A wave of frustrated anger swept over her and she tried to tamper the fury. When she finally got her hands on Declan O'Hara, a bunch of nasty demons were going to be the least of his worries.

To the left was Club Doom. She glanced in that direction and took a step forward. Declan had been there for a reason. But what was it? Her eyes narrowed and she headed toward the club. The blond demon might know something. Ana's fangs throbbed. She was in the mood to kick ass big-time.

She'd taken only a few steps when a tingle crept up the back of her skull. Someone was there, just behind her. She cracked her fingers open slowly, though she was careful to keep them at her side. She continued along, her steps sure, measured, but all her senses were open, seeking that which stalked her.

The mist was so thick she couldn't see her feet and grimaced as she slid over a sticky substance. Her chest tightened, muscles bunched.

She took another step and whirled around, a dirge of hair, nails, and fangs. Her nose immediately connected with a hard chest. She dug in, smiling as her nails cut through leather.

But the bastard was too large, too strong, too much demon. Dark shadows erupted around them, swirling about their bodies, and she closed her eyes—it's not like she could see anyway—and went limp.

"What the—?" He was surprised. *Good.*

She hissed and lunged forward, her claws grasping him around the shoulders as she went for the jugular. His hands twisted into her rib cage and he applied just enough pressure that she felt one of them crack.

She knew she wasn't strong enough to defeat him. Not physically. She let go and was thrown to the ground. The cobblestone was uneven and she landed on her side. *Hard.*

Ana lay there for several seconds, her breaths falling in painful draws. Her teeth had grazed his flesh. She'd scored a drop of his blood, and it had been enough to tell her he was more powerful than she'd first thought.

It wasn't juiced up with the poison the lower ranks carried in their veins. It was pure, raw power.

She turned over slowly and glared up at the demon. The fog parted just so and a sliver of light illuminated him from behind. He looked like a bloody angel.

He grinned down at her, had the audacity to stretch out

his hand as if to offer help. She tossed him an are-you-fucking-joking-me look and carefully got to her feet.

"Feisty little thing, aren't you?" The tall demon's hand dropped back to his side, but she was well aware he held his arms loose, at the ready.

"You get your kicks stalking women who are smaller than you?" She made an effort to keep her voice neutral but wasn't so sure it was working. His smiled widened and she wanted nothing more than to punch the asshole. To smash his nose and mar what was without a doubt one hell of a handsome face.

He studied her in silence and Ana tried not to panic but she knew she needed to play this cool. She couldn't chance being outed. She needed to get to Declan.

"We're in District One. Anyone is fair game. You'd best learn that, newbie."

Fear clutched at her. *Newbie.* Did he know? She eyed him warily and took a step away, wincing as a shot of pain splintered across her rib cage.

Christ, it felt like he'd broken at least two ribs. She exhaled slowly and grimaced.

"Still"—her gaze swept the area—"there's something sad about someone your size taking on a lady."

The demon stepped toward her. He was wearing large aviators and he removed them from his face. Ana kept her cool but the truth was, his freaky eyes were unnerving. Everything about him screamed Hollywood from the thick, dark hair atop his head, the classic cheekbones and cleft chin, but those eyes . . .

He smiled, tilted his head as if they were having a Sunday afternoon conversation over coffee, and spoke. "You're no lady."

She opened her mouth to retort, intent on keeping him off his game, but his body moved quickly, so fast she didn't see it. And then he was there, so close she saw flames flickering in his eyes.

"Can you stop that?" she ground out, surrendering to the anger inside.

He arched an eyebrow and she saw interest. *"That?"* he mimicked.

"The freaky eye thing. I don't like it."

The demon laughed; a throaty chuckle that echoed into the night, bouncing off the walls until it surrounded her in a wall of sound. He leaned forward, sniffed along her neck, and twirled a finger around a long piece of her hair.

"You are delicious. I can see why he lusts for you."

Ana's eyes narrowed and she took a step back. And then another until she had some space between them. "Who the hell *are* you?"

He watched her closely, the smile never leaving his face. "Ana, I'm disappointed you don't recognize me. Though, sadly, any renderings I've seen of myself in the human realm are less than flattering."

Ana's eyes widened. She noticed the vibrant tattoo along the side of his neck. It was a dragon. She didn't need to hear anymore. "Samael."

"Beauty, brains, and apparently strong enough to break through powerful wards put in place by your boyfriend." Samael's smile vanished. "Which, I feel the need to point out, wasn't a very smart thing to do."

Ana watched the powerful demon warily as he paced a bit, though his eyes never left her.

"You've created a problem for me." Samael shook his head. "I don't like problems."

"I'm not leaving until I find Declan."

"You should not have come here." He glared at her, his jaw tight. Shit. He was pissed.

"I shouldn't do a lot of things." She shrugged. "It's part

of my charm." Ana knew she sounded flippant, but her mind was racing, searching for a way out. She decided the direct approach might work best. Declan had indicated Samael had given him a serum, something to help him blend in. It was obvious the demon was helping him in some way.

"What's your part in all of this?"

His hand was at her throat before she could blink and he lifted her into the air, slammed her back against the wall. She grunted at the force of the hit, ignoring the pain in her side as she struggled to breathe.

Desperately she tried to free herself but ceased her efforts after a few seconds. It was no use. He was much too strong.

"You will leave here or you will die." He spit the words at her and let her fall to the ground.

She was up in an instant, hissing and baring her fangs. Ana was livid. She was sick of men—be they demon, sorcerer, or fucking Seraph—charting her path. A crackle of energy teased the edges of her fingers.

Did she have enough mojo left? Was there only a limited supply?

Declan's blood had provided an added boost, a bit of magick she'd not expected. She didn't know the why or how of it, and didn't care, but she'd used it to escape the hotel room, successfully blasting through the charmed window.

Samael's grimace softened. He studied her, an unreadable expression on his face. "You would still challenge me?"

"Time's running out. I need to get to Declan. Can you help me or not?" Ana threw the question out there. What did she have to lose? "He has a much better chance of getting those kids out with my help."

She watched his face darken, refused to budge when he took the last few steps toward her.

His nostrils flared once more and he leaned down. "You drank from him." It was a statement, not a question.

She nodded. "He forced me to. Said his blood would mask my scent." She glared up at him. "Said you supplied the serum."

Samael's eyes narrowed, though he remained silent.

"I have no clue what your involvement is and honestly don't give a shit as to your reasons. If you know where Declan is, share now or get the fuck out of my way."

"What would you do, what deal would you sign, in order to get what you want?"

Ana swallowed carefully. What the hell was he getting at?

"I don't want to play games, demon. I'd do anything." A lump of dread rolled over in her belly and she hitched her breath.

For Declan, she'd sell her soul.

The heat of his breath touched her skin and she tried not to grimace, though the distaste she felt was more than apparent. She'd never been this close to a demon before. Their energy was intense, but tainted with such darkness that it made her nauseous.

"Good to know," he whispered, "because where you're going you might very well have to sign your pretty little ass over to the queen bitch of Hell."

"Lilith," she whispered.

Samael nodded. "She has a hard-on for your boy. She won't play nice with anyone she sees as a threat."

Ana bit her lip. "What do you mean?"

Samael pushed away from her, turned, and walked for a bit. "He's not shared his time in Hell?"

"No." Ana stared at him, wishing the unease that filled her would go away. She thought of the scars that adorned Declan's chest. Of the pain that sat in his eyes when he thought no one would notice.

"It's not my place to spill another's secrets." Samael turned to her, his fingers crooked as he gestured for her to come to him. Slowly she took the steps needed until she was inches from the demon. "You are brave, I'll give you that. Most would run, hide from me."

"Most don't have something worth losing."

He placed his hands upon her shoulders and stared directly into her eyes. When he spoke, his lips didn't move, though his words echoed inside her head.

I know you've pledged your allegiance to Askelon, whom you know as Bill. It is for that reason only I've not ended your life. You will not mention my name to anyone, or my affiliation to your sorcerer. If you do I will end you. I've no problem doing with that. Understand?

Ana nodded, her mouth dry. His words were direct, cold, and there was no doubt he meant them.

The sorcerer is on his way to a demon, Seth. This demon hates Lilith more than anyone, save perhaps for your man O'Hara. I will get you there, but be warned, you're on your own.

A flash of light had her wincing as a rush of wind ripped through her hair, and a roaring in her ears left her off balance. Ana staggered back and when the world righted, when everything stopped spinning, she stilled.

It was like she'd been dropped into the middle of the Sahara except there was no sunshine, only the eternal fog. It slid between huge sand dunes that surrounded her. The air was dry, biting, as it caressed her skin.

Her hand clutched a large, serrated dagger. She stared at it in confusion.

Howls erupted to her left, the kind that signaled something new stalking the night. It was familiar. Ana crouched low, her eyes scanning for a way out. She knew what was out there amongst the shadows.

Hellhounds. She smiled, a harsh slash of white in the gloom. Guess Samael wasn't such a bastard after all. He'd plunked her down in the middle of a rabid pack of dogs, yet he'd supplied her with a weapon.

A real gentleman.

Growls, moans, and howls lit up the night. Ana had no choice and took off running, desperately trying to seek cover. Her boots sank in the sand and she found it hard to keep her balance. She scrambled up a large dune, crested it, and fell head over heels all the way down the other side.

Jesus fuck! She spit dirt from her mouth but was up and running. The damn things could be heard, their stench rose into the air but she couldn't see them.

Yet.

She slid between two large dunes, the long mounds giving some sort of cover from the endless wind and sand. Her chest was heaving, her mind on red alert. A whisper of energy caught her attention. Shadows moved along the edge of the dunes but she was afraid to venture deeper into the crevice for fear she'd become trapped.

Ana cracked her neck, welcomed the rush of adrenaline that slid through her veins. She was gonna need a shitload of it, too. It sounded like she was surrounded by more than a just few of the bastards. Her fangs hung, ready for attack, and she held herself as loose as she could, considering her feet kept sinking into the soft sand.

A howl rent the night and her hair stood on end as a cacophony of growls accompanied it. Heavy breathing blew down the pike and she wrinkled her nose as the otherworld stench of the hellhounds came with it.

"Bring it on," she whispered. She shook out her fingers but luck was not hanging with her this night. Any extra mojo she'd ingested from Declan was long gone. There wasn't even a tingle.

She held her breath as everything faded away and when several sets of fiery eyes appeared, all emotion fled.

She needed to survive this. She *would* survive.

The beasts were impressive in height. Tall, shaggy things with powerful jaws that held several rows of serrated teeth.

She glanced down at the dagger in her hand. Somehow it didn't seem fair.

The leader sported two heads; the smaller one blew plumes of fire at her as the hellhound stopped a few feet away.

Long moments stretched between them and a wave of nervous energy rolled over Ana. She hissed, showed her fangs in defiance, and shouted, "What the hell you waiting for?"

Ana DeLacrux had never been a girl who waited for the shit to hit the fan. She'd rather be the one flinging it.

She flashed the dagger, rolling it easily in her hands as she advanced toward the pack. There were five of them. All of them were massive, easily topping her height of five-foot-two. Their hair was long, coarse, and they stank like the foulest shithole imaginable.

She would have only one chance to surprise them. Ana decided the best defense was to attack and take out the leader. Lightning bolted across the darkened sky, cutting through the strange red sheets of energy that shifted in the wind.

The hellhounds howled once more, but Ana was already on the move, her small body twisting in the air as she aimed her dagger at the double-headed pack leader.

She spiraled as high as she could, a savage yell falling from her lips as she slid through the darkness and fell between them all.

CHAPTER 24

Declan heard howls in the distance as he trudged through the dunes. Hellhounds, no doubt. Seth would use creatures such as them to guard the many treasures he held.

The cold, biting wind and sand were constant, pounding his body as he headed toward Seth's compound. It was not far, hidden between two massive mounds of sand.

The demon had an impressive display of collectables, stolen from both the human realm as well as every corner of Hell. There were whispers that he housed several items taken from the Holiest of places—Heaven itself. Pieces that had been lost for thousands of years.

Seth was in fact a cross between an art collector and a garbage man who had some strange ability to land on both sides of the fence without getting burned.

He answered to no one and was free to come and go as he pleased. For reasons unknown, Lucifer had bestowed on the demon great boundaries in which to exist.

It was one of the reasons Lilith hated him so. And why she'd stolen one of his most prized possessions over five hundred years earlier, the stone of the Nile, an ancient necklace worn by Nefertari herself.

Seth had been trying to retrieve it ever since, with no

luck. Declan planned to get it back for him—as long as Seth agreed to accompany him to District Three.

He was well acquainted with Lilith's private quarters. He'd seen the prize. He knew where she kept it. If it wasn't around her slimy neck it was hung on a golden rod near her bed. His mouth thinned at the thought of Lilith. Rage, pain, and fear mingled, forming a toxic soup that waited to be unleashed.

He'd love nothing more than to rip her head from her body. He wanted to make her suffer for the things she'd done to him. The things she'd made him do.

He shook such thoughts from his mind as he ventured deeper into the dunes. He needed to focus. His goal was the teenagers and Ana. Nothing more.

Thoughts of the vampire warmed him, bled through the cold that had settled upon his soul. He felt the strength she'd imparted to him, the vampire blood that now fused with his. It was a marriage of power—the brute, cunning strength of a vampire and the seductive magick that lived inside him.

He might be a fool but for the moment Declan felt invincible.

The sky above him flickered, with sheets of white energy rippling along the ribbons of red that hung there. Yet another storm was brewing. Everything down here was extreme and Declan pulled the collar of his leather coat higher as he picked up the pace, and jogged through the sand. By his calculations Seth's compound was just beyond the next dune.

A sharp howl, followed by a scream, ripped through the night and Declan paused, his nostrils flaring as he whipped his head around. What the hell was that?

Fog slithered over the sand, whirling in a macabre dance with bits of garbage and sheets of mist. Adrenaline flooded his body and a tingle rippled along his skull. It was a weird sensation and at first he didn't know what it was. What it meant.

He took another step and was about to take another when he dug in and came to an abrupt stop. A familiar scent rolled over his nose and his gut clenched hard.

Ana. What the fuck? She was at the Soul Sucker. Wasn't she?

Quickly he darted between the shadows and he flicked his hand, charming the cool mist up his body. It enveloped his tall form, effectively hiding him in plain sight.

His power lay coiled in his chest and he tapped into some of that juice, welcoming the familiar wave of energy that rippled over his skin.

He smiled savagely. His magick was free. He could spell and charm as much as he wanted. Lilith had no dominion over that part of him anymore.

His heart slowed, his mind cleared as he carefully slid around the largest of the dunes. Ahead, he saw shapes moving slowly, in a predatory manner. They were large animals, their growls unmistakable. Definitely hellhounds

Declan watched the shadowy figures, eyes narrowed, body primed to attack. They stalked a prize, and as Ana's familiar scent hung in the air, he swallowed the fear inside.

He knew how fucked up things were down here. How easy it was to fall victim to the mind crap that was everywhere. Rarely was anything as it seemed. There was no need to panic just yet.

Declan threw his hand forward, the edges of his fingers glowing as they emitted a luminescent light that swept before him. It enabled him to see clearly.

There were five hellhounds at play, their large bodies trembling with excitement as they growled and whined.

Yet it was the small form amongst them, the petite

woman who drew his attention. He hissed sharply as his newly formed fangs erupted, and the growl that fell from his lips was anything but happy.

The hellhounds whirled around, their tongues lolling, their mouths agape. His eyes connected with Ana's and he glared at her.

Ana held a dagger in front of her, which she took the time to wave at him. "I am so going to kick your ass when this is all over, O'Hara."

Declan arched a brow, didn't trust himself to speak; instead he threw an energy bolt into the pack, killing one of the hounds instantly. Howls erupted from within. The beasts snarled and all hell broke loose. He saw Ana whip her small body into the air, and she landed upon the largest of all of them. A hellhound with two heads. The leader.

He squared his shoulders and methodically picked off the remaining animals. His energy was red hot and he easily sliced three of them in half as they rushed toward him. Declan ignored the bits that flew at him and walked with purpose toward his woman.

Her hair was a wild mess, streaming behind her as the wind took it. She cursed an impressive blue streak as she sank the dagger into the neck of the larger of the two heads— all the while trying to avoid the fire-breathing second.

The hellhound bucked madly and Ana nearly fell off, barely able to keep her balance as she pushed the dagger in deeper.

Declan watched the entire scene, and though his anger was still at the fore, he couldn't help but feel admiration for the woman.

She was magnificent. Fierce.

She was also knee-deep in his shit and he wanted her gone. There was no way in hell Lilith was getting anywhere near the vampire. It was a sobering thought and one that fed the urgency of the situation.

Ana glanced up and shouted, "What the hell are you waiting for? Blast this thing!"

The animal bucked madly as it tried to unseat the vampire. He thrust one massive grade A energy bolt at the hellhound. The damn thing exploded and Declan smiled harshly as Ana shrieked and went flying, followed by gory bits of beast.

She landed hard, rolled over. And then was still.

Declan arched an eyebrow. What game was she playing now?

He glanced around, aware that they were out in the open, deep in the heart of the dunes.

"Get up, Ana." His voice was curt and a muscle worked its way across his cheek. "We need to get our asses in gear because I've got to get you back to the hotel. I'm not taking you down with me so forget it."

The air shifted with traces of something powerful. Declan cursed and dropped all pretense as he jogged to the vampire. His annoyance vanished when he reached for her.

Blood was spattered along her throat, a macabre splash of crimson against the ivory of her skin. Her eyes were closed. She looked like a broken doll.

Panic hit and he fell to his knees, his hands running up her body until he cupped her face. "Ana, for Christ sakes, answer me!"

His anger abated as fear took its place. What had he done? His fingers trembled as he traced her lips, her cheeks.

"Shit, babe, I'm sorry I didn't mean—"

Her eyes flew open and her hands were around his throat before he had time to react. Two seconds later, he found himself on his back, with the spitfire vampire straddling him.

"How dare you leave me in that shithole," she shouted at him, her lips inches from his.

She was pissed. Well so the fuck was he.

Declan's hands crept up and he buried them in her hair as he cradled her skull, effectively holding her prisoner. He was not letting go. She couldn't be trusted.

"I had my reasons." His eyes narrowed as he fought the anger inside. She couldn't be here. Not now. He had enough on his plate.

"I'm taking you back." He tried to unseat her, but she held firm.

"That's not going to happen." Ana was breathing hard. Her eyes were round balls of blackness that stared at him in anger.

"I don't want you here," he snarled.

"You should have thought of that before you made me drink your blood." She spat at him. "I told you I didn't want this bond."

"What the hell does that have to do with anything?" He pushed up, this time sending a line of fire out his finger-tips, and smiled savagely when she rolled off him. "The only reason you weren't attacked in that fucking club was because of me. Those demons would have been all over that delectable ass of yours if it weren't for the fact my blood masked your scent."

She cradled her abdomen. Declan was on his feet and stood behind her, his hands clenched at his side. The turmoil he felt was indescribable. It was a mix of mental and physical. It packed a serious punch, and along with it came resentment.

Would he ever achieve balance? Contentment?

"You don't understand," she whispered hoarsely, "what this means."

Declan stared down at her slight form and fought the urge to grab her into his arms. To bury his nose in the thick mess of the hair at her neck. His mouth ached and an unfamiliar longing swept over him.

He wanted to sink his fangs into her flesh and take from her again. Sweat beaded his brow and his gut tightened as another wave of hunger rolled over him.

"We can't be apart. We're bonded whether you like it or not." Ana turned her head to the side. "That's on you, O'Hara." She got to her knees and then stood, though she kept her back to him. "You think I will let you feed from another?"

Declan grimaced. He'd not thought about that.

"Let you hold someone close and take their essence into your body?" Ana whipped around and he was taken aback at the fury that colored her eyes deep crimson. "After we've bonded?"

She stalked over to him. Her fangs were fully distended and he smelled her hunger, her *need* as she stared up at him defiantly.

"You woke the beast, my friend. Let me explain exactly what that means." She lunged forward, her hands on his shoulders, her body pressed against his, and she sank her fangs into the side of his neck.

Instantly he was flooded with hot need and he grabbed her, held her in place as she fed, baring his own fangs as the need inside him grew. The connection was instant and fucking glorious.

She broke away, her chest heaving as she fought for control. His own was thin and he growled in frustration. He was left hungry, full of a need that had not been met.

The wind whipped her hair into the air furiously. Ana tugged it out of the way and plunged forward. "This thing that's between us is permanent. It's not like you can return it or ignore it when you don't want to deal."

She thumped him in the chest and he gritted his teeth as he stared down at her. Energy lit the air and the feel of something powerful permeated the entire area as the storm gathered. Everything in him screamed get the hell out, yet he couldn't move. He was mesmerized by the woman in front of him.

"You're inside me, Declan . . . *living* inside of me." Her eyes widened, they glittered with the sheen of what looked to be tears. "Can't you feel it?"

He nodded. There was a ruthless hunger that had been gnawing at him since he'd left her. Declan had assumed it was some weird vampire thing but now he knew better, because as he stood inches from Ana, the twisted, wild place inside him was calm.

"Your energy feeds mine, keeps me sane, and fulfills my needs on every level." Her voice lowered and he strained to hear. "I don't want another. You are my soul now. I will not let you exist without me."

He heard her pain, but dammit, there was no time for consoling. For the big I-love-you-we'll-live-happily-ever-after kind of chat. Something was coming. He could feel it.

"I can't . . ." he began, and grimaced as his voice trailed into nothing. He didn't want her exposed to what existed below. The depravity and decadence were unparalleled, and the things he'd done . . .

He didn't want her to find out the truth of his relationship with Lilith. Would she still want him if she knew? Bond or no bond?

"I need to get you out of here." He tried to grab her, but she moved quickly. He'd forgotten how fast she was.

Ana grinned down at him as she stood atop a sand dune ten feet away. She wanted to play hard, so be it. He took a step forward, unaware of the forces gathering close until it was too late.

Two large demons appeared out of thin air, one on either side of the vampire. She didn't have a chance and cursed a blue streak as she was taken into custody. Before he could do anything, he, too, was surrounded. He hissed his displeasure, his dark eyes narrowed accusingly onto Ana.

She stared down at him, chin raised, lips tight.

"Trespass." The word was grunted from the demon closest to him. Declan arched a brow. "That's a good word. All you got?" It never ceased to amaze how fucking dumb most of these soldiers were. He knew better than to put up a fight. There were too many. He needed to conserve his energy. To plot.

His only hope was that the demons worked for Seth. If not, his and Ana's trip to the dunes of District One was going to be short.

And painful.

CHAPTER 25

They'd been separated for what seemed hours. Declan was nearly going mad, and not just because he had no freaking clue where they'd taken Ana.

He was hungry. He closed his eyes and the world was washed in crimson. Blood was all he could think about. If he could, he'd charm a fucking keg of the damn stuff into his prison, but that was beyond his capabilities.

His booted foot kicked the door again, though a yell didn't accompany it this time. It was no use. No one was there to listen.

His gaze traveled the small room he'd been tossed in, methodically running over the gray stone walls for the hundredth time. He growled in frustration. The entire area was fortified with iron. He could feel it and knew the bloody stuff severely hindered his magick.

He ran his hand over the stubble that covered his jaw. *Fuck me.*

An echo outside his chamber had him holding his breath, coiling what power he had into his gut.

He might be in for a major ass kicking but he'd give as good as he got. He clenched his hands into fists, spread his legs, and eyed the door. Footsteps sounded, slow and measured. His breaths were coming faster than he'd like, but it was next to impossible to tame the beast within him.

It wanted out. It wanted the darkness.

When the footsteps stopped outside the door he readied himself to fight. Slowly it swung open.

It was Ana.

Her eyes were downcast, the long lashes hiding whatever was reflected in their depths. He saw how her hands trembled and the rage that he felt, the hot anger that swept over him nearly brought him to his knees.

What had they done to her?

Someone was there, just beyond the doorway.

"If you've touched a hair on her head I'll rip you to pieces," he barked.

Ana looked up then and he was taken aback by the sorrow in her gaze. It was quickly hidden and she looked away from him.

An uneasy silence fell into the room. What the hell was going on?

A tall man strode by her. It was the demon Seth. His face was grim.

"O'Hara." Seth nodded as the door closed behind them. "You're one sorry son of a bitch I never thought to see again." The demon was tall, with powerful shoulders, white blond hair, and winter blue eyes. They were unnerving and he knew it. He was dressed in leather, with many tattoos adorning his flesh. None were the special kind that Samael sported.

Seth arched a brow and frowned. "You have a death wish these days?"

Declan glanced at Ana, but she was still overly engaged in staring at the stone floor.

He turned to Seth. Time was running out.

"I want back into District Three."

Seth's mouth tightened. "I know."

Declan shot a look at Ana. What exactly had she shared?

"I'd like to speak to you in private."

"There's no need. I know what it is you seek."

Declan blew out hot breath, cracked his neck in an effort to relieve the tension that knotted his shoulders. Ana was now staring at him as if he had two fucking heads.

"You'll get me in?" he asked again, ignoring the vampire even as he took a step toward her.

"*Us* in . . ." she interjected quietly.

"Ana, you will stay out of this." Anger bled through his words. Would the woman never listen? He turned from her and addressed the demon. "I want her out of here. Topside."

Seth snorted. "You seem to want a lot for someone who's my prisoner."

"I don't have time for games," Declan growled, and flexed his fingers. He knew he wasn't at full strength, but damn, he could still do some damage. *Inflict pain.*

"What's in it for me?" The demon's eyes lingered on Ana and Declan growled, not liking the way his eyes rested on the vampire.

"Don't go there unless you want me to rip you a new one."

Seth laughed. "Still so arrogant." The laughter quickly died. "In case you haven't noticed, sorcerer, you're on my turf"—he gestured—"and I have dominion over all of it."

"No shit," Declan growled. He took another step until his tall frame effectively cut Ana from the demon's view. "I'm here to make a deal, so can we get on with it?"

Seth exhaled slowly, as if he were bored, or would rather be elsewhere, but Declan knew better. The demon hated Lilith. Their animosity was legendary.

"For safe passage to District Three"—Declan nodded—"for the return of Ana topside, I will get you Nefertari's stone."

"Nice try, Declan, but I'm not going anywhere," Ana piped up from behind him.

Declan clenched his jaw painfully. He was irritated,

pissed off, but ignored the vampire. Instead he watched as Seth considered his words. He knew his bargain held interest. The necklace was the demon's most coveted prize and Lilith had it. He'd had an obsession with the Nefertari for thousands of years.

Seth turned to him, his answer abrupt. "Done."

Declan smiled and nodded.

"Except for the part where I return Ana topside."

Declan's smile turned into a growl. "I'm not negotiating."

Seth shrugged. "I've already made a deal with your vampire. Sorry." The demon waved his hand and the door flew open. He paused. "I'd work out your differences if I were you. District Three is unforgiving." He nodded toward Declan. "I know it's been, what, two years? Trust me, nothing's changed."

Seth stepped out into the hall. "You've got one hour so make the most of it. I will make the arrangements."

The door closed, leaving them alone.

Declan paced. The anger, the *hunger* inside was nearly too much to bear with Ana so close. He couldn't look at her. He didn't know what he wanted to do more—fucking strangle her, kiss her silly, or grab her to his body, sink his fangs into her neck, and feed.

It scared him, this beast that now existed inside. A loss of control skittered along the edge of his mind, but he pushed it back. He needed to focus.

"Declan." Her soft voice was hesitant and yet it set him off, unleashed the fury inside him.

"What the hell are you thinking?" He turned on her and took two strides until he was inches away. His mouth ached, but Declan held on, forced his fangs back. He would maintain control. He would figure this out.

A blush crept into her cheeks as she stared at him. Her eyes glittered and he could tell she was as angry as he. But there was something else there. He didn't like it. Defiance.

"I'm not going anywhere other than"—she gestured toward the floor—"down below."

Images assaulted him and he swore he could smell District Three. Pain had a scent all its own. It was sharp and left a bitter aftertaste.

"You have no idea what awaits us there." Bitterness laced his words. "The most horrific things you've ever encountered cannot compare to Lilith's domain."

"A little refresher, Declan. *I died.* Sorry, but that was pretty awful."

He shook his head. "That's not the same thing and you know it."

"What are you so afraid of?" she asked suddenly. "It's not like we've never stared down the face of evil before. Hell, it's the mainstay of our diet."

He stepped away and closed his eyes. Did he have time to list them all?

Declan felt her hand upon his arm, winced as her fingers slowly caressed their way up to the shredded flesh underneath his left pectoral. Her touch burned through the fabric of his shirt.

"I know she did awful things to you." Ana's words were barely a whisper but he was in no mood for softness, for comfort.

He wrenched away from her touch. "You don't know shit."

"Seth told me"—she faltered and his frown deepened—"you were her property for months. He said she makes Lucifer's work look like child's play. I mean I . . . don't know specifics but I'm sure it wasn't pleasant."

Declan stopped in his tracks. "Not pleasant?" He was incredulous. "That's the fucking understatement of the year." In that moment he wanted to shout, to cry out his anger and frustration. Yet he gritted his teeth and remained silent, tucked all emotion away.

"What did you promise Seth?" he asked instead. Pain

lashed across his gut and he groaned, closed his eyes. Instantly crimson bled before his eyes. His fangs slid out and he hissed as his stomach muscles cramped.

She was there. Her body next to his, her hands upon his face. "Declan, you need to feed."

"What did you promise Seth?" he spat out, unable to look at her for fear he'd eat her alive. His hands trembled. He tucked them into fists and hung on.

She stared at him intently. "It doesn't matter. I did what I had to do and don't look at me like that. It's no different than what you did."

He growled and grabbed her by the shoulders. "Every single thing you do matters to me. It always has, but now we've gone to the next level, you and I. There is no in between. No halfway for us. So yeah, if you've signed your soul over to the demon I need to know this shit."

Declan broke away and took a step back. It was too much. The hunger, the fear, and the overwhelming need to protect. He looked at her, his heart in his eyes, "I don't want you near her poison. Understand? I don't . . ." He blew out a breath. "The things I did . . . we did . . ."

Declan snapped his mouth shut. His body was wound tight, every muscle corded into a band of pain.

Ana's mouth trembled, just a bit, and she bit her lip. "It's too late. What's done can't be taken back." Her hand crept up to his cheek and something loosened inside. Like a balloon of pain and longing had burst. "For either one of us. I'm not interested in what you did, what you *had* to do to survive down there."

She laid her head against his chest and slipped her arms around his body. Declan inhaled her scent and for a second let the balloon linger, slowly leaking from his body in a tight flow of pain.

He couldn't fight it. He groaned, hugged her close. And let it go.

She nuzzled his flesh, her cheek gently rubbing against the damaged skin.

"I'm only interested in two things," she whispered. "Getting those teenagers out of District Three, and you—that's it. There is nothing else."

He felt the rise and fall of her chest, heard the beat of her heart. "You need to feed," she breathed against him. *"I need to feed."* Her voice deepened.

Declan felt the scrape of her fangs against his skin and his hold tightened. The severity of his situation faded away. Seth. District Three. All of it.

He closed his eyes and everything was a wash of crimson—his thoughts, emotions, his wants and needs. Her blood had infected them all, had woven its way into his heart and soul until there was nothing else.

"Declan, look at me."

His eyes flew open and the raw hunger that he saw in her face left him weak. His hand sank into the thick, silky tangle of hair at her nape as he gazed into her eyes.

"I love you."

Those three simple words nearly did him in. In that moment he would have sold his soul ten times over in order to push back the clock, just so he could hear them again. And again. *I love you.*

"Ana." He cupped her chin and bent until his lips were inches from hers. He opened his mouth wide and took her lips with a fierce need that made him tremble. Her mouth was soft beneath his, her tongue silky as it teased along his own, but it was the taste of her that inflamed his senses.

She tasted like home.

"Ana," he whispered again into her mouth as his hands held her firmly in place. "I can't remember a time when you weren't the thing I wanted the most. It's like I have no memory before you walked into the briefing room at Quantico." Her eyes widened at his admission. "I knew my path had just been altered and even though you were involved with Diego I was willing to wait." A half smile tugged at his mouth. "Christ, did you make me wait." He brushed his lips across hers once more. "Now that you're mine I refuse to let you put your life in danger. If anything happened to you . . ."

His face darkened, his voice was grim. "I saw you die once, stood by helplessly while my father ended you." He shook his head. "I will not go through that again. Lilith makes my father look like a punk-ass Dr. Evil. He had nothing on her. She's ruthless, conniving, lethal. She feeds on fucking children, for Christ sakes."

"I don't care."

An exasperated grunt slipped from him. "You should care very much. This trip below won't be a holiday. The chances of surviving are pretty goddamn slim but I have to try. She cannot be allowed to gather the mark of seven"—his voice was hoarse now—"or all will be lost."

"There's no way you can stop me, and besides"—her eyes glittered in a strange way, the blue depths shiny like iced diamonds—"you need me." She angled her head slightly and he groaned as his eyes feasted on the expanse of smooth skin. "I can smell your hunger. You need to feed."

Quiet fell between them. "I need to feed," she whispered.

His fangs ached terribly and for a second, time stilled and the floor beneath his feet shifted. He would have fallen save for her strong arms around him.

"Do it, Declan." Her hands were in his hair, guiding him toward ecstasy. His tongue flicked across her flesh, his teeth scraped along the hollow of her neck. The pain inside him was fierce. He crushed her tightly and sank his fangs into her skin.

Instantly his senses were flooded with an overwhelming surge of power. His cells were on fire, electrified with an insane energy, and one only she could provide. Declan took from her, pulling long draws of blood, and it was all sorts of darkness, power, and sex.

She shuddered against him, her slight body melted into his large frame, and he reacted fiercely. He was hard, his body filled with carnal need. Blood and sex.

Ana's fingers crept up to his skull and she wrenched away from him, her chest heaving, her eyes gone fully black. "My turn," she said hoarsely. Her fangs were fully distended, her hair was about her shoulders in a mad tangle of auburn.

She was the most beautiful thing he'd ever encountered and the emotions that pummeled him as she gathered him once more, and sank her fangs into his flesh, was indescribable.

His hand slid down to her ass. He held her tight against his erection and they moved together slowly, their bodies gyrating to a rhythm only they could hear.

Each draw of blood she took from him had his cock twitching hard and he groaned as she continued to feed. Awash in the knowledge that he sustained her. It was a powerful thought. Sobering.

Declan had no clue how long the two of them rocked together, oblivious to their surroundings and the path they'd be taking soon. It could have been minutes or hours.

A not so subtle cough ruined the euphoria and intensity of the moment. Reluctantly he loosened his hold, resting his forehead against hers as they evened out their emotions.

"Snack time's over, kids. Your ride to Lilith's Hell leaves in five minutes."

Declan raised his head and nodded. He glanced down at Ana and knew there was no way to stop her. He shook his head. "Are you sure?"

She nodded but remained silent.

Declan stepped away, rolled his shoulders, and tossed a smile at the demon, Seth. "Let's do this."

Ana followed Seth from the room and he pushed down

the cold lump of fear in his gut. Hell knew, he'd led a life most unexpected. One filled with extreme highs and lows. Was it about to end for real? He knew Lilith would fry him alive if she had the opportunity.

He just hoped he was able to get the teens to safety and his woman out before she did.

CHAPTER 26

The trip to District Three would take about an hour. Seth had arranged for Declan and Ana to replace the guards who escorted newbies sentenced below. They loaded up just outside the dunes and headed into the center of the largest one. A gaping hole opened allowing them entrance and then swallowed them.

The uniforms they'd been given rocked, the fabric was black, light, and form-fitting. Declan told her they were fireproof.

Ana could barely keep her eyes off Declan as he adjusted a pair of dark glasses. Hers were already in place, which was the only reason she could look and not get caught.

She tore her gaze away. The transport shuttle was an elderly piece of crap metal that shook something fierce as they began their descent. The cargo was a motley bunch, an eclectic group of souls that included both human and otherworld. Their fear was thick. The scent of it nearly overwhelming. They'd been aboard for nearly forty-five minutes and she felt the tension rising rapidly, the closer they came to their objective.

Declan stared out into the darkness, his face grim. She felt him pulling away and hated the distance between them.

She sighed as her gaze traveled to the front where a large

glass partition allowed her to see outside the shuttle. They were in a tunnel, one that was similar to a mine shaft. There were overhead bulbs that glowed, the eerie light throwing macabre shadows against rough-hewn walls on either side.

It was hot. The kind of dry heat that burned harsh. Ana's body self-regulated her temperature so she was able to adjust with no difficulty. The humans amongst the bunch, however, were already suffering miserably. She could only imagine what it would be like once they reached their final destination.

She exhaled, leaned against the steel at her back, and closed her eyes. She ached to touch Declan, to keep his body close to hers, but that was impossible. They were guards, not lovers, and it was imperative they keep their cover intact. The potion he'd ingested, the gift from Samael that had bled into her, would keep their scent masked.

It was up to them to do the rest.

She shook her head, a slight smile tugging at her mouth. Even though the circumstance she found herself in was extreme, it wasn't unlike many a mission she'd run with Declan years before.

God, how she missed those days.

Slowly her eyes slid open. A jolt ran through her. Declan's dark eyes were intense as they rested upon her, his glasses gone. They glittered strangely. Instantly her heart sped up and she fought to remain passive. There was much pain reflected in their depths but it was gone just as fast.

She opened her mouth, wanting to whisper some kind of comfort, but he nodded, a sharp jerking motion, and looked away. Ana bit her lip and concentrated on pushing her feelings aside. She needed to tap into the cold bitch that lay in wait, the one who'd do anything to survive and win.

The large weapon she carried was heavy and she adjusted it, her eyes resting on a woman who huddled in a shaking mess two rows back. How the hell she could be cold in this inferno was a mystery. She was filthy, her thin arms covered in needle marks. Her blood scent was sickly, filled with the chemical influence of several different types of illicits. She was young, that was obvious.

Ana wondered how she'd died. What had led her to a path that had taken her straight to Hell. She winced as the woman jerked, her body convulsing in an unnatural manner.

The woman moaned softly, clutched her belly, and then turned to retch. A large shifter sat beside her, his huge frame crammed against the side of the shuttle. He swore loudly and slammed his fist into her face, breaking her nose, sending blood spurting everywhere.

The cry that fell from her mouth was pathetic. Ana took a step forward. It wasn't her nature to stand by and watch the weak take such abuse. The shifter turned his attention to Ana and growled as his hand went around the woman's neck. She struggled as he tightened his grip, yet his gaze remained focused on Ana. The bastard smiled, licked his lips.

She took a step forward, a snarl escaping as she took another. The large weapon she carried was quickly pulled into her arms and she pointed it at the shifter.

"Release her at once."

Declan moved beside her and she was aware that all eyes were now focused on the two of them. She didn't care.

"Do it now or I'll blow your fucking head off."

"You think I care?" the shifter rasped. "I'm already dead and would like nothing more than to escape the shithole I'm headed to." He barred his teeth. "Do it," he goaded.

Another moan slid from between the woman's lips and her legs began to shake as he twisted harder.

"You think if she blows your head off"—Declan nodded toward Ana—"*that* will be your ticket out of District Three?" Declan's gaze traveled the room as he spoke. "Sorry to burst your bubble, asshole, but that ain't the case. You've been sentenced to District Three and that means Lilith has you by the balls for as long as she wants." He aimed his weapon toward the shifter as well and snarled, "Head or no head. She'll put you back together but you won't be as pretty as you are now."

The shifter growled, enraged, and threw the woman onto the floor as he leapt over her. His intent was clear. Ana did not hesitate. She planted a blast dead center of his forehead and felt nothing as his head exploded into a shower of blood, brains, and not much else.

Complete silence filled the shuttle and Ana stepped back, carefully avoiding the mess on the floor. She would have reached for the moaning woman but Declan stepped in front of her.

"Move," he hissed, his voice low.

He then bent down, yanked the woman back to her seat, ignoring her shriek of pain. He glared at the rest of the group. "I don't want to hear so much as a whisper 'cause I sure as hell have no qualms about using the rest of you for target practice." He arched a brow. "Remember, you can't die here unless Lilith wishes it." Declan spit on the headless body. "Trust me, he should have played it cool. Lilith has no patience for this shit. He'll be avoiding mirrors for at least the next century."

Ana took another step back as Declan turned and nailed her with a furious look. He was at her side in a second and bent low, his breath caressing her cheeks as he whispered in her ear.

"You show weakness like that again and we're blown wide open. Everyone will know we're not what we seem. There is no room for mercy down here. At all. Do you understand?"

Ana nodded.

"Move to the door." His voice was dead serious. "And don't do anything."

The shuttle started to shake something fierce. Ana glanced out the windows. Long fingers of mist crawled along the side and then twirled upward, sliding along the stone walls like ribbons of smoke.

Up ahead the heavy weight of gray that blanketed the shaft they traveled was slashed through with a reddish glow. She could see another shuttle in front of them, and beyond several more.

"We're nearly there." Declan watched the prisoners carefully, before cocking his head to the side and speaking in low tones. "Stay close, do not touch anything, and for God sakes, keep your mouth closed."

Ana kept her face calm, uttered not a sound, though inside, every curse word she knew flew about her head.

The shuttle picked up speed and the noise was so loud that nothing else could be heard. Ana stared out the window at the rapidly approaching glow. Hell was not at all what she'd expected.

A screeching sound erupted as the brakes were engaged. The entire cabin shuddered and Ana struggled to keep her footing. Within a few seconds they came to an abrupt halt.

There was nothing but silence. Ana saw the fear in the newbies' faces and her eyes lingered on the addict. Her thin arms were wrapped around her body as she tried to pull some kind of comfort from what little was there.

The doors slid open and two guards appeared, dressed in black like Ana and Declan, with massive weapons held firm in their grasp. They were demon, the scent was unmistakable.

"Let's go," the nearest one shouted.

"Everybody up," Declan said, waving his weapon at them, "and be quick about it. I'm feeling a little antsy."

Ana stood back as the entire shuttle emptied, all prisoners taking care not to step anywhere near the still twitching body of the shifter.

She and Declan followed the last one out and Declan nodded to the large demon closest to him. "We've got a body that needs a pickup."

"No shit." The demon laughed. "There's always at least one." He turned and shouted for a cleanup crew and then smiled at Ana. "You staying with him?"

Ana nodded. "Yep." Her answer was curt and didn't invite conversation.

The demon grinned. Its human facade was in place and she'd be the first to admit he was handsome. Demons thought humanity weak, pathetic, yet they loved playing dress-up in human skin.

How ironic.

"We'll take over from here," Declan interrupted. "Once the cleanup crew is done with the shifter, you boys can head back."

"Yeah, looking forward to some R&R in District One. It's been a while."

Ana followed Declan onto the platform where the group of newbies huddled together. The heat was indeed much worse and she took a moment to study the terrain as Declan consulted with another demon.

The cavern was large, with walls carved from stone that rose to well over two hundred feet in the air. The ceiling was covered in long, deadly, staccato-like stakes. They glistened as if made from glass and a reflection of fire danced inside them. She watched closely, surprised as long drops of water fell from several of them, to splash into steam as they hit the surface.

To her left a smoking river of lava slowly drifted by, disappearing through a crevice at the opposite end of the cavern. In the center of the cavern lay a huge gaping hole. It sported occasional surges of fire, flames that erupted at least fifty feet into the air.

The platform looked like any found in the subway of a

metropolitan city in the human realm. Their shuttle was but one in a long line of nearly one hundred.

The entire scenario was unreal, something out of a nightmare. There were hundreds of bodies milling about. Ana shook her head. By her estimation, at least eighty percent of the occupants on the platform were human, from every race and social status—rich, poor, educated or not.

Sinning, it seemed, knew no boundaries.

It was sad, how easily they were swayed. The demons' influence was much too strong.

No one met her gaze, they were much too afraid.

Regret was a bitch that would eat at them for the rest of their days.

"Okay, we're heading out." Declan indicated their group should follow the long line ahead of them. Two large doors swept open, loud creaks echoing into the cavern as they did so. From between them thick fog swirled outward, falling along the floor like long tentacles.

There was a sickly green tinge to it. Ana heard murmurs, confusion, as unease swept the crowd. There was nowhere to go but through them.

A rumble sounded into the bizarre night. Ana glanced back in time to see the row of shuttles, humming and shaking before they moved backward, heading up to District One.

She bit her lip. They were on their own.

Her eyes found Declan's tall form as he guided their load of prisoners down the path and she quickly fell into step beside him. They didn't speak but the feel of him next to her was enough.

As they neared the large doors a new sound swept into the room; a weird, whistling noise. She glanced at Declan, but his gaze was firmly set ahead, his jaw tense, his mouth tight.

She kept pace with Declan, her gait relaxed, or as relaxed

as a guard in the fucking pits of Hell was supposed to be. When she was finally able to see beyond the door, it took everything inside her to keep her mouth from hanging open.

Sweet motherfu—

"Do not look in their eyes."

The sad souls in front of her, those prisoners on their way to a true hell, were eerily silent.

Ana was aware of movement on all sides, of the ghostly forms with gaping holes in their skulls where their faces should be. Of their maggot-infested hands and feet and the stench that followed in their wake. They floated just above the ground, and the god-awful sound that rushed from the holes in their heads was like nails on chalkboard.

"Keep moving," Declan shouted, shoving the edge of his weapon into the closest body. It was a vampire, and judging from the scent of him, an ancient. The tall, thin male turned and Ana was astonished at the bald fear she saw.

A large body floated close by and the vampire turned to avoid it, but instead the creature moved quickly and the vampire was caught, his eyes bulging out as he stared into the depths of depravity.

He opened his mouth to scream and as the ever-present fog continued to swirl, thicker and faster, the wraithlike creature opened wide. A disgusting suckling sound came from its throat and Ana nearly gagged as it decimated the vampire's face.

Declan forced her to keep going and she ignored the sound as the vampire's limp body fell to the ground, its scream dying inside the wraith's mouth.

Up ahead she saw several similar scenarios. "That is how these creatures are made," Declan whispered. "Do not look at them."

Her heart was beating heavily and sweat broke out along her forehead. It was a true testament to the stress level she was feeling considering it was fucking cold as hell.

Pun intended.

She let her left hand fall to her side into a fist and slowly relaxed, stretching her fingers. His hand was there, ever so briefly, but the touch gave her strength.

Ana kept her eyes averted, concentrated, and blocked out the endless moans and harsh noise that was around her. The wraithlike bodies continued to glide beside them, eagerly searching for new victims. They moved amongst the fog like phantom corps.

After several tense minutes the fog parted, the cold swept away revealing a dull gray chamber, much smaller than the first they'd arrived in. Ana took stock. The group had thinned somewhat; by her estimation it looked like they were missing at least a hundred bodies.

"What is the point?" she was truly bewildered.

"It is a way to cull the weak." Declan muttered before stepping past her. She held her weapon at the ready, her eyes never leaving him, and watched as he consulted with several of the guards.

He motioned toward a dark tunnel to the right but by this point most of the prisoners were hysterical. One of the guards near the front blasted into the crowd, mowing down several of them. It was a sure way to get their attention.

"Move," the demon shouted.

The line shifted forward and one pale, frightened face stood out. It was the young woman—the addict from the shuttle—and she stared at Ana, her entire body trembling.

Though her heart broke, Ana looked away. She couldn't afford the distraction. She was aware of Declan and not much else as she followed behind, her gut twisting as the fear and the tension inside her escalated.

In no time the darkness swallowed her whole.

CHAPTER 27

The darkness, the absolute silence, lasted a mere five seconds. They were through the tunnel and spilled into what could only be described as controlled mayhem.

The lighting was harsh, sterile, and the room resembled a medical lab. It was filled with all sorts of machines, and monitors lined the sides. Several demons shuffled about wearing lab coats, their massive forms looking somewhat comical in such understated attire. They were in their true form and stood nearly eight feet in height.

She watched them walk through the crowd, murmuring amongst themselves as they wrote notes on their clipboards.

"We'll take over from here." Ana tore her eyes away from the prisoners and glanced at a tall guard. His uniform was different than hers. The same crest adorned his left shoulder, but he was dressed head to toe in crimson. He smiled at her and she caught a glimpse of serrated teeth. They were platinum gold.

Declan nodded. "Have fun. They're a pathetic bunch."

The demon laughed and shook his head. "Aren't they always?"

Declan indicated she should follow him. They made their way through the room and paused before two large steel doors. There were several guards in line ahead, waiting. It was a checkpoint and she watched, a sick feeling in her gut, as each of them paused for a full body scan.

"You'll be fine," Declan whispered in her ear. "The serum is active and the chip Seth implanted underneath your forearm is good."

Ana remained silent and when it was her turn she walked forward calmly. The crimson guard looked bored as hell, but he activated the scan while she held her breath and prayed.

Ana DeLacrux had found religion. It had taken only three hundred years.

A tingle of electricity sizzled along her skin as the scan slid over her body, lighting up her flesh in a warm glow. It was over in less than five seconds. The guard pressed a button and shouted, "Next."

A door slid open and Ana moved toward it like a good guard would do, and when it shut behind her the sound reverberated inside her head. The brightness that assaulted her was nearly blinding. She felt the warmth of it on her cheeks and winced as she blinked her eyes in an effort to see clearly.

"You're new here." His voice was harsh and belonged to a guard with the same uniform as she. He was tall, well built, and like so many of the demons she'd met, his facade was human. His eyes, however, were a deep shade of crimson and the intensity of his gaze as they rested upon Ana put her on edge.

She shrugged. "It's been a while." Her eyes widened and though she tried to remain calm, Ana wasn't sure she was successful. She was standing in a freaking meadow, with blue sky and a blazing sun overhead.

She'd not walked in full sunlight. Ever. The closest she'd gotten was an overcast day in the jungles of Belize.

She whirled around and panic clogged her throat. There was nothing but long grass and blue sky for as far as she could see. Scratch that. In the distance a tall tree stood proud, its branches outstretched and full of green foliage.

Was she dead? Had one of the wraiths grabbed her, sucked her dry, and she didn't know it? Where the hell was Declan? Her scan had taken maybe five seconds. She'd been standing here for at least a minute.

"You coming?" the demon asked.

"Uh, where?" she asked hesitantly. There was no way Ana was heading anywhere without her sorcerer.

"To Succubus Blues, the queen's place. I'll buy you a drink and we can have sex."

He would have grabbed her arm but Declan was there, appearing from nowhere.

"She's with me." His voice was curt.

The demon flashed a sloppy smile, "I don't mind sharing. In fact it makes things more interesting."

"Maybe some other time." Declan's hands slipped around her shoulders and he nodded toward the tree. "Let's go."

A second demon appeared from thin air and the tall guard dismissed them, immediately propositioning the male. Guess the dude swung both ways.

"What is this place?" she asked quietly. "I've never in my three hundred years experienced what I've just seen." Ana closed her eyes and drank in the sunlight. "For some, this would be Heaven, not Hell."

"Don't worry," Declan whispered, "this is the only slice of Heaven you'll find down here." They were halfway to the tree.

"It's like the opposite of everything I've ever read or imagined Hell to be."

Declan snorted. "This whole place is a warped version of Lilith's mind and she is fucking psycho."

"What happens to them? The newbies we just brought down?"

"They'll be evaluated and sorted for whatever needs

Lilith has. If they're lucky, they won't catch her eye. They'll be sentenced to grunt work in the bowels of District Three for eternity."

"That sounds pretty harsh."

"Those souls are the worst kind of fucking crap there is, Ana. Murderers, drug pushers, rapists, and pedophiles. Why do you care?"

She thought of the pale woman from the shuttle. "I just . . . I think some of them are lost and not through their own fault. If they had a light in their lives, a chance to grow without darkness, they'd be different."

He shrugged dismissing her softness. "At least they have a chance to work their way out, make it up to District One. It's not so bad up there."

Ana paused, moistened her lips, and asked the question that had been haunting her forever, it seemed.

"Where did you end up . . . when you were down here?"

They'd reached the tree. The trunk was massive, spanning nearly eight feet in width. The thickness of the canopy blocked out the sun and the coolness of shade caressed her cheeks. She welcomed it, not used to the sun.

Declan glanced behind them. The two guards were still several hundred feet away.

He turned, looked down at her, his lips tight. He blew out a hot breath and spoke quietly. "I caught her eye."

They stared at each other for several long moments and Declan moved so that his hand hovered over the bark of the tree. "Stay close to me and be silent. I'll do the talking if need be. We don't have a lot of time."

Ana nodded and then grabbed his arm. "She won't be there, will she? In this Succubus place?"

"I hope not," Declan said as his hand slammed against the bark. "We didn't exactly part on good terms."

The tree shimmered and Ana watched in astonishment as the center liquefied. It expanded and then melted away leaving a gaping hole big enough for them to walk through. Seriously, Hell would be a lot easier to navigate, to *understand*, if it was actually the fire and brimstone she'd imagined. This was just weird. The only lingering connection was the ever-present aroma of sulfur.

"After you," Declan said.

Ana didn't hesitate even though everything inside her was screaming no. She squared her shoulders and stepped through.

Cold dread sat like a lump in Declan's gut as he followed Ana through the portal. Long-ago memories threatened, but he pushed them back fiercely. He would not relive the horrors from his time here.

Yet they were always there: images of long blond hair, entwined limbs, and the rot of evil.

As soon as they cleared the threshold, the insanity that was Succubus Blues embraced them fully. The music, the mayhem, the drugs—most of all, the scent of fear and the taste of pain.

Happy hour was in full swing, but then again it was always happy hour down here. An overabundance of illicits and alcohol fueled the crowd into a frenzy most nights and there were always casualties. The bodies were piled outside in the square, taken back to the bowels of District Three. There they'd regenerate so that their pitiful existence could happen all over again.

It was a true fact. There was no escaping District Three or the reach of Lilith.

As far as he knew, no one but he and Julian Castille had managed to do it, and that was only because of Bill. If the little bastard hadn't pulled Declan's ass out when he did, there was no telling what he would've become.

No, it definitely wouldn't serve him well to run into Lilith until he was ready.

Declan flexed his fingers, felt the power that lay beneath his flesh. It was there, not cut from him like before, impotent and useless.

He glanced at his timepiece. They had less than two hours to accomplish their goal. Seth said he'd have a shuttle waiting for them, commandeered by one of his own men. If they didn't haul ass and get back to the platform by the agreed upon time, they'd be stuck in District Three indefinitely. There would be no changeover for the guards for at least another two weeks.

His gaze rested upon Ana's small form. The serum he'd gotten from Samael would never last that long.

"What now?" Ana asked, her eyes trained ahead, taking everything in.

They stepped out of the way, letting the two guards who'd been behind them by.

"Follow me and remember what I said, no—."

"Talking," she interrupted sarcastically. "I get it, you Tarzan, me Jane."

In the midst of all the chaos that surrounded him, he fought a smile. "That would be right," he murmured, and added, "Keep your eyes low, do not encourage contact with anyone."

They'd given up their weapons at the last checkpoint. No one was allowed any sort of weaponry in this part of district three. Lilith preferred her subjects dummied down to their basest natures—which, considering they were in fact demons, meant that a lot of physical pain was doled out hourly. Disagreements were settled the old-fashioned way. If you didn't like someone, you kicked the crap out of them and moved on.

The two of them slid through the crowd, avoiding spilled beer, the occasional mess of spilled guts, and an abundance of crude jokes and come-ons. A band was onstage, loud guitars wailing and hypnotic vocals falling from the singer.

He ignored all of it and stayed the course, following a direct path to the doors on the opposite end of the club. They led to the square, the central gathering place here in Lilith's corner of District Three. From there they'd make their way to the bitch's palatial estate.

He shouldered his way outside, grunting from the effort it took. He knew Lilith would never stash something as valuable as those children anywhere but close to her.

He gritted his teeth. He knew exactly where they'd be, or at least hoped he did.

The square was empty, which wasn't surprising considering the party was full tilt inside Succubus Blues.

"Unreal," Ana whispered as they walked along the silent street. Shops lined either side, facades that said Gucci, Tiffany and Harrods.

"Lilith loves Hollywood. Everything about it. Her favorite movie is *Pretty Woman.*" Hell, she quoted the lines verbatim, played the role of Vivian with ease, whore that she was, except she didn't have the required heart of gold.

"I'm not surprised," she murmured. "This has got to be the craziest, most screwed-up place on earth."

Declan snorted. "You haven't seen anything yet."

They continued along the street until they reached the end where a wall of black hid anything beyond a few inches. It was as if the world, or *this* world, ended.

"This way," he said, a little impatiently as she hesitated.

"But there's nothing here."

"Not that you can see."

Declan glanced around and when he was sure there was no one about, drew a spell in the air. His fingers sizzled with the powerful energy inside him, and he smiled harshly as the translucent weave of magick shimmered and then disappeared.

He'd have to thank Lilith if he got the opportunity. She'd fed him steadily for six months.

He let his hands rest as the blanket of dark peeled away like the rind of an orange.

"Jesus." Ana moved a few paces away. "I've never seen anything like it."

Declan paused as he gazed across the vast expanse of manicured lawns and gardens. He saw two black swans in the distance, slowly circling the large pond that was dead center. Behind them, sitting upon a hill, was her home.

"It looks like—"

"Buckingham Palace, I know."

"Is this *Alice in Wonderland*? 'Cause it sure as hell feels like it."

Declan grabbed Ana's hand. "We don't have a lot of time."

He pushed her through and followed as he waved his hand in the air. Instantly the darkness slid into place behind them.

The soft strains of a harp drifted on the breeze. A garden party. How she loved her garden parties. The notes were sad, melancholy, and some were off key, the pitch all wrong. The music was laced with a dark undertone. Such was the way of it here, nothing was as it seemed.

Declan nodded toward the trees. "The serum will block our signatures but we need to proceed with caution. I want as little contact as possible."

Once they gained the cool interior of the pine forest that lined the estate, he came to a full stop, his eyes falling to Ana's pale face. She looked up at him, her expression earnest, fierce, and the wave of longing, the intense love he felt for her tightened his chest. He found it difficult to breathe and rasped loudly as he bent over, his hands resting upon his upper thighs.

If something happened to his vampire . . .

Her hand was at his back and slowly traveled up until she sank her fingers into the thickness of his hair.

"Declan."

He straightened and pulled her close, his chin resting

upon the top of her head as he took a few moments to savor the feel of her in his arms. He groaned as a vision of her atop him rolled before his eyes, her small breasts full and round, jiggling slightly as she rode him hard.

He looked into her eyes. The deep blue depths held such secrets, such desire and promise. He cupped her chin, held her jaw steady.

Such love.

She inhaled. Her heart beat rapidly against his and he bent low. His lips scraped the softness of hers and with a groan he opened wide, taking her mouth with an aggression that signaled how close to the edge he was riding. She answered in kind and he knew they both were there. Near the precipice.

He hoped like hell they didn't fall in.

She pulled away and he felt the sharp prick of her teeth upon his neck, and his mouth watered with anticipation as she broke skin. It was over quickly and she offered her neck to him.

"Drink, Declan," she said hoarsely. "You need it."

He didn't hesitate, his fangs were ready, and when he was done, when he licked the last of her precious blood from his lips, he cradled her head once more and kissed her mouth. It was a gentle pass, filled with much emotion.

"I love you, Ana DeLacrux. Remember that."

Ana pulled away from him, her brow furrowed. "That sounded like good-bye, not a declaration of love. *Remember that.* What's that supposed to mean? The last time you said that corny line you knocked me out with a goddamn sleeping charm." She was angry now. He could see it.

His gut told him the truth. Things might not end well but it wasn't for the reasons she was thinking. Declan was confident he'd get the children out. He would do whatever it took to get them and Ana back to the platform in time.

"I'm not saying good-bye Ana, I just . . ." his voice trailed off as he looked into the distance. The house was barely visible through the trees, but he didn't need to see it to remember. To know that the evil she'd tainted him with lived inside his soul, no matter that he'd hidden it. He could feel the sickness of it rushing through his veins.

He'd been weak and would pay the price forever.

But would Ana be willing to stay with him? When she found out the truth?

"What are you afraid of, Declan?"

She whirled around. The wind lifted long tendrils of hair that had escaped the tether at her nape, and they snaked into the wind. Her skin was rosy, flush from a feed, and her eyes were jeweled blue.

No good could come from this conversation. He would not confess his sins to her. He wasn't ready.

"We need to go," he said roughly as he tapped his timepiece. "Not sit here, hold hands, and sing 'Kumbaya.' Time's running out."

She was before him in less than a second, her body a blur, her heat upon him as her eyes flashed. She was more than pissed. Declan would hazard a guess the vampire was livid.

"Whatever the hell baggage you're carrying must go." She swallowed and his gaze rested upon the delicate lines of her throat. He saw the twin marks that were there, near the crook. His marks.

Her hands slipped up and she caressed the stubble that now shadowed his cheeks. "I don't care about any of it." She shook her head. "I don't, Declan. Every moment of our lives has shaped us into what we are. Every decision, every act . . . all of it."

He tried to jerk his head away but she held firm. "Listen to me, sorcerer. I love you. All of you. What you were and what you are now." She rose on her toes and kissed him gently, before turning to whisper into his ear. "So don't you dare say good-bye to me."

Declan pulled away. "I think you'd change your mind if you knew the juicy details of my stay here in Club Lilith."

"No."

There was no time to argue the point. He'd let fate come into play, there was no other choice.

"Let's go." They crept through the forest, the off-key lilt of the harp calling them like the Pied Piper.

CHAPTER 28

Shouts of joy, mingled with screams of pain, echoed into the sky as they approached the main house. Declan winced as a particularly loud moan of anguish went on and on.

"What are they doing?" Ana's brow was furled; concern lined her features.

"You don't want to know."

"But—"

He put his hand on her forearm. "Trust me on this and leave it alone." He nodded toward the palace. "We're damn lucky Lilith is having one of her *parties*, it will make it easier to get inside."

They'd just passed the pond, and the black swans paid them no mind as they crept closer to a large garden. It was picture-perfect. A slice of English summer with a border of rosebushes and a lush green maze set out before them. Overhead, the robin egg sky warmed his face.

He ignored it all. He knew it was nothing more than an illusion, a fake skin to cover the truest of evils.

"This way." Declan pointed toward the maze. "We'll go through the maze. It's the only way to remain unseen from those attending Lilith's garden party."

They slipped inside and immediately there was a drop in temperature. The lush boxwood was nearly eight feet in height and afforded the best cover possible. But it was dangerous. This he knew from personal experience.

"Stay close and don't—"

"I know, touch anything. For fuck sakes, O'Hara, you sound like a broken record."

He blew a hot breath but didn't bother replying. Instead he concentrated, drawing upon the well of power that sat in his gut. The energy was hot, licked at his insides with hunger.

He held his fingers loose. He was ready.

Swiftly they maneuvered down the narrow path, his feet sure, his gait steady. He'd run through them before, wet, cold, out of his head in pain, and it felt like yesterday.

Sweat broke out along his brow and he wiped it away impatiently. They came upon a break in the path, a fork that led to two possibilities. Without hesitation Declan turned to the right and came to an abrupt halt.

A large animal sat on its haunches, sides heaving, mouth frothing. It was a hellhound and its eyes burned crimson as it flashed an impressive set of canines and growled.

"Shit," Ana said. "That does not look like a friendly. Can't we go the other way?"

He rolled his shoulders and shook out his arms. "Nope."

"That's what I thought you were going to say."

She cracked a smile, and in spite of the gravity of the situation, there was a hint of laughter in her voice. For a second, his here-and-now faded to nothing but her eyes. They were like liquid cobalt and reflected the deepest parts of her soul. Her fierce loyalty, her passion . . . her love.

He knew he'd never find another woman like her, no matter what realm his ass happened to be parked in. He reached for her and claimed her lips, eating her surprise as he opened wide. Declan kissed hard and fast and when he wrenched his mouth from hers, he whispered, "I'll do whatever it takes to get us out of here, to make a life with you."

He stared into her eyes, aware the hellhound was now on its feet, panting heavily twenty feet from them.

"Okay," she whispered, "you might want to start with the fire-breathing fur ball."

The hellhound snarled and took off, its long legs gathering speed as it gunned straight toward them. Declan whirled around, his arms going wide as the power inside erupted. He pushed Ana back and sank to one knee, smiling into the dead eyes coming at him.

The power inside spiked hard, like an electric shock of energy. He grunted, relishing the feel of it as it rushed through his body. He cocked his head to the side, felt it burn through his mind, and kept his eyes trained on the animal. When it jumped up at him, his hand shot out and clamped around the hellhound's neck. He held the beast firm and bared his teeth as he forced the animal to the ground.

He could have killed it. Easily.

Slowly he stood and let go. The hellhound was trembling and fell to the ground. It rolled onto its back, tail between its legs, and began to cry.

"What a pussy," Ana murmured. "How'd you do that?"

"I TiVo *The Dog Whisperer* every week."

He pulled her past the hellhound, smiled as she snorted. "You're full of crap."

"Yeah, I am."

Silently they cut through the maze without incident and in no time stood near the exit. Ten feet away was a terrace and beyond that garden doors.

The haunting sounds of the harp still echoed around them, the notes wrapped around laughter and pain.

He stepped forward, took a cautious glance around, and turned to Ana. "We need to be quick here. From this point until we reach those doors our asses are on the line, totally exposed. Understand? Invisibility charms don't work down here."

She nodded, her face grim. "Like the wind," she said, and before he could react she was gone.

Her preternatural speed carried her forward so quickly, the only evidence left behind was the gentle rustle of the large potted plants that lined the stone steps.

"Son of a bitch," he muttered as he took off after her, pleasantly surprised when he was able to navigate just as fast. No doubt due to his vamped-up blood.

Declan closed the door behind him and stilled. He was assaulted by the scents of lavender, licorice, and fear. A god-awful combination.

The sound of flies buzzing about rang in his ears, and he shook his head in an effort to clear it. Nothing had changed.

"You okay?"

They were in the dining room. Sunlight streamed through the windows, the beams falling upon a table in disarray. Food that had been left out was rotting, meat already infested with maggots. Glasses were overturned, wine spilled along the floor, and as he approached the table, the scent of blood was added to the mix.

And sex. The unmistakable musk was everywhere.

Ana was talking to him but the words were just sounds. His mind was spinning and images flashed before him, memories from his time here. In this room.

He backed away from the table and swallowed though his throat was dry, his tongue like sandpaper.

"Declan!" Her whisper was harsh, but it was the clawlike ends of her nails that finally snapped him out of it. She dug into his flesh and drew blood.

"We need to go."

Declan gave himself a mental smack down and felt instant relief when the sounds, smells, and images disappeared.

"This way." His tone was urgent as he headed for the exit.

They immediately headed upstairs. There was not a soul

around—no sound to be heard except faint noises coming from the party at the back of the grounds.

"Are you sure she's outside?"

They'd reached the landing and Declan crossed to an impressive window. Its treatment was heavy damask; the crimson folds ran floor to ceiling as if encasing the glass in blood. He stood to the side and gazed down at the orgy below.

Lilith was in the middle of it all. She was hard to miss. Her long blond hair hung in silken waves to her ass and her lithe form was covered by the thinnest of silk that did nothing but enhance her figure.

She reclined on a settee of satin, drinking wine and watching her subjects engage in all sorts of nasty business. Her left hand clutched a whip. His mouth tightened. How he'd love to wrap the fucking thing around her neck and pull until her eyes popped.

"Never mind, I see her," Ana whispered as she stepped close to him. "She's beautiful."

"She's an evil bitch and I hope to never lay eyes on her again." He turned. "Down here."

The hall narrowed into a thin line as he gazed toward the opposite end. Her private quarters were there, the double doors nondescript. How fucking ironic.

He made his way there quickly, his footfalls silent on the luxuriously thick carpet.

"Why are there no guards here? It seems careless." Ana frowned and shook her head. "It doesn't make sense."

Declan snorted. "Sheer arrogance on her part, but be prepared. Once we gain access it will be a different story." He nodded. "Stand back."

He waited until Ana was a safe distance away and then closed his eyes, concentrating, willing the magick inside him to triple in strength. It stirred. He felt it like a fist in his gut, pushing forward, reaching for him.

Declan's hands were inches from the door and he began to weave a spell into the air. Her wards were powerful and he concentrated as his charm shone in luminescent splendor. They were long, spidery fingers that bled into the door, infiltrating her protection ward with tenacious intent, like a parasite on the rampage.

When he heard a slight click, Declan's eyes flew open and he paused. His heart was beating steadily, his nerves cracking wide open.

Declan squared his shoulders and reached for the handle. It was time to face his demons.

Ana reached for him, her fingers inches from his back, but Declan turned the latch and the door swept away. He stepped through and she followed suit.

And her mouth fell open. Literally.

Lilith's private quarters were the most opulent, gaudy, shiny, and disturbing rooms she'd ever seen. In the middle of it, on a raised dais, was a massive bed. It was round and draped in layers of velvet and satin. Red and black seemed to be Lilith's colors of choice, and the gauze that fell from the ceiling to embrace one half of the bed was shot through with both.

The covers were rumpled and the smell of sex permeated everything. Ana made a face and turned away but not before an image of Declan, naked on the sheets, assaulted her.

Declan was staring at her, his expression unreadable. Something flickered in his eyes, a flash of pain? Regret?

She opened her mouth to speak and closed it again. There, behind Declan, was a man chained to the wall. He was unconscious but his bindings kept him upright. She sniffed. He was human, tall, and from what Ana could see, Hollywood handsome. He looked vaguely familiar. Her eyes widened when she realized who it was.

Jack something or other, an actor who'd died several

months earlier. A result of too much partying and too many illicits.

What a waste.

He was naked; his torso was covered in a series of marks that were red and raw. She saw more of them along his inner thigh.

"What are those wounds?" She watched Declan closely. He paused before answering and she knew he was uncomfortable.

"Lilith is a succubus. She feeds her power through sex." He nodded toward the unconscious man. "Those would be teeth marks."

Ana's gaze fell once more to the actor. "I bet he never thought this is what his end would be," she murmured.

Declan scooped up a large dagger that had been lying on the floor. It was stained crimson. He stared at it for a moment and then tossed it to Ana. She grabbed it, held it tight. Her nostrils flared as she inhaled the putrid scent of stale blood.

Declan shrugged. "He made his bed, now he'll be lying in Lilith's until she grows tired of him and moves on." His eyes narrowed. "Everyone down here has a touch of darkness in them, Ana. Don't feel sorry for them." He nodded toward the human. "That is no innocent, but a man who was weak and danced on the dark side. He lost and now he's Lilith's bitch."

She knew he was right, but it didn't negate the sadness of the situation. Her mind was asking questions, things about Declan's stay that she had no right to ask.

But she had to wonder. Had her lover suffered like the human chained to the wall? She thought of the scars that adorned his chest.

I caught her eye.

His words echoed in her brain and she took a step forward, hand outstretched.

"No," he said softly. "I can't go there."

Ana pulled back. "Okay. Let's get the children." She glanced around the large room, her gaze shifting past the gaudy furniture, the reams of clothes that adorned the floor.

Beside the bed was a table, and once again the remnants of rotting food were present, along with several bottles of wine and a plate of sweets. The flies were thick, their buzzing the only thing she heard past the beating of her heart.

"Where are they?" she asked, tearing her gaze away.

Declan answered, the sound muffled, "In here."

She found him inside a walk-in closet that was the size of the entire main floor of her house in New Orleans. Again it was a disaster. Clothes were strewn everywhere, as were jewelry, shoes, and expensive bags of every brand known to man.

"You think she'd employ a maid," Ana mumbled.

Declan stood before a nondescript door. It was between two large armoires.

His fists were slowly unclenching, long fingers stretching out before tightening up once again. Ana slid beside him and grabbed his hand into hers. She looked up at Declan, saw the pain though he tried to hide it, and she held his wrist against her cheek.

She didn't say anything. It was enough to just be with him.

He gently extracted his hand from hers. It was time.

Declan's face was grim. "Our objective is to get the kids out safely." He arched a brow. "Understand?"

She nodded.

"I'll get us in. They'll be on the left side of the room—bound, of course—but you should have no problem setting them free. There will be a hellhound or two. Do you think you can handle them?"

And held the deadly dagger he'd given her loosely in her hands and smiled. "I don't think I'll have a problem."

"Good. Concentrate on the kids and leave the others to me."

"The others?"

Declan shook his head. "Don't ask and don't look at them. They make those maggot-infested shitheads look like playthings." He glanced at his timepiece. "We have exactly one hour to get back to the platform or we're on fucking vacation in the land of the lost."

Adrenaline pumped through her. Ana cracked her neck. She was ready. "Okay, let's do this."

"One more thing . . ." She looked at him questioningly and stilled as his lips descended to brush over hers with a whisper of heat.

"Be safe, and when I say run, you run, got it? Do not hesitate. Get those kids out and into the forest." He opened his hand and she stared at a glimmering ball of energy. "Take this."

It was hot in her palm and quickly hardened into a solid mass. "What is it?"

"If something happens, if we get separated, use this to open the black shield at the end of the forest where we came in. You'll have to retrace your steps to get back to the platform." He paused. "Succubus Blues has a direct portal to the platform. It's on the upper level."

She shook her head, opened her mouth, but Declan gave her no time to speak. His eyes were intense. "There's nothing to say. The situation is what it is. I need to know if you'll get them out, back to Succubus Blues without me if need be. That's why we're here."

She nodded as Declan stepped back. He could believe what he wanted. There was no way she would leave him behind.

"Ready?"

Ana stared at the door. She let out a breath, centered herself, and prepared to fight.

CHAPTER 29

The memories inside Declan's head sickened him. He wanted to close his eyes and push them away. He wanted to hang his head in shame.

Instead he focused and took all the pain, hatred, and fear inside his soul and fed on the darkness that accompanied them. It was powerful shit and at the moment he'd tap into anything he could find.

Declan glanced at Ana. His love for her was also full of a power he could tap into and use.

It gathered in his gut and he held his hands outward, palms up, as the energy inside him burned and pulsed. It traveled through his veins, firing his cells and infusing them with his powerful essence.

His senses were in hyper mode. Since he'd taken from Ana, fed from her, everything was much more vibrant, *clear*, and his nostrils twitched as the scents that surrounded him settled in his chest.

He stared at the door in front of him and had a moment when everything faded away, like a wall of reality had been peeled back. He heard the breaths falling from his chest, the flies buzzing madly around the food and the screams.

They filled his head, gaining strength as they ripped along his skull. How many had he watched suffer at her hands? How many times had he participated in their torture?

Anguish sat in him. It was heavy but he ignored it and instead focused on the absolute hatred he felt for Lilith. It was potent—exactly what he needed to fuel his magick.

He touched the handle and winced as a bolt of energy shot up his hand. Lilith's wards were strong but not nearly strong enough to keep him out. He smiled.

Dumb, arrogant bitch.

Declan whispered ancient words, *powerful* words, while his fingers wove a tapestry of magick in the air. They were beautiful, luminescent patterns that shimmered for several seconds before disappearing. As his hands worked faster, his breaths increased, his heart beat madly in anticipation.

His fangs broke skin.

He smiled as Lilith's protection wards started to crack, and when he felt them crumble he looked to Ana. She stared up at him and he was humbled that she was willing to risk her life for him.

"Let's do this," she whispered. He saw the tips of her fangs, white against the red of her lips, and his heart ached. Ana DeLacrux was his and he would do whatever it took to claim their destiny.

He just needed to take care of a few things first.

He blew out a hot breath and flexed his fingers. They were ready.

"You get to those kids and let me deal with the others. If all goes well we'll make it out at the same time. If not . . ." He shook his head as his words drifted into silence.

Her eyes shone something fierce and a blush rose in her pale cheeks. "I'll get them to safety, but I'm telling you right now if you don't get your ass out, I will come back for you."

A spark of anger touched him and Declan frowned. "You will do no such thing."

She rolled her shoulders and tucked a long strand of hair

behind her ear. "First of all, you're not the boss of me." She glanced up at him, and unease rifled through Declan. The look on her face was one he was familiar with. He didn't like it. It usually meant the shit was about to—

"And secondly, I'm sick of this place. It's dirty, cold, full of creeps, *and* I need a bath. A long, hot soak in the tub. So I suggest you"—her booted foot shot out and splintered the door in two—"get your ass in gear 'cause I'm done talking."

Son of a bitch!

The door was now on its hinges and she was through it before he had a chance to react.

"If you're a good boy I'll let you join me." Her words drifted back to him and galvanized him into action.

Declan jumped through, his hands loose and ready, his fingertips sizzling as his magick burned hot.

He was hit with a wall of cold, his nostrils tightening in reaction as he exhaled. The smell of fear, pain, and suffering was tenfold. Fog slithered along the floor, licking his legs as he stood, gathering his bearings. It was the same as he remembered. A large, cavernlike space, with cold, wet stone walls that jutted up nearly twenty feet.

Water dripped constantly, the sound of it echoing into the silence—which was thick, solid, and eerie.

The entire room was a wash of gray. There was no color, no life—only a dull palette of pain.

Images, scenes from his past, played out in front of him, and Declan had to blink his eyes in an effort to banish them. Yet he could taste it, *feel it* in his mind, and the intensity of them hit hard.

Long blond hair, limbs entwined around his own— blood—there was always so much blood. Screams and the echoes of long-ago sins.

"Declan!"

He shook his head and stared down into the face of the one woman who could save him.

"Let's do this. You and I. Don't let the ghosts overshadow you."

Swiftly his lips grazed hers, his tongue passing over her mouth, infusing her body with a hot zap of energy. Her eyes widened, their liquid depths glistening, and she smiled.

"I love you," she whispered, and turned away, disappearing into the swirling fog.

Hissing noises intruded on the moment and Declan squared his shoulders, his arms flung wide as he turned to face Lilith's pets. A savage smile tore at his mouth and he moved forward with purpose. He was no longer a weak, castrated man, but a sorcerer filled with power, infused with the strength of a vampire.

"Come on, you slimy bastards." His eyes carefully scanned the room. "Let's have at it."

The tallest one appeared first, his massive frame emerging from the mist in a lazy I-don't-give-a-fuck kind of way. The creature was well over eight feet in height, humanoid in looks except for the fact that its skin was hard-shelled scales that shone an iridescent blue.

And it had two heads.

Two sets of eyes were trained on him, both glowing crimson as two long, forked tongues flickered out into the air, testing the vibrations that hung there. He knew the demon couldn't see all that well, but its sense of smell was powerful.

The mouths opened and spoke in unison. "We are surprised you've returned." A hiss escaped, like air leaving a balloon. "We look forward to imparting much pain. The queen will be pleased."

Declan was light on his feet as he moved to the right. "I see you boys still talk like E.T." He flashed a smile. "Want some Reese's Pieces?" His smile turned dark and he snarled, "Or would you prefer I send your fucking ass home?"

The tall creature hissed loudly and rushed him, its long arms outstretched, the claws deadly sharp. They could cut out his entrails in one swipe. He'd seen it up close and personal on several occasions.

Declan ran toward the beast, his hand outstretched, and blasted as much energy as he could, aiming dead center for its chest. He managed to knock the bastard off its feet, but wasn't certain if it was from the strength of his hit or the fact he'd surprised the crap out of him. Of course the demon would assume he was still powerless.

An agonized roar fell from its lips and it flailed madly in an effort to gain its footing. The beast was massive, clumsy. Declan leapt over it, barely managing to avoid a swipe of its claws, when a shadow moved to his left and caught his eye.

Declan tucked his body into a roll and hit the stone floor hard, yet still the heat of a bullet cut through the air where his body had just been. He called the shadows to his form, knowing it wasn't foolproof.

He moved with stealth, tapping into the preternatural speed he wasn't yet used to. In less time than it took to blink, he was behind the second creature. This one was demon, not nearly as large or as fierce as the two-headed bastard on the floor.

Declan's hands went around its neck in one swift move and he snapped it, then threw the demon to the floor. He needed to move quickly. Nothing died down here and he knew it would be on its feet in no time. Its neck would still be broken, bent at an unnatural angle, but it would be mobile, therefore dangerous.

He grabbed the weapon from its hands and stalked over to the two-headed creature. It was up, both heads frothing at the mouth, spittle flying in all directions.

"We will kill you," it shouted like a petulant child, its body trembling with anger.

Declan shook his head. "You could try, douche bags, but the only one who can do the killing would be your queen, and she's busy having sex with a goat in the garden."

The creature bellowed in rage. "Do not speak of her." It rushed him, a blur of madness. Declan aimed his weapon and fired off two shots in rapid succession, planting two bullets right where they mattered most, between the beast's eyes.

It kept on, but he held out his hand and as the creature began to wobble, Declan's magick held it aloft. He increased his hold and watched as the creature trembled and struggled to breathe. Shock and surprise appeared within the depths of its eyes.

"Not so much fun when the playing field is even," Declan growled.

"We will kill you." It managed to squeeze the words out though they were weak.

Declan snorted. "I don't think so, ass wipe." He turned, smiling as he heard it fall to the ground. He had mere minutes before it, too, would be up and about, gunning for his ass. He heaved the weapon over his shoulder and slid deeper into the fog.

The enemy he sought was still here, hiding from him. Other than Lilith, this was the one piece-of-shit entity he dreamed of nightly. Was it man or woman? He had no clue. The bastard changed skins as easily as a snake.

Declan had no more time to play games. He snarled into the gray mist. "Show yourself, dickhead. I know you're here."

A tingle of energy slithered along his skin and then the air rippled, creating a swirl of mist that evaporated into nothing. A space opened up, like a black hole, and a shape materialized.

He saw a face he'd thought never to look upon again, but really, should he be surprised?

Father.

Declan stared into the cold, dark eyes of Cormac O'Hara and smiled as the energy inside him stirred hot.

Was it really his father? Or the skin shifter demon he'd come to know so well during his stay here? Did it matter?

The familiar face cracked as a stiff smile swept over his features. He saw the nostrils flare as he gazed behind Declan. White teeth showed brightly as he smiled in wonder. They were serrated. It was definitely not his father, but he'd play along.

"I smell Ana DeLacrux. I thought I nailed that bitch cold. How in the hell did your vampire come back from the dead?"

Declan glared at him, his face darkened with anger. He knew the skin shifter showed itself in any form it thought would bring mental pain. Hell, how many times had it appeared as Ana? How many times had he been forced to watch the woman he loved engage in all sorts of sordid acts?

"This must be my lucky day," Declan said, his voice deadly as a sneer lifted the corners of his mouth. His father held no sway where he was concerned.

Cormac O'Hara's frosty eyes narrowed into twin slits of blackness. "How so?" the shifter asked, his voice silky smooth.

Declan took a step forward and glowered. "Because I get to kick my father's ass again and then I'll have the pleasure of blasting him into tiny little pieces." He flexed his fingers and growled, "Again."

"Come now. Is that any way to speak to dear old dad? The man responsible for giving you life?" The skin shifter's eyes narrowed. "For giving you power?"

Declan snarled. "He was nothing more than a sperm donor."

"His blood flows inside you and that is not something you can deny."

Declan watched as the shifter moved toward him. He waited, held his power tight. He needed the right moment.

The fog continued to swirl, faster and thicker. Declan heard a groan behind him, followed by a bellow of pain. He knew he had to act quickly.

"You think to steal the two marks from the queen?" The skin shifter's voice was low, neutral, yet Declan sensed the anger that simmered below the surface.

He shrugged. "They don't belong to her."

"You arrogant piece of shit," he spat, and then lunged.

Declan was ready. He blasted an energy shot into the floor, using the force of it to propel himself up and over the shifter. He landed behind him, hard, and grunted from the force of it as he rolled to the side and was on his feet in a second.

With his right hand he drew a charm in the air and with his left he shot another energy bolt directly at the shifter's chest. The eyes, so like his father's, blazed with a blackness that glittered like diamonds.

It did nothing more than slow the skin shifter down, and the creature bellowed in rage. Declan watched as his fingers elongated, the tips lengthening into razor-sharp claws. He waved his hands in the air.

"I'm sure you remember the pain these bring."

Declan's chest began to burn and the scars that had been embedded deep within his skin tingled painfully. Hell yeah, he remembered. After the bitch with the dagger was done with him and had torn his skin to shit, the skin shifter loved to run his long claws along Declan's raw flesh. Sometimes he'd poke around inside, twisting and turning, while Lilith watched with her entourage.

The pain had been incredible and Declan was ashamed to admit that after months of abuse, he'd been broken. The darkness—*Lilith*—had been much too strong.

That was when he'd truly danced with the devil and it was only because of Bill that he'd not surrendered wholly. He was man enough to admit that if the little bastard hadn't yanked his ass out of Hell, he'd still be Lilith's bitch, tied up to the wall in the outer sanctum.

Engaging in all sorts of unspeakable acts.

He snarled and faced the skin shifter. "I remember everything, asshole." A harsh smile swept over his face. "Like how pathetic you are. Always under Lilith's skirts, begging for a piece of ass you'll never get."

"You will not speak of her in such a manner." The shifter was livid and his words echoed into the air, falling like stones in the quiet. "She is our queen and respect is called for."

Declan was nearly finished with his charm. "Respect is earned. You should know that. You've been groveling for, what, ten thousand years? And you're still the douche who hides in the corner. Playing dress-up for Lilith when she commands," he snarled, "wearing whatever face she desires, and watching her fuck anything and everything while your lust is never satiated."

The skin shifter's eyes bulged and for a moment the air around him shimmered. Declan chanted ancient words in his head but he stopped as the face and form in front of him changed. His father's countenance disappeared and it was now Ana who stood before him, her tight, lithe form clad in sheer wisps of gauze.

"I watched you have sex with Lilith," she purred, her legs moving slowly as she moved toward him. "I watched her feed from you as you screwed her in every way possible."

Declan tried to ignore the words, tried to maintain his composure and work his charm, but it was difficult.

"I watched your face as you spread her legs and inhaled the darkness that clings to her like candy." Laughter fell from the shifter's lips and Declan gritted his teeth. "It's like a drug, no?"

Don't let him fuck with your mind.

Ana's visage wavered and then she was gone. Nothing but silence and cool air filled the space where she'd been.

Declan exhaled a long, torturous breath and as quick as he blinked, Lilith stood before him. She was naked, her long blond hair falling about her perfect, alabaster skin in silken

waves. Her blue eyes were iridescent. They shone like bea-
cons, little pieces of the artificial sky from outside.

She opened her mouth and smiled widely, her teeth even
and pearly white. Alarm rifled through Declan.

Her hands tweaked the tips of her rose-colored nipples
and as they moved lower, down to the golden thatch between
her legs, he noticed the necklace that swung between her
breasts.

Bingo. Nefertari's stone.

Small giggles fell from her lips. "Declan, I knew you'd
come back to me." Her face darkened, and for a second, her
true self was revealed. It was ugly, vengeful, petulant. He
knew this was no longer the skin shifter, but the real deal.

His eyes narrowed. The game had just changed.

She licked her lips as a slow grin crept over her features.
"I've been starving since you left."

CHAPTER 30

The stone floor was damp and each cautious step Ana took echoed much too loudly. She tried to be careful but it was no use. At this rate she might as well scream and announce her entrance.

The steady drip of water mingled with the rapid breaths that fell from her mouth. Her senses had kicked into overdrive and an adrenaline rush fed her body. She glanced ahead and though her eyes usually had no trouble seeing in the dark, down here the thickness of it was nearly impenetrable.

The dagger was held loosely in her hands and her muscles screamed for action.

She heard muffled sounds from behind her, but they were distorted, and that made her nervous.

Her booted foot hit a rock or something like it and she cursed as it went flying, scraping across the floor as it rolled.

"You've got to be kidding," she muttered, and stopped as a foreign scent rifled across the cool wet air. She inhaled sharply and gripped the dagger a little tighter. "Come to mama, you little piece of—"

Her words were cut off as two red eyes appeared a few feet from her. They were as high as her chest. A rumbling growl sounded and she was silent as a large hellhound slipped through the bands of gray mist.

Each breath it exhaled was like a ribbon of fire and buckets of spittle dripped in globs from the exposed teeth.

Which to be honest were impressive.

Ana stared at the damn thing and squared her shoulders. It was one hellhound and she was a vampire, a three-hundred-year-old vampire with a hate-on that could tear it apart.

A second growl joined the first and she swallowed heavily as two more sets of eyes joined the first.

Shit. Okay, must reevaluate.

"Not fair, boys," she said as she moved a few paces to the side. The wall was inches away, the hard surface slippery with the constant dripping water. It was then that she felt the subtle energy traces that signaled the presence of a human. Or two.

Excitement shot through her. She was close and needed to keep cool.

The first, the largest hellhound, turned its massive head and blew out one long, lingering breath. The heat of it wafted in the air and she wrinkled her nose as the constant rumble of their chests permeated the space in a wash of sound.

Her hand tightened on the shaft of the dagger and her eyes narrowed onto her prey. Take out the leader and the rest will follow.

Wise words.

She hissed and jackknifed her body into the air so that she ran horizontally up the wall and pushed off with a mighty kick. She flew through the air, her body spiraling so that she looked down at the beasts as she passed overhead. The large hellhound snapped its great jaws and she felt a tug as a chunk of her hair was ripped from her skull.

She flew by so quickly she was surprised the bastard

managed to snag a piece, and hit hard, her feet sticking the landing like an Olympian. She whirled around and jabbed the dagger into the hellhound's haunches. One quick shot to each leg.

She was away, barely avoiding the snap of the smaller bitch to the right as she jumped back. It would have charged, but the leader turned on it and sank its fangs into the smaller beast's neck, tearing a huge gaping hole into its neck and tossing the animal to the side.

"You want me for yourself?" Ana shouted. Anarchy was a good thing in a situation such as this. Her fangs erupted and she relished the aggressive push that came with them.

The hellhound bellowed and charged. Ana stayed her ground, the dagger held tight, and when it hit, she sank the blade into its chest, forcing it deep as they crashed to the ground.

The beast's jaw snapped in rapid succession like a jackhammer. Ana barely managed to avoid the danger as she yanked on the dagger. The damn thing weighed a ton and she felt her strength waning but held on.

Her left hand sank into the coarse hair at its neck and she pushed hard, giving herself a couple of inches' grace from the deadly teeth that growled and snapped.

Pain ripped along her right side as its razor-sharp claws tore into her flesh. Her anger and steely determination gave her the boost of energy she needed and she heaved with all her might, bucking and kicking at the same time. With a grunt she flipped the three-hundred-pound animal onto its back and held the dagger aloft.

The smell of blood was in the air—hers—and it enraged her. Ana's eyes were fully dilated, her fangs extended as she hissed at the hellhound.

"I'm going to carve your heart out and feed it to your friend." She held on as the animal struggled to unseat her, and bared her teeth as she drove the blade through its chest walls. She heard the sound of bones breaking and flesh tearing.

Dark, putrid blood sprang from the wound like a geyser and Ana jumped back, pulling the dagger from the hellhound's chest as she did so. She'd hit pay dirt.

It scrambled, trying to get to its feet, and she sliced into its side, grunting savagely as the dagger scraped along each and every rib. The hellhound cried out and with a final heave managed to find its footing.

"Tenacious bitch, aren't you," she muttered under her breath as the animal glared at her. Its eyes still glowed fiery red, but the rasping that fell from its lips signaled she'd injured the beast and had done a good job of it.

It stumbled forward a few feet and then collapsed inches from her, raspy moans and growls falling from its trembling mouth. Ana gave it the boots, her heel connecting once more as she silenced it.

Her chest was heaving but there was no time to rest. She ducked as the third hellhound flew at her. It had waited patiently, watching from the shadows. Ana cursed, dropped, and rolled. The pain in her side was becoming sharper and she knew she was losing blood.

She needed to get to the kids and get the hell out.

An eerie sound drifted through the thick air and startled her. Declan? She hesitated, and it cost her.

The hellhound was on her in an instant and though she twisted her body she couldn't avoid the hit. Her right arm was caught between herself and the beast, the dagger was pinned tight. Useless.

The animal stared down at her and a cry of frustration erupted from her throat. The hellhound blew hot air against her cheek and she thrashed violently, trying to unseat the bastard and avoid the deadly canines that dripped poison.

A hot sting inched across her face as drops fell from its mouth to land on her cheek. She managed to wriggle her arm up an inch but as she twisted her neck back, Ana knew the chances of avoiding the dangerous teeth were slim. Her side ached and she was losing a lot of blood.

She lunged forward, one last desperate attempt at attack, and fell back as the hellhound was flung from her body like a rag doll. Ana rolled over and staggered to her feet, her gaze wild as she circled the room.

What the hell?

A vortex of wind filled with hail the size of footballs spun like a tornado, surrounding the hellhound and holding it prisoner. She watched in awe as the fury of the wind lifted the large animal and slammed it against the wall. The hellhound was stunned, a ball of fur and mangy growls against the wall, and then it went still.

She clutched her side, took a step, and stopped as a voice cut through the mist.

"We're over here." It was young, on the cusp of change. Definitely a teenaged male with the high-pitched cracks to prove it.

Ana ran toward the voice and as the cool mist evaporated she came to a halt.

They were safe, bound to the wall with iron chains, but safe. The young girl, Francesca's sister, stared at her in fear, and beside her was the boy. He looked to be no older than thirteen or fourteen at the most, yet his eyes were hard, his hands trembled at his side. He was on the small side, with a thick crop of inky black hair and skin as pale as hers.

"Is it down?" he asked, his voice rough. "Hurt bad?"

Ana rushed to their side and assessed the situation. She looked down at the boy. "The hellhound?"

He nodded as quick, hard breaths escaped from between his lips.

"You did that?"

Again, a nod.

"Impressive," she answered with a quick smile.

"It won't stay down for long," he answered quickly. "Nothing does down here."

Ana looked at the bloody dagger in her hands and eyed the two teenagers. "I'm getting you out, so listen closely. You do as I say, no questions asked, all right?"

"How do we know we can trust you?" The boy's eyes narrowed.

Ana paused, her gaze settling on the girl. Her large eyes were full of pain, confusion. "Francesca sent me and I promised her I'd bring you home."

A single tear wove its way down the teenager's face and she began to tremble.

"You're a vampire," the boy said.

Ana retracted her fangs. "We don't have time for chitchat." Ana glanced at the heavy iron chains that bound them. "Don't move."

She held the dagger tight and leapt forward, striking the iron as hard as she could. The force of the hit reverberated along her forearm and she barely managed to hold on to the dagger.

It didn't do a thing.

"Dammit!"

"The key is over there."

"What?" Ana looked at the boy, not impressed with the grin that now swept over his face.

"The key for the chain is on that table." He nodded behind her.

Ana whirled around. *Smart-ass.*

She retrieved the key and seconds later freed the teenagers.

"I'm Daniel," the boy said. "This is Alex but she doesn't talk much."

"Ana." She glanced behind her, worry for Declan weighing her down. She felt a shift in the air.

"Oh crap," Daniel muttered.

Ana turned to the boy. "What's happening?" Alex was

trembling, her slight form shivering madly, and she was unable to hold the sob that escaped her tight lips. This could not be good.

"She's back." Daniel's eyes were wide, his lips thinned. "Lilith."

Ana had a moment—a second of thought that said she was never getting her ass out of this hellhole. Her side ached and the need to feed was pinching hard. She'd lost a lot of blood. She could hear the hellhounds behind her stirring and that galvanized her into action.

"Let's go." She looked at both of them. "This is the only shot we're going to get so you need to listen to me. Stay close and do exactly what I say." She arched a brow. "We clear?"

Daniel nodded, his hand slipped into Alex's. The girl flinched but didn't pull away. Ana was worried about her. She seemed off, her mind in another place. She eyed Daniel. "You need to keep her in line. There's no room for error." Ana squared her shoulders and turned. "Let's go."

She felt the presence of Lilith. Her power was undeniable, her lust overwhelming.

And Lilith was gunning for her man.

They slid through the shadows, melting into the dullness of it as they headed toward Declan. Ana sensed him, could feel his anger, frustration.

Muffled voices wavered in the air and became clearer as the seconds ticked by. She was so intent upon them that she nearly stepped on a large, writhing lump of demon. If not for the whispered warning from Daniel she would have.

Without pause, Ana struck swiftly, slicing through bone and tissue. A guttural gasp escaped and then whatever the hell it was lay still.

Score another for the vampire.

She paused, her thoughts swirling madly. She knew she should take the teens out, get them back to the forest, but she couldn't leave Declan.

She wouldn't.

Ana turned and bent low so that her face was inches from Daniel. He held Alex's hand tightly and though the girl was taller than him it was clear his courage was holding her up.

She shoved the dagger into his free hand, took a moment to gather her bearings as best she could, and whispered softly, "Wait by the door. It's several feet to your left. If anything comes close, use this, all right? I can't leave without Declan."

Daniel blinked, a frown falling upon his face. "The sorcerer? He's here?"

"You were expecting him?" A fresh dose of unease punched her in the gut and Ana clenched her teeth tightly.

Daniel shook his head. "No, but Lilith talks about him a lot." He glanced at Alex before his wide gaze rested upon hers again. "Like he's her . . ."

Ana blanched at the teen's words. "Her what?"

"Um, her . . . like boyfriend or something." Daniel glanced away.

Hot anger ripped through her and she hissed at the ferocity of it. "Go now and hold tight to your position near the door." She turned and peered through the swirling fog. "Can you make this thicker? Dense?"

"Sure."

"Do it and wait for me."

Exhilaration rushed through her. A cool wind swept along the ground and teased the fog into a heavy shroud that coated her fully.

Boyfriend? She tossed the notion aside. *As fucking if.*

"He's mine," she muttered.

Her booted feet crept silently upon the stone floor. She was wound as tight as a rattlesnake about to strike, yet her hands were loose, at the ready.

Carefully she crept toward the voices. One—Declan's—was raised in anger, while the other—Lilith's—was coy, smug. She saw soft light ahead, filtered through the dense fog.

She hoped with the cover afforded by Daniel, Lilith wouldn't be aware of her presence. She took another step, her breath held in anticipation of the fight.

"There you are. I've been dying to meet the little bitch Declan pined for the entire time I had him."

The voice was sickly sweet, plastic, and full of shit.

It was Lilith. Her cover was blown. The pretense was over as quickly as it had begun.

Ana slid from the darkness and stepped into the light.

CHAPTER 31

The woman was a whore.

Every inch of her naked flesh screamed wanton tramp. She hid it well, behind the mask of an angel, but Ana saw past it. The decay was there, beneath the surface, you just had to look.

Ana kept her face emotionless as she stared at the naked bitch; her own mask of sorts. Inside rage lingered, festered, and pulled at her until she was barely able to contain herself. She wanted to rip her nails across the perfect, creamy flesh and choke the life out of the witch.

It was impossible of course. Lilith was one hell of an adversary. Ana would have to play it cool if they dared grab a chance to leave this screwed-up version of Hell they'd fallen into.

Instead she squared her shoulders and stood with legs spread wide, hands loose at her side. She knew Declan was there, just beyond Lilith. She could smell him.

"This is your vampire?" The tall blonde arched an eyebrow and laughed. "Declan, I'm surprised." Lilith moved aside, uncaring of her nudity, and gently swept a long golden curl behind her ear. Her breasts lifted, just so, and the smile that graced her lips would make a Cheshire cat proud.

Ana's gaze narrowed onto drops of blood near her right

breast, twin smears of crimson against porcelain. Lilith turned slightly, looked behind her, and shook her head. "She's less than ordinary and so small."

She saw him.

Ana's breath caught in her throat and pain lanced across her heart. Declan was shirtless. The scars along his chest, the ones she'd kissed with love, were smothered in blood. *His blood.*

She swallowed, her gaze rose slowly, and she blanched when she met his eyes. They were flat, his face hard, full of anger. His gaze narrowed and Ana was more than a little pissed to realize his anger was aimed directly at her.

There was accusation, disbelief thrown in as well.

She tried to ignore the crimson that shone upon his lips, but couldn't.

He'd fed from Lilith.

"She doesn't smell like a vampire." Lilith's gaze returned to Ana. "She smells like demon." Her eyes narrowed. "You've been feeding from my boys." The china-doll face cracked, the eyes no longer sky blue but crimson. "You've been feeding from my Declan."

It took all sorts of mental strength for Ana to remain quiet.

Lilith was inches from Declan and she sniffed, her face wrinkling in distaste. "She's the one who *turned* you. I should have known. You're not as sweet as you once were."

Her long, elegant fingers reached out and she ran them down Declan's cheek. Laughter bubbled from inside her, falling like musical notes. "No matter." The laughter stopped abruptly. "I shall be your breakfast, lunch, and dinner."

"You will not touch him." Ana's anger erupted but she underestimated the queen's power. Lilith had her by the throat before her words had even left her tongue. The demon held her aloft and her legs thrashed wildly as she struggled to break the grip. She didn't need to breathe per se, but it would take nothing for Lilith to snap her neck in two.

"I will end you." Lilith glared up into her eyes. "And since this is my Hell, I will look forward to repeating it, every single day."

A ribbon of black bled through her vision and Ana hissed, her fangs fully extended as she tried to break the queen's grip.

"Put her down," Declan growled. His tone commanded attention and Lilith paused, a perplexed expression marring the perfect features.

Lilith squeezed a little harder, her nails digging into Ana's flesh, and the smell of her own blood filled Ana's nostrils. Shit, she'd already lost too much. She was weak and ceased her struggles.

Lilith arched a brow and let Ana fall to the ground. A loud groan escaped as she hit the stone hard. She rolled over and staggered to her feet. Declan was at her side in an instant. His face was full of concern, but he was angry.

"Not a great time to disobey my orders."

"You would do the same," she rasped, her gaze never leaving Lilith. Her throat was fucking killing her. Why didn't Declan attack?

"When the moment's right, you run. Got it?" His words were a whisper against her ear.

Lilith leisurely fingered a long strand of her blond hair as she paced in front of them. Her full lips were softened by a smile that never left, and it widened as she stopped abruptly.

"Does she know the details of your stay down here, sorcerer?"

Declan tensed beside Ana and his hand dropped from her waist.

"What's done is done and I don't care to know." Ana glanced at Declan as she spoke and hated the way his face was closed, his emotion turned off.

Lilith ignored her; her electric eyes never left Declan. Her hands dropped to her naked breasts and she slid her fingers over the plump flesh. "Remember what it felt like? To be my lover, to have your hands on me?"

Ana was sickened by the pink tongue that escaped as the demon started to pant. The bitch was aroused.

"To be inside me?" Lilith's face changed, and once more Ana saw the true monster behind the mask. "To *kill* with me?"

An invisible hand was once more upon her and Ana grunted as she was thrown to the floor. Her arms and legs were spread wide.

Declan's gaze followed a trail of blood that was now flowing freely from her side and frustration brought tears to her eyes. She tried to move but it was no use.

"She looks yummy, doesn't she?" Lilith asked. She knelt beside Ana and beckoned to Declan. "Don't you want a taste? I don't mind but you'll have to wait." The demon grinned and Ana watched helplessly as the bitch's fangs slipped from between her lips. "I'm not standing in line, sorcerer. I've never been one for sloppy seconds."

Ana glared at her, all the hatred and fear inside, coloring her eyes to midnight. "I'll never let you take from me."

Lilith smiled. "You insignificant bitch. That's what they all say, even your precious sorcerer. A little secret?" She glanced up at Declan before bending lower. Ana flinched as the warmth of Lilith's breath slipped across her skin. "I don't care."

Ana's muscles tightened. She gathered what strength she could and looked up into Declan's eyes. They were cold, flat. The air around him shimmered, but Lilith couldn't see this. She was much too busy licking Ana's skin as she slowly made her way toward the beating pulse at her neck.

What arrogance. To assume Declan was no threat. To assume he would follow like a pathetic fool. Lilith had no fucking clue.

In that moment she knew Declan would get them out. He would settle for no less.

"Take your hands off my woman." Declan's words were spoken slowly, each one enunciated with care.

Lilith gazed down at Ana, tucked a piece of auburn hair behind Ana's ear, and shrugged. "I'm going to enjoy eating you." She ignored Declan and continued, "And then I'm going to have sex with my sorcerer and we'll both feed from you." She giggled. "You won't like it, but I sure as hell will."

The ground shook and the energy around Declan erupted into a shower of sparks.

Lilith's face contorted into a grimace and she snarled as she turned from Ana to confront Declan. She rose and her body started to twitch as if she was unable to control the anger inside her. "You think to challenge me? I am the queen, you belong to me."

The invisible restraints slipped from her limbs but Ana remained still, biding her time. And of that, there wasn't a whole hell of a lot. She was getting weaker by the second.

Declan snarled and took a step toward Lilith. "Things have changed. I'm no longer without magick. My power has been infused by your darkness, why else would I take from you now?"

"You belong to me," Lilith hissed.

Declan ignored her. "My power has been balanced and magnified tenfold by the Seraphim." He snorted. "I've got a newsflash for you. You're the queen of fuck-all."

He charged forward and smacked her so hard, a tooth went flying. The shriek that escaped Lilith was wretched enough to break glass. She staggered backward and Declan kicked her hard once more.

He turned to Ana. "Run."

She rolled over and was up on her feet, though a wave of dizziness made it difficult to stay upright.

"You will regret this," Lilith bellowed. "No one touches me like that." She growled like an animal and lunged forward, screaming in frustration as she tried to get to Declan, but was held back.

"The only thing I regret is the fact I can't toast your ass when we leave." Declan's hands wove a spell and though the queen fought like hell, her arms slowly fell to her sides and her mouth was sewn shut. "That's better. You're more annoying that nails on chalkboard."

A strangled sound escaped her, but nothing more fell from Lilith's lips.

An arm touched Ana's shoulder and she turned, shocked to see Daniel and Alex.

The three of them watched as Declan stood inches from the impotent queen of Hell. His hands hovered above her face and Ana felt a sliver of triumph when she saw the demon flinch.

Declan's fingers lifted the heavy chain that hung from her neck and he yanked it over her head, hard, taking a huge chunk of hair with it. Lilith fell to her knees, chest heaving as she struggled against the invisible restraints.

"You will never be free of me." She spit the words out and fell over, exhausted from the effort it took to speak.

Declan turned, his eyes pained as they connected with Ana's. "That I don't doubt," he muttered.

Ana wavered on her feet. She needed blood. Declan offered his wrist and she latched on as he addressed the teens. "We need to vamoose. My magick won't hold her for long." A growl slid from the ever-present fog. The hellhounds were stirring.

"You got enough?" He was breathing hard. Ana licked one last drop, ignored the "ew" that Daniel muttered, and shook her head. She was good to go.

"Declan . . ." *I'm so sorry. God, what you went through.*

Declan started forward. "We need to get out." His face

was harsh and it was obvious conversation was the last thing on his mind.

They exited the room and rushed down the stairs. Daniel and Alex had no trouble keeping up, but with the urgency of the situation and rescue close at hand, it wasn't surprising.

They flew across the terrace and as they entered the maze shouts and screams followed behind them.

Declan shouted. "Move, faster!"

Ana grabbed Alex and dragged her along, her legs flying over the path they'd trod earlier. The hellhound was where they'd left it, and she leapt over the animal, Declan and the boy close on her heels.

Dark, thunderous clouds gathered overhead, an insane screech flew from within their depths. Alex whimpered and Ana chanced a glance upward. Hundreds of small, black, daggerlike things flew from their midst and her eyes widened in horror as they focused.

They looked like deranged cockroaches with giant wings and big-ass fangs.

Ana had never seen anything like it.

"They're full of poison. Don't let them get close enough to bite." Declan shot a bolt of energy up at the sky as they plunged into the cool depths of the forest. No words were spoken, fear clogged her throat.

They skidded to a halt near the black wall and Declan peeled back the layer of darkness. Ana shoved the girl through, clenching her teeth as one of the roaches zipped by. She jumped after her and whirled around as Declan and Daniel slipped through.

Declan held his hand aloft and the wall fell in place, though a roach squeezed by at the last second. Its fire engine red eyes blazed as it locked onto Ana. She snarled, but Declan toasted the little bastard before it could reach her.

There was no time to talk, Succubus Blues was around the corner.

"We've got five minutes." Declan's voice was tense. "There's no room for fuckups. Keep your head low and don't make eye contact with anyone. Understand?"

Ana nodded. "Let's go."

"I'm serious, Ana." Something in his tone made her stop and look up. "I can't lose you." His lips were tight. "Not now."

Ana whispered, "I'm not going anywhere"—she flashed a smile—"but up."

Declan led the way and they followed the sounds of music, voices, and general mayhem that spilled into the street from the club. The square was full, lots of bodies milling about, some fighting, some sexing.

They ignored all and headed straight for the door. A huge mountain of demon was at the door. Ana didn't remember him from before. She stopped, uneasy.

"No illegals allowed into the club." The demon nodded toward Daniel and Alex.

"We're escorting them back to processing," Declan said smoothly.

"On whose orders?" The demon was not going to make it easy.

"Lilith's. So unless you want to explain to her why these two puny exports from the human realm were late for processing, I suggest you move your ass." Declan glared at him and took a step forward. "She wasn't exactly in a great mood. Her garden party was interrupted."

The demon stood back though his eyes followed them closely. "Go straight to processing. I don't need any problems. My shift is almost over."

The club was loud, the energy even more frenetic than just an hour before. Ana held tight to the teenagers as they followed Declan through the crowd. She felt eyes upon them but ignored everyone save for the man in front of her.

They reached a set of stairs that led to a small alcove up

top. Declan paused. He turned around and she didn't like the frown on his face. He looked down at her, his voice tense.

"Mountain man is still watching us. A bunch of guards are gathering." He looked at the teens. "Once he sees us take the stairs they'll be after us." Declan nodded toward a non-descript door, half in shadow near the end of the bar. "That leads to processing but we're heading for the phone booth up there."

Ana thought she'd heard and seen a lot of crazy shit since coming to District Three but this one was clearly bizarre. "A phone booth? Are you for real?"

Declan flashed a smile, seeming to enjoy the absurdity of the moment as much as she. "I told you Lilith is all about Hollywood." He turned and glanced upward. "That would be her ode to Superman."

He glanced at the kids. "Ready?"

They nodded.

"Let's go."

They took the stairs, legs pumping hard, the kids first. Ana ignored the shouts from behind, though a blast that took out the railing beside her was almost too much. Daniel had the door open and Declan brought up the rear, latching it into place behind them as they piled in.

Alex screamed as a blast hit and they shook from the force of it.

The small booth was in complete darkness. There was no sound and then a blinding light swept over them. Ana experienced a weird distorted sensation. She blinked once and when she opened her eyes, they were standing on the platform.

"There's no time. The shuttle is moving." Declan shouted.

The four of them ran like lunatics and panic hit hard as shouts followed in their wake. The shuttle was moving slowly, gearing up to leave; however, once it reached the tunnel there was no way they'd be able to climb aboard. There wasn't enough room between the vehicle and the wall.

Things slowed down, noises receded into the background. Ana felt like she was one step behind but reached the shuttle first. The door was open and she saw one of Seth's men motioning, his eyes fixed on the action behind her. She leapt up, ignoring the twinge in her side, and grabbed Alex, hauling her up while Declan cleared the landing with Daniel in tow.

The door slid shut and the shuttle made a loud, creaking noise as it shuddered madly and then accelerated.

The demon looked disgusted. "Nice entry, O'Hara," he muttered before heading up front.

Ana licked her lips. They were dry. She shivered and began to tremble. Declan's eyes were huge pools of chocolate and she exhaled a shaky breath as she gazed into them. His arms wrapped around her and he pulled her close, burying his head into the mess of hair that lay in tangles at her neck.

They said nothing and she was content to bask in his embrace, and take what comfort she could. Lord knew she needed it. Her journey was far from over.

There was still vampire council business to attend to.

CHAPTER 32

The trip topside from District One was relatively painless considering the last twenty-four hours had been a mess. Seth gave them safe passage from the dunes and Declan got his group to Samael's private portal. It had taken less than half an hour.

After all that.

He inhaled a crisp shot of cool New Orleans air and glanced down at the woman beside him. She was subdued, and that made him uneasy. Ana was hiding something. His gut told him it involved Seth and the deal she'd struck with the demon for passage to District Three.

She wouldn't pony up and spill the details, which pissed him off. He frowned. Nothing was for free.

"Someone's following us." Ana sounded tired.

"They're Ransome's men."

"I'm starving," Daniel piped in. "Shit, I haven't had a burger in like days. I hope you have food. Lots of it."

"Are we almost there?" Alex's voice was tremulous.

"Just around the corner," Ana answered. Declan felt sorry for the girl. She was clearly out of her element and just about done.

"Francesca's there, right?"

Ana nodded but remained silent.

An owl hooted as they approached the boundaries to the DeLacrux mansion. The darkness was thick, not a star in the sky, and the wind was chilled. He felt the eyes of the dead upon him and pulled the collar of his jacket up a little more.

They stopped in front of the iron gates and he quickly wove Daniel and Alex's signatures into the protection wards. Two minutes later they stood upon the large porch. The kids looked a little shell-shocked and unsure.

A howl sounded behind them, echoing into the night. It was a signal from one of Ransome's wolves. They were home.

Ana's hand was just reaching for the handle when the door was wrenched nearly off its hinges. Nico stood there, shirtless, fierce. Declan stared at the jaguar warrior in silence.

"Cool Mohawk." Daniel was in awe. "Cool tattoos."

Nico's nostrils flared as his gaze traveled the group. They rested upon Ana before narrowing onto Declan.

"You look like shit," Nico observed, moving to the side to allow them entrance.

Declan followed the group into the foyer. "Yes, but at least I've got a full head of hair."

"And you smell bizarre," Nico stated warily.

The sorcerer snorted and flashed his fangs at the jaguar. "You have no idea."

Surprise lit up Nico's eyes. He glanced at Ana and then back to Declan. He opened his mouth to speak but was interrupted as Francesca flew down the stairs, Ransome close on her heels.

"For Christ sakes, she fucking kneed me in the groin." The werewolf was livid but no one paid him any mind.

Declan stood back as the necromancer enveloped her sister in a hug that was full of tears and words that were hard to understand.

"Where's Kaden?" Ana asked softly.

"Here." The teenager shuffled forward, his hands tucked into the pockets of his jeans. He wiped the remnants of a beignet from his mouth and hunched his shoulders forward. "You made it back." His eyes were on Ana. "That's good."

"Good for you, my friend," Declan snapped. He pushed past Ana and crowded the teen. "I gave you an order."

Kaden didn't shrink from him. "Yeah, well, I don't take orders from you."

Declan bent down until he was close enough to count the fuzz patch sprouting along the teen's jaw. The anger inside him was dark. "I don't negotiate with children."

"Declan, stop. He did what I asked." She yanked on his arm and he turned away. She glanced up at him and his breath caught at the look in her eyes. They smoldered with heat, promises, yet he saw sadness as well.

"Anyone hear from Bill?" she asked.

Nico shook his head. "There's been nothing. Cale was by this morning. He's heard nada."

Ana turned to the gathered group. "Let's call it a night and get some rest. We'll regroup, catch up, and figure out our next move in the morning."

She started for the stairs and didn't bother to look back. "Alex, you're with Francesca. Daniel, there's a room beside Kaden's, he'll show you." She paused, hand on the railing. "Ransome, if you're staying, the sofa in the parlor is all I've got left."

Declan watched as her small form disappeared at the top of the landing. He turned, catching the look in Ransome's eyes. "Spit it out, LaPierre."

The tall shifter's eyes were narrowed. "Just never thought I'd see the day, is all . . ."

Declan shook his head. "I'm not in the mood for riddles. Say what the hell you mean."

The teens slipped by, with Francesca leading the way up

the stairs. Ransome's eyes lingered a little too long on the necromancer in Declan's opinion.

"She's slave to Samael."

Ransome snorted. "Don't worry 'bout me. I'm not the one with a problem." Ransome smiled widely and cupped his crotch. "Ana's got you by the balls." He laughed softly. "Vampire, sorcerer . . . that's some fucked-up shit. Are you officially a hybrid?"

"You're an asshole."

"Yeah, but I'm ball and chainless."

"Fuck you." Declan started for the stairs.

"I've got business at the club, but my men will patrol for the remainder of the night. We'll talk tomorrow."

Declan grunted an answer. He was nervous. They were out of Hell and back in the real world. It was still the same twisted reality he'd left behind, but his personal situation had done a 360.

He belonged to someone.

He reached Ana's bedroom and slipped inside. The lamp near her bed glowed softly, casting an arc of light that cut through the dark. His breath caught in his throat when he spied her. She was naked, her pale form glowing eerily as she stood beside several large canvases along the wall.

"I paint," she murmured, affording him a side profile as she turned slightly. "My father taught Jean-Charles and me." A long, shuddering breath escaped her. "So long ago."

Declan could not take his eyes from her.

"He was . . ."

He felt her pain. It punched him in the gut and yet he found himself baring his teeth, jealous at the thought of the mysterious Jean-Charles. "Who was he?" The question slipped from his lips before he could stop himself, and he grimaced. Christ, Ransome was right. The woman had him in knots.

A soft smile tugged at her mouth and she turned fully.

Her face was half hidden in shadow, but the red of her lips burned through the gloom and he focused on them as she ran her tongue along the bottom.

"He was my twin brother." She took a step forward, her eyes shimmering like liquid glass. "My best friend, and for nearly two hundred and fifty years my constant companion."

Declan unclenched his hands and strode forward until he was able touch the softness of her cheek.

"Where is he?" He thought of the crypt with Jean-Charles's name inscribed and felt like an ass for asking the question.

Ana leaned into him, her head resting against his chest, and his arms slipped around her to hold her tight. She whispered so lightly he barely heard her reply. "I don't know. I haven't seen him in nearly sixty years."

Declan was torn. He figured something pretty bad had happened to separate her from a brother she clearly loved. Should he pursue it or leave well enough alone?

She wriggled out of his embrace. "You smell of Lilith." She pushed away and took a step toward the ancient bathroom off her room. "Coming?" Gone was the sorrow from moments before. It had been replaced with raw hunger and need.

She slipped away and ran into the bathroom. His eyes fell upon the paintings, but they were deep in shadow and he couldn't see them clearly.

The sound of the shower tore his gaze away and jumpstarted him into action. Declan's clothes were hastily shed. The hunger inside was gnawing heavily, as was the need to hold Ana close.

Steam was already rising fast as he entered the large room. The decrepit light fixture that hung from the center of the ceiling didn't throw much illumination, but it was enough. His gaze found her immediately.

The tub was a mammoth thing, with four clawlike feet

holding it in place. She stood inside, staring at him in silence as water fell from above, running over her porcelain skin, touching the places that belonged to him.

If he could take the time to just watch her, he would. He'd memorize every nook and cranny, every single dimple and curve of her body. But there was an urgent need in her eyes and his energy fed off it. It propelled him forward until he was beside her, touching her and claiming her with his hands and his lips.

The spray was hot and felt like heaven against his skin. It seemed as if he'd been cold for days. The wetness slid between their bodies as they strained together. His hand held her head firmly while his mouth skated across her jaw, nipping lightly as he worked his way to the open mouth that he craved.

He ate the groan that slipped between her teeth, his tongue aggressively tasting everything she had to offer.

God, that he had her now, after so many years of want. He growled and the darkness inside him stirred. The need to protect was powerful and he trembled from the ferocity of it. He would kill anyone who would harm her.

"Ana." Her name fell from his lips as he broke away. He couldn't shake the sense of doom hanging over his head. There were still so many unanswered questions.

"No words." Her voice was hoarse. He saw tiny veins appear beneath her skin. Her fangs poked out and the now-familiar ache spread inside his mouth. She grabbed a bar of soap. There was no washcloth or bath sponge, just fingers and slippery smooth bubbles.

He stood still while she slowly ran her hands along his shoulders. His eyes moved lower, fixated by her small, round breasts as she rose on tiptoes to accomplish her task.

She spread the clean-smelling soap along hardened muscles and damaged, scarred skin. Her eyes claimed his and never left as she moved lower, her fingers kneading, massaging. When her fangs became fully distended, when they scraped along the side of his straining cock, she did not waver.

He hissed when her fingers closed around his erection and when her tongue teased, stroking in tandem with her hands, he started to pant, and a growl did indeed escape.

His eyes bored into hers. "Keep that up and it will be over before we start." He slid his hands along her body, yanking the soap from her grasp. The tub was now nearly full of hot, silky water. He turned off the tap and slid down into the welcoming depths, pulling Ana between his legs.

His body raged with need and yet he knew somehow that she needed comfort. Her back rested against his chest and he took his time, running his large, soapy hands over her skin.

Declan cleaned every single delicious inch of her body and took special care to massage her delicate feet, running hands along the arches and in between her toes. She was mush in his hands when he was finally done and the water was no longer hot, but tepid.

Declan scooped her up and slid from the tub, grabbing a large towel as he moved into the bedroom. Gently he laid her on the bed and she stared at him in silence as he rubbed the moisture from her body.

When he was done he tossed the towel aside and rested on his haunches as he gazed down at her. The moon had found her way out and small slivers of light drifted through the slats in the blinds. They caressed her pale flesh in a wash of stardust.

She looked like a fucking goddess.

She sat up and placed her hands upon the torn, scarred flesh of his chest. Her shoulders trembled and she shook her head. "If I could take this away I would." Her eyes were wide, their blue depths darkened, intense. "I would do anything for you, Declan." She rose the last few inches and he groaned as her hands cupped his head. She lowered her mouth and kissed his lips, a butterfly touch, but one heavy with meaning and emotion.

Her tongue wove a path of desire along his jaw and she whispered, "Anything."

The energy changed and it was no subtle thing. Declan frowned, a sliver of unease subduing the passion somewhat. He tensed as her fangs broke skin on his neck and closed his eyes as she pulled from him, taking his blood. It was an exquisite sensation, one that overrode any feelings of danger.

Each draw was like fire over ice. He groaned as his head started to spin and a host of erotic images fluttered in his brain. His own fangs were ready, his body filled with need.

He tried to shift but Ana was astride him now, her grip firm, and he was unable to move her. He'd forgotten how strong she was. Too late he realized something was wrong. She was taking too much.

His eyes flew open but he couldn't focus. He was losing himself.

There was pain. He started to thrash, but her claws dug in and held him tight. And then there was nothing. The connection was broken.

Declan fell back onto the bed, his head limp upon the pillow. He was cold, disoriented. A whisper of warmth touched his face and forced his eyes open.

Ana's blue gaze held him firm, but she could not hide her anguish and regret.

"I'm so sorry, Declan. I had no choice."

He closed his eyes, surrendering to the darkness that called, and her scent lingered in the air long after she fled.

CHAPTER 33

"Hey lady, watch where you're going—"

Ana hissed and pushed past the tall eighties wannabe rocker as she slid into the darkened interior of the Voodoo Lounge. The Quarter was still hopping and it was no different inside the club.

She paused near the bar, her gaze moving quickly over the crowd. There was only one face she wanted to see and irritation slid over her when she came up empty.

Where the hell was he?

"Can I get you anything?"

She turned, her gaze falling upon the hardened bartender she'd met a few evenings before. The faded eyes narrowed and the woman frowned.

"What do you want? 'Cause I sure as hell know we don't serve the kind of refreshment you seek."

The woman made no attempt to hide her dislike. Ana smiled. Like she gave a damn.

"I'm looking for Asher. He around?"

Surprise flickered in the depths of Sarah's eyes, but she quickly hid it. She nodded toward the mezzanine. "Ransome hauled his ass up there 'bout half an hour ago." She shrugged. "As far as I know he's still chewing the slimy bastard out."

Ana pushed away from the bar.

"How's the magick man, O'Hara?" Sarah was concerned. It was obvious in her tone. Ana paused, her lips tight. "He's fine."

"Lady, as long as he's got the hots for you, I highly doubt it."

Ana ignored the comment and headed toward the stairs. Once on the landing she strode toward Ransome's office and pushed the door open. The air was thick with the putrid taste of hatred, a healthy dose of blood, and an insane amount of testosterone.

Ransome stood near his desk, hands loose and bloody at his side. He was shirtless, his powerful chest showed signs of a fight. Long smears of blood ran along his pectorals and down his abs.

The scent hit her hard and Ana's eyes widened, the blue receding to black as she glanced toward Asher.

The werewolf was breathing heavy. His face was a bloody mess and his arm was held at an awkward angle. Definitely broken. She smiled and hoped it hurt like hell.

"Out for a stroll?" Ransome smiled, though his eyes hardened. He knew this wasn't a social call. "Where's Dec?"

Ana ignored the question and responded with one of her own. "What's going on? This some weird werewolf fore-play or what?" She took two steps until she stood in front of Asher.

The werewolf looked up at her, his left eye swollen shut, and sneered. "What do you care?"

"Actually, I don't." She bent low and let her fangs slide into view. "At all." She smiled. "I came to see you."

The werewolf's eyes narrowed and he straightened, hissing as he held his arm close, tight. "Whatever do I owe the pleasure?"

"Cut the crap, Asher. You hate me as much as I hate you." She let the anger inside flush her skin, loving the boost of energy that accompanied it, and clenched her hands together tightly. "I want to know where council hides these days. I need to see them."

"The Velvet Rope is at the far end of the Quarter," Ransome butted in, his large frame sidling alongside the two of them. "Same as it's always been."

Ana's eyes never left Asher. "I'm not talking the club. I'm more interested in their lair. "

"This is my city and even I don't have that kind of information." Ransome sounded more than a little annoyed.

Ana snorted. "Asher knows. He's been in their back pocket for over a hundred years. How else do you think he's managed to keep that slimy neck of his attached to his head?"

Ransome growled and bared his teeth. "That sure as hell doesn't surprise me." He shoved his face in Asher's. "And you thought to challenge for alpha? On what fucking planet? LaPierres do not get into bed with vampires. That kind of alliance never ends well." He paused and glanced at Ana. "No offense."

"None taken."

Asher's face whitened and he tried to back away but there was nowhere for him to go. The wall was at his back. The bastard's eyes were huge and Ana loved that his whiny voice trembled slightly as he spoke.

"I can't give you that information. You know the rules. Only those invited are allowed inside. There is no negotiation."

"I don't care," Ana bit out. "You will tell me or I'll drain you dry right now." She smiled brightly. "How's that for negotiation?"

Ana pushed past Ransome and sank her long nails into his broken arm. Asher screamed and tried to shake free but she was too strong. Stirrings of Declan's magick, remnants of their joining flooded her and she considered trying an energy blast, but her fangs seemed to do the trick.

He broke immediately. How fucking pathetic.

"They're living in English Turn."

"Where the hell is that?" she spat. "Never heard of it."

"It's a gated community full of new money," Asher managed.

Ana twisted his arm and smiled as he screamed.

"Why, thank you, asshole. Before I leave, I need another piece of information."

Asher stared at her with hatred, his chest heaving, his eyes flat, black stones.

"I know it was you who tipped off council as to the whereabouts of Jean-Charles and his lover. You put the blame on me. If I hadn't been out of my mind with grief I would have ended your sorry excuse of a life sixty years ago." She grabbed him by the neck and brought his face so close she could see the tiny veins that ran beneath his skin. "Why? We were all friends. Why would you betray them?"

Asher's face was pale, but the growl that erupted from his chest brought a fresh wave of heat to his skin. He bared his teeth and spat, "She was mine. She was always mine."

Ana fought the sadness she felt as the memories of that tragic night from so long ago swept over her. It welled up until her chest hurt from the breadth of it, and then she let it go.

She dropped Asher to the ground, and smacked him hard across the face. Blood spurted in every direction as he slid into a pathetic heap of animal. She stared down at him for several long moments and then turned, her voice barely a whisper.

"Sadly, Cerise belongs to no one, because you ordered her execution. I wonder how you live with yourself."

"What the hell are you planning?" Ransome was once more fully clothed and spoke from across the room. He was directly in her path to the door.

"I don't have time to explain and you need to get out of my way."

"Lady, I'm not moving and don't make the mistake of thinking I'm some weakling like that piece of shit over there."

Ana knew his type. Alpha—used to getting his own way—and strong as hell. "I need to get something from that house."

"For who?"

"A demon, Seth."

"Christ, lady, I thought you were smarter than that. No deals with demons. They always bite you in the ass."

"I had no choice."

His eyes narrowed. "So spill the details."

Ana hesitated and then plunged forward. Some secret corner of her heart was relieved to be able to share. "Declan and I are joined now. We've bonded and there's no turning back." She swallowed and exhaled a shaky breath. "But there's consequence. In my world, we're not allowed to make vampires. It's forbidden. If it happens"—she glanced down at the now-silent Asher—"council will destroy the fledgling and banish said maker, to wherever. *If* said vampire is lucky enough to escape with their life."

"But he is Seraph, one of their soldiers. That has to count for something."

She shook her head. "My queen's rules are absolute. They will hunt Declan when they find out."

"If that's true, how will this demon be able to help you?"

"Seth wants something they have. He says if I get it for him, he'll use an outstanding favor and guarantee Declan's safety."

"And you believe him."

"Like I said, there was no choice." Her eyes were beseeching. "It's late and I need to do this."

"And Declan's okay with this."

Her cheeks darkened and Ransome took a step forward. "What have you done to him?"

"He doesn't know. I left him in a weakened state, but he'll be fine when he awakens." Her lips tightened. "He *can't* know. If he goes anywhere near them, they'll kill him without question. These are ancients. Their powers are fierce and their loyalty to the queen unbreakable."

Ransome grabbed his leather jacket from the hanger near his door. "Let's go."

Ana shook her head. "No."

Ransome ignored her and opened the door. He glanced over to Asher and growled, "When I return I want your ass gone from New Orleans, or better yet, get the fuck out of Louisiana. Because I will kill you. That, my friend, is a bona fide LaPierre promise."

Ana stared at the wolf in disbelief. "Why would you do this for me? This could be a suicide mission. You understand that, don't you?"

Ransome shrugged. "It's not my nature to stand by while a woman heads into danger. Can't do it, besides"—he arched a brow—"O'Hara will use his mojo crap to fuck me over huge if I let something happen to you. Christ, the last time someone pissed him off he spelled the worst kind of shit imaginable on the poor son of a bitch." He shivered and grabbed his crotch. "Every time he had sex his dick nearly fell off. That would not be good for me."

"This is serious."

He spoke quietly. "I know."

How could Ana argue with that?

"So what exactly are we stealing?"

She couldn't be sure, but was that a hint of glee in his voice?

"The elixir of immortality," she said quietly.

"Fuck me."

Definite glee.

Declan awoke with one hell of a headache.

He rolled over and stumbled from the bed, his gut clenched tight, temples throbbing. Damn, but he hurt all over.

His eyes peeled open and though he tried to get his bearings he was having difficulty. The hunger was overwhelming and the scent of blood was everywhere. Declan focused and swallowed. Painfully. His throat felt like dried cotton.

The blood, where was it?

The rickety table by the bed held the treasure he sought and he leapt toward it, groaning as he slid across the mattress. His hands eagerly entwined around the large glass decanter. It was full, filled to the brim with crimson gold.

His body was covered in sweat and he felt like a junkie jonesing for a fix. Never had he felt so on edge, so fucked up. He drained the decanter, wiping any remnants he saw with his tongue.

As his body relaxed, his senses sharpened and he looked around. Images assaulted his mind, Heaven and Hell all wrapped into one insane collage, with one constant thread: Ana. Unease slid over him.

He walked toward the scattered canvases along the wall. His mouth fell open as he studied them. They were of him. All of them, amazing portraits that looked alive, painted with a brush that felt love.

He frowned. The last one was of a stranger. A handsome man, with blue eyes and dark auburn hair. Jean-Charles no doubt.

Fear clutched at him. Where the hell was she? Last thing he remembered was lying beneath Ana, her fangs distended, and then she . . .

A growl escaped as he cursed a flurry of words. She'd drunk from him until he'd passed out.

But why?

Declan grabbed his clothes and quickly threw on jeans, shirt, and boots. He was down the stairs and swore when he saw the last fading rays of sun filtering in from the stained glass on either side of the front door.

Christ, he'd been out for nearly twenty-four hours. Panicked, his long legs ate up the distance to the back kitchen in no time. Everyone was there. He could smell them.

Everyone except Ana.

"Where the hell is she?" He stalked over to Nico and swung his gaze toward a stranger. He was tall, lean—a werewolf—one of Ransome's.

"Ah been waiting on you," the wolf said, his words a slow Louisiana drawl. "Got a message from Ransome."

Ana was in trouble. He could feel it.

A wave of dizziness washed over him and he grunted with the effort it took to stay on his feet. He hissed, "Why didn't you get me?" His question was directed at Nico.

"I tried." He shrugged. "You were dead to the world." Nico's face darkened as he frowned. "She drained you near dead, though it was a nice touch—leaving a gallon of blood."

His hand snaked out and he slammed the werewolf against the wall. "Where is she?"

The werewolf growled and the air around them shimmered as his animal shifted beneath his skin.

"He can't answer if you're fucking choking him," Nico hissed.

Declan slowly let his hands fall and the werewolf moved away, his hands rubbing his neck. "I was ordered by my alpha to give you a message—no one else—if he didn't return."

"Where are they?" Declan roared.

"They've gone to English Turn."

"Where the hell is that?" Declan rasped, glancing at Nico as he struggled to keep his emotions in check. At least she'd not planned another trip below.

"It's across the river." The werewolf paused, his face strained. "He said he was going with your Ana to pay a visit to the vampire council, but they should have been back this morning."

"What possible reason would she have . . ." His voice trailed off as his mind worked overtime. *Seth.*

Kaden started for the door, Daniel on his heels. "We have to go after her."

"You will do no such thing." Cale entered the kitchen, and behind him, Samael. "I'm here to take the kids back to The Pines. They'll be safe until Bill makes contact and we can figure out what to do with them." He paused. "Where is the girl?"

"Upstairs." Nico nodded. "With the necromancer."

"I'm not going, not until Ana's safe." Kaden glared at Declan.

"Don't worry about Ana, I'll bring her back." Declan's eyes met Cale's. The tall Seraph nodded.

"I will see you soon." Cale turned to the teen boys. "Let's go." They started to protest but he silenced them with a wave of his hand. "Now." His tone brooked no argument though Kaden's angry glare shot bullets at his back.

"Take care of my necromancer, brother. I've unfinished business with her, but for the moment"—Samael glanced at Declan—"I'm otherwise occupied."

"You're not coming?" Cale arched a brow.

"Can you not handle the children?" The sarcasm was hard to miss.

"No worries there. I didn't lose them, you did."

Samael smiled and flexed his hands. *"Touché."* He turned to Declan. "I think I'll come along, if you don't mind."

Declan eyed the demon lord closely. He was unsure of the demon and his motives, but if he was willing to help Ana, that was good enough—for now. He turned to Nico. "You ready to hunt?"

The tall warrior grunted. "I've been ready for days. Babysitting a bunch of teenagers isn't what I signed up for."

"Let's go." Declan headed for the door. He paused and scooped a bag of goodies, filled to the brim with charmed daggers and special weapons used on supernatural beings. As the three of them stepped into the fresh night air, they startled a squirrel on the railing of the porch. It froze and then scurried away, disappearing into the gloom.

Declan flexed his arms and called upon the power coiled in his gut. His gaze swept the now-empty porch.

Smart little bastard. He wondered if the vampires would be as accommodating.

He looked at the demon and jaguar warrior and then stepped down.

Somehow, he didn't think so.

na sat in the corner of the sparse room and ignored the cameras protruding from every corner. The bright light overhead was harsh, the tiled floor cold. She was stiff, her face blank, but inside emotion raged hard and fast.

Ransome was pacing. He'd been pacing ever since they'd been escorted inside, which was hours ago. She knew it was now early evening. Why the hell hadn't council come for them?

The whir of the camera sounded as it followed the were-wolf. Ana fought the urge to throw up her middle finger and wave it. Actually she'd like nothing more than to take some-thing long and hard and shove it up Alistair's—

The door opened suddenly and a tingle of anticipation rolled through her. Good. It was about fucking time.

She stretched, took her time, and slowly rose to her feet. Ransome stopped his endless pacing and glanced at her. He arched a brow.

Showtime.

The tall vampire didn't move and she felt the weight of his stare upon her back. She let her hands fall loose and cracked her neck. Her long auburn hair fell wildly about her shoulders. She tucked an unruly curl behind her ear and smiled as she turned to him.

Alistair—member of the local vampire council. He was an ancient, a cold son of a bitch, the vampire who'd hunted and killed Cerise. He was in fact the council's executioner and head of their security.

He stepped into the light, his dead eyes clear and filled with anticipation. He was dressed in black, a long duster made of velvet that touched the floor as he walked. He took another step and crossed his hands behind his back and smiled. It quickly turned to a sneer as he spoke.

"I hope you're both well rested."

Ana's urge to slam her fist upside the vampire's head was violent, but she lowered her eyes, took a second to compose herself. She needed to keep to her plan. Play it cool.

"I don't know about rested, but I sure as hell could use some red meat," said Ransome.

A snort of disgust fell from Alistair. "You will not speak unless I ask it, wolf." He turned his black gaze to Ana and stepped aside. "Shall we? It's time we had a little chat. We're most interested in finding out how you became aware of our location and why you've dared to bring a wolf into our midst."

Ana started forward, her steps unsure, hesitant. She kept her eyes lowered—didn't trust that the hatred she felt was hidden—and she prayed he wouldn't sense the undercurrent of magick that empowered her blood. It was the ace in her pocket. Of course the fact that Alistair believed all women were inferior could only help. His tendencies, both sexual and political, swayed toward the male of their species, and the only female he pretended to admire was the queen.

Ransome fell in behind her and she was grateful he held his tongue. The tall wolf wasn't used to taking shit from anyone and she knew he would like nothing more than to rip into Alistair.

Wolves and vampires had a longstanding grudge, most of which was empowered by ignorance. Those stuck in the past, such as Alistair, would never change their shortsighted view of the world.

Two guards stood outside and led the way toward the main house. She and Ransome had been held in one of the smaller outbuildings. The night was crisp, the air cool on her face. In the distance an owl hooted, its cry sad, melancholy. A shiver rippled over her flesh at the sound.

Not a good omen.

The main house was impressive, if you liked over-the-top, gaudy architecture. It was a large, gothic-looking monster with stone gargoyles and several turrets that seemingly had been put there just because. Retro was in and she was amused to see the vampires had jumped on the bandwagon.

The foyer was large, opulent, filled with shades of gold, crimson, and black. A huge staircase dominated the center of the room and her gaze traveled upward, resting on several paintings that lined the wall. A stab of longing fell over her as she settled on a portrait of her parents. As direct descendants of the queen they were honored in this way.

What would they think of her choices? Would her mother understand?

"This way." Alistair nodded to the right, toward a small alcove. She stepped through and into a large elevator which they rode down in silence.

She knew they'd have one shot at getting to the vault. One shot at getting the elixir for Seth. Tucked into her boots lay the magick ball Declan had given her in Hell. It had the power to peel back layers of reality. Ana hoped it was enough to peel back a huge iron vault.

If not, both she and Ransome were fucked. She cleared everything from her mind. When the elevator halted and the door opened, her fangs slid out.

She heard Ransome growl. It was low, full of menace, a promise of things to come. Ana snarled, turned, and attacked.

"So what's the plan, sorcerer?" Samael eyed the property closely, his arms crossed, legs spread wide.

"I don't have one." Declan studied the ten-foot walls. They were charmed, the wards impressive. "Was thinking we could ring the bell but something tells me that ain't gonna work."

Nico joined the two of them. "I scouted the properties on both sides. They're occupied by humans. Bet they'd shit their pants if they knew what lived next door."

Samael cracked his neck and removed his aviators. "Boys, I think it's time for a little chaos, don't you?"

Declan glanced at the demon. "What do you have in mind?"

"Watch and learn, sorcerer."

Samael slipped his aviators back in place and walked toward the gate. Declan glanced at Nico. "You ready?"

The warrior smiled harshly and held his dagger loose, while slinging an impressive-looking rifle across his back. "Let's do this."

Samael smashed the console near the entrance and immediately alarms sounded. He whipped out a cell phone, dialed 911, while behind him several vehicles, including the one they'd arrived in, exploded.

Two vampires appeared on the other side of the gate. They were livid, their fangs fully engaged, eyes aflame with crimson lust. Declan reached Samael and nodded. He was impressed. "This should do."

The vampire closest to them snarled and rushed forward, leaping over the gate with no problem. Nico intercepted and the two went down hard. In the distance sirens sounded, signaling that police were on their way.

"Go!" Samael shouted. "We'll meet you inside"—he flashed a grin and eyed the second vampire—"in a bit."

Declan's body thrummed with adrenaline. The energy in

the air was sharp, dark, and powerful. He ran forward and jumped the fence easily, landing nearly ten feet away.

The vampire mojo had kicked in and he grunted, welcoming the rush.

Declan called the shadows to him and wove a protection spell that would hopefully be strong enough to cloak his body from the vampires within.

He sensed several vamps running toward the gate, their preternatural speed propelling them forward so quickly he barely had time to duck behind one of the large oak trees that lined the driveway.

Once they passed he made his way toward the main house, slipping through the shadows with ease. Ana's scent was strong, as was Ransome's—they'd trod this path recently.

He crept up the front steps and opened the door, drawing out a charmed dagger as he did so. No one was around and he figured the incessant alarms had pretty much called all available bodies to the breach near the front gate.

Declan didn't hesitate. Ana's scent was like a trail of bread crumbs he had no problem following. It was dark, pitch black, and the sirens sounded loudly. He strode across the large foyer and slipped inside a small alcove. An elevator door was all it housed. He gritted his teeth and pressed the button.

Less than five seconds later the doors slid open and he snarled, his fangs erupting painfully. It looked as if a bucket of crimson had exploded inside. A body was sprawled awkwardly. Its head had been severed. It was vampire.

Declan jumped inside, ignored the carnage at his feet, and pressed the only option available, which was down.

The alarm still sounded but it was muted here below the main house, and though it was dark, his eyes had no problem adjusting as he moved forward.

Another body lay ahead. It stirred as he approached,

moaning softly as it rolled over. The large male vampire opened his eyes and hissed, but Declan rendered him useless with one deadly swipe of his dagger.

The smell of fear, violence, and pain lingered madly and he panted as his focus faltered and thoughts of Ana infiltrated his mind. Up ahead a small glow cut through the darkness. He *knew* Ana was there, just beyond his sight.

Declan called on his power, loving the sizzle of energy that ran along his arms. It rested in the palm of his hand, and he exhaled. The smell of burned flesh infiltrated his nostrils and he growled. It was wolf, no doubt Ransome.

He squared his shoulders and moved forward, his eyes on the glow at the end of the hall. He heard raised voices.

"What havoc have you brought to this house?" It was male.

A groan sounded softly and his insides turned to ice. *Ana.*

The floor trembled and a glass case on the wall exploded, showering its contents all over the floor. Declan ran the last few steps and halted, his gaze cold as he surveyed the scene before him.

Four vampires stood to his left. They glanced up at him in surprise. At their feet lay Ransome, his pallor gray, his eyes shot through with blood. Several wounds bled through his leather jacket and as he struggled to right himself, the vampire nearest him gave him the boots. It was a wicked blow that sent the werewolf flying.

Ana's eyes met Declan's and the fury that laced hers a deeper shade of blue was impressive. She was pissed.

A tall, pale vampire held her.

The bastard gave him a once-over and sneered as he spat at Ana, "I knew it was only a matter of time until you followed the path of your brother."

Declan would have moved forward but the sharp knife the vampire held at Ana's throat stopped him cold. Small rivulets of blood rolled down her skin. She'd already been cut.

The vampire laughed, his whole body shaking from the joy he took in Ana's pain. "No matter," he said to her, "we won't make the same mistake we did with Jean-Charles. Once we destroy this"—the vampire nodded toward Declan—"abomination, we will cut your head from your body and dump your remains in the Mississippi."

He pressed the knife in and she hissed, her eyes never leaving Declan's. Her hands clutched a small package of emerald silk.

"Take your hands off her." Declan spoke slowly, enunciating his words carefully as he took a step forward.

"Do not speak to me." The vampire dismissed Declan as if he posed no more of a threat than a pesky fly, or human.

Totally wrong fucking thing to do.

Declan's arm flew out and with it, an incredible surge of energy. It engulfed the four vampires who watched at his left, their countenances almost bored. He snarled as surprise flickered across their stony features.

Two of them were knocked back so hard into the wall that the entire room shook from the force of it. The others shrieked—enraged—and scrambled for footing as they turned toward him, fangs at the ready.

Bring it on, assholes.

Ransome rolled over and took the nearest one down, his body a blur as he shifted into his animal form. Declan saw Ana struggle and swore as the vampire who held her clocked her upside the head. She staggered from the force of it, falling to the ground.

The remaining vampire attacked Declan and he tore his gaze from Ana as he focused on the bastard. The vampire was strong as hell, most likely an ancient, but Declan lunged forward, his fangs sinking deep as he tore at its throat.

The vampire roared in pain and head butted him in an effort to break his hold. The dagger went flying, but no matter. The power inside him tripled, a mix of magick, vamp juice, and sheer determination. He grabbed hold of the vamp's neck and twisted as hard as he could while they rolled upon the floor. With a mighty heave, Declan snapped his neck and threw the body to the side.

He was up on his feet in an instant, just in time for his world to stop cold. Blue eyes stared into his, large round pools of regret. Everything faded into the background, save his woman.

The vampire was locked onto her jugular and it was obvious his intent was to kill. Each draw he took from Ana reverberated deep in Declan's soul.

"No!"

The savage cry erupted, torn from his chest. Ana struggled against the vampire who held her and managed to toss her emerald prize in the air. "Take this and run!" she shouted hoarsely as she tried to twist away from her tormentor.

He watched the bag as it floated in a perfect arc. It moved slowly. Time had stopped. Confusion reigned.

Then a hand slid through, parting reality in a shower of light.

"Oh my, it's been a while since I've played catch." A short, round, balding man appeared from nowhere and smiled widely at everyone. Bill. He tossed the silken bag into the air once more and moved to the side, speaking behind him. "Yes, almost forgot."

A tall, blond man appeared, sliding into view in the same way Bill had just done. His strange golden/black eyes were flat as he glared at the vampire who held Ana.

It was Azaiel, the fallen. "I suggest you remove your hands from the lady, Alistair."

The vampire looked shocked. He dropped Ana at his feet and moved away, his fangs retracting as he did so.

Declan was at Ana's side instantly and he scooped her slight form into his arms, cradling her closely.

"Why?" he asked, shaking his head, not understanding.

Her eyes fluttered opened and she smiled, shakily, but in that second he knew she was going to be fine. "Your safety," she managed. "Seth."

He ignored everyone, sliced into his wrist, and held it over her mouth. As he gazed down at her, felt her take life-giving blood from him, Declan knew his path had been forever altered.

That she would be willing to sacrifice herself so that he would live was humbling. The woman he held completed him, made him whole. He would never give her up.

"This is not your concern." Alistair had managed to regain his composure and his dark eyes were centered on Bill and Azaiel.

Bill laughed and shook his head. "Oh, but it is." He nodded toward Declan and Ana. "They are Seraph and as such are part of my family. They are under my protection." Bill's hand was upon Alistair's throat before the vampire had time to react. "The Seraphim."

He bent forward, his face inches from Alistair. Light emanated from his body and the horror that was reflected upon the vampire was sobering.

He'd just had a sneak peek at Bill's true nature.

Bill dropped Alistair and smiled down at the now-cowering vampire. "The Seraphim don't like to get involved in day-to-day squabbles amongst the otherworld. However, I've always been more hands-on." He shrugged. "I bend the rules, and sometimes I break them. So, vampire, be forewarned, anyone who is under my protection is off-limits. If you touch them I will destroy you."

"Alistair, we will not be dictated to."

Ransome growled at the last vampire standing other than Alistair. The large wolf had him cornered. Bill didn't bother to look their way; he waved his hand and the vampire slid to the floor, forever silenced.

Bill patted Alistair as if he were a dog. "Now then, I've

business to attend to, run along." The small Seraphim stood back and Alistair's form shimmered and disappeared.

He turned to Declan and Ana, his meaty hand clutched tight around the emerald bag. "I should like the pleasure of returning this to Seth." His eyes widened. "If you don't mind, Ana."

Though Declan would have preferred to hold her close and not let go, she slid from his arms and enveloped elf man in a hug. She whispered something into his ear and Bill's face reddened considerably as she let go.

Bill stared at the two of them for a long moment and sighed. "A dark wind is coming, my friends." His eyes glittered, "Go with Azaiel to The Pines. There is much to discuss."

And then he was gone.

Ransome shifted back to human form and gathered the tattered remains of his clothes. "Damn, I need a drink," he murmured to no one in particular as he pulled his jeans up. "You guys coming to the Lounge for one last hurrah?"

Declan slipped his arm around Ana and shook his head. "Next time, LaPierre." He shook the wolf's hand. "Thanks for everything. I'll be in touch and if you ever need a hand . . ."

"No worries there, my friend. The company you keep is kick-ass. I won't hesitate to call."

Nico appeared in the door and nodded. "Samael is waiting."

Ana looked at Declan and slipped her hand into his. "Let's get the hell out of here."

Declan bent, his lips grazing hers as he whispered, "I'm thinking a long, hot bath and hours of undisturbed sleep."

Ana smiled against his mouth. "After I'm done with you, a week's worth of sleep will not be enough."

Declan groaned. "Promise?"

They were outside now and Declan eyed the sleek limo parked in front of the house. On the street great plumes of smoke still poured from the vehicles Samael had set on fire. Ana tugged on Declan's sleeve. "Cross my heart."

They slid inside, followed by Nico and Azaiel. Ana settled against him. He held her close and glanced at Samael. The demon's hands were clenched tightly, the set of his mouth tense.

Declan turned away and closed his eyes. He didn't want to think about the bad shit. Not yet. Not when the feel of the woman he loved made everything all right.

He'd waited forever, it seemed. He would savor and worship her —never let her go.

"We made it," she whispered, moving against him and relaxing in his arms.

He kissed the top of her head. He wouldn't think of the bad stuff.

There would be time for that later.

"We sure as hell did."

EPILOGUE

"Sorry to keep you waiting."

Bill bustled into the room, full of energy and smiling like a lunatic. It was overdone, of course, an attempt to mask the pain and shock he felt. The news he held close to his heart was grave indeed.

In his hands were two large bags of candy, which he tossed onto the table before grabbing a glass of water. He smiled once more and took a good long, drink. He needed a moment.

The men and women seated were silent, respectful. He held the glass, his stubby fingers absently rubbing the cool moisture that collected along the side. Some of them were meeting for the first time and he saw the nervous stares, the carefully controlled posturing. He'd never gathered them like this, together in confined space.

Natural adversaries, coupled with fierce natures, made for strange bedfellows indeed.

He glanced at Cale and Samael. They were two prime examples, and yet they'd learned to get along.

They were smart. They knew they couldn't survive without the other. Every soul present had taken a sacred vow to protect the status quo, to make sure neither the upper nor lower realm achieved too much power.

They were in fact the scales of justice by which the human realm was able to exist. Without these creatures, culled from every corner of the otherworld here and beyond, there was no hope. Chaos would rain down upon the heads of man and all would be lost.

His eyebrows furled. He would hold them to it.

He turned quickly and asked for another glass of water. The pitcher was handed to him, and once his glass was filled he looked at the group. Where to start?

His eyes rested upon Declan and Ana. They were happy, and he supposed after all they'd been through, they should be. Declan would continue working on behalf of the Seraphim, but was now part of this secret sect, the League of Guardians. He'd also claimed the jaguar warrior Nico. There had been no other choice—they knew too much.

His gaze moved to Ana. It had always been his plan to include the vampire in the fold.

Funny how things worked out.

Ana looked worried. He'd grown close to the vampire over the last while. She knew his moods.

"The children you recovered have been moved to a safe haven. We can watch over them, guide them, and track down the others before they are found." He smiled though there was no joy inside him.

"What about the list?" Declan arched a brow. "We never recovered the other names."

Bill sighed. "I've no knowledge of a list and as far as I know, the remaining four marks have not been recovered."

"What of the necromancer, Francesca?" Samael flashed a smile and removed his aviators.

Bill's eyes narrowed. "She's with her sister and the others. I'm not happy she wears a slave collar."

Samael shrugged. "It was the only way to get her to co-operate . . . initially."

"You will remove it."

Samael shook his head. "No, brother, I will not."

Bill eyed the demon lord closely. There were times when it was prudent to pick his battles. This was one of them. "If the collar remains, you will refrain from engaging it, understood?"

Samael remained silent, but nodded his agreement.

Bill cleared his throat, and for a second the enormity of the news he held was overwhelming. He took a few extra seconds before he addressed his team. He glanced at the empty chairs. Some were on assignment and hadn't been able to make it. It was the others that troubled him. The ones he couldn't locate.

And the one who was never coming back.

"Cara is no longer among us." He watched them closely. "She's been . . . eliminated."

"What the hell does that mean?" Cale frowned.

"She was murdered," Bill said softly.

Shocked silence followed his announcement. Cara had been an important member of his team. She was an elderly woman of magick, a white witch, and had been three days shy of her seventieth birthday when she'd been found, her body beaten, tortured, and branded.

Cale's hardened features turned to him, his voice barely a whisper. "How? Why?"

Bill turned to his oldest, most trusted confidant. "The details are horrific."

"Was it otherworld?" Samael's lips were tight, his aviators back in place.

Bill grabbed a handful of Gummi bears and chewed them thoroughly before swallowing. "Most definitely." He shook his head and made no effort to hide the sadness, the utter despair he felt. "I fear we've been discovered. After working for millennia to keep the balance in our worlds, we may have a betrayer in our midst."

Silence greeted his words. Bill let his gaze wander the

room. So many noble, fierce warriors and each of them, he'd trust with his life.

"Do we know this for certain?" Azaiel spoke from the shadows.

Bill shrugged. "No." The small man leaned on the table and let a glimpse of his power—his rage—shine through. "But we will find out. If there is a betrayer among us"—he arched a brow—"here in this room, or posted in any realm we inhabit, they will be hunted and held responsible."

"We need to find out what happened to Cara," Cale said quietly.

Bill nodded. "Azaiel will leave at once."

"You would trust him with such a delicate mission?" Cale stood so quickly, his chair skittered across the wooden floor.

All eyes turned toward the tall figure in the corner. Azaiel sat alone, his long, denim-clad legs crossed in front of him as if relaxed, but the tight set of his mouth told the truth. The fallen was on edge.

Bill cocked an eyebrow. "I would trust him with my life."

Cale's face was red, angry. He snarled and strode for the door. Samael sat back, crossed his arms, and shrugged. "I don't usually agree with Cale, but in this instance, I gotta say, I think you're making a mistake."

"I thank you for your concern; however, I have the greatest of faith that Azaiel will perform admirably."

Bill grabbed another handful of candy. "He will leave as soon as transportation is made available."

"I don't think Cale is gonna want to give up one of his prized Harleys."

Bill ignored Samael and nodded to Azaiel. "It's time, my friend."

Azaiel stood. Six feet, six inches of intensity. "Where am I headed?"

"Salem, Massachusetts. A bed-and-breakfast called the Black Cauldron."

Azaiel turned without another word, though he paused at the door. "I'll see what I can find out and report back within the week."

Bill watched the fallen leave and knew the coming days were going to be dark. He popped one last Gummi bear into his mouth and grabbed a third glass of water.

He had faith in Azaiel. He just hoped the fallen angel had a healthy dose of his own.

Or they were in big trouble.

Read on for a sneak peek at

KING OF THE DAMNED,

the next book

THE LEAGUE OF GUARDIANS series,

coming December 2012

from Juliana Stone

and

Avon Books.

> There's nothing like a trail of blood to find
> your way back home.
> SIXX: A.M.

Darkness had fallen hours earlier, leaving only the moon's glow to illuminate the house on the hill. Rowan cut the engine of her rental, a frown furling her features as she stared at the large, rambling home.

The wind whistled and moaned, whipping dead leaves from the ground into a chaotic dance across her windshield. In the distance a once-vibrant red sunset settled along the edge of darkness that encroached from below. The day was dying and soon nightfall would be complete.

She glanced at the parking area next to the gift shop and was surprised to see it empty. The Black Cauldron was one of the most popular bed-and-breakfast stops in Salem and there were always guests in residence. At least there used to be.

An uneasy fist turned in her gut as she narrowed her eyes and gazed toward the house. The porch light was out and the evening's early shadows nearly hid the newspapers piled up next to the door. Leaves and debris clung to the corners of the steps leading up to the porch. It looked as if it hadn't been swept for days.

She pursed her lips and frowned. It was too dark, too silent. Something was wrong.

Very wrong.

Rowan pushed her car door open and grabbed her overnight bag as she slid from the car. Cool wind caressed bare legs and a shudder wracked her body as she paused beside the vehicle. She was still dressed for Southern California, not fall in Massachusetts. The ice blue silk blouse wasn't going to cut it.

She smoothed the lines of her short linen skirt, exhaled, and strode toward the house.

Her nana had left a message on her machine days ago asking her to come home, but she'd been in Europe on business for the firm. Now that she was home, she was anxious to see her.

She swept a pile of twigs and maple leaves from the corner of the door and bit her lip as the knob turned beneath her hand. The house looked closed up and yet it was unlocked.

"Shit," she murmured as her eyes adjusted to the gloom. "Nana?" Her voice tentative, Rowan set her bag on the floor and locked the door behind her.

She bit her lip. Nana never left it unlocked.

Her hand felt along the wall and she flipped a switch, bathing the foyer in a soft glow. It looked exactly as she remembered. Delicate roses adorned the wallpaper in the entry though the bottom part of the walls sported golden oak trim. The floor at her feet was worn, the oak planks smooth from years of use and polish.

To her left was an antique Queen Anne side table. It held Nana's guest book and sported a large vase. It was always filled with fresh flowers taken from the gardens out back. Depending on the season it could hold a riot of color or the fresh greens of November. Not tonight. The water was dark and the droopy remains of sad-looking sunflowers hung over the side. Their leaves were brown and curled, their centers moldy.

And the guest book? Well, from what she could see it was gone.

What the hell was going on? Was Nana ill? Why hadn't she called sooner?

She headed toward the back of the house. Just off the

kitchen, Nana kept a small apartment. As Rowan neared the kitchen something made the hair on the back of her neck stand on end.

She paused. A cold shot of *something* slid across her skin.

Hell, who was she kidding? She knew what that something was and it wasn't anything good. Not in this part of Salem anyway. It was dark energy. Scratch that. Dark, *powerful* energy.

Dammit! Fear for her nana pushed Rowan forward and she jogged the last few steps, her out-of-place stilettos clicking across the hardwood in a thin staccato.

"Nana?" she whispered hoarsely as she rushed into the kitchen. Her heels slid across the smooth hardwood floor and she barely avoided a fall as her hands grabbed the edge of the large kitchen table.

"You've got to be kidding me." She nearly went down again as she struggled to maintain her balance. "Shit!" she hissed, pushing a strand of long, dark hair behind her ear—the wind had pulled it loose from the tight ponytail she sported.

The window above the sink rattled as a wall of rain hit the panes.

She nearly slipped again and her gaze fell to the floor. A large stain marred the golden planks, leaving in its wake a macabre splash of dark art. Nausea roiled in her gut and her eyes widened in horror.

It was blood. There was no mistaking that coppery stench. *A lot of blood.*

The silence was broken as music erupted from inside her nana's apartment, "I Fall to Pieces," a sad lament sung by Patsy Cline. It had always been Nana's favorite.

Her heart was pounding crazily as she sidestepped the sticky mess and moved toward her nana's rooms. The door was ajar and soft light fell from inside. She paused, fighting fear and anxiety.

She hated Salem, the memories, the nightmares, the danger—the legacy that had taken many of her ancestors and driven her mother mad. It was the reason she'd left. Her nana wouldn't have called unless things were bad.

Oh God, things must be bad.

Where was she?

Rowan slipped inside and was careful to keep to the shadows. It was an automatic reaction and one that she welcomed. Old habits might die hard but they sure as hell were there for a reason.

The room appeared empty but she knew in this world she inhabited—one with layers most people were unaware of—looks could be deceiving.

She crept toward Nana's bed, holding her breath as she did so, eyes moving toward every corner. Her fingers grazed the stereo on the night table beside the bed and Patsy was silenced.

Rowan exhaled and glanced around the room once more, past the heavy crimson coverlet that was turned down. Past the robe flung across the chair at the foot of the bed. Past the book that lay open upon the pillow and the reading glasses that rested alongside it.

Her hand trembled as she picked up the book. A sad smile lifted the corners of her mouth as her fingers touched the yellowed pages. *To Kill a Mockingbird.* How many times had they read the book together?

She held the novel tight against her chest and tried to clamp down the fear that bubbled inside but it was hard. The blood in the kitchen filled her with dread.

"Nana, where are you?" she whispered.

A sound echoed from somewhere in the house and it was one she knew well. It was the loose board near the front stairs—the one that she'd fast learned to avoid as a teenager when sneaking in late at night. She froze and her breath caught at the back of her throat in a painful gasp. When she heard it again sweat broke out on her forehead as a sharp stab of fear punched her in the gut.

She put the book back, just as it was, and reached for her cell phone, cursing beneath her breath when she realized it was in her bag.

Which was in the foyer.

Shit.

Someone was out there—she sensed the energy and knew it was someone powerful. Or rather, *something.* At this point she had no idea who or what the hell it was but she knew it didn't belong. Not here in her nana's bed-and-breakfast.

Rowan blew out a shuddering breath and centered herself. She needed to be calm.

She crossed to the sitting area beside the stone fireplace. An iron poker rested against the hearth and she grabbed it, holding it tight as she melted into the dark corner nearest her. With her back protected she felt more in control and had a clear view of the room.

She closed her eyes for a second, concentrated, and felt the familiar pull of energy sizzle along her fingers. There was no way she could charm or spell because her power was weak—ill used—but it would have to do.

She heard a step echo and then another. Anger washed over her skin in a hot wave that left her teeth clenched, her fingers tight, and her resolve firm. The bastard was playing with her.

Come on, asshole. Let's do this.

Rowan slipped out of her heels, tossed them aside, and spread her legs slightly as she balanced on the balls of her feet.

Someone passed beyond the door and then there was silence. It stretched long and thin until she wanted to scream. Rowan's heart was nearly beating out of her chest but her eyes never strayed from the door.

She called to the shadows, coaxing them so that they

slithered along her flesh and covered her body with their darkness. A small thrill shot through her. She'd denied her gifts for so long she'd forgotten how good it felt to use them.

Suddenly the door swung open. Something big stood there, just beyond her line of vision. She couldn't see it but she sure as hell sensed it. She grimaced, pissed at herself for letting her powers get so rusty.

She heard a scuff, like a boot scraping along the floor, and held her breath in anticipation. Who would have predicted ten hours ago she'd be hiding in her nana's room, gripping an iron poker from the fireplace, waiting to attack?

Back in the day, before she'd reinvented herself, it had been the norm and something she'd taken great pains to distance herself from. Yet it seemed as if the ghosts of her past had found her.

A tall shape came into view. Impressively huge.

Rephrase: The ghosts of her past were about to kick her ass but good.

The door creaked as it slowly slid all the way open. She heard her breaths falling lightly as she struggled to keep it together and forced them to quiet. She needed to focus.

Rowan's eyes widened as the intruder strode into the room and cast a long shadow along the threadbare carpet. It was a very large, very *male* form.

Denim and leather adorned his powerful frame, emphasizing long limbs and wide shoulders. He moved with the grace of an animal—a predator—and she held her breath as his gaze swung toward her.

Was she safe? Could he see her?

His face was in shadow but the square jaw was visible. He reeked of power; even in her weakened state she was able to sense the enormity of it, and a sliver of fear bled through her determination.

Something awful had happened in her nana's home. Had this man been involved? If so, what did he want?

He took a step forward, moving into the light, and her mouth went dry. His eyes were intense, an unusual shade of gold that was piercing. A day's worth of beard shadowed his chin, covering it in scruff that was model-perfect. Dirty blond hair as thick as sable framed a face that was, without a doubt, the most devastatingly handsome one she'd ever seen. Hollywood had nothing on this guy.

Rowan knew she couldn't take him. There was no way in hell. The man was well over six feet in height and (a) she'd just tossed her heels, and at five-foot-six she didn't even reach his chin, and (b) the power that clung to him was incredibly strong. It cast a fractured light around his frame, one bled through with gold and black.

She'd never seen anything like it.

The stereo erupted once more and Patsy's mournful soprano sliced through the quiet. Rowan's heart took off, banging out of control and she tried to swallow her fear as the stranger turned fully in her direction.

For one sweet second she thought she heard her nana's voice whisper to her. *Always keep them off-kilter. Do the unexpected.*

It pushed her into action.

Rowan fell from shadow and stepped forward. "Who the hell are you and where is my grandmother?"

Surprise flickered across his face though it quickly disappeared. She swallowed tightly as the stranger's eyes narrowed. He raised his hand, and her fingers clutched the iron poker so tightly, they cramped.

She flinched as he flicked his wrist—it was a subtle motion that silenced the music.

He arched a brow. "Granddaughter?"

His eyes glittered, a strange shimmer deep within their depths. His voice was low and she detected a slight accent when he spoke. She couldn't place it.

"I won't ask again." Rowan straightened, glad her voice

was firm, no matter that her insides were mush. "Who are you and why is there blood in the kitchen?" A small tremor caressed the end of her sentence but it couldn't be helped.

She was freaking out, scared as hell, and there was a mountain of muscle between herself and freedom.

The stranger cursed, words she didn't understand, but they were definitely curse words. His tone and scowl told her so. "No one mentioned a granddaughter." He cocked his head to the side and frowned. "We've got company."

He crossed to the window and yanked the drapes into place in one quick motion. At the same time the glow from the nightlight was extinguished.

Rowan didn't know what to think but she was starting to get pissed off.

"This is crazy, where is my nana?" She took a step forward.

"Cara is . . ." His voice trailed into silence as the windows began to shake, the panes rattling against an onslaught of wind and rain.

"She's what?" Rowan's eyes were huge as she stared up into a face devoid of emotion. There was a coldness there that was unsettling.

"I'm sorry," he said abruptly. "She's dead."

The iron poker slipped from her fingers as she stared up at the stranger.

She heard the words but her brain wasn't translating them. Rowan shook her head. "I don't . . . that can't be, I'd know . . ." She couldn't articulate what was in her head. None of this made sense. Her eyes fell to the book on the bed, the reading glasses, and she felt something inside her break.

Nana.

In that moment she knew the truth, the pain and the guilt. *It's my fault.* The whisper slid through her mind. *I never should have left.*

A low keening erupted, one that shot up several decibels

within seconds until the window shattered. Glass blew everywhere and shredded the curtains into billowing tatters. They were long plumes of crimson silk that fluttered like crazed feathers in the wind.

Rowan winced at the sharp sting of shrapnel as it sliced into her arms and legs. Searing pain ripped across her cheek but she paid no mind. The wind pulled at her, whirling into the room with a hazy cloud of freezing mist that made it difficult to breathe.

The touch of his hand on her flesh pulled her from the darkness. The roaring dialed down and as she stared up at him, her lungs expanded and she was able to draw a shuddering breath.

"Who . . . who did this?" she rasped. She had no idea who the hell he was but in that moment she knew he meant her no harm. The darkness, *the evil*, wasn't in this room. It was out there beyond the broken window.

"I think your answer is there." His eyes were no longer gold, but solid, flat black, and the white of his teeth flashed through the gloom as he spoke. He pointed outside and Rowan turned to the window. Thunder and lightning had joined the chaotic dance of rain and wind. A bolt of energy streaked across the sky, illuminating the entire front yard in a sizzle of white.

It was a quick, precise hit, and gave just enough light for her to see seven hulking figures standing in the pouring rain.

Their scent reached her and she nearly gagged on the thickness of it. *Demons.*

Their eyes glowed red. *Blood demons.*

A weird calm settled over her. She'd come full circle, it seemed.

Rowan squared her shoulders and glanced up at the man beside her. "Who sent you?"

He was silent for a moment. "Someone who cared deeply for your grandmother."

She felt her stomach twist. She didn't like the stranger's vague answer. If what he'd said was true, her nana was dead and outside seven blood demons called—his presence was no coincidence.

A guttural cry rent the night—a harsh echo that slid like nails against a chalkboard, and her hackles rose. She didn't have time to worry about the details.

"I'm Rowan. What's your name?" she asked as she grabbed the iron poker off the ground.

"Azaiel."

She arched a brow. "Okay . . . that's different."

The demons began to howl in unison, their voices rising into a crescendo of noise and then it dropped suddenly until there was nothing. The silence was heavy. Eerie. It was the calm before the storm.

The tallest of the demons grunted and began walking toward them, a deadly machete trailing behind him. Another series of lightning strikes crashed across the sky and its ugly horned face split open into what she supposed was a grin.

"I'm sorry but it looks like things are about to get nasty," she whispered, her gaze focused upon the gathering outside, "but then again with a name like that, I suppose you've not forgotten."

"Forgotten what?" he asked, moving beside her.

Rowan whispered, "What it feels like to get your ass kicked."

The door opened behind Logan Winters, bringing with it a gust of wind, the faint scent of pine, and complete silence. Like a ripple effect, conversations stopped, laughter faded, and eyes were averted.

Logan glanced up at the bartender, took notice of the stubby fingers grasped tight to the bottle of Canadian whiskey—the bottle Logan had been waiting for—and scowled.

The Neon Angel was a sad excuse of a drinking hole. It had seen better days, and from what he could tell, so had most of the staff and clientele. The bar was a rickety shack on the edge of a town he had no name for. It was the place he'd ended up at—no reason other than timing—and for a brief moment it had been the heaven he'd been seeking.

His eyebrows knit together tightly and his lips tightened. All he'd wanted was a drink. *Just one fucking drink.*

He exhaled and shifted slightly, giving himself more room as he pushed his bar stool back a few inches. The couple that had been sitting to his left was already on their feet, a wad of cash thrown onto the bar as they slid into the shadows that wrapped around the room.

The blonde who'd been eyeing him up but good downed her wine and smiled a crazy I'm-getting-the-hell-out-of-here kind of smile before wiping the corner of her mouth and turning away.

Guess he wasn't getting laid, either.

Logan swore, a harsh string of words no one would understand, and nodded to bartender. "I'll take that shot now."

The large man ran his free hand through the thinning gray scalp atop his head and swallowed hard, his watery eyes wide as he glanced toward Logan. Thick bands of wiry gray brows curled crazily above round balls the color of peat moss.

His soft arms, bared to the world thanks to the faded black wife-beater T-shirt he wore, was filled with tattoos that jiggled as he rubbed the scruff on his chin. "Dude . . . not sure if that would be a good . . . uh . . . idea."

Logan's ice blue eyes narrowed as a snarl caught in the back of his throat. He felt the heat beneath his skin. The burn. The itch.

A rumble rose from his chest—a menacing warning—and the bartender took heed, his body jerking in small, quick movements as he jumped. Logan nodded toward the bottle, his low rasp barely containing the irritation he felt. "Pour me the drink." He'd have his whiskey and then deal with whoever the hell had decided tonight was a good night to fuck with him.

The bartender swallowed nervously, his Adam's apple bobbing through the thick folds of skin at his neck. The man didn't know what to do. Run from whoever—or whatever—had blown into the place or pour the damn whiskey and be done with it.

His eyes darted to just behind Logan once more but he jumped when Logan barked. *"Now."*

The bartender poured a generous amount of whiskey into the tumbler and though he tried to be careful, his hands shook so much it was a damn miracle he didn't spill the precious liquid all over the place.

The sound of clinking glass echoed into the dead silence and when the bartender was done, he set the bottle to the side and stepped back. A pronounced tick pulsed near his left eye and he swallowed nervously as he stood there, shuffling his feet, eyes shifting from Logan to the door. He was unsure. *Afraid.*

Logan tossed some cash onto the dark-grained bar and

stood, his six-foot-six-inch frame unfurling with the un-
canny grace of an animal, which considering his origins
wasn't surprising.

Tension settled along his wide shoulders as he reached
for the glass, but along with it, a shot of anticipation. He was
itching for a fight. He'd just not known it until now.

He tipped his head back. Amber liquid slid down his
throat and he welcomed the smooth, sweet taste. It burned—
all the way down—yet he closed his eyes and savored the
sensation.

Logan had been pretty much everywhere—in the human
realm and beyond—and he could say with certainty, Cana-
dians knew how to brew their whiskey better than anyone
else.

He let the liquid fire settle in his belly and then carefully
set the empty glass back onto the bar. He arched a brow and
nodded, a slight jerk to the right.

Now would be a good time for the bartender to leave.

Sweat beaded along the man's top lip. It was quickly
wiped away by a thick, meaty hand and then the bartender
took a step back before he, too, disappeared into the shadows.

Logan slowly rotated his head and turned.

Two men stood just inside the door of the Neon Angel,
their tall frames bathed in shadow. They were big. Well built
and muscled.

And they'd not come to socialize.

Logan had no idea who they were, but judging from the
otherworld scent that clung to them, he had a pretty good
idea where they'd come from. But that was the tricky part,
wasn't it? Which realm did they call home?

No scent of demon twisted in the air and yet . . .

His hands fisted at his sides. He could take them. Hell, he
wanted to take them.

"Shit, that didn't take you boys long." Logan nodded
toward the now-empty bar. "You cleared the room in less

time than it takes for a junkie with a needle in his vein to get high."

Nothing. There was no expression or words.

Logan remained silent for a few moments and cocked his head to the side. He studied the two creatures—and creatures they were—there was not one drop of humanity in them. His nostrils flared as the subtle scent of pine drifted toward him once more and he frowned.

A memory stirred and with it a flush of heat, a dirge of anger.

Slowly his fists unfurled to hang loose at his side and Logan leaned back against the bar, crossing his long legs in front of him.

"I'm not much for one-sided conversation so unless you've got something to say I'd suggest you turn your asses around and leave." Logan grabbed the bottle of whiskey off the counter. "'Cause I've got some drinking to do and that sure as hell *is* something I prefer to do alone."

A low keening vibration rippled through the room—an invisible thread that electrified the air and sent his radar crashing into full-on red alert.

Bright light lit the men from behind, beams so intense Logan took a step back and winced. His skin burned as if it had been touched by flames and the control he had was fast slipping away.

Stars danced in front of his eyes and he shook his head aggressively as he moved forward, his mind emptying of all thought except one. Survival.

There was power here. Old, ancient power—the kind that always signaled shit was about to hit it. *Hard.* Logan was determined that any ass kicking in the immediate future would not involve his own.

The sifting beams of light sizzled and popped, and for a second he saw nothing but glitter, small pulsating fragments of gold that drifted on the breeze and whirled around the shadowed forms. They merged, twirling faster as the keening vibrations became louder, and they melted together into one large vortex of light.

Logan glared straight ahead, his gut tightening as the pine scent that hung in the air sharpened. It was fresh, tangy . . . and all too familiar.

His anger spiked as one form emerged from what had been two, a smallish, round bit of a man who looked nothing like what he truly was—Seraphim—and *he* was one of the original seven. Humans might call him angel, though in this form he bore no resemblance to the golden creatures popular in lore.

This was no cherub.

"Askelon," Logan said smoothly, his anger in check, his facade calm.

"Let's not be so formal, my friend."

Glittery gold lamé lapels glistened against his gray jacket as the small man moved forward. His pants were ill-fitting, a little too snug around his generous belly, and his dress shirt sported gaping holes between the buttons. Something was smeared alongside his mouth—ketchup? And in his hand a bag of—Logan sniffed—candy was held.

Good to see his sweet tooth was still intact. "A little theatrical, even for you, don't you think?"

Askelon arched a brow and shrugged his shoulders.

"Your bodyguards?" Logan continued dryly.

The small man laughed. "Ah . . . that was nothing. Parlor tricks really. I somehow doubt this room would have emptied if I stood alone and I do so want a private chat. We've lots to discuss."

Logan's eyes narrowed as he watched him walk to the bar, throw his bag of candy—which Logan could now see was filled to the brim with colorful Gummi bears—and with a little effort, settled himself onto the bar stool Logan had just vacated.

Pudgy fingers grasped a napkin and wiped away the stains on his face as Askelon turned to him. For a second his eyes shimmered—a weird translucent silver color—and Logan saw the power that shifted within their depths.

"Please"—he smiled and nodded—"call me Bill."

"Bill?" Logan's eyebrow arched in disbelief.

Bill grinned, shrugged, and proceeded to pour himself a glass of whiskey. "It's plain, I know, but suited me at the time." He poured one for Logan and handed it to him, raising his own in a toast.

What the hell do you want with me?

"I'll explain in a minute, but first let's drink, shall we? That is why you came here tonight isn't it? To drink? Perhaps forget?"

So he was a mind reader now.

The tension that had fled moments earlier was back, pinching his shoulders as Logan reached for the glass and tossed back the tumbler full of whiskey.

The little round shit was responsible for his banishment as surely as if he'd—

"You know that's not true, Logan."

Logan's chest heaved. He gritted his teeth and slammed the glass back onto the counter.

"Stay the fuck out of my head, Seraphim." Logan moved forward until he was close enough to see the veins in the little shit's eyes. His nostrils flared and his chest grumbled. Beneath his skin, the beast stirred.

"Your banishment was unfortunate." Bill sipped the whiskey, his eyes shimmering as they regarded Logan closely. "But you knew there would be consequence when you joined the League."

Logan snorted. "Yeah, well. Your so-called League can go screw itself."

Bill set his half-empty glass onto the counter and twirled the liquid slowly with his finger as silence fell between them.

He turned to Logan and though his voice was soft, there was no mistaking the hard glint in his eyes. "That's not how it works, my friend."

Logan snarled and whirled away. He was a hellhound. His job was to retrieve souls that were beyond redemption and escort them to District Three—one of several levels in Hell—for processing.

He neither liked nor hated his job but he sure as hell was the best kind of animal for it. He was an elite hellhound shifter, born from the depths of Hell and destined to straddle the realms. His hunting capabilities were legendary, his sensory skills unparalleled.

Logan's lips curled as the faint smell of pine tugged at him once more. He stared at the mirror that hung on the wall in front of him. At a reflection so bizarre it was laughable. Askelon had outdone himself. His human mask was nothing short of brilliant. No one would ever suspect the short, round, balding man was in fact one of the most powerful beings in existence.

Anger spiraled through him and Logan took a step toward Bill, uncaring that the ancient could dish out a hell of a lot of damage with nothing more than the flick of his wrist.

He growled and passed his hands through the thick hair at his nape.

"Why are you here?" The last time he'd seen the little fuck, Logan's life had taken a header right into the fires of Hell. Literally. He'd defied direct orders from his handler because Bill had asked him to. He'd led a child back into the human realm—one he'd been ordered to retrieve for processing—and Logan had been brutally punished.

He'd been sentenced to the pit—the shithole beneath District Three. It was the one place in Hell that everyone avoided. If they were smart. It was saying something that a creature born of fire and brimstone had nearly been broken by it.

"I need your help, Logan."

Logan paused, his face incredulous. "What part of shove your fucking League of Guardians up your ass didn't you understand the last time?" He arched a brow and smiled, his lips tight in a sarcastic grin. "Or is this something else entirely? You pulling a Vader and crossing over to the dark side, Bill?" He flexed his arms, let his beast shift beneath the surface. "You want a ride down? Is that it?"

"The girl has been killed."

"What girl?" A frown crossed Logan's face. He didn't like where the conversation was headed.

"The same girl you were ordered to drag to Hell fifteen years ago." Bill sighed, rubbed his temples. "The one we saved." If Logan didn't know better, he'd think the little shit was tired.

"We? Seems to me I did all the work and had my ass kicked for thousands of years because of it." Logan shook his head. No way was he getting involved again. "I'm done. I don't give a flying fuck about that girl." Did the Seraphim think he cared if the girl was dead? As far as Logan was concerned she'd been on borrowed time. If anything, she'd been granted a reprieve while he'd rotted beneath District Three.

Time moved differently there. In the pit. What had been fifteen years to the human girl had been nearly fifteen hundred for Logan.

"Tsk, tsk . . . language, my friend." Bill turned fully and nailed Logan with a direct stare. "You should care. We all need to care."

"You're talking in circles, old man. You'll need to elaborate."

"She cannot perish. Her future is hidden in the fabric that binds us all, and it needs to be protected."

"Seems like a moot point considering she's already dead."

Bill's eyes narrowed. His face darkened. Gone was the

pleasant, middle-aged human. In his stead a powerful, enig-
matic creature stood. Two realities converged and Logan had
to admit, the little shit's mojo was impressive. Bill's voice
vibrated, falling in layers that encircled Logan and filled his
head. There was no mistaking. The Seraphim was livid.

"She is not meant to die—not yet. Someone is trying to
alter her destiny and I need you to retrieve her for me."

"She's not my problem. Find some other dog."

"Oh but she is your problem. I need someone who can
track her. Someone who knows her scent." Bill leaned closer,
his voice amplified even more. "Someone who's tasted her
soul."

Logan had had enough. He growled, bared his teeth. "I
don't take orders from you. Not anymore. I don't know why
I ever agreed to it in the first place."

*Liar. If he was being truly honest, Logan could at least
admit he'd only agreed to join the League because he hated
Mallick's guts. The demon was getting much too powerful
as far as he was concerned. Something had to be done.*

Bill sighed, grabbed his bag of candy, and helped himself
to a generous amount. He chewed and stared up at Logan
thoughtfully, though the hellhound was wary of the expression that now rested upon his features.

"You will do this for me."

Logan crossed his arms over his chest and spread his
legs. The Seraphim was going to have to do a hell of a lot
better than that.

Logan reached for the nearly empty bottle of whiskey
and dumped the last of it into his glass. "You've wasted a
trip, old man." He was dancing on the edge. Tossing insults
to one of the most powerful creatures in existence.

And he didn't give a shit. Such was the way of it these
days. His stay in the pit had altered him in more ways than
one.

"You will do this because of your vow to the League and

because I know your true origins." The words slid between them. Silky. Dangerous. Bill's ace in the hole.

Logan paused, the glass nearly to his lips. His throat tightened and his teeth clenched hard.

"I know who your mother is."

The glass shattered in Logan's hand as a snarl erupted from within his chest. His fist closed around Bill's throat and he shoved the Seraphim back into the bar with such force that the walls shook, sending bottles and glasses crashing to the floor.

Logan's skin shifted and the beast shone through, his eyes morphing to bloodred as he stared down at the small man held tight in his grip.

Several long moments passed and eventually Logan pulled back, curses in an ancient tongue flying from his mouth as he stepped away.

He closed his eyes, forced his body to relax, and crooked his head to the side. "Where's the girl?"

There was a pause.

"Purgatory."

Logan swore. "And her body?"

"The Regent Psychiatric Institute in Florida." At Logan's arched brow the round man finished quietly. "Morgue."

The word had barely escaped Bill's lips and Logan was already gone.

Next month, don't miss these exciting new love stories only from Avon Books

A Blood Seduction by Pamela Palmer

Quinn Lennox is searching for a missing friend when she stumbles into a dark otherworld that only she can see. She has no idea of the power she wields . . . power that could be the salvation or destruction of Arturo, the dangerously handsome vampire whose wicked kiss saves, bewitches, and betrays her.

Winter Garden by Adele Ashworth

Madeleine DuMais's cleverness is her greatest asset—one she puts to good use as a spy for the British. When she meets Thomas Blackwood, her partner in subterfuge, duty gives way to desire and she discovers their lives are no longer the only things in danger.

Darkness Becomes Her by Jaime Rush

Some might say Lachlan and Jessie don't play well with others. But they're going to have to learn to, and quickly. Because they are the only two people in the world who can save each other— and their passion is the only thing that can save the world.

Hot For Fireman by Jennifer Bernard

Katie Dane knows better than to mix business with pleasure, but when she finds herself working side by side with Ryan, the sexy heartbreaker of Station One, playing with fire suddenly feels a lot like falling in love.

At Avon Books, we know your passion for romance—once you finish one of our novels, you find yourself wanting more.

May we tempt you with . . .

- **Excerpts** from our upcoming releases.

- Entertaining **extras**, including authors' personal photo albums and book lists.

- Behind-the-scenes **scoop** on your favorite characters and series.

- **Sweepstakes** for the chance to win free books, romantic getaways, and other fun prizes.

- Writing **tips** from our authors and editors.

- **Blog** with our authors and find out why they love to write romance.

- **Exclusive content** that's not contained within the pages of our novels.

Join us at
www.avonbooks.com

AVON

An Imprint of HarperCollins*Publishers*
www.avonromance.com

Available wherever books are sold or please call 1-800-331-3761 to order.

FTH 1111